RED RIVER

Also by Lalita Tademy

Cane River

RED RIVER

LALITA TADEMY

WARNER BOOKS

NEW YORK   BOSTON

Warner Books
Hachette Book Group USA
1271 Avenue of the Americas, New York, NY 10020

Printed in the United States of America

Warner Books and the "W" logo are trademarks of Time Warner Inc. or an affiliated
company. Used under license by Hachette Book Group USA, which is not affiliated
with Time Warner, Inc.

ISBN-13: 978-0-446-57898-1
ISBN-10: 0-446-57898-3

Book design by HRoberts Design

For Nathan Green Tademy, Jr.

Daddy, I owe you

RED RIVER

1 9 3 5

C ome closer. This is not a story to go down easy, and the backwash still got hold of us today. The history of a family. The history of a country. From bondage to the joy of freedom, and
almost ten hopeful years drinking up the promise of Reconstruction, and
then back into the darkness, so fearsome don't nobody want to talk
about the scary time. Don't nobody want to remember even now,
decades removed, now things better some. Why stir up all that old mess
from way back in 1873? I don't hold with that point of view. I was
there, watching, like all the women done, up close some of the time but
mostways from a distance. They all dead and buried now. I outlast each
one, using up my time on earth and some of theirs too. One hundred
last birthday, trapped in this wasted body. All I do now is remember and
pray the story don't get lost forever. It woulda suit Lucy fine, everybody
forgetting. Lucy and me, that the only thing we usta argue about, when
we was both clear-minded and had more juice to work up, but those
talks never last too long. She just shut her mouth and shut her mind,

refusing the truth. I still got heat around the subject, but where to put it now? Lucy gone last year. She turn one hundred five before she left this earth. Was two of us held on for such a long time, me and Lucy. Outlasting our men—our husbands, our sons, even some grandsons. We all had it hard, but the men, they had it worse, 'specially those what come up on life from the front. Women is the long-livers at the base of the Tademy family tree.

They don't teach 1873 at the colored school. Wasn't for my husband, wouldn't be no colored school for Colfax, Louisiana. That the kind of man Sam Tademy was. Could carry a vision in his head and stick to it no matter what the discouragement. Some men good providers, got a way with the soil or a trade. Some men been given a singing voice take you to glory, or magic in they bodies to move in dance and make you feel alive. Some men so pretty you gaze on them with hunger, or so smooth they get hold of words and make you believe any nonsense come out they mouth. Some got the gift to make you laugh out loud, and others preach strong and spread the word of God. My man, Sam, he quiet after his own way, look after his family, not afraid of the tug of the plow. He done some preaching, and some teaching, but always thinking about the rest of the colored. Not wanting to get too far ahead without pulling forward everyone else willing to work hard at the same time. Education mean everything to that man. Once he set his head on a colored school in Colfax, wasn't nothing could crush the notion. He mortgage his own sons to the plan, and it come to pass.

We been writ out the history of this town. They got a metal marker down to the courthouse tell a crazy twisting of what really happen Easter Sunday sixty year ago. The ones with the upper hand make a story fit how they want, and tell it so loud people tricked to thinking it real, but writing down don't make it so. The littlest colored child in Colfax, Louisiana, know better than to speak the truth of that time out loud, but the real stories somehow carry forward, generation to generation. Those of us what was there catch a retold whisper, and just the mention got the power to stir up those old troubles in our minds again like they fresh, and the remembering lay a clamp over our hearts. But we need to remember. Truth matters. What our colored men try to do for the rest of us in Colfax matter. They daren't be forgot. We women keep the wheel spinning, birthing the babies and holding together a decent home to raise them in. We take care of them what too young or too old to take care of theyself, while our menfolks does battle how they got to in a world want to see them broke down and tame.

Was a time we thought we was free and moving up. When forty acres and a mule seem not only possible but due. First we was slave, then we was free, and the white call it Reconstruction. We had colored politicians. Yes, we did. It was our men vote them in, before the voting right get snatched away. We losing that sense of history, and it seem wrong to me. Young ones today, they don't carry memory of our colored men voting. Like those ten years of fiery promise burn down and only leave a small gray pile of ash under the fireplace grate, and don't nobody remember the flame. Not like the locals made it easy, but we had our rights then, by law. We was gonna change the South, be a part of the rebuilding after the War Between the States. We owned ourself and was finding our voice to speak up. Some on both sides of the color line talked about us going too fast. No matter how hard times got then, when wasn't food enough for the table and the debt growed too fast to pay off at the general store, or a homegrown pack of the White League terrorize us or string up one of our men to keep us in our place, still our hearts and heads swole up with the possibilities of Reconstruction. Our men was citizens. We had the prospect of owning a piece of land for ourself. Ten years. Don't seem so long when you reach over one hundred years in your own life, but more hope and dreams in those ten years than the slave years come before or the terror years after. Back then hope was a personal friend, close to hand. Seem anything could happen. Seem we was on a road to be a real part of America at last.

I think on those colored men in the courthouse every day. They was brave, from my way of seeing, dog-bone set to fight for a idea, no matter the risk. Not all the old ones see it the same. Lucy used to say by stepping up, the colored courthouse men bring the white man down on us, but what foolishness is that? Some white folks never change from thinking on us as they own personal beasts of burden, even after freedom. Those ones down on us already.

But we got the strength to outlast whatever trials is put before us. We proved it. There a special way of seeing come with age and distance, a kind of knowing how things happen even without knowing why. Seeing what show up one or two generations removed, from a father to a son or grandson, like repeating threads weaving through the same bolt of cloth. Repeating scraps at the foot and the head of a quilt. How two men never set eyes on each other before, and, different as sun and moon, each journey from Alabama to Louisiana and come to form a friendship so deep they families twine together long after they dead. How one set of brothers like hand and glove, but two others at each other throats like jealous pups fighting for the last teat. How two brothers from the same house marry two sisters, sets of bold and meek. How men come at a thing nothing like what a woman do, under the names dignity, pride, survival. The words alike, but the path not even close between man and woman, no matter they both trying to get to the same place. Making a better way for the children. In the end, making a better life for our children what we all want.

Eighteen seventy-three. Wasn't no riot like they say. We was close enough to see how it play out. It was a massacre. Back in 1873, if I was a man, I'da lift my head up too and make the same choice as my Sam and Israel Smith and the others, but there was children to feed and keep healthy and fields to harvest and goats to milk. Those things don't wait for history or nothing else. But I saw. I cleaned up after. I watch how 1873 carry through in the children that was there, and then in they children years later.

My name is Polly. I come to the Tademys not by blood but by choice. Not all family got to draw from the bloodline. I claim the Tademys and they claim me. We a community, in one another business for better or worse. How else we expect to get through the trials of this earth before the rewards of heaven?

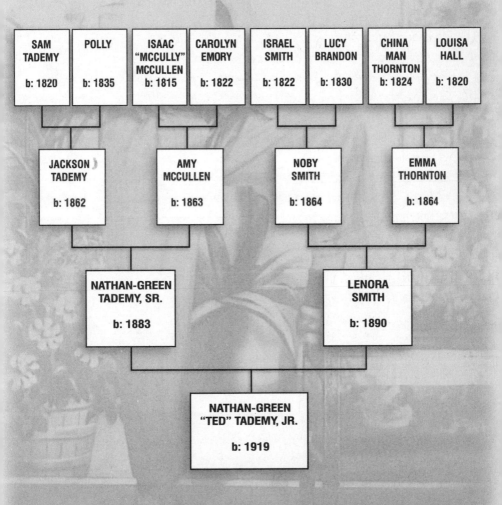

Figure 1. Nathan-Green "Ted" Tademy's pedigree

Part One

Before

1873

1

*L*ucy pushes herself up from their bed an hour earlier than usual, quiet and purposeful. Off to start the cooking fire, Israel thinks, fully awake now, but he says nothing. The sleeping room of the small cabin borders on pitch-dark, with only a hint of the moon's light coming from a single small window. He intended to be first up this morning, and gone before the inevitable rehash of last night's quarrel and resulting standoff, but that's no longer an option. The Bottom is calm the way only early morning brings, before the rooster's crow, and Israel's mind races, thinking about going into town, into Colfax. Yesterday he heard from a neighbor sharecropping the next plot that the last steamship from New Orleans had come and gone, with no Federal troops on board. The new officeholders arriving today would need local protection from the colored men of Colfax.

Lucy pauses to smooth the quilt over their boys, still asleep on their shared moss-filled mattress, and then slowly pads her way toward the front of the cabin. Her step is heavy with the additional weight of the new baby she carries inside her, a soft, rhythmic waddle as her wide feet slide across the planked floor, oddly reassuring. Israel assumes she knows he is awake. Lucy always recognizes his moods and his habits, and he follows her unspoken signal and gets up too, drawing his cotton shirt and pants on over his sleeping union suit, and gathers up his worn leather boots from the corner. He stops at another bed in the room to shake two of the boys awake. He lets the younger children sleep.

"David, Noby, get on up, you covering my chores today," Israel whispers.

Since he has missed his early getaway, he heads out to the shed in the darkness to relieve the cow of her morning's milk. By the time he enters the cooking room of the cabin with a half-filled pail, the fire is lit and starting to blaze up in the fireplace, and Lucy has already pulled on her faded housedress and wrapped her hair in a tight kerchief. She is packing up cold foods for him to carry away in a bucket, an acknowledgment that she has lost the argument. Deep circles under her eyes give away her exhaustion.

"Pone, tack, and taters," she says. "Three days' worth."

"More than enough," Israel replies. "Might be home tonight." He pulls the straight-back chair to the old traveling trunk that serves as their eating table and begins to eat the biscuit and fried chicken's egg Lucy lays out for him. "Soon's the Federals come, I hightail it back, least in time to preach Sunday's sermon. You'll see."

"Can't nothing but grief come from you showing yourself like this."

"We been over this, Lucy. I'm going." Absently, with his thumb, Israel rubs the length of an old scar like a question mark split deep along his cheek and down to his jaw, lighter in color and raised like a welt.

"We free and movin' up, Israel, and you throwing away our

work of the last seven years." She whispers, but her tone is urgent. "We come from nothing, less than nothing, and now we owns our own wagon, and the cow. We got the Reconstruction, and laws be on our side. Colored politicians sitting side by side with white down in New Orleans, and our colored men up here vote different-thinking men in to Colfax, fair and square too. We might could own this land one day if we keeps low, but not if you go down to the courthouse and rub the white man's nose into the politics. Stay home. This not like you."

Israel doesn't look forward to confrontation, either at the courthouse or in his own home. Against his better judgment, he steps into the carryover of last night's row.

"Why the colored man risk everything to vote if the Republicans we vote in just be turned back when the time come to take office? That's all we trying to do. Get the old guard in Colfax to stand down long enough for the new appointees to catch hold."

"This not like you," Lucy says again. "Mixing in white man's business. We done fine by keeping out the gaze of white. Let the new sheriff handle it."

"We got a sheriff coming in today, elected, but they got a sheriff too, don't want to give up his place. Colored men meeting at the courthouse 'cause we got a job to do till the Federals come. White business and colored business not so separate no more."

David and Noby shuffle barefoot into the cooking room, still sleepy-eyed, dressed in the shabby mismatch of their everyday homespun shirt and trousers. David is two years older and over a head taller than his younger brother, rail-thin legs too long for an eleven-year-old boy. His skin is pale and heavily freckled, and the light sandy hair falling into his face without curl or nap makes it seem he has been accidentally left with the wrong brown-hued family. His fierce gray eyes, so light as to be mistaken sometimes for blue or green, scrutinize and judge everything around him, and never seem to leave Israel's face, as if searching for clues. Noby, at nine, is somewhere between the caramel color of his mother and the walnut tinge of Israel, and although it is difficult to know when the growth spurts will start and stop, he seems to be a little replica of his father, brooding brown eyes, high forehead, nappy-headed, sturdy of body.

The boys approach cautiously, waiting in the morning chill to see which way the household wind is blowing. Not once last night or this morning have they heard their parents' voices rise above a regular speaking tone, but there is a tautness in the air of unresolved difference. Their mother almost never answers back against the wishes of their father, and they have seldom heard so many words at once from their father unless it is Sunday and he is delivering a sermon. Despite the tension, David separates himself from Noby and steps forward.

"Papa, if you go to town, can I come too?" he asks.

Finished, Israel pushes his tin plate aside and jams his hat on his head. "Noby might's well come with me," he says.

"Why take the boys?" Lucy asks.

"This a man's job, a *citizen's* job," Israel pronounces carefully. "Noby need to understand."

"Then take David." Lucy moves quickly toward the two boys and throws her fleshy arm around David's shoulder. "David the oldest."

"David need to stay and cover the chores," says Israel. He motions to Noby, and when the smaller boy comes to stand near his side, Israel touches him lightly at the neck to shepherd him outside. David's pale face flushes deep red, and he flinches as if struck, but Israel is already on the move away from the table.

"That's settled," Israel says, satisfied. "We be gone, then."

Lucy keeps her arm around David, but he shakes her off and trails behind Israel and Noby for a few steps as they move toward the front door of the cabin.

"All right," Lucy says. "We watch over things here till you

home again." Suddenly, she seeks out the straight-back chair at the table and sits down hard, as if her wind has given out.

"You see us soon," Israel says. He lifts both his and Noby's jacket from the wall hook, and the two of them head off down the twisting, mud-crusted road on foot.

David shadows his father and his brother as far as the edge of the yard in front of the cabin, near the vegetable patch, staring at their backs until they are obscured from view by the thick of pine trees to the north. Neither father nor son looks back.

The steely sky with its dark-tinged clouds feels heavy, and for Israel it is almost as if he carries an extra burden, like a woman balancing a heavy wash basket on her head as she walks. The sun struggles to punch through, and intermittently succeeds, but Israel and Noby get caught in several brief showers, only enough wetness to damp down the dust and muddy the cow and horse trails. In long-leaf Pine Hills country, they pass a small cluster of naked cypress trees, the spindly, brittle branches seemingly dead, used up, bare and sheathed in gray, with a few curled brown leaves that still refuse to drop. Spanish moss hangs from the gray trees like rotting flesh from a skeleton, ghostlike.

"Spring coming," Israel tells Noby. "Them Resurrection trees gonna get green again soon."

They walk in silence, and when they come to Red River, Israel and Noby follow the bank, paralleling the course of the water through the bottomlands on their way to Colfax. A large brown heron begins flight at the river's edge, outstretched wings so heavy they bat the water several times before the bird gains the air, creating brief ripples before settling. Noby runs to the bank, picks up a rock, and skips it along the river's surface.

Some of the good cropland they pass remains fallow, not planted out since the last flood, but of the land in cultivation, most is in cotton and corn, the rest in sugarcane. It is unusual to head into the village for a purpose other than to bring back supplies from the general store. Colfax isn't such a far distance from The Bottom, but Israel makes the journey to town only two or maybe three times a year, a few more if you count the visiting trips to nearby Smithfield Quarter.

"How long to Easter, Papa?" asks Noby.

"Go look at that pecan tree, tell me what you see."

Noby races to a twenty-foot tree in the direction of the river, studies it, and runs back to where Israel waits. "The tree got buds, and little leaves starting."

"How big the leaves?"

"Size of my thumbnail."

"Spring don't come to Louisiana till the pecan trees leaf out, leaves at least big as that quarter dollar we got buried in the backyard," replies Israel. "Easter come about the same time. We got almost three weeks till it safe to plant new in the garden, otherwise late frost likely come and steal up all our labor."

They make good time, less than ninety minutes through the woods on the walk from The Bottom, past Calhoun's Sugarhouse and into Colfax's center. They hurry to the hub of the small town, the courthouse, a dusty-red wood and brick structure that squats on its designated patch of land, blocking the view of the Red River.

Israel and Noby arrive unobserved and slip to the rear of a clutch of two dozen or so colored men standing around in front of the courthouse doors. Noby doesn't recognize many of the men, particularly the handful of whites at the front doing most of the talking, but Isaac McCullen is well known around Colfax, and stands toe-to-toe with one of the white men.

The large colored man takes off his trademark slouch hat, a weather-beaten wreck of a fedora that at one time must have been sleek and velvety brown but now is faded blotchy and dull. A small but showy blue-gray heron feather is tucked securely into the wide band above the brim, and the man waves the hat in an arc above the ground with a flourish. "My name be Isaac McCullen, but just call me McCully," he says to the sheriff. "Only problem we got is getting in, but someone small slip right through that side window."

McCully turns to the waiting men, scrutinizing them like a bloodhound on the scent. Noby Smith freezes in the oversize man's critical gaze. His hand-me-down shirt, torn through at the elbows and threadbare after so many seasons of use, barely keeps out the early-spring dampness. There is only one other boy among the townspeople gathered, smaller and shorter than Noby.

"Sheriff Nash carry the key, but that don't mean we stuck outside," McCully says.

"Ex-sheriff Nash," says the white man. "I'm sheriff of Colfax now."

Most of the men nod in agreement, but some shake their heads, resisting the notion of breaking any parts of the law even if the new replacement sheriff, white and seemingly in charge, stands in front of them encouraging them to do just that.

Noby takes notice of everything around him, as his father has taught him to do when navigating the woods. He observes the beginnings of the white sheriff's impatience, the crowd's shifting mood, Mr. McCullen's confidence, his father's scowl, the nervousness of the new men in town declaring themselves friends of Colfax coloreds, the long white-pine crates of guns that the strangers brought with them into the parish on the steamboat this morning, stacked like coffins in front of the locked double doors of the Colfax courthouse.

Noby swallows hard and steps away from his father. "I can do it, Mr. McCullen, sir," he says. Noby is uncertain whether to try to look smaller than his nine years, so they will believe he can fit through the half-open courthouse window; or bigger, so they think he is up to the task.

15

"Go on, then, boy," says the sheriff. "Sooner we get inside, sooner we establish Republican rule and stand up for our rights." He has a tarnished silver star on the lapel of his jacket and a small pistol firmly seated in a worn leather holster at his hip, sheriff for only a few hours. He waves a folded piece of paper he says is from the governor of Louisiana.

Noby stands still, looks back to his father and Mr. McCullen. Israel doesn't make eye contact, with Noby or anyone else, staring down at the ground as if there is a secret hidden in the dirt at his feet. Israel Smith is not a man to act in haste, especially with whites around. Several long moments pass.

"A good choice," McCully says into the awkward silence. Out of respect, he waits for Israel to give a sign. The two colored men stand with Noby between them.

Outside of the protection of his own home, Israel Smith has an odd, almost hypnotic way of pausing before he speaks, signaling his desire to make a pronouncement, as if asking permission. He loosens and tightens the muscles around his lips, building up the required momentum for the thought to be delivered, giving the impression that the journey from thought to speech is dangerous, weighed down by the boundless possibilities of ominous and unforeseen penalties. But Israel doesn't speak. He only catches Noby's eye, briefly, and then nods, a slight tilt of the head. The crowd waits to see if there is more.

Israel lets his gaze fall downward, and Noby knows his father has resigned himself to the outcome. Noby has given him no option, no real decision to make. Israel Smith would have to go against the wishes of a white man to speak his true mind. His father, like a possum. Laying low in public, going limp in the face of danger.

Noby sprints toward the window, and McCully follows behind to the side of the courthouse at a measured pace. Effortlessly, the thickset man lifts the boy up on his shoulders until Noby's chin is even with the middle of the tiny window. Noby snugs the callused soles of his bare feet on Mr. McCullen's shoulders and finds his center of balance. He feels for the reassuring stiffness of the hidden reading primer tucked securely in his waistband before reaching out to establish a toehold on the high windowsill above.

Noby's palm rests on McCully's coarse hair, just the briefest moment of contact. The big man's fiercely tight hair twists are slightly damp from scalp sweat, giving off the flat scent of yesterday's farm chores and dotted with as much gray as black. Not like Israel's hair, nappy but inky black all the way through, with a softness that yields easily under Noby's fingers.

The men watch the surety of Noby's movements, all eyes on him. Adrenaline pushes Noby forward, but another, more cautious part of him registers the colored men he doesn't know, has never seen. Not to mention the handful of too cordial, unfamiliar white men, as suspect as old, gamy pork.

Noby anchors his bare foot on the ledge, wiggles it through the opening, and contorts his body to follow. He drops down inside the courthouse, out of his father's sight. Later, for his refusal to seek permission first, will come the strap or extra chores, maybe both, Noby's refusal to cry, his mother sneaking him a biscuit or a cold bit of ham if there is any left.

Noby makes his way to a room dominated by a high pinewood counter, with oversize bound books squeezed so tightly along the walls they look like cut logs stacked on end. He is tempted to linger in a place that holds so many books, as if being in such close proximity will help him understand the wonder of the words they contain. One day, he tells himself, he will be able to read these books. Already he can write the year, tracing it in the dirt with a stick, following the swirls and shapes of each of the four parts to form 1-8-7-3, 1873. Already he can write his own name, first and last, Noby Smith. Hansom Brisco, his godfather and owner of the land his father sharecrops, is teaching him how to read and write in the woods, wrapping his big, blistered farmer's hands around Noby's small, eager ones, first guiding the stick and then expecting him to repeat the motion on his own, smiling at the boy's keenness to learn, calling him a natural. Already Noby has mastered some of the sentences in the primer tucked into his waistband. *This is a fat cat on a mat.*

Noby follows the darkened hall past several rooms, some with long pine or oak tables and rows of mismatched chairs, stacked and pushed to the side. The air inside the courthouse smells musty with what Noby assumes is the potent combination of paper and power. He continues around toward the front of the building, where the double doors stand locked, but when he tries to turn one of the knobs from the inside, the door won't open.

"Twist the bolt, boy," a voice calls from outside.

Noby twists and turns metal in random order until the doorknob spins, and then he opens the double doors to both the men and the stacked gun crates outside.

They are in.

The building seems bigger inside than it looked from outside. Israel enters the wide double doors along with the others, unsure what they will do next. He makes sure Noby is safe, watching from the corner of his eye as his son settles himself in a corner. Noby sits small, curling himself into invisibility while the men debate what to do now that they have possession of the courthouse. Though Israel can see Lucy in the boy, her quietness, her reserve, her competence even under crisis, he sees himself in larger measure, not only physically but in the occasional mirrored image of his own moodiness staring back at him, and the impending menace of the red rages. Noby is so obviously from his seed, and David is so obviously not. Noby, his stolen child. Stolen from slavery. Stolen from death. The first of his seed to live with him in freedom.

The sublime blessing of freedom is exacting its price, is demanding his participation here today, and he wants his son to see his bravery. Lucy and Israel came together from Alabama into Louisiana during the War Between the States, during an era when bravery wasn't much of an option. They didn't start out as a couple but came together at the same time, brought in by the same master. Lucy was newly pregnant with David then, but she didn't tell anyone until much later. Israel and Lucy's pairing made sense. Her man was left behind, as were Israel's woman and the children they had together who hadn't already been sold away. The plantation where they lived and worked was put up for sale along with everyone on it, and the slaves went out in all directions, to other parts of Alabama, to North Carolina, to Louisiana, and down deep into Mississippi.

No explanation was given for why they didn't sell Lucy and her man as a pair, but Israel knew he was younger by quite a few years. Maybe the new master thought there was more work left in Israel. Lucy and Israel traveled into central Louisiana by wagon with their new master, a hard, stingy man. By the time they had made the trip and settled into their new surroundings, Lucy and Israel considered themselves together, a pair, making do the best they knew how. They were like-minded enough to be all right with each other.

David was born while most of the white men were away fighting for the Confederacy. Israel thought he was fully prepared to embrace Lucy's child as his own when David came, even though he was the issue of Lucy's other man. But Israel was sickened when he saw the boy-child for the first time; he had felt his insides become a hard knot of disgust and rage. The boy Lucy named David was pale as dried hay, with deep-set eyes an unnatural, grayish color, and wisps of straight, light brown hair on his head. He even smelled different. In between the normal baby smells of milk and spit-up and night soil, Israel thought he sniffed out a thin, sharp odor of ruin, a sullied stink. For Lucy's sake, Israel tried to interest himself in little David, to hold him close, but all he could think about was which white man on the old place had forced himself on Lucy and planted this child. Lucy never apologized or made excuses, and Israel never asked who or what or when. He tried hard to swallow back the revulsion he felt for the boy who grew up to call him Papa, who stared at him with those strange, begging eyes.

Noby was born two years later, after the domination of the North ushered in the miracle of freedom in Louisiana and swept along with it the promise of a new kind of life. Israel was relieved to see his nappy-headed brown son, although the baby was puny and sickly from the start. Lucy did what she could for Noby, but the boy seemed always to be crying or choking or both. There was no medicine, only what an old black nurse-woman on the place could do with herbs while Lucy and Israel worked the field. More important, there wasn't enough food. Sickly babies didn't have much chance to survive, and Lucy was already heavy with another. The war was all but over, and the land in disarray. White men came back from the front, some in anger, most in defeat, and colored men were on the move too. With the children in tow, Lucy and Israel set out from the hill country down toward Alexandria and got work on one of the Calhoun plantations.

Israel remembers the Sunday in the middle of that sweltering summer when they gave up hope for little Noby, the baby listless for several days already, barely responding. Together, Israel and Lucy laid the child out in the back of a wagon, knowing he wouldn't live another week, maybe not another day.

Israel sat vigil alone with Noby, checking to see if he still drew air, trying to get him to drink a drop or two of water, wiping him down. It was the least he could do for the boy, the first son he and Lucy had made together. Noby was lethargic, his breathing dangerously thin, and Israel rigged a shade blanket over his head to mute the sun. Wrapped in his own waiting and grief, Israel was startled when a colored man on a sorrel bay mare passed.

"What you got in the wagon?" the man asked. He was a working farmer with calm brown eyes, fit and well fed, dressed in dirty overalls and a rough homespun shirt, a little younger than Israel.

"This my son, taking his last breaths," Israel said. His tongue worked against him around strangers, and he had to push at the words to make them come out. "We laying him out for the Lord."

"What's wrong with him?" the man asked. He spoke almost like a white man.

Again, Israel tried to judge the man who talked to him from a high perch on his horse, to assess if he posed any danger. "Don't know what he got. He weak-like from the day he born."

The man dismounted and came closer to the wagon. He lifted the thin burial cloth tucked around the lower part of Noby's body. "Skin and bones," he observed.

"Don't none of us have too much to eat," said Israel. "I done lost every son of my flesh before they was ten, from either them or me being sold, and now we got freedom, my boy getting ready to be snatched away before he turn two."

The man reached out to feel the baby's forehead, then took one of Noby's small hands into his own.

Weakly, the tiny baby curled his small fist around the stranger's finger. The man looked surprised. "Can't eat, you say?"

"We got lots of mouths to feed. Noby get his share, but there's not much."

"He got any catching disease?"

"No, sir. None of the rest of the children got this."

"You work here on the Calhoun place?"

"Yes, sir."

"My name is Hansom Brisco. You let him, this baby gonna die right here. Why not give him a chance? My wife will look after him."

Israel didn't understand. "Pardon me, Mr. Brisco?"

"Let me take the boy and see if we can help him."

"The Lord ready to take this boy for His own, sir. What you be wanting with him?"

"Might be nothing wrong but not enough to eat." Brisco sounded angry. "There's enough senseless death to last a lifetime around here."

"Why my boy?"

"Why not?" The anger drained out of Brisco's voice and was replaced by a bargaining tone. Brisco ran his thick and callused hand, the one Noby didn't have hold of, slowly across the smooth cheek of his sunbaked face, buying time. "Look, there's nothing to lose. If the boy dies, I bring him back and you bury him, like you planned. If he lives, in a few days or weeks or months, I return him to you healthy. I'm less than half hour's ride from here."

"Don't seem natural, taking a dying boy from his mama and daddy."

"What they call you?"

"Israel. Israel Smith."

"All right, Israel, who take care of the boy tomorrow while you in the field if he don't oblige and die today? You let me try to save this boy's life, I'll pack up food for you and your family, whether he makes it or not, and deliver it to you here tomorrow."

Israel felt cornered. Hansom Brisco seemed well intentioned, and the rest of the family could use the extra food. They were all hungry. Maybe the man really could save Noby. Israel wanted to believe things like this could happen. "You bring back his body?" he asked.

"Yes. But I hope to bring back a boy made well."

They wrapped Noby tighter in the blanket and transferred him from the back of the wagon to a spot Hansom Brisco made in front of him on his horse.

Israel watched the small trail of dust that swirled behind them as Hansom Brisco rode off with his son.

True to his word, Hansom Brisco brought food for the family and came to visit with periodic reports of Noby's good progress. Two months later, he delivered to Israel and Lucy a vigorous baby boy, strong of lungs, with flesh filled out around his ribs.

"He's your son, always be yours, but they belong to all of us," said Hansom Brisco. "We can't spare a single one. I be watching this boy, not only for health but for what use he put it to."

"You give me back my son. I can't never pay you back enough," Israel said. "But anything in my power I can ever do for you, just ask and it be done. Anything."

"Then let's start now," said Hansom. "I'd like to be godfather to this child, see him to manhood."

Israel, grateful for this unexpected smile of fortune, was thankful to comply. Noby Smith had been stolen for the first time from death.

The courthouse smells stale and damp but protects them from the nipping cold of the wind. The men set about the business of organizing themselves, and the newcomers bark out orders to the colored volunteers, breaking them into groups. There are three white officeholders—the wiry sheriff, with deep lines grooved in his forehead from too much time in the sun; a pasty-faced judge with a thin nose and wide belly; and a small, runtish tax collector. The sheriff takes the lead, and the tax collector sets off down a hallway looking for an office, while the judge keeps taking off his black hat and running his hand over his thinning hair before replacing the hat on his head. The three colored men with the newcomers aren't officeholders and have lived in Colfax two or three years, ex-soldiers in the United States Army in the War Between the States.

Israel is assigned with two others to pry open the wooden crates outside so rifles can be distributed, then joins the rest of the men digging a long trench for a barricade about forty feet in front of the courthouse. Within two hours, the sweat-sheened men have a good start in hollowing out the reddish soil in sections around the courthouse, digging up slimy mud to form a series of trenches that look like a series of narrow, shallow graves. Noby makes himself useful by running water to the men outside and carrying off displaced dirt and mud.

In the early afternoon, they halt to eat, and Israel shares the contents of his dinner bucket with Noby.

"Time for you to go on home now, son," Israel says. He mentions nothing about Noby's part in the morning break-in. "You able to find the way. Follow Red River and then Bayou Darrow."

"Can't I stay with you?" Noby asks.

"Too many guns here. This not a place for a boy after all. Tell your mama I might be staying longer than I thought."

A good number of the men have finished eating and are already back to work, stabbing at the hard ground with pickaxes and shovels. With all the movement, the square has the feel of a disrupted anthill. Noby says goodbye to his father and sets off, alone this time. Retracing the same path in reverse of the morning, Noby pictures his mother in their small cabin, what she is likely to be doing right now. Lucy is always in motion, scrubbing, cooking, cleaning, or sewing. Tending and mending, his father says, and there is fondness to it.

Last Easter, his mother made a new collar for his father's Sunday shirt and passed the old frayed collar down to David. There are too many sons and daughters in their family for his mother to manage new clothes for everyone, or more than a mending and pressing of her own Sunday dress, but she sees to it that each one sports something white.

Lucy Smith is soft-spoken, yielding, always in some stage of creating babies. Unlike this morning, she usually defers, with a calm acceptance demonstrating her unshakable belief in the

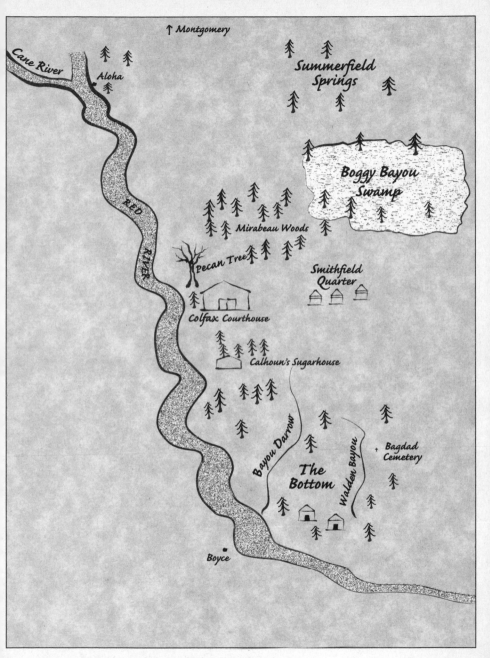

Figure 2. Map of Colfax and surrounding areas

inevitability of life. She delivers the most baffling answers to questions that explode in Noby's head all day long. She doesn't shush him or shoo him away, but her answers seldom fit the questions he asks. The serenity of her voice soothes him nonetheless.

"Mind your father," she says after Noby asks if he can go off to school in Montgomery when he gets older. "God is great," she says when asked why possum tastes different than chicken. "The husband shall rule over the wife" is her response when Noby asks if she tires of wearing the same faded dress four seasons in a row.

Lucy Smith and the other women in The Bottom will make sure there is plenty of food Easter Sunday. Noby assumes Mr. McCullen and his father and the rest of the colored men of Colfax at the courthouse will be finished standing up for their rights by then.

It is only the third week of March.

2

In the calming stillness of Tuesday's earliest morning hours, Israel Smith wrestles with how much time has passed in this place. Today marks the first day of April. It is a full week since the takeover began, and the defenders dwindle. Not all at once, in a mad rush of panic or confusion, but in an unremitting seeping away, hour by hour. Colored men throw off the cause and go back to their homes to try to catch up on farmwork they have missed, or jobs where they have been too long absent, or simply to check that their families are safe. Most have slipped off in the last two days, open in their dismay that the Federals haven't yet arrived in Colfax, and that no one seems to know when they will.

Prior mornings, waking to the foreignness of the courthouse, Israel has risen after waking and stumbled outside to relieve himself. Years of habit have conditioned him to be firmly entrenched in his day's work by sunup, but not today. Reluctantly, he throws aside the blanket and unballs the old homespun jacket serving as his night pillow. He forces himself to his feet and draws the jacket around his shoulders, a comforting warmth against the morning's chill. Mindful of the men still sleeping on the floor around him in the cramped room, he rolls the blanket and stuffs it into a corner before grabbing up his tin cup and boots. It is already light outside, and others are stirring. He stops on the front steps to pull on his boots, not sure whether he should wait for the day's courthouse assignments or just turn in the borrowed rifle and start the long walk home.

Instead, he follows his nose to the coffee, already boiling, and a small group of volunteers, idling. Sam Tademy and McCully are deep in conversation, already on their second cup.

"Brother Sam, when you get here?" asks Israel.

"He set out before daylight, just walk in this morning," McCully answers for Sam. "Musta knowed how much we need more men."

"Polly too sick for me to come earlier," adds Sam. "But I check on Lucy yesterday. They doing all right."

"Thanks to you, Brother Sam," says Israel. Lucy and Sam's wife, Polly, often fish on Walden Bayou together in the early morning before the men go off to tend crops on their different farm sites, and Israel receives, secondhand, much of his neighborhood news from those exchanges.

"You think the Federals come today?" Sam asks. "I don't fancy leaving Polly and the children too long alone on the farm." Sam is short and slight, with carved features. He too is a preacher, with a small congregation in The Bottom.

"We all just waiting," says Israel. "Bad situation, us here, families there. I hope The Bottom far enough away."

"Leastways in town we got guns and numbers on our side," says McCully. "But it not clear how long these men gonna hold. More coming in, but more leaving every day too."

Israel nods and drinks his coffee. While hot enough to be helpful, the foul-tasting liquid is both sour and weak, as if someone has neglected to clean out the pot from the days before. Lucy would never serve such poor coffee. His wife masks the flavor of even the greenest or the oldest beans with chicory or sage, if they are lucky, or at least willow leaves if not. Still, Israel is glad to be out of the close confines of the courthouse and out in the open air, away from the invasive, lingering smells of too many men forced together for too long.

Lucy won't be able to make do without him forever on their rented farm. The crop work has surely fallen behind. Just a day or two more, he tells himself, and one way or the other, he will go back home.

"How the day pass here?" asks Sam.

"I do lookout from the roof, and Brother Israel here patrol around town," McCully says.

Sam looks up. "What they doing putting you on the roof?"

"The roof where I ask to be," says McCully. He walks, surprisingly graceful for such a big man, uncoiling like an oversize spring, full of energy, his dirt-caked overalls stiff with ground-in grime. McCully motions for Sam to follow. "Come up. See for yourself. You might's well come too, Israel."

The two men follow McCully up the pine ladder leaning against the side of the east courthouse wall up to the flat roof.

"Fine day to take the courthouse," McCully says with a grin when they get there.

"This not a game," Sam snaps, his voice testy. He is angry about leaving Polly and his boys alone with the farm, angry that he's jeopardizing not only his job overseeing old man Swafford's place but his hard-won reputation for dependability, angry that all he has to show for eight years of freedom is more children, a mule and wagon that aren't yet his, a few saved coins buried beneath the live-oak tree by the smokehouse, and a stumbling dream on which he has yet to make good.

"No, 'cept for us voting Republicans in office in the first place, this here the most real thing this town done, far as I remember." McCully chooses his words deliberately, chews on each one. The grin never leaves his face, and his eyes never leave Sam's.

Sam looks away first. "We put everybody at risk coming here."

"Name a time we not at risk." McCully looks at Sam as if sizing him for a new suit of clothes. "You a front man, Sam. Some born to follow, but your ideas put you in front, no matter that's where you wanna be or not."

Sam gestures to the rifle McCully holds close and easy by his side, gun barrel down. "That's not the way," he says.

"Now, that's a conversation worth our time. Way I see it, this here the *only* way to get to those things you always talking about." McCully warms up to his subject. "You don't demand what's yours, you live with nothing or with leftover. White man won't give us nothing worth having if we won't fight for it ourselves. Don't expect nothing, don't get nothing. We the ones gonna change the South. We need the Federals for now so white men pay attention, but we got the equal rights."

"Not all white men bad, McCully. Look at the ones in the fight with us."

"Why everybody talk about good white men and bad white men? I'm here because it supposed to be my boy Spenser or one day your boy Green or Israel's boy Noby holding papers from the governor, giving orders. Folks need to get used to Republicans in Colfax, so next we get us colored Republicans for the big jobs. Your sons or my son."

"You too impatient, McCully," says Israel. "It take time."

"How long you think we got to wait? We three men already old."

"Just 'cause we over fifty don't mean we too old to know what we up against here," Sam replies.

"You deny we need to keep the courthouse for the Republicans we elected till troops come from New Orleans?" McCully closes the distance between himself and Sam, enough so Sam can feel the heat of his breath. There is an intentional intimidation to the man, as if McCully purposely leans into his weight to give Sam less room to move. "You saying if the colored man don't step up to claim our rights, those rights still be there next time we go look for them?"

"I come. I'm here," Sam says wearily.

"Why?"

"Why what?" asks Sam.

"Only a handful of colored Colfax citizens backing what we doing here. The rest going about their business just hoping for the best." McCully drops his teasing tone. "You coulda stay out to Mr. Swafford's, running his place, without coming to town and showing your hand. Why you here?"

Sam hesitates. "I tell you why, Brother McCully," he says carefully. "I walk all the way out of Alabama into Louisiana on a barebone hope to find some better way to live free, make a family and keep them close, work hard enough to sweat on my own piece of land, and pass what I earn to my children when my time on earth is done. Before, I get sold from place to place whenever it suit somebody else. Pick up and go without no notice, no reason why, follow some new master, one more place worse than the last. Not supposed to be no thought of who's left behind." Sam takes off his hat, delaying the words. "I'm home now. Colfax and The Bottom my home. Hard and slow and ugly sometimes, but this mine, and I got the duty to make this town a place easier for my children than it be for you or for me. I'm here because it late in life, and you right. We getting old, and it up to us to move the race forward whenever and however we able."

"Amen, Brother Sam," McCully says, nodding slowly in agreement. "You preach the truth."

"How long you think we be here?" Sam asks.

"Until these new Republicans make peace with the old guard, or Federals come from New Orleans to force the law. Whichever come first."

Sam looks doubtful. "These old boys around here used to giving the orders. Sheriff Nash not gonna step to the side for a new sheriff just because colored vote him out. And Federals not gonna stay in town forever."

McCully removes his brown fedora, extends it like a live, fragile thing, runs his fingers along the feather in the brim, holds it out to Sam for inspection. "See this here hat?" he says. "This my voting hat. I wear it the day we vote them men in, and I keep on wearing it till they take up the office for good. Just like this here phoenix feather, we gonna get stronger and stronger and rise from the ashes where we been."

"What you talking now, McCully?" asks Sam. "That feather come from one of the birds common as dirt around here."

"I'm disappointed in you, Sam," says McCully. "You showing a terrible failure of imagination. This here a rare feather from the phoenix bird what lived in the desert for five hundred years, go up in flames, and raise itself up brand-new from the ashes."

Sam is used to McCully, doesn't contradict him, and McCully returns the hat to his head. "We got to protect the Republicans until the Federals get here," McCully says. "I don't care nothing about them white officials, but I care about the Republican Party. They set us free, and I vote with them every time. I glad to die on top of the party if it come to it. After the Federals leave, then we deal with whatever the good colored citizens of Colfax got to do. We prove they can't scare us off from voting. Now we got to protect our choice. There's more of us colored than there is white around Colfax. We got the majority."

From the vantage point of the courthouse roof, Colfax lies neatly below. There are five or six dwelling houses in Colfax proper, spaced far apart, to house a population of only seventy-five that includes several outlying sections. Not far from the courthouse is the general store.

"Look yonder," says McCully. "A perfect view of Smithfield Quarter." He points northeast to the closely packed colored settlement directly outside the town. "From here," he goes on, "I almost can look into my house and see what my wife got cooking in the pot for supper."

"It is a good lookout point," Sam agrees. "And you got your fair share of kin down there."

"Over this way, Mirabeau Woods." McCully turns north and gives a broad sweep of his arm. "Clear line of sight all the way to the trees." He turns toward the river. "Only thing I can't see is the river side, between the oaks and cypress, and the drop-off to the Red River bank. Too overgrown."

Sam takes it all in. "They tell you what you supposed to do from up here?"

"Look for trouble," McCully says, and laughs. Several men below look up. The laugh is too loud and too long. "I gets the easiest job," McCully goes on. "Trouble never too hard to find."

Sam changes the subject. "I just come to be useful."

"First thing is get you one of these rifles they pass out. That old worn-out shotgun you dragging probably fire once and blow up."

"They passing out shotguns?"

"Not shotguns. Almost-new Enfield rifles, left over from the war, if you serious about staying. Can pick out a man almost from here to Smithfield Quarter. I got some pull. I get you one before they run out."

"I wouldn't hardly know how to use a rifle that shot straight." Sam gives McCully another look. "What you up to, McCully? What you want?"

McCully acts hurt. "Why so suspicious, Sam? We been friends a long time."

Sam doesn't answer, just continues to give McCully the fish-eye.

"Plain said," McCully finally says, "it too late for my boy Spenser. But I been thinking about my younger ones. I want to send them to your colored school."

"You know good and well there ain't no school yet. Not till we get land and a building and a teacher. No matter if you get me a rifle or not, if I start a colored school, Amy and the others be welcome."

"There'll be a school, all right, assuming we get you out of here in one piece," McCully says. "You a front man, Sam."

All three men climb down from the roof to find an Enfield rifle for Sam. Once again, as he has each morning for over a week, Israel decides to stay another day to defend the Republican officials.

They drill for almost an hour before setting off on morning patrols. Those with Enfields watch their assigned group leader demonstrate the thirteen steps of loading and reloading the rifle. Levi Allen, a colored war veteran, carries himself in such a way that his clothes seem clean and ironed even though, like everyone else, he has slept in them for almost a week. He has a square-shouldered look about him, so full of discipline that the other men appear lax and unkempt in comparison. In order to preserve powder and cartridges, none of the men actually fires or loads. Mostly, they practice as units, marching together in assigned groups back and forth in front of the courthouse with their weapons drawn or hoisted onto their shoulders.

Levi divides them into three groups, with ten to fifteen colored men of Colfax in each, and assigns another half dozen to stay on the grounds around the building with their weapons visible. McCully remains overhead, spotter on the courthouse roof.

Sam Tademy joins Israel's unit, and they cut back behind the courthouse to begin the day's patrol, footslogging along the bank of the Red River, past the Pecan Tree, around to the northern tip of Mirabeau Woods, east to Smithfield Quarter, almost down to Calhoun's Sugarhouse, and back to the courthouse again. "Sweeping the perimeter," Levi Allen calls it. They can't cover as much distance on foot as the mounted men. Those few who have horses form a separate patrol that ventures out in a wider arc to check the entrances to Colfax, displaying their strength to the townspeople, white and black.

They make their first wide loop, through piney woods and riverbanks, across the one well-traveled wide road but more often over dirt trails, patrolling single file or by sloppy pairs in lazy circles around the town. Every man on patrol is required to carry a firearm, but the unfamiliar weight feels all wrong to Israel, not centering wide across the back as with the plow, or through the middle as when lovemaking, or through the shoulders as while fishing.

On their third elliptical march around town, just past the old Pecan Tree, they hear a warning signal from the direction of the courthouse, two pistol shots in succession. Levi holds up one hand, stopping the men in their tracks, and waves them into position, spreading them in a loose ring across the field. There is minor confusion, since they have never practiced this maneuver. It doesn't take long for the white men to make themselves visible, riding in along the riverside, coming out of the woods almost right on top of the patrol.

Israel counts nine on horseback, advancing slowly down the wide dusty road. The white men have been caught off guard, the surprise on their faces easy to read. There are more colored men on foot than white horsemen, but that gives Israel small comfort.

To Israel's right, Sam Tademy tightens his grip on his Enfield, and Israel follows suit. This is uncharted territory. There is no reliable script for how the two opposing groups are supposed to act toward each other if the colored men refuse to give way.

"I'm J. W. Hadnot, from Montgomery," the lead white man says. "We got business at the courthouse."

Israel recognizes this man and hopes the memory is not mutual. There are Hadnots spread from Montgomery to Alexandria, in the towns and in the backcountry, known for both their political connections and their commitment to white supremacy. This particular Hadnot's name is Smokin' Jimmy, presumably for the pipe he keeps clenched between his teeth, lit or not, and he is high up in the ranks of the White League. In the woods outside of the polling place last year, Smokin' Jimmy Hadnot and a handful of others in the White League intercepted and challenged every one of the hundred colored men traveling to Montgomery to vote, threatening to kill them on the spot if they didn't turn back before casting their ballot. A majority of the colored men traveled in armed groups, and although most were intimidated, they were not deterred. It is well known that the main job of the White League is to terrorize white and black Republicans, to keep them away from polling places, but the organization has obviously expanded its charter.

"Only Republicans got business in the courthouse today," says Levi.

Smokin' Jimmy Hadnot regards him quizzically, as if Levi is a pet dog that suddenly knows how to talk.

"Who are *you*, boy?" he asks.

"My name is Levi Allen. Captain Levi Allen."

Smokin' Jimmy Hadnot pointedly ignores Levi. He eyes the other men of the foot patrol one by one, willing them to acknowledge his authority.

"Most of you are good boys," Hadnot says, barely shifting in the saddle. He delivers his words with the sluggish, thin-lipped smile all of them recognize as threat. "You don't want to be throwing in your lot with carpetbaggers."

He takes his time, removes the pipe from his mouth, leans to the side of his horse, and spits at the base of the trunk of the Pecan Tree. Israel holds his breath, knowing better than to meet the white man's cocksure gaze. He is just one of the faceless colored men he hopes Hadnot won't remember.

"Time to get back to your own concerns while you still got the chance, go back to your homes. You know better. You dealing with something you can't understand here. Let us take care of the politics."

Levi stands his ground. "We got the right to be here. We hold the courthouse for officers duly appointed by the governor of the state of Louisiana."

Once again, Hadnot ignores Levi. "What you boys think you doing with those weapons, scaring all the decent people in town?" he asks.

"We ask you to turn around and go back to Montgomery," Levi says.

Hadnot finally turns to Levi, his eyes a searing blue buried deep under hooded lids. "You in over your head, boy."

"These townspeople protect the appointed officers and the courthouse, sir." Levi seems unruffled, his body all but hidden from view by the massive bulk of his sky-blue military greatcoat, which makes him look bigger than he is. Israel, on the other hand, feels the runoff of sweat from his scalp and the widening dampness around his armpits. He doesn't want to call attention to himself by wiping his face, so he lets the sweat run off the slick surface of his skin to splatter in little droplets to the ground.

"I wanna talk to someone in charge," Hadnot says. "Are the white men at the courthouse?"

"We can't allow you further into town. We ask you to turn around and ride out. Those are our orders."

Hadnot's face turns a mottled red, as if someone has hands around his throat, choking him.

"Who you think you talking to, boy?" he sputters. He has a long-nose pistol tucked in the side of his saddle, and reaches to draw it out.

The other men on horseback reach for their guns too, as if it is an orchestrated, singular move. They carry an assortment of weapons, mostly pistols and shotguns, although two of the men on horseback are armed with nothing more than the long-standing assumption of privilege.

"Trouble's not what we want," Levi says evenly, "but each of us ready for it." He brings his Enfield rifle to his shoulder, pointing it directly at Hadnot's chest, with his finger on the trigger lock.

The colored men follow Levi's lead. Israel lifts the heavy weight of his rifle, hoping the shaking of his arms and legs isn't noticeable, to either the men on horseback or the men on the ground. He hears heavy drags of breath coming from men on both sides as he points the gun in the general direction of the horses.

Hadnot pauses, assessing the situation. "Bring me the one calls himself the new sheriff," he says finally. "I won't waste my time talking to a colored boy."

"Unless you got special business in Colfax, no one comes in," Levi says.

"Only business with you got a bullet or rope connected." Smokin' Jimmy Hadnot waves a piece of paper over his head. "This a warrant for the arrest of the black radicals. That include you. Go get me the new sheriff. His scrap of paper don't make him legitimate, but least he's white."

"The Republicans won on Election Day, and they in office now," Levi says, as if explaining a simple lesson to a dull-witted child. "A warrant from Montgomery is no good here. We asking you to turn around and go on your way, peaceable."

Hadnot turns halfway in his saddle so the men on horseback can hear. "Carpetbaggers," he says with disgust, shaking his head. The other men nod in agreement and laugh, but there is tentativeness in it.

"You from Montgomery, Mr. Hadnot, not Colfax." Israel sees Levi steady the angle of the Enfield rifle, tightening his index finger around the trigger as he talks. "I been appointed by the governor of the state of Louisiana."

"We don't accept you or the governor, neither one. We run Grant Parish without outside meddling. You leading these local boys someplace they be sorry to find themselves later."

"These *men* plenty capable to protect their own rights," says Levi.

"These boys can't do their own thinking, we all know that. And you can't stay forever. You gonna give them work too, after you gone? Shelter their families?"

"The party in office changed, Mr. Hadnot," Levi says. "Time to turn around."

Neither Hadnot nor Levi moves for several long seconds, and the men on both sides wait. At last, Hadnot gives a firm squeeze of his heels, unhurriedly, edging the dapple-gray mare toward the ragged line of men on the ground.

Levi fires once, a quick shot gotten off just in front of Hadnot's mare, and Hadnot pulls back sharply on the reins. The mare prances nervously, whinnying and snorting, but Hadnot quickly gets her under control. It is all heavy breathing and hearts pounding, but no one else fires.

"Time to turn around, Mr. Hadnot." There isn't a quiver in Levi's voice. He brings a pistol out from under his coat and aims it squarely at Hadnot's head. "The next one won't miss."

Israel feels a sickness in his stomach. He would rather strain against the plow in hard labor, ass side of a mule, than bear the self-defining weight of his gun for one minute more, but he forces himself to pull up on his rifle as well. All the men on the ground do the same.

Hadnot's barely disguised rage hardens into stony resolve. He gives a signal to the men on horseback, an abrupt wave of his hand. "You not worth the bullet to put you in your place, and you don't understand how we do things here. Yet." With exaggerated, careful movements, Hadnot tugs on the reins to turn his horse. "Sheriff Christopher Columbus Nash is the real sheriff of Colfax, and he won't like this one bit. Count on us coming back."

The other mounted men turn in a wary arc away from the center of town.

After the white men retreat, the colored men look nervously at one another. Israel isn't sure who delivers the first big whoop, but before long, they all let loose in an excited churn of voices.

"They know we mean business," says McCully's son, Spenser, bringing the sight of his rifle to his eye and aiming the long barrel in the direction the horsemen just rode. "This our town now."

"Settle down," Levi says, not only to Spenser but to all of the men, and there is a startling quiet as the adrenaline begins to drain away. In contrast to the rest, Levi's voice seems infinitely sad. "It's only the beginning."

Even before Levi finishes the words, Israel knows what he says is true.

As soon as the patrol reports back to the courthouse, the new sheriff holds a general meeting in the area surrounding the giant Pecan Tree.

"I'm calling for deputies," he says. Sheriff Shaw's pale face is flushed, haggard and drooped as a hound's. Rigid muscles around his thin lips do little to hide his anger. His entourage, including Levi Allen, moves close together behind him in a show of solidarity. "We got word a group out of Montgomery planning to attack Colfax tomorrow. They threatening to replace all the Republican appointees with their own party and hang the black radicals. Two things we need. We need to hold the courthouse to protect the lawful appointed Republican officers, and we need to keep the peace."

Sam Tademy steps forward. "Where the Federals at?" he asks. "The Federals supposed to be here if the election men have trouble taking office. That be the understanding."

As the colored men talk among themselves, uncertain, McCully elbows his way forward in the crowd, his brown fedora jammed down low on his head.

"I voted Republican last November," he proclaims loudly, his voice at full pitch. He goes quiet until he reaches a spot directly opposite the sheriff, not over three feet from the politicians standing near the base of the Pecan Tree. "You might could say it was me voted you folks here in the first place." McCully holds himself very straight, towering over the men around him, refusing to be either dismissed or ignored. "Where you from, Sheriff Shaw?"

The sheriff's face tightens, and he makes no attempt to hide either his puzzlement or his annoyance. "Philadelphia, by birth," he says reluctantly.

"I don't know how it be where you from, but any colored man vote Republican in Colfax may as well walk up to the devil, introduce himself, and slip his own neck into the hanging noose." McCully stretches out one arm and waves it in a broad motion, indicating everyone present. "Every man here got a story, but I'ma tell you about my family. We got more than a few McCullens around Colfax.

"The white man at the livery stable tell my brother Eli he see him in hell 'fore he let him vote Republican, but Eli vote anyhow. Next day no more job. After five years doing whatever that white man ask. Best livery hand this town ever seen, but Eli don't get no more work from any white man in Colfax."

The crowd responds. "Amen, Brother McCully."

"My brother Abe vote, get his ribs kicked in behind his shed the next night by three white men don't even bother to hide they faces. In front of his woman and children. Nothing happen to those men. They brag on it and come out meaner the next time."

"Preach on."

"Instead of marching together right up the road to Mr. Calhoun's plantation to vote, like we done in 1868, last year the polling place move way out almost to Montgomery, where we couldn't hardly get to it. The few colored could get hold of a mule or horse carried others out with them, and the rest of us walked, took near the whole day. We put our votes through."

"What's your point, McCully?" asks the sheriff, barely keeping his tone level as he clenches and unclenches his fists at his sides.

"White men here in Louisiana determined. You got a letter from the governor in your pocket, don't mean we won much of nothing yet. Colored men here already prove we able to protect the courthouse and the Republican Party. But keep the peace? That a whole different bucket of slop, unless you talking about things going backwards to how they was before. That the only peace we likely to get. The colored citizens of Colfax gone too far down the road now to give up that ground."

There are a few echoes of "That's right," but most of the men stay quiet and uncommitted, tracking the exchange between McCully and the sheriff like a horse race, not yet choosing sides.

"You can't protect the courthouse and keep peace at the same time," McCully says. "Sam's right. We need the Federals, but we need Colfax colored men even more to force change on this town. We risking everything, but long as we got guns, we at the level of the white man. We got majority. We got right on our side. We got law. Even if they bring in every white man from Grant Parish."

"We Republicans too, me, the judge, the tax assessor, throwing our lot in for change," says the sheriff. "We got plenty to lose. This don't go down easy for any Republican, white or colored." Irritation settles along the deep creases of his face. He lets go of a bit of the tobacco juice he holds in his cheek, spitting it out in the dirt. "You volunteering for deputy or not?" he asks McCully.

McCully takes off his fedora and, in an exaggerated, theatrical gesture, raises it above his head. The light plays off the colors of the heron feather, from blue to gray and back again. "I volunteers," he says. "And my son gonna volunteer too."

The sign-ups go slowly at first, but before long, there are six-teen new deputies sworn in among the colored men of Colfax.

Israel packs his dinner pail and his other belongings into the blanket, balls it tight, twists a knot, and flings his possessions over his shoulder. One last look around the room convinces him he has left nothing behind. As he prepares to leave, he almost collides with McCully and Sam.

McCully eyes his bundle. "You not doing your children no favor, quitting now."

When McCully comes around, Israel feels small, as if he has something to apologize for. "We in too deep. Lucy alone on the place. I got to go back."

"You call one thing right," McCully says. He enters the room and leans his weight against a heavy oak table. His beard is thick and full, dotted with gray, his hair uncombed, and his clothes filthy from a week's worth of tar and grime on the roof. "What you call right is, we in too deep to back down now," he says. "This a test. Because of this morning, they see us now. We visible. You know what that is, Brother Israel, how important that is, to be vis-ible? It mean now we something they got to deal with."

Israel comes back sharply: "I know visible, McCully. You not the only one know some big words. I got to think of my own."

"True again. Lucy and the children the reason you need to stay."

"What good it do if we dead?" Israel wishes he had slipped away sooner, without the need to explain himself.

"There's worse than dead." McCully steps closer. "Look here, Brother Israel, nobody talking dead but you."

"You think the Federals still coming?" Israel asks.

"We got to get more men to stand up. That way, when troops come or troops leave, the old guard know they can't mess with the colored men of Colfax, like before. Us men here, right now, got to break that way of thinking. Break that way of living."

"We only sign on to hold the courthouse for a day or two. Now there's shooting, going head-to-head with white men, and promise of more. We running out of men and food. This can only go one way."

"Don't know no such thing," says McCully. "When we ever stand together as men and ask for what's coming to us? Food be scarce now, but food easier to come by than men. Yes, some don't want nothing to do with us courthouse men, don't want to be seen drinking out the same cup, like we dogs gone mad. Looking over they shoulders like they afraid the white man see us talking and think they one of us. Why a few white men getting run off more important than all the colored shot and hung? Time to think a new way, Brother Israel."

"A few days or weeks marching around town don't make us ready."

"What example you putting forward to your sons?" McCully says. "First scuffle, and you ready to go off with your tail between your legs."

"Nothing but words. Still got to think about Lucy and the children."

McCully doesn't hesitate. "Sam and me just been talking. He gonna bring his family up from The Bottom to stay with my brother in Smithfield Quarter, where we able to watch over them. And my wife happy to make room for Lucy and your children till this thing over."

Israel wavers. He thinks about the patrols, the unwashed men in the courthouse, the shacks filled with defenseless women and children on the farms that ring the borders of Colfax. He thinks of his sons Noby and David and what sort of future they have in Louisiana.

"We doing this for the children," says McCully, as if reading Israel's thoughts and giving a final push. "You come this far. What say you now, Brother Israel?"

Israel looks to Sam Tademy, standing quiet behind McCully. Sam nods.

Everything suddenly seems too heavy, and Israel drops his rolled blanket in the corner of the courtroom.

"I hope you right, Brother McCully," Israel says.

Israel Smith bears the added weight of his new Enfield rifle as he trudges along the last bit of the road home. Under different circumstances, the novelty of today's warm spring sun would coax a more hopeful mood, but even the respite from the gloom of winter and the promise of increasing green in the landscape do nothing to calm his nerves. At his first glimpse of his cabin, the ragged brick of the fireplace, the familiar contours of the sloped log walls, his reaction is a sharp, euphoric rush. He is tempted to run through the field, burst through the door, find Lucy, and kiss her square on the lips in broad daylight. As if miraculously bidden outside by his need, she comes out of the cabin with a tin of slops and dirty wash-water to throw to the pig. Intent on her task, she doesn't see Israel at first, and he studies his wife as if he has been away years, not a single week.

Lucy has gone stouter with each successive baby. She is significantly shorter than he is, so short he can look down on the top of her kerchief when they stand side by side. She has a broad, agreeable face and thick, powerful arms equally adept at cradling a baby or splitting logs for the fire, and the early graying of the hair around her temples somehow softens her. She carries this baby low, and Israel knows this one has made her movements slower than usual, her hand often at her back as a counterbalancing weight. In the courthouse, even the quietest men have taken to talking about their wives aloud, longingly, even those whose wives are known to be scolds. None of the volunteers is a stranger to crowded living and crowded sleeping quarters, but at home they are surrounded by the rhythms and habits of their own families, not jammed tight into small courthouse rooms, set adrift among nervous, snoring men with personal habits as annoying as their own.

Israel keeps the run out of his step but fast-walks toward the cabin, and when Lucy finally catches sight of him, she hastily throws the slops toward the pig and waits on him in the front yard.

"You back," she says, relief so evident in her face that Israel feels a stab of guilt at leaving her alone for so long. She looks him up and down to assure herself he is the same as when he left.

"Not to stay," says Israel.

Lucy stands still for a moment, then turns her back to Israel and moves toward the cabin. "You'll be wanting to eat," she says.

Israel follows her inside. While Lucy spoons up a thin stew from the kettle in the fireplace and cuts him a wedge of two-day-old corn bread, Israel breathes in the familiarity and comfort of his cabin. He eats, comforted by the familiarity of his wife's cooking.

"Where the boys?" he asks.

"'Round back cleaning out the barn. We hard pressed to keep things going without you here. They working sunup to sundown."

Israel nods, continues to eat the tepid fish stew, unwilling to begin.

"I seen Polly Tademy just this morning, down to Walden Bayou," says Lucy. "Polly say Sam swallowed up by the courthouse too, same as you. Say we got to keep each other strong while our men stand up. Say if she wasn't a woman, she be down to the court-house with the rest of you."

"Polly speak out too much like a man to suit me," says Israel. When Lucy doesn't respond and the silence threatens to go stony between them, he adds, "But I know how tight the two of you is."

Lucy dishes up more stew for Israel, and he eats this helping at a more leisurely pace. Finally, he makes a start. "This afternoon the new sheriff put the call out for deputies."

Lucy drops all pretense of calm, unable to mask the alarm in her voice. "You didn't step forward, did you, Israel?"

"Nah. McCully and one of his sons signed up, but Sam and me didn't."

"Praise be."

"Sixteen colored men official deputies now."

"When you home for good, Israel?" Lucy asks. "Supposed to be the Federals defending the election men."

"I only come back today to carry you all to Smithfield Quarter," says Israel. He doesn't look Lucy in the eye. "We can't leave go of the courthouse till the Federals come, and the ugly got a face to it now. Smokin' Jimmy Hadnot the one intending to take the courthouse back."

"The head of the White League? How a sprinkling of colored farmers gonna hold off the White League?"

"We almost sixty men strong, with guns." Israel doesn't admit to the dwindling numbers of the last few days. "Smithfield Quarter closer to Colfax, closer to our patrols and our rifles. You safer staying with McCully's wife in Smithfield Quarter than out here alone. Some of the others moving they families too."

"Polly don't say nothing this morning about moving."

"Sam coming for her today, same as me for you," Israel says.

"Our life is out here in The Bottom, Israel. We got crops in the field and animals to tend. What you thinking?"

"Hansom Brisco refuse to join with us at the courthouse, but he gonna look after our place here best he can while we gone. I talk to him just before coming. We packing up what we can and bringing the cow. This the way it gonna be, Lucy."

Lucy only stares at her husband for a moment, enough to come to terms with the hardness of his face and the resolve rooted in his eyes, then gives a small, resigned shrug. She calls for the children and begins to pack up the few belongings they will need for their journey into town.

3

ucy doesn't enjoy living in someone else's house. Already she misses their farm. Smithfield Quarter is foreign, as different from The Bottom as her sons are from each other. The colored settlement only a half mile from the courthouse is a dense warren of close-set log and plank cabins. Fifteen or so houses spill out along the length of the community on either side of bisecting dirt paths. As spring weather turns, newly washed clothes flap on cord lines strung behind cabins, occupants blanket the reddish soil of their small garden patches with thick layers of pine straw to protect their root vegetables from the possibilities of late frost, chickens boldly strut across the cut-through walking trails. Children play noisy games of hide-and-seek or marbles in the middle of the dusty thoroughfare, burning off energy until called in for the evening. Old folks sit on their front porches day and night, greeting passersby, and housewives bring out baskets of their darning and sewing work to join them. Stray lean-ribbed dogs forage, feisty cats chase mice. Compared to the self-contained isolation of more remote farms, life teems in Smithfield Quarter, the families here used to being cheek by jowl. The vast majority of the townspeople in Smithfield Quarter stay neutral, refusing to display defiance, despite the drama taking place in the courthouse and the town only minutes away.

They look of a type, these one- or two-room cubes in this section of the quarter, with a single small window by the front door, peeking out to the porch. Each has narrow wooden steps leading up to a raised, warped porch in front and back; each has gaps between the wall boards patched with crisscrosses of wood and tin, and each has some sitting place, a stump, bench, or chair out on the porch, under the eaves. Without exception, every one of the small wooden houses is propped up at each corner on stacked blocks, raising the wooden slats off the ground by several feet. When the inevitable floodwaters rise above the sunken ground level each year or two, the added height is sometimes enough to save belongings or an entire house from washing away. The tilt of the porch depends on how much the ground underneath has shifted since the last flood.

Lucy feels no safer at McCully's house near town than she did two mornings ago waking in her own bed. Big-bellied pregnant, she sleeps in the bed with McCully's wife and her two youngest. Six of Lucy and Israel's children sleep on the floor alongside the McCullens' four, a sea of brown and tan child-flesh tussling for coverings, quilts, and space, a jumble of jabbing elbows and knees fighting for a crowded night's sleep. Israel spent only enough time to oversee the transfer, and then he was off to the courthouse again, leaving Lucy to her own devices.

"I thanks you," Lucy says to McCully's wife, Carolyn, in a rare moment of quiet. "All these children too much for anybody's house but mine. Mighty kind of you to take us in."

"We no stranger to children in this house. You already been a help, what with the meals and the cleaning," says Carolyn. "And the cow benefit mine and yours both."

Lucy's youngest wakes with a startled cry. What starts as whimpering soon becomes a steady wail of abandon, building in volume.

"Teething," Lucy says with an apologetic shrug as she picks up the baby and begins to massage his gums. "Maybe sassafras tea help this time."

Carolyn sympathizes, but the constant crying just adds to the chaos of the household and keeps everyone on edge.

By the time evening comes, Lucy is exhausted. Of the six children still with her, the two girls are the only real help with housework and the baby, and both are still too young, at seven and eight, to take charge completely for very long. The girls have fallen fast asleep inside, cocooned together on the front-room floor near the fireplace. The baby has had a particularly bad day, has barely stopped crying even to eat. Lucy breaks off a small piece of the sassafras bark she used to steep the sedating tea potion and ties it around her baby boy's neck. Despite the chill in the evening air, she takes him out to the front porch, away from all of the bodies crammed inside. He continues to bawl, his face a contorted mess, his wriggling body a rebuke to her ineffective efforts to soothe him.

Lucy is surrounded by people she doesn't know very well, in a strange place, under an enormous, indifferent night sky. Her husband, normally cautious, has thrown his lot in with radicals carrying guns and challenging white men, and she doesn't have control of her children. She sits and rocks. A smattering of people pass the cabin along the dirt path out front. Lucy speaks to each, just enough to be polite, lost in her own misery, until a tall, familiar figure walks briskly toward the house and turns up the trodden path leading to the porch. She would recognize Polly Tademy's simple olive housedress anywhere. Her neighbor from The Bottom is five years younger and lanky, a wisp of a woman, especially compared to Lucy's girth. Her inky-dark hair is without a trace of gray, pulled back in a severe style, and fastened at the nape of her neck with a strip of cloth.

"I hear you all the way down the road," Polly says. "I know the baby be teething, so I brung something for him."

"Israel say you coming to town too," says Lucy. "Can't say I'm sorry to see a friend in this place."

"We staying with McCully's brother 'round the way, three houses down."

Polly storms the porch as if it is her own and pulls Lucy's baby into her arms. "This one unhappy boy," she says. She pulls out a small glass vial of a brownish liquid and balances it on her palm.

"What's that?" asks Lucy.

"Just a bit of whiskey," says Polly.

Lucy looks over her shoulder to see if anyone is watching. "You know good and well Israel don't approve," she whispers. "Neither do Sam. Whiskey the devil's work."

"Is they here?" asks Polly. "Is they the ones with new teeth coming in or wanting some sleep?"

"But whiskey, Polly. Where it come from?"

"I got my ways. Come on, Lucy, this sassafras bark not doing no good tonight for the child. Some whiskey on the gums give him some release. And the rest of us too."

"Israel won't like it," says Lucy.

"Israel don't need to know every little thing. We two roads going to the same place, men and women, and don't need to share each bump and scrape along the way." Polly rocks the fussy baby, who already shows some signs of quieting. "Men got they own kind of business."

"Anything new happen at the courthouse today? I ain't seen Israel since morning."

"Sam just leave from his evening visit. Seem the new sheriff just capture the old sheriff and holding him down at Calhoun's Sugarhouse. And some colored break into a white man's house in town and run him and his family out. Things is building to a head fast. Too fast."

"Sam or Israel any part of that mess?" Lucy asks.

"Nah. Spenser McCullen and a few of the young ones gone off on they own and go a little wild."

"They gonna get us all killed," says Lucy.

"Seem to me we sometimes coming at the Reconstruction too soft, willing to settle for too little, 'cause we was so use to worse before. It got to be hard for someone young as Spenser to understand why things change so slow. Why it seem like everybody want to see our menfolks meek?"

"You not scared for Sam?" asks Lucy. "We farmers, not fighters."

"There's something to be scared of every day," says Polly.

"I'm afraid for Israel. Israel and me, we not like you and Sam," says Lucy.

"You be surprised what a person got in them to do when the time come."

"Our men in the courthouse gonna bring the white man down on us," whispers Lucy.

"Them what gonna be down on us, down already," Polly says, dismissive. "They's a time for sitting still and praying the wind blow over you, and they's a time to rise up and face the storm."

"Wish I be bold like you."

Polly laughs. "One of me more than enough." She quickly becomes serious. "Tomorrow let's us go down to the courthouse, carry some food over for the men, and do some cleaning. With all them guns, they say the courthouse the safest place in town."

"I don't know," says Lucy. "The children—"

"The children look after each other while we gone, and Carolyn's here. Always a help to me to see a thing with my own eyes before it get a chance to grow too big and be discouraging. I'm thinking we both needs to see this courthouse from the inside. We be back here soon enough."

Lucy doesn't commit. She doesn't say yes, but she doesn't say no either.

She and Polly sit out on the porch together in the cold, until the baby falls asleep.

Early on Friday, Israel finds an unoccupied place on the front stoop of the courthouse and settles himself on the wide planks. He pulls off his boots, lets his legs hang over the side, and tries to stay out of the way. It is still a little chilly for bare feet, but airing his toes feels good. He knocks large clumps of dried, crusted mud off his boots by banging the soles together, and uses an old moth-eaten rag from the back storeroom to buff up the leather. There is little point to the exercise—the boots will muddy again on patrol later in the day—but he has been consumed all morning with the need to tidy up around himself, as if less dirt can inspire more logic and order.

Israel loses himself in polishing the rough-stitched cowhide the faded color of rotting pecans, worn dangerously thin and soft at the heel. They need mending again. From the corner of his eye, he catches sight of the skirt hems of a pair of women coming past him up the steps to the front doors of the courthouse. He moves aside for them, forced to glance up from his work.

"Morning, Lucy. Morning, Sister Polly," says Israel, surprised, and touches a finger to his hat. His wife wears her everyday long skirt, its soft pleats covered by her bleached-white cotton work apron. "What you ladies doing here?"

"We hear it's a disgrace, the way you men living in there. We come to clean," says Polly. Lucy carries a large tin pail of water and several rags, and Polly holds a short-handled straw broom.

"This no place for women," grumbles Israel. "You supposed to stay in Smithfield Quarter."

"We gonna do our part too," Polly says matter-of-factly.

"The politicians meeting in there."

"We clean around them, then," says Polly.

Polly takes Lucy by the arm, and they climb the steps and disappear through the wide double doors of the courthouse. Within minutes, Sam Tademy comes out into the sunshine to join Israel.

"They run you out too?" asks Israel.

Sam nods, chagrined, and squeezes himself in next to Israel on the front steps.

* * *

Polly goes room to room, surveying, pulling Lucy behind her. They are assaulted by mingled, rancid smells the men have grown accustomed to in the last two weeks. Odors lay one on top of the other—musty sweat, spilled homemade wood alcohol, coffee, decomposing food, a sharp trace of urine. The rooms are filthy, strewn with snuff chaws and snuff spit, sticky residues of unidentified origin, tracked mud, blankets carelessly tossed aside. The women are prevented from entering one of the rooms by a man with a rifle at his side. It is blocked off for a meeting where the women are clearly not welcome.

"Plenty other places to clean," Polly says, sniffing, but she takes note of Lucy's tentativeness. "This a big job, and I'ma start out here. You go on back to the storeroom and see if you find us some sacks and cord or something to haul out the garbage. Won't be no menfolk in your way there."

Lucy retraces her steps along the narrow central hallway connecting the front and back rooms. Toward the back of the courthouse is a small, jumbled storeroom, stuffed almost floor to ceiling along the back wall with mops, tin buckets, small cans and bottles, kerosene, worn-out brooms of stiff straw, bottles of ink, and miscellaneous bits of this and that.

Propped against the far wall is an old, battered humpback leather trunk, the clasp broken and hanging crookedly at the front, fastened by a grimy rope. On top, packed in stacks higher than Lucy's head, are boxes of various sizes, and on top of the boxes is a dusty half-bolt of material of some flowery pattern for dressmaking or curtains. A small ball of twine is nestled on the bolt, almost hidden from view. Lucy stands on her toes, stretches, and almost has hold of the ball when the twine rolls off and falls down behind the trunk, beyond her reach. She lifts each box off the trunk, one at a time, and stacks them on the other side of the small storeroom. When she tries to pull the trunk out from against the wall, it refuses to budge, caught. Underneath are two loose floorboards, and one of the misfit planks holds the trunk fast.

She jimmies the trunk forward, a few inches at a time, jerking side to side, the floorboards kept in place only by the trunk's weight. Lucy pulls at one of the planks, and the old rusted nails and rotted wood separate. The board comes free easily. Loosened, the ball of twine rolls in a slow, wobbly line along the tilt of the floor and disappears into the gap. With barely a tug, Lucy gets the neighboring board free, revealing a crawl space below the court-house floor, maybe two feet from the ground.

It is too dark to determine how wide it is. Lucy tests whether any of the other boards are loose. At least four more planks could be removed, but she is reluctant to fiddle with other people's prop-erty. Lucy goes back to the front stoop to get Israel.

Both Israel and Sam follow her to the storage room. Sam inspects the crawl space, retrieves the ball of twine, now covered with thick spider webbing, and even considers lowering himself down into the hole to explore. Instead, he replaces the two boards and carefully returns the various boxes to their previous positions.

"Rats, fire ants, who knows what down there," Sam says. "Best left alone."

Lucy takes the twine and several burlap sacks, leaves the men in the storeroom, and joins Polly. They clean for three hours, hauling out filth and garbage and dumping it behind the courthouse. They subdue the worst of the odors with vinegar and water, but for all their effort, the courthouse still hangs on to some of its stench.

Polly was wrong. Seeing the courthouse close up doesn't calm Lucy at all, has not punctured the bubble of fear growing steadily larger within her chest, fear for Israel and the rest of the colored Colfax men.

4

Noby Smith shivers on the damp front porch of Isaac McCullen's house in Smithfield Quarter, waiting for his father to round the curve of the dirt road leading from the center of town, from Colfax. He has been waiting since before dawn. If Noby were home now, he would be foraging for kindling outside in the semidarkness near their shack in The Bottom, or toting an armful of oak or pine split logs for the fireplace so his mother could set the water to boil for breakfast. Noby blows into his hands and tucks them under his armpits to stay warm, aware of the moist staleness of his skin under his thin shirt. He is slightly numb, not because of the nip to the air, so typical of the Louisiana run-up to spring, but because of the possibility his father won't show. What if he doesn't come this morning as he did yesterday? As he did the day before? The only way to see his father alone is before he enters this unfamiliar house crammed full with too many people, before Israel Smith disappears into the attentions of his wife and other children.

Before he is pulled by Smiths and McCullens, young and old, to produce the latest news from the courthouse.

The roosters have crowed, and Noby hears serious stirrings from inside the house, announcing the early risers are up, yawns and throat clearings and bare feet slipped into unlaced shoes for the trip to the backyard outhouse. Just as Noby begins to think his chance is lost, Israel Smith comes into view carrying a rifle, walking fast down the road, his hat pulled low over a tangle of black kinky hair. Israel's eyes dart, right and left, on alert for unusual movement, and he holds himself rigid. Noby runs to intercept him before he turns onto the dusty path to the house.

"Papa," Noby says.

Just saying the name out loud is a relief until he looks into his father's face, and at the familiarity of the old curved scar just under his right eye. Noby has seen his father in all of his moods, his temperament fueled by nervousness of one flavor or another. His father is afraid.

"Noby," Israel says, distracted. He looks back over his shoulder but never slows his pace.

Noby trots behind to keep up. "Papa, I want to come to the courthouse. To help."

Israel focuses on his son, anger replacing preoccupation. He puts a heavy hand on Noby's shoulder and shakes him hard. "Stay away and out of trouble. You not even ten yet. Hear me, boy?"

Israel leaves Noby standing in the path and hurries into the house. By the time Noby catches up, his father has found Lucy amid the dense mass of sleeping bodies and pulled her outside behind the back sleeping porch. There are so many adults and children of all ages squeezed into the small rooms, awake and asleep, McCullens and Smiths, so many eyes and ears, outdoors is the only place to attempt privacy.

Noby trails behind them and hides himself behind the door to the sleeping porch.

"White men gathering at Summerfield Springs today," Israel says to Lucy in a whisper. "We don't know what they planning."

"Yesterday you say Sheriff Nash captured and locked away at the sugarhouse." Noby can tell by the rise in his mother's voice that she too is afraid. "They don't got no leader. And we got the law."

"It what we counting on, Lucy. But still no sign of the Federal troops."

Noby creeps away before they see him, and goes back to the front porch. He wants to be a citizen too, like his father said when he first took Noby to the courthouse. He wants to be a part of what the colored Colfax men are doing. If his father can step up, so can he. Noby knows where Summerfield Springs is, and a nine-year-old colored boy by himself can slip in and out of places none of the men in the courthouse can.

Despite the warm promises of spring everywhere else, the deep woods rimming Colfax remain damp and dark. Noby follows the coastline of Red River as long as possible instead of heading inland, preferring a route where at least he can feel the sun on his face while he walks. He keeps close to the banks of the river, northward, the easiest part of the trip. First up the river, cut inland to the twisting curves of Bayou Grappe, and along the banks of the bayou until Summerfield Springs. Noby has always been good at course-plotting, as his father taught him, interpreting the clues offered by the sun, stars, or moon, observing wildlife and vegetation, monitoring where moss grows on trees or how the mistletoe drapes. His sense of direction is keen and specific, and once he travels a path, the most obscure landmark is implanted in his head from that day forward.

Noby knows two ways to get to Summerfield Springs. Just three months before, he made the same trip from The Bottom with Sam Tademy, taking different routes coming and going. The possibility of buying a healthy mule for Mr. Swafford from a white farmer in the piney woods presented itself, and Mr. Tademy asked permission from Israel for Noby to accompany him on the buying expedition to Aloha, an hour of walking past Summerfield Springs. Noby and Mr. Tademy and his two oldest sons took the water route to get to Aloha, following the Red River and cutting inland on the bayous; but coming back, leading the newly purchased mule, they traveled the entire distance through different sections of the deep woods.

There is no trick at all to the first ninety minutes of walking, merely following the Red River north. It is only a couple of hours after dawn, so early and cold-damp that Noby sees his exhaled breath outlined in the air. There isn't much river traffic. Only two skiffs float past, both crudely made, one going upstream and the other down. The first dugout heads slowly toward Colfax, gliding dangerously low in the water. A small, thin colored woman with a scarf tied around her head pulls resolutely at both oars from the back bench seat, holding one sleeping child in her lap, while three other children, none older than Noby, hold on to the sides in the front. Noby waves to them, and they all wave back, although no one smiles. Later, the second skiff floats past holding five occupants, headed north toward Montgomery. A white farmer rows this boat, weighted down with supplies, while his wife sits rigidly and quietly toward the front with their three children. The farmer has a shotgun at his side, propped up in the boat with the barrel pointed skyward. No one waves.

Noby continues on until he recognizes the markings of the spot where he needs to turn inland toward Bayou Grappe. He feels confident along the river, but there is no getting around the shadows of the woods if he is going to make it to Summerfield Springs. He reaches his hand to the small of his back, and through the rough cloth of his homespun shirt, for courage, he runs his fingers along the stiff binding of *Sheldon's Primer*, tucked into the waistband of his trousers.

The woods aren't quite so dark as Noby had feared, but they are still a brooding place, giant virgin pine trees with trunks grown so close that there are places a full-grown man would have trouble squeezing through, the tree-branch canopies twenty feet overhead so dense and tightly interlaced it seems they conspire to keep out any real view of the sky. Noby walks faster, east this time, while he recites in his head one of the book lessons from the primer.

The terrain changes abruptly, a thinning of the trees and a swampier feel to the ground, pine trees giving way to cypress. Noby remembers this exact spot from his trip with Sam Tademy, a point where they had to make a decision. Directly ahead are the meandering, twisting marshes of Bayou Grappe; to the left is the footpath leading west that will take him to the town of Aloha; and through the woods to his right, a more direct route to Summerfield Springs.

Noby is still trying to decide which path to take when a horseman appears on the footpath from the direction of Aloha. The white man seems enormous, wide around the middle, his girth almost ridiculous in proportion to the smallish mare underneath him. The thinning beard that hangs from his fleshy jowls is more salt than pepper. His slouch hat is cocked low over his ears, but not down far enough to hide his muttonchop sideburns. The man is about Noby's father's age.

"Say, boy," the white man calls.

Noby stops. "Yes, sir," he says.

"You know where Summerfield Springs is?"

Noby points north. "That way, sir."

"What about a clearing by Bayou Grappe?"

Bayou Grappe is the route Noby favored to take himself. "I don't know nothing about a clearing, but this the start of Bayou Grappe here, sir," Noby says.

"Mr. Narcisse Fredieu," the man says.

"Beg pardon, sir, Mr. Fredieu, sir."

Noby feels the watery, piercing eyes of this man sizing him up in a way most white men don't bother, as if he is figuring a troublesome puzzle. "Any your people mixed up in that courthouse ruckus in Colfax?" Narcisse Fredieu asks.

"No, sir, Mr. Fredieu," Noby answers, quick. For emphasis, he says it again. "No, sir."

"Better not be. Bad business. Can't be allowed to drag on." Abruptly, he pulls rein on his horse and heads off in the direction Noby pointed.

Noby is certain he has been handed an essential piece of information. The meeting will be held in a clearing in Summerfield Springs, just off Bayou Grappe. This morning when he set out, he hadn't thought much beyond simply getting himself to Summerfield Springs, but if he travels the winding bayou path by foot, it will take him an extra hour to get there. He decides to cut through the woods and hope he can find both the clearing and a hiding place.

At a point not far from the second bend of the bayou, the terrain changes from marshy swampland to a wide clearing off to the north. Noby keeps close to the undergrowth as he works his way along the bank, and angles to get a better view. A small hill rises up at the far end, and Noby freezes. He hears a high-pitched whinny from a horse in the distance, and the unmistakable sounds of men talking. He dares to lift his head for a better look. There are four white men gathered in the clearing already, relaxed and sitting in a semicircle, talking casually. Their horses are just as lackadaisical, nibbling at the grass in the clearing, their reins dragging the ground.

The men's voices are low and mostly indistinct. As Noby strains to catch their words, the topics drift from a recitation of a difficult calf's birth to remedies for the weevil infestation that has plagued Colfax farmers for the last month. One man, impatient, grumbles about when the meeting will start. Noby is sure he is in the right place.

Noby moves more cautiously now. The banks are sodden and slippery, not so firm as they will become in just a few weeks, when the weather settles and turns warm for good. The damp, siltlike mud oozes between his toes as he struggles to keep his balance. He finds a good resting point at the edge of the bayou, but the long, jutting clumps of grass that keep him hidden are damp. He loosens the rope belt around his trousers and gently removes the slim, stiff-spine book loaned to him by Sam Tademy, held in place at the hollow of his back. His skin is clammy under his shirt from walking, and the book feels damp. He chooses a saw-palmetto leaf just bigger than his two hands together, rubs at the wet with his shirt until the book feels dry, then wraps it in the leaf before returning it to its hiding place at the small of his back. Noby reties the rope belt and gives his pants one more reassuring tug to make sure that the book is secure.

"They gonna bring him directly here, and then we figure what's next," someone in the clearing says. Noby doesn't know who they are talking about. The white men aren't in a hurry, and Noby is bored.

Again he takes out the book, unwrapping it from the water-proof leaf covering he has fashioned. Borrow-time with the book is precious; he must return it tomorrow. After Hansom Brisco first taught him to recognize each individual letter of the alphabet in its separate box on the first page, Noby devoted himself to the task of understanding how those letters came together in different ways to form distinct words. It didn't take long to master *This is a fat cat on a mat*, once he saw the trick of changing just one of the memorized letters and making a whole new meaning. For a long time, all that Noby understood of the primer's cover was the chubby white girl sitting on an overstuffed pillow. In one hand, she clutched a doll, a miniature golden-haired replica of the girl herself, and with the other hand, she waved, although it was not clear whom she was so happy to see. The picture upset Noby. An open book was carelessly placed at the white girl's feet, and she wasn't even trying to read it, as though she knew the book would always be there if she wanted it. By the time Noby learned enough for Hansom Brisco to teach him the words on the cover, the little white girl's lack of appreciation didn't bother him anymore. None of the words started out as familiar, but with Hansom Brisco's teaching, he memorized all of them. *Sheldon's Primer.* Scribner Armstrong & Co. New York.

Figure 3. Sheldon's Primer, *1871*

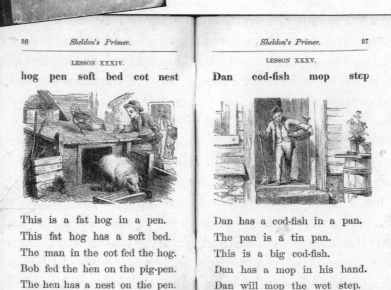

Noby turns to page 37, his favorite section, letting his mouth fill silently with the words he finds there:

Dan has a cod-fish in a pan.
The pan is a tin pan.
This is a big cod-fish.
Dan has a mop in his hand.
Dan will mop the wet step.
The mop Dan has, is a rag mop.

Noby has gone through every page of the book many times, and it is the only picture with a person in it who looks a little bit like him, not like the uninterested girl on the cover or the man he met on the road who asked him questions about the courthouse. Not a single adult in the book resembles any of the colored men in the town, not his father or Mr. McCullen or Mr. Tademy. Noby repeats his favorite passage over and over. The sun is warm, and in the background the white men in the clearing smoke and tell lazy fish stories. Noby drifts toward sleep to the quiet whispers of the birds in the trees and the loud croaking of toads along the river. Even from just a few feet away, he looks like an insignificant curl spot in the tall grass.

Noby wakes of a sudden and, for a moment, doesn't know where he is. The book is pressed against his small chest but is undamaged. He could never face Sam Tademy if he ruined the primer, a teaching book meant for everybody, too important to be his alone. He knows better than to rise up and show himself or make any sound. An uncomfortable dampness chills him through his clothes as he sifts through the sounds of the white men's voices. There are more of them now than before, and their voices are louder, with a dangerous edge. They no longer talk crops. Noby doesn't know how much he has missed.

"Without the carpetbaggers, our colored gonna fall back in line," someone says.

Noby wants to lift up his head to see who is talking, but he is trapped. He remembers one of the lessons in the book, a picture of serious white men under the open sky discussing important matters, and he envisions that image as he listens.

Ten men sat on a den.
The men had on vests and hats.
The ten men had ten vests.
The ten men had ten hats.
Ned and Ben sat on the den.
Ben has on a vest and a hat.

White men with vests and hats.

"Why wait?" someone interrupts. "I say run them to ground, sooner the better."

"Taking care of a few upstart coloreds and politicians and tangling with the Federals two different things."

"We shoulda took care of this the first week they took over the courthouse."

"I agree with Smokin' Jimmy. More colored coming to Colfax to join the rabble-rousers each day. We wait too long, who knows what the carpetbaggers able to get our boys to do? Must be hundreds of them in town now."

There are at least four men talking, and maybe more who haven't spoken. Noby hears one of the horses nearby, foraging, coming closer to his hiding spot. He is tempted to try to ease down the bank of the bayou and slip away, but he isn't sure his body will obey his mental commands. This is exactly what he has come this far to do, and he wills himself steady. He keeps still and listens hard, trying to remember every word.

"Nothing we can't handle if we get more men."

"What about the Federals, Hadnot?"

"If they not here by now, maybe they won't come up this far from New Orleans."

"But maybe they will. There's middle ground. We can talk these boys into going back to their crops. We don't want to go up against troops." Noby recognizes the voice of the man he met on the road.

"You sound like a Negro-loving Republican, Narcisse." Noby starts to place a few voices. This last, Smokin' Jimmy Hadnot, does most of the talking. "You sure you found the right camp? We got our own ways on Red River, different than how you carry on in Cane River." There is contempt in his tone. "Democrat by day and Republican by night, seem to me."

"We not talking my personal business here," Narcisse says sharply. "Any fool with common sense knows to be careful with the Federals."

"We need to clean out the courthouse and worry about Federals later," Smokin' Jimmy Hadnot says.

Noby waits for Narcisse Fredieu to respond, but he doesn't.

"It's up to us to teach the black sons of Canaan a lesson. 'Specially the black radicals. We got to string them up."

"There's more to this than getting back at some colored boys because they turned a few of you back from town, Hadnot."

Noby doesn't recognize this speaker. His voice is soft-edged but commanding.

"My cousin can collect men over to Catahoula Parish. And those Sicily Island boys know how to stop a thing like this cold. White men from Winn, Rapides, Natchitoches, Sabine, Tensas, and Caddo parishes all turn out for us."

"That's right, Sheriff Nash. We'll put out the call to the White League. Plenty out there back us up."

Sheriff Nash? His father told his mother Sheriff Nash was locked up in Calhoun's Sugarhouse. Nash was supposedly a prisoner, but here he is. If Noby slips away now, he has something big to tell the men in the courthouse. He begins to move himself slowly down the bank, but the grass is slick and damp. Before he can get a good foothold, he starts a fast slide down toward the bayou on his backside and stops only when he bangs against a protruding rock at the river's edge. One of his legs is thigh-high in the chilly water, and he braces the other at an awkward angle on the bank so he won't go all the way into the stream. The wind suddenly shifts, and a quick chill seizes him. Before he can stop himself, he sneezes, not once but twice.

Noby stops short, afraid to move a muscle, and listens hard while trying to calm his breathing. The men in the clearing have stopped their conversation. He dares not call further attention to his position. Although Noby doesn't hear anyone approaching, he frantically looks up and down the banks of the bayou for an escape route. If they come to the water after him, he is in the open, and he will have to decide whether or not to run. He waits.

"If y'all talked less, and done your job last November to keep them from the polls, we wouldn't have this mess to clean up now," one of the men says.

Noby is so relieved they haven't spotted him that he almost cries. Although he can't seem to stop his body from shuddering, he holds himself as quiet as he is able, one leg still in the bayou.

"No need going back to what we shoulda done, Hadnot. Anybody see clear over they shoulder. If we can't vote the Negro down, we knock him down. End result's the same."

"We agree, then. Put the word out to neighboring parishes, and make sure they bring guns to blast them out. As of today, we at war."

A few of the men stay in the clearing at Summerfield Springs for another hour, talking in small groups and drinking before mounting their horses and riding away. Noby takes his leg out of the chilly water but keeps down and waits them out. What seemed an elaborate game until a few hours ago has become something very different, and he is paralyzed with the visual image of his own small body hung from the neck by a rope thrown over the nearest pecan tree. He doesn't move for another thirty minutes after all sounds of the men have faded.

Noby climbs up the bank from the bayou and forces himself to back away through the tall grass slowly, carefully, afraid with each reverse step that a heavy white hand will clamp down on his shoulder or over his mouth, and he will disappear forever from everyone he knows.

It is an easy matter to follow the curves of Summerfield Springs Bayou and Boggy Bayou, and zigzag back toward Smithfield Quarter. Noby plays back the words of the white men at Summerfield Springs and their tone, remembering exactly who said what, without thinking too much about what they meant. It is too hard. This time Noby seeks out the dark, wooded areas with as much cover as possible, straining to hear any unfamiliar sounds of white men prowling about. Right now he wants to sit down in the middle of the soggy marsh and not think anymore. He wants someone to tell him how to get out of hostile territory and to lead him somewhere that is safe. He wants his father.

When at last he enters the familiarity of Colfax, he begins to run for the first time. He holds his head down and puts everything into the churning of his legs, his heart pounding hard against his bony chest and his lungs so raw he thinks they might burst. He runs headlong in the general direction of the center of town and the courthouse, as if he is being chased by demons, no longer cautious or carefully picking his way, no longer listening to anything other than the whizzing of wind against his face and the beating of his own heart.

Noby crashes through a small grove of pecan trees and barely feels the nick on his cheek from a low-lying branch as he continues to throw himself forward. The running consumes him, and by the time he registers the men sitting in the grove, he almost slams into one of them. His vision fills with the tiny cylindrical hole of the pistol leveled at his head.

Eli McCullen holds a 9mm sharpie, and he is as surprised as Noby. There are six armed men in the grove, one of the smaller colored patrol units. Noby runs to Eli McCullen before anyone can stop him.

"Mr. McCullen, sir, please don't shoot me." Noby takes big, gulping breaths, but that's all he can get out.

"Slow down," Eli says. "You Israel Smith's boy? You and your mama staying at my brother's house?"

Noby nods, still winded.

"We don't shoot our own, son."

"I got to go to the courthouse," Noby says. "The old sheriff loose, and they calling for more men to take the courthouse back. It's a war."

"Where this news from?" Eli McCullen asks.

"At Summerfield Springs, they talking about bringing white men from Sicily Island. And other parishes too."

The other men press closer to Noby and Eli. "I thought they had Sheriff Nash in the sugarhouse," says one colored man. "Sheriff Nash never been one to turn the other cheek."

"What else you hear, boy?"

Noby feels damp through and through. "Said they gonna run the carpetbaggers out. They gonna hang the black radicals. They say they calling in the White League." The men grow deathly quiet. "Can I go to the courthouse now?" Noby finally asks.

"This news got to get to the top quick." Eli McCullen looks to the rest of the patrol, but each has retreated into his own thoughts. "I take him myself."

Noby follows blindly behind Eli McCullen on the way to the courthouse. They cut through an overgrown part of Mirabeau Woods where low-hanging branches from the trees push at Noby. Thankfully, Eli doesn't talk to him or expect him to talk, stopping only to lift Noby over a fallen trunk or hold open twisting vines for him to squeeze through. Noby follows, stumbling more than once, unaware, glad to have someone else in charge. Eventually, they come to the courthouse and see Mr. McCullen climbing down the ladder from the roof.

"What you doing here?" McCully says. "Why you got the boy, looking like a crazy man?"

"Sheriff Shaw inside?" asks Eli.

"They all in there. Something big going on. They got some letter."

"Had to bring this boy in. Sheriff Nash escape up to Summerfield Springs, and white men getting ready to attack the courthouse."

McCully addresses himself to Noby. "How you come by this?"

"I go to Summerfield Springs this morning and hear the white men talking. Sheriff Nash there. He say this a war."

"How you get all the way up to Summerfield Springs? Who go with you?"

"Walk, by myself," Noby says.

McCully furrows his forehead, studying Noby. "You full of surprises, son. You done a fine job."

"The sheriff gotta hear this. You gonna take him inside?" Eli asks his brother.

McCully nods, places his big hand at Noby's back.

"Please, Mr. McCullen, can I see my papa?" Noby asks.

"Run and get Israel Smith," McCully says to Eli. "He on the last patrol toward Smithfield Quarter."

McCully leads Noby inside the courthouse.

The politicians and leadership inside the courthouse huddle together in one of the anterooms. Twelve men, four white and eight colored, hunch over a table, reading and arguing about the two-page letter in front of them. They barely look up when McCully barges in, annoyed at the interruption by the big man and the small boy at his side.

"This a private meeting," snaps Cap'n Ward, the most vocal of the colored politicians. He is a round, dark man with unforgiving features, dressed in a hodgepodge of leftover Union Army uniform pieces, boots, shirt, cap, and jacket. Although shabby, they exude, if not authority, at least a certain official feeling.

McCully isn't cowed. "This boy got news you want to listen to. Go on, Noby," he prods, "tell these men what you just hear."

"Sheriff Nash at Summerfield Springs," says Noby. He repeats his story.

"We know Nash escaped," says Sheriff Shaw. "Now we know where, for all the good that does. They lost him from the sugar-house this morning. Eight men busted him out. It's too late to do anything about that. Right now we got a peace proposal from the constable and J. W. Hadnot in Montgomery to answer."

Noby recognized the name. "Smokin' Jimmy Hadnot at Summerfield Springs too," he offers. "He the one say they gonna blast the courthouse and hang the radicals."

Cap'n Ward snatches up the piece of paper the men have been studying and throws it to the floor. "Hadnot sends in a peace proposal while he plots to attack?" he says. "I told you not to trust them."

"We still gotta answer," says Levi Allen. "Hadnot don't speak for everybody. This proposal sound like a reasonable place to start." He retrieves the paper from the floor.

"Read it again," says Cap'n Ward reluctantly.

McCully mutters to himself as Levi reads the proposal out loud.

In order to settle the present disturbed condition of affairs in the Parish of Grant, restore quietude to the people and protect all citizens in the enjoyment of life, liberty and property, it is agreed by the undersigned parties to:

—Disband all armed forces in the parish—individuals to be permitted to return to homes quietly without being disturbed

—All citizens driven from homes be permitted to return and live undisturbed

—All white and colored citizens be allowed to travel on the public highways and visit the town of Colfax without being disturbed or insulted

—All offenders of law surrender themselves to proper authorities to be dealt with as the law directs

— That in future all political topics be avoided in conversation and more friendly and better feeling be cultivated between the two races.

Signed,
J. S. Payne
Special Constable

Figure 4. Letter to commanders of the force at Colfax, from Montgomery

"'Restore quietude to the people,'" McCully says. "Ask us to lay down like a whipped dog, more like it."

Noby just wants to go home to The Bottom, back where the most important thing is squabbling with his older brother or punishment for not doing chores.

The light of day has already crossed over to the dim of evening by the time Israel arrives at the courthouse. He bursts through the front door, a man on fire. Noby runs to him and throws himself on his father.

Israel holds Noby away from his body and crouches down to get at eye level. "They say you hear the white men's plans in Summerfield Springs," he says.

Noby nods.

"Don't you dare put yourself in harm's way like this again." Israel takes Noby by the shoulders and shakes him. "You hear me, son?"

Noby nods again.

His father places his arm on Noby's shoulder, lightly rests it there.

"Those white men gonna kill you, Papa?" Noby asks.

"We both gonna make your tenth birthday," says Israel. "Once Federal troops get here, I come on home, home to you and your mama."

Within the hour, the men in charge draft their response to the peace letter. Each signs his name to the return document, and they fetch someone to deliver it to the Montgomery men.

Response of the Commanders at Colfax:

We the undersigned pledge ourselves and the men under our control to cease all hostility towards the citizens of Montgomery, and use all due politeness toward all citizens of Montgomery and vicinity while in Colfax, and afford to them protection while in Colfax. We will not make any armed demonstration against the people of Montgomery and vicinity so long as they keep the peace themselves. If any of the citizens at Montgomery join Hadnot then this agreement is not in force any longer.

Figure 5. Response from Colfax commanders to Montgomery

5

*O*n Saturday, Colfax cautiously flirts with the fragile hope that goings-on inside the courthouse will end the standoff. A swelling crowd of men mills around the grounds, on break from patrol, sticking close to await word of progress. Messages have been delivered back and forth for two days between the white Democrats of Montgomery and the colored and white Republicans of Colfax. Despite stubborn posturing by both camps, the two sides have finally arranged a face-to-face meeting to talk out their issues. Now men with decision-making power sit across the table from one another inside the courthouse. They have been at it for two hours.

A colored man emerges at a gallop from the thick foliage of Mirabeau Woods, past the Pecan Tree on the river side. He holds on to the reins with one hand and waves his slouch hat in a high arc above his head with the other, hollering into the wind.

"Here come Eli McCullen," someone shouts. "Riding like the devil hisself chasing him."

"They shot Jessie McCullen through the head," Eli yells. He reins in the dark gray mare, in full lather, snorting and heaving. "At his farm, shot through the head."

Everyone pushes and shoves to gather around Eli, forming a tight circle. Pressing him for details, they barely give him time to dismount or catch his breath.

McCully scrambles down the wooden ladder from the courthouse roof at high speed, hand under fist, two rungs at a time, and forces his way through the throng of men to get to the front, shoving without apology. He grabs Eli's arm, spinning him around until they face each other.

"What happened?" McCully asks.

"You know Jessie's place, down Bayou Darrow," Eli says. "His wife say Jessie mending the fence, patching where the cow push through. White men come on horses, five, maybe six. They ask what he think about coloreds at the courthouse don't know their place."

"Jessie say, 'I don't know nothing about that mess. I tend my fence, mind my business.' His wife tell me he say it three or four times, but they keep asking, pushing him back and forth between them, one to another."

"Jessie dead?" McCully asks. His dark face is ashen, drained.

Eli puts his hand on McCully's arm, his own grief plain. "Gone from this life."

McCully flinches as if the touch burns, and shakes Eli's hand away. "His wife and children?" he asks.

"They hole up on Mirabeau plantation. His wife and a neighbor put Jessie's body in a wagon and carry it over to her stepfather. Mr. Calhoun let them keep the body on his place for now, and he let the kin stay too, till it safe to go back home."

"Who done it? She know the men?"

McCully's features arrange themselves in a peculiar way. There's a moment when a man goes a certain way in his mind, and his body follows. A moment when anger has the power to transform itself and its vessel into something else entirely. A man can explode into rage or retreat into madness. A man can break. Those in front of the Colfax courthouse stay quiet, waiting for what McCully will do.

"Don't matter who done it, McCully," says Eli. "Just white men sending a message. Anybody serve the purpose, long as they colored."

"We going after them what done this," McCully says. "Colfax our town. We got the numbers. We got guns and men. We ready to fight back this time."

Israel, usually mute in a crowd, comes forward. "What more we can do? They own the stores and farms, run the politics."

McCully pulls himself from his own thoughts. Color has flooded back into his face, and he seems massive. "Ain't you tired yet of living like a whimpering stray dog, Israel?" McCully asks. His voice quivers. "Is begging scraps at the white man's table enough for you?

"Is we men?" McCully shouts, and he holds his rifle out in front of his body. A small, slick bead slides down the side of his face and all the way down onto his grimy shirtfront. He doesn't bother to wipe it away. "Is we men?" he says again. He drops to his knees and raises both arms over his head, cradling the rifle in his palms, as if in offering. "Has You forgot us?" he whispers. "When can we be men?"

Israel Smith melts back into the crowd, and the other men wait, unsure.

Sam Tademy steps forward and takes hold of McCully around both shoulders. He unlocks McCully's grip on the Enfield, transferring the rifle to his own hands, and urges him up from the dust.

"The Lord with you in your time of darkness, Brother McCully," says Sam softly as he helps him stand upright. "So is we."

McCully looks at Sam as if they are the only two standing outside the courthouse, as if the crowd doesn't exist.

"Jessie the baby," McCully whispers. He shakes his head, disbelieving, as if in checking, he will find it all a mistake and his little brother is still alive. "He the only one of us refuse to take the courthouse, and they cut him down noway," he says to Sam. In his grief, stooped, he looks like an old man, tired of the struggle. "Why He not take me instead?"

"Wasn't your time," replies Sam, his tone both soothing and assured. "The Lord work in mysterious ways, His wonders to perform."

McCully shakes Sam off and storms toward the courthouse, disappearing between the double doors.

"What's going on in there?" Eli McCullen asks, finally registering the half-dozen saddle horses tied up at the east side of the building.

"Montgomery men in there two hours, trying to hammer out peace," says Sam.

"Peace?" Eli snorts an ugly laugh with no humor in it. "They talk peace in there but murder us out here?"

Eli strides toward the courthouse, only a few steps behind his brother.

Within minutes, all six of the white men from Montgomery spill outside on the run, faces tight as they make a beeline for their horses. A phalanx of colored men gives chase, close at their heels, like sheepdogs herding an errant flock. One of the white men loses his hat, but he doesn't retrieve it, racing for his mount. McCully appears at the courthouse door, struggling against two colored men holding him, just as the last white man swings into his saddle. They pin McCully's arms back, blocking his access to his gun.

"How dare you act like you talking peace while you shoot my brother," McCully yells after the men. "We coming after you next."

The white men gallop toward Mirabeau Woods, trailed by two colored horsemen assigned to ensure they don't stop until they are beyond the town limits.

* * *

The murder of Jessie McCullen jolts the colored populace. Sketchy but disturbing reports fan outward to more remote parts of the parish, from Smithfield Quarter, Bayou Darrow, and The Bottom, up to Boggy Bayou and Montgomery to the north, and as far as Pineville to the southeast. Another colored farmer is taken from his home in Mirabeau Woods and is feared dead too. Every colored citizen of Colfax immediately understands the real meaning of the stories, the implications, without the need for exact details. Many who stayed their ground earlier in the week abandon their homes and flock into Colfax.

The roads around Colfax and the surrounding woods choke on the desperation of entire families on the run. There is barely a nod, friendly or hostile, between the nervous sets of people crossing paths in opposite directions, whether on foot, on horseback, or in wagons or boats. On the roads there is practiced avoidance, deferred glances, studied nonconfrontation, even by the children, as if the situation is too peculiar and unpredictable to risk upsetting a delicate balance. All the people flowing into town are colored, and all fleeing out are white.

It is a completely different story when one group meets another going in the same direction. Relief revives the fellow sojourners. They form hastily banded-together packs, joining one another in travel for as long a distance as possible. Anyone fleeing in either direction has the same fear of isolation and vulnerability, of suddenly finding themselves picked off and alone, eager to fall in with greater numbers of their own kind, swelling their ranks, increasing their odds.

At various intervals along the roads and riverway are squads of colored men in groups of three, four, six, as many as a dozen, with guns. They don't stop or interact with any of the white groups leaving Colfax. Most of the white caravans include at least one or two older males with weapons. But the Colfax defenders are steadfast in their refusal to allow entrance to any white person. If there isn't already an armed colored man in a group coming into Colfax, a patrol unit assigns a man with a gun to escort the cluster of families seeking refuge inside the town limits. Asylum seekers arrive in Smithfield Quarter anxious and sweating, almost always in groups of ten or more.

White men patrol too, mostly along the banks of Red River, and it is inevitable that opposing patrol squads, colored and white, cross paths. Mostly, the two sets of tight-lipped, armed men glare in silence across the distance at each other, or briefly exchange coarse taunts. In a few cases, they exchange gunfire as well, but no one is seriously injured.

The precarious relationship between colored and white in Colfax crumples like a wobbly wagon wheel that finally capsizes the cart. White men are angry that Negroes who just weeks before knew their place now flex their muscles, their numbers increasing on a daily basis. Colored men try on rebellion as a naked man would a suit of clothes. Some of the younger ones, including Spenser McCullen, become intoxicated with the idea they are one step closer to the freedom granted after the Civil War, when they believed they would receive forty acres of land and a mule instead of never-ending work for a succession of white men.

Terrified colored families pour into Colfax and overrun Smithfield Quarter, already stretched beyond its limits. Opposing forces close rank, black versus white, Republican versus Democrat, plantation riverbed people versus hill people.

The colored men meet outside the courthouse at noon to change patrols and exchange news, comparing notes. There are hundreds of them now, and they spread themselves out from around the building all the way out to the Pecan Tree. Men mill everywhere around the courthouse square, sitting, standing, lying down.

McCully, Israel, and Sam sit together under the Pecan Tree, and Spenser McCullen joins them late, arriving on foot from the direction of the steamboat landing. He waves a packet of papers at the older men as he approaches.

"What?" McCully asks. His face is set in grim lines. The teasing that his eyes usually convey has been extinguished, but he looks more in control of himself than a few hours before, after hearing about Jessie.

"A newspaper from New Orleans, on the upriver boat," Spenser says. "The captain say we in it."

"We best take it to the courthouse and see if the politicians tell us what it say," says Israel.

"Politicians don't tell us nothing till it suit them," Sam says. "Go to Smithfield Quarter, find my son Green, and bring him here. We sent that boy to school for a reason."

While they wait, the men handle the newspaper, passing it back and forth, studying the drawings and regularity of the lines of print, speculating on the contents. Eventually, they abandon the newspaper.

"Mr. Hadnot and some other men from Montgomery come again this morning, near Coptic Point," Israel says. "They call us names, even fire a shot. We fire too, but nobody hit nothing but dirt. One fall when his horse spook, but he just dust hisself off and get back on the mare."

"Coptic Point where white men get Charley Harris alone and carry him out to the woods," Sam says. "No body yet, but he gotta be dead."

McCully says nothing, and Israel and Sam fall silent too, until Spenser comes back with Green Tademy. Green's younger brother, Jackson, tags along behind the two older boys. Both of the Tademy boys are handsome in the same dark, chiseled fashion, with Indian features in the sharpness of their nose and smooth, high foreheads, though at fourteen, Green already sports hair on his face, and the beginning of sideburns. Green has a compact, athletic body, almost sculpted, and Jackson, at eleven, shows signs of the same body type. There is no need to explain that they are brothers. Only the age difference separates their looks. The biggest contrast between the two is that Green has a mischievousness about him, even as he carries the weight of expectations of a firstborn, and Jackson is more serious-minded, determined not to disappoint. Their crudely made shirts and pants are from the same bolt of material, differentiated by size and the patterns of whatever was at hand at the time of mending. Green usually speaks for both of them. Giving direction to one is as good as giving it to the other.

Green studies the newspaper, turning the pages until he finds a small article buried in the rest of the news. He reads out loud to the men haltingly, stumbling over some of the words, unable to recognize or sound all of them out, but he manages to convey a majority of the newspaper account.

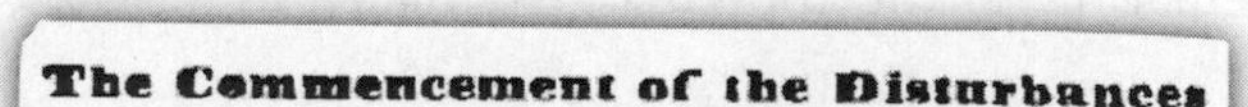

> **The Commencement of the Disturbances —Calm Statement by Citizens.**
>
> *From the New-Orleans Republican, April 12.*
>
> The steamer St. Mary, which left Colfax on Wednesday morning at daylight, brought down to the city quite a number of gentlemen who were witnesses of the recent tumult in Grant Parish. They report everything quiet at the time they left Colfax, all the attacking parties having disbanded. Capt. D. W. Shaw, sheriff of the parish, with his deputies, was in charge of the court-house, and there were no apprehensions of further trouble. Measures have already been taken by the authorities here, State and Federal, which will insure peace hereafter.

Figure 6. New-Orleans Republican, *April 12, 1873*

"See. The authorities on the way," says Israel when Green has finished.

"On the way not the same as here," says Sam.

"Last of the white folks leaving Colfax," says Spenser. "We come across a family with a wagon so full, pots falling off the pile like it raining supplies. They don't stop to pick them up neither. We let them pass."

"I hear they put the word out to the colored reverend in Montgomery for the colored there to help us."

"Somebody got to do something," says Israel. "Federals too slow, and everything else too fast."

"They didn't have to take Jessie," McCully mumbles.

"No, they didn't," Sam says into the uncomfortable silence that McCully's reminder brings. "We need to take a pause and put up a service for your brother. Respect his passing. Tomorrow Palm Sunday, no better time than that. The women can bring food, and we each say a few words. And Brother McCully, tonight you need to go home, be with your family. We do fine here one day without you."

"Lucy say they low on rations in Smithfield Quarter," says Israel. "And now there more people than ever."

"The Lord will provide," says Sam.

"Yes, He will," echoes Spenser McCullen.

Colfax La
April 5th 1873

Rev. Jacob Johnson,
Dear friend, as I reserve your answer you
will do me and all our colored people all the
help in the world at this time. Our people
are in trouble and I ask you in the name of
our liberty and our children's rights. Come
to our assistance as many as will and can
and that feels that we are citizens. I can
command; all I lack is help. I have been
engaged 3 days and this day I had a battle
did not amount to but little. One man I
think wounded. By all account he fell, but
got off and between now and Monday we
will have heavy times.

I am in need of all the help we can get. If
it was Grant Parish men we could manage
this but I seen men today from Winn
Parish and the rebels kill Jessie McCullen
today and they taking Charley Harris and
carry him off in the woods today and I am
satisfied that they have killed him. And
gentlemen, we are in need of all the help we
can get. I hope the Brothers will come to
each other's assistance as the white does.

Very truly yours,

Capt. Wm. Ward

Figure 7. Letter from Captain William Ward to Reverend Johnson, Montgomery

Chapter

6

*A*fter patrol, as Saturday turns toward evening, Sam and Israel sandwich McCully between them along a path from the Colfax courthouse to Smithfield Quarter, escorting him to his house for the night, as though they can somehow shore up the big man if they position him just so. They avoid direct reference to the long day: Jessie's murder, the breakdown in peace talks, McCully's unpredictable mood. The three men cross over to the low side of Colfax to enter Smithfield Quarter, navigating the narrow dirt roads, passing a group of shacks so close to one another they almost touch.

Smithfield Quarter before the siege was always crowded, but now it spills out over itself, like the swollen waters of the Red River during flood. Every available inch houses a family in need of safe haven. Front and back stoops are pressed into service, newly made into sleeping porches. Floors and kitchen tables become beds. Towels and washrags double as blankets. People in every house make do, giving up what they can to put up fellow townsmen, whether they agree with the courthouse seizure or not.

Each house they pass brings a "Hello" or "How's the family getting on?" or "I'm sorry to hear about Jessie." Israel and Sam wave soberly and pay their respects to the people porch-sitting or walking, but they don't stop beyond the obligatory politeness of Sam informing each that there will be a service for Jessie tomorrow. The sun dips lower in the sky, and the trio picks up their pace.

"Who gonna sort out Jessie's service?" Israel asks.

"Once we get McCully home, Polly be good at organizing the food and the women," says Sam. "And we all preachers. Whoever want to speak about Jessie, free to speak up."

They cut between two small shacks to get to the parallel road, Israel in the lead, navigating the twisting streets. At the bend of the road leading toward McCully's house, they come upon a thick cord of men, women, and children standing patiently in a ragged line, talking and visiting to pass the time. One old woman pushes a small wooden wheelbarrow, dilapidated and wobbly, and others in the line carry an assortment of feed sacks, gourds, baskets, and canvas bags.

"How you fixing to carry away the food?" the old woman asks when she sees the three men are empty-handed.

Israel and Sam look at each other, puzzled. They push toward the front of the line to get a better idea of what the attraction is.

"Look here, Brother, we all waiting our turn," an elderly man says.

"Just looking, Brother," Israel says.

On the buckled front porch of McCully's house, Polly and Lucy measure and transfer small quantities from several large sacks of flour, rice, cornmeal, and sugar to people waiting in line. Behind them are two large smoked hams and a keg of molasses. Polly stands at the head of the steps, introducing herself, rationing supplies, setting the pace and keeping the line moving. Her voice carries as she gives orders. "Service for Jessie McCullen at sunup tomorrow. What you able to bring? Sweet-potato pone sound fine. Make as much as you can. Give her a little extra of the dark corn syrup, Lucy.

"Young man, you help Miz Johnson here home. And don't leave till she unload all this food," Polly commands.

"Look like your wife already got the word," Israel says to Sam. Sam nods. Polly is a generation younger than Sam, taller by several inches than her husband, and as far as Israel is concerned, would be especially attractive if she wasn't so forward.

When Lucy sees Israel, she smiles. Her chocolate-brown skin is slick from physical exertion, and an escaped wisp of wiry, gray-streaked hair peeks from her head scarf. The baby is asleep in a basket at her feet, and the long sleeves of her dark dress, her apron, and even her exposed wrists are coated with the fine white flour she scoops. She looks happy at her task. She gives Israel a short wave and goes back to spooning out flour for two small boys, each holding a handle of the #3 washtub they carry between them. Israel slowly waves back.

"Where all that food come from?" asks Sam.

McCully speaks for the first time since they started out for the quarter, his voice a little flat. "Spenser and some others get supplies from Craft's store."

"That much food got to cost a pretty penny," says Sam. "Whose account old man Craft gonna charge?"

"The account past due, I expect," says McCully.

"What that supposed to mean?" Sam stares at the food that hasn't already been packed up and taken away. "Mr. Craft gonna make somebody pay. Who got that kind of money? The politicians?"

"Nah, not the politicians." McCully releases a bitter grunt. "We out here the better part of two weeks, Sam, and now our women and children drawn in too. We running out of everything. The general store cut off credit to any family they know got a man at the courthouse."

"Somebody still got to pay," Sam insists.

"We already pay, ten times over," says McCully. "We pay all our lives. A bit of food don't put a dent in what's owed."

"Spenser *stole* all this food?" Sam asks slowly.

Israel keeps quiet, listening. He doesn't think it right to take food from the white man's store without asking, but he worries about Lucy and the children. The last time he visited, Lucy was reheating and adding more water to the same weak soup they had served each of the last three days, and there wasn't meal for corn bread.

"It ain't right, McCully," Sam says. "Mr. Craft never done nothing to us."

"You wrong, Sam," says McCully. "Only two sides now, and when it come down to it, I tell you which side Craft be on."

"Do people know where that food come from?" Sam asks.

"Nobody want to know. Nobody care. That what scared and hungry is."

"There ain't no excuse to take what ain't ours," says Sam.

"We come too far to turn around. We got to outlast them." McCully summons up a little of his old spark. "Tomorrow we do Jessie's service like we supposed to, and the children gonna eat. Monday, colored men of Colfax go back to the courthouse and fin- ish what we start, clear a path for change to visit this town. That all anybody need know."

The women cook late into the evening and early in the morn- ing before the sun comes up. Almost every cabin has some contri- bution, a still-bubbling pot of seasoned stew, fatback and limp dandelion greens simmered for hours in its own pot liquor, rice and thickened gravy, twice-risen bread. Plenty of pork is threaded through the dishes, no longer the poor fare they have rationed the last few weeks. Those who don't have basics to cook or vegetables from their garden plots to offer use their portion of the food doled out the day before. No questions are asked, no explanations are offered. Against all odds, a faint but stubborn strain of optimism hangs in the air as families take pleasure in being reunited. They make a clearing along the widest, longest road in Smithfield Quarter, just in front of Eli McCullen's place. The weather is warmer, and they set up tables out-of-doors. Almost everyone in Smithfield Quarter turns out for Jessie's service, whether newly arrived or longtime resident.

Preacher Johnson speaks first, a gray-haired man about eighty, a well-known minister from Montgomery. Two men help him to the makeshift pulpit they have set up on an elevated part of the road.

"Jessie McCullen a good man, a good husband and father, and he cut down in his prime," Preacher Johnson begins. "All he ever want is to serve his God and serve his family. We all just want to live in peace. We got no call to mix in white folks' matters. Give up the guns and the courthouse, and go back to the families waiting for you. Give up now before you bring the white man down on all of us. God give us our just rewards in the next life, if not in this one. We got to wait. We got to be patient. That all I want to say." Johnson takes his seat again.

Scattered *amens* erupt from the gathering, and many heads nod in agreement. A few other men stand and address the congregation with similar sentiments, although the words differ.

McCully rises from his chair and walks forward slowly, letting his height and carriage settle in the minds of his audience before he says his first word. He looks across the breadth and depth of the crowd, catching one eye after the other in a conspiratorial connection, as if he assumes they know what he is going to say and they already agree. He lets the silence build until it is uncomfortable. Babies start to whine and children squirm. He waits until adults fidget in the beginnings of confusion and annoyance, some pitying him for his loss and others barely containing their anger or discomfort. Only then does he begin to speak.

"We want our turn," he says.

His words are so soft and indistinct that those beyond the first few rows of listeners have trouble understanding he has begun at last. There are those who can't quite catch what he says and lean over to a neighbor to ask. But McCully himself repeats the words, stronger and louder this time.

"We want our turn," he says again, and he shakes his fist as he says it. "We done waited too long a time, and now we want our turn.

"We was free once, and they cast us into bondage. We waited to be delivered again.

"At last we was set free one more time. All of us remember like it just come this morning. No words possible to capture that certain sweet joy what come on Freedom day. But the land we work and the land where we leave our sweat and our blood don't belong to us. No. We don't get no part of that land, even though our hands and our backs bring up the fruit from the soil.

"Most of us still on that land, or some mean little piece just like it. Still not ours or our children's. But we say, 'That's all right. We just wait a little longer. Because we free now.' We decide to be patient some more.

"They tell us we got the right to vote. But if we get to the polls set up in white folks' section of town, white folks say we don't have no home to come back to. They threaten us. They beat us. They kill us. We don't get no work from them, even the ones on the land by rights should be ours.

"Did we not march? Did we not march to the polls anyhow, one hundred black men here in Colfax, in 1868, cast our vote one after the other for the party of Lincoln, the Republican Party? Did we not make our voice heard? They turn out our families then, and we move them from one piece of land that weren't ours to another. We vote for a set of white men taking the place of the ones been in charge too long, thinking the new ones treat us better. Treat us fair. But now is time to help our own self. Give our children what their children get."

McCully stares down at the crowd, fierce. "Eye for a eye." He has a cruel cast to his lips. "That come straight from the Bible. They take one of ours, we got to take one of theirs. We got to take two of theirs."

The rhythmic nods in the gathering turn cautious, uneasy.

"It's our turn now. Our children's children still be waiting if we don't stand today. You think you safe looking the other way, going on with the life you living now? Ask my brother Jessie. Ask him what he done to deserve a bullet to his head. Ask him what good the safe choices done him. No. You can't ask Jessie. Jessie dead."

McCully pauses for a long time. He points to several family men in the gathering, key in the community, one after the other, without saying their names out loud. "Less than half the Smithfield Quarter men join up so far. How about the rest of you? What you waiting for? For the white man to make a promise about better times coming? To die a old man in what you calling peace without scratching together nothing to leave your children? To hope nobody notice you and just let the days pass, one to another, without lifting up your voice for what is surely ours? What good a extra day of life if you don't move something forward? You think those white men out there gonna all a sudden change their way and give us anything we not willing to take ourselves in blood? All you people trying to stay in the middle. There ain't no middle. Ask the White League and the Democrats, turning everything into white against black. We in a war, and they pull every white man into it against us before they let one of us have something. Yes, my brother Jessie was a good man, a man like you. He think by staying out the way, staying in the middle, not doing no harm to nobody, the white man leave him alone. He don't vote. He don't come with us to protect Republicans. He work old man Thornton's place five years, and he weren't no closer to owning his own mule or wagon than when we first get to Louisiana.

"Don't we all want our children to get a better life? I know what

I want for mine. They free, just starting out, but that's not enough. I want more. I want them not only free but with the chance to do better than me.

"We need more men for our patrols, till the Federals come stand with us. We need more men to step up and make a difference now, when it mean something.

"Jessie just as dead playing the fool to the white man, not asking for nothing. The time for waiting is over. Our time is right now, this very day. We want our turn."

McCully's voice cracks at the very end, and he stops talking. There are no more dramatic pauses or impassioned pleas. The big man suddenly looks as confused as a child who has lost sight of his mother.

Israel leaves Lucy's side and pushes forward to where McCully stands rooted. He takes McCully by the elbow, a light touch, and leads him back to his seat. McCully sits, not once glancing at Israel or any of the others gathered, and sinks his face forward into the arc of his big hands.

Israel stands directly behind McCully as Sam Tademy takes the preacher's spot, the last to speak.

"We all understand and sympathize with Brother McCully's grief," Sam begins. "We all want a better life than the one put on us. The question is how to get that life. Brother McCully think the time for settling scores is now. A eye for a eye. I say we need to take a good look around us. If we say we need more men for this fight, we get twice the local colored men we got now. If Sheriff Nash put out the same call, they get five times more white men, bringing their own guns.

"We farmers, most all of us, better at land than at rifles. I want land and education for my children. My boys gonna read and write. They gonna use both their minds and their backs to get their chance. My oldest son, Green, go away half the year to the colored school in Montgomery." Sam pauses and nods in the direction of fourteen-year-old Green Tademy standing in the congregation. Next to Green stands his little brother, Jackson.

"Green already know how to read. And one day, Lord willing, we build a colored school right here in Colfax. My other children, and your children too, go to that school one day. We need education, not bullets. That the only way we win. Not all these white men bad. We got to make stepping stones out of stumbling blocks. That the only way progress last."

Amens drift from the congregation. Hands wave slowly in the air.

Preacher Johnson leads them in a final prayer, and the hastily formed choir sings. They have had only the morning to rehearse, but when they lift their voices, the hymn is strong and they are in harmony. Everyone in the congregation is moved, no matter which side of the courthouse question they are on. The women dish up the food, and everyone gets as much to eat as they want. The service is over.

7

onday morning, the courthouse square is congested with men, women, and children camping out. Neither Smithfield Quarter nor the courthouse can contain the latest torrent of people surging into Colfax. Some are old hands, in town since the beginning of the siege two weeks before, but most are newcomers, just arrived in Saturday's latest big wave.

"Some service yesterday," Israel says to Sam Tademy over mid-morning coffee.

"Polly and the boys look mighty good to my eyes," says Sam. "Been too long."

"You got afternoon patrol?"

Sam nods.

"McCully back on the roof?"

"Took first watch this morning."

"More women in the courthouse today than ever, Lucy and

Polly right up front. Can't seem to help themselves, cleaning up behind us no matter where we is. Lucy want to go back home to The Bottom, say it too crowded at McCully's. What you telling Polly to do?"

"Stay put till we get a sign. Maybe Federals show up now we in a fresh week. This thing got to have some end in sight, or nobody gonna keep to it much longer."

They sit in silence for a while.

"You think McCully shoot at a white man from up there?" Israel asks.

"McCully bullheaded, but he not a fool," Sam says. "Trouble I see is too many guns in too many hands, white and colored."

"Education, not bullets," says Israel. "Fine preaching yesterday."

"Something need saying to cool the sting of McCully's eye for a eye."

"My Noby listen close to you yesterday." Israel stumbles over his words, twirling his cap around in his hands. "Noby study that book you give him all day and night if he could. He want to be like Green, but we can't send him off to school. He got to help on the farm."

"Best twenty-five cent we ever spent," says Sam. Last year Sam pooled cash with two other farmers to buy a secondhand copy of *Sheldon's Primer*, dog-eared and worn. The little book makes the rounds in The Bottom, lent and rotated among children learning to read. Green is already beyond the lessons, but Jackson still uses the primer when his turn comes.

"Noby got a temper," Israel says. "I pray on it. He a good boy, but lose himself sometime. Nothing that boy want more than reading. Might calm him some." Israel glances at Jackson expectantly.

"What you asking?"

"A place for Noby in your school when the time come."

"Every child welcome," says Sam. "But the school ain't real

yet. No telling how long before it start. Not many white want a colored school in Colfax."

Israel acknowledges with a nod.

Men mill around, waiting for their patrol duty shift. Others seem lost, the routines and discipline of the last weeks disrupted as they are pressed instead into domestic chores in service to the large numbers of families camping outside. Sam spots Levi Allen under the Pecan Tree, slightly apart from the others, smoking the stump of a cigar.

"I'ma talk to Levi," says Sam, standing. "Coming?"

Israel trails Sam toward the Pecan Tree. The military man seems uncomfortable, surrounded by the unruly throng, but relieved to see Sam and Israel.

"Must be four hundred people here," Levi says.

"How many guns we got?" Sam asks.

"Maybe eighty." Levi scans the tumult of the square. There is a sea of makeshift shelters and tents, separate cooking fires, transported pots and dishes, children running in all directions, kindling and firewood stacked in heaps, bags of foodstuffs, dogs rummaging through discarded garbage, hastily dug sewage mounds. "Meeting be over soon, I suppose."

"When the Federals coming, Levi?" Sam says. "No more dodging."

Levi seems to debate how to answer, which official party line to give, but then he shrugs. "No way to know, exactly," he says. "We expected them before now."

"Our wives inside cleaning for the general meeting, but unless something change in the next hour or two, you gonna have a spotless courthouse and most men taking their families back home." Sam rests his Enfield rifle against the base of the Pecan Tree. "I'm thinking that way myself," he says. "What's today's meeting about?"

"We gonna open the court and deputize more men. And if the boat from New Orleans don't bring troops today, we gonna send Cap'n Ward down to talk to the governor in person," says Levi.

"We got families to worry over, not political careers," says Sam.

"Why don't you get sworn in this morning, Sam?" Levi asks. "You too, Israel."

"Without those troops, don't matter if you make every colored man in Colfax a deputy," Sam says. "You got to know that, Levi."

Levi takes a long draw on the fat stump of his cigar. "Spread the word about new deputies," he says, but before they have a chance to respond, someone begins ringing an old plantation bell at the front stoop of the courthouse to signal the beginning of the general meeting.

Sam, Israel, and Levi head toward the sound.

Polly and Lucy, already inside the courthouse, have managed to save four seats in the second row of the judge's meeting room. Sam and Israel push toward the front of the crowd and join their wives. The few chairs quickly fill, and the rest of the men and women of Colfax and surrounding towns stand anywhere they can in the small room. Hundreds of people cram inside or wait outside.

"Never been in a courtroom with a judge before," Polly announces to Sam. Her brown eyes shine; she is like a youngster with her first candy treat. Eight years with this woman, and Polly still surprises Sam. The uncompromising fullness of her pouty lips even now has the power to stir him.

"Tangling with the law in a courtroom usually don't mean nothing good for colored," Sam corrects. "We got danger here."

"Times is changing, Mr. Tademy," retorts Polly.

Judge Register, one of the original three white elected Republicans who arrived in town at the beginning of the siege, beckons Sheriff Shaw and the rest of the politicians to his side and opens the courthouse for official business, the first time since the administration change. With a great show of pomp and dignity, the judge gavels the courtroom to silence. "I call the first session of the only official and recognized court of Grant Parish to order.

"This court and its officers are duly appointed by Governor Warmouth of the great state of Louisiana, and we will not tolerate interference in performing our duties on behalf of the local citizens of Grant Parish." The judge embodies new-order legitimacy, hope that the escalating patrols of armed men gathering up and down the river and in the woods, black and white, are an oddity that will pass. "We have two orders of business before us this morning.

"First. We issue a citation against Sheriff Christopher Columbus Nash for attempting to violate the civil rights of Sheriff Shaw, the legal officeholder."

A burly middle-aged colored man, lucky enough to claim one of the few seats in the front row, stands. "You be able to do that?" he asks.

"We are Republicans, the ruling party, recognized by the state," the judge says. "We hold the court, we hold the law, and we hold tax assessment powers for Grant Parish."

"What's a citation?"

Sheriff Shaw, at the judge's elbow, speaks. "A citation sends a message that we serious. Give us the power to arrest their agitators if we have to, like they trying to arrest some of us. Trust me. A citation is proof for New Orleans that we got trouble, and once they see it, they gonna send armed troops lickety-split. None of these local troublemakers gonna stand up against that. Then we go after the renegades who kill Jessie McCullen, arrest them, and bring them to justice. This citation gonna turn everything around."

"That sound good to me," the colored man says, and sits back down.

"Which brings us to the second order of business," says Judge Register. "To keep the peace, we will accept more deputies. All men prepared to defend the town and our rights who weren't sworn in before can sign up now with Sheriff Shaw."

There is an immediate buzz in and around the courthouse room. The standing-room-only crowd parts for four men who come forward, eager to sign. A few more men approach, trying to decide.

Judge Register pounds his gavel a few times for effect. "Court is hereby adjourned," he says. "Deputies sign up at this table."

Less than fifteen minutes has passed.

By eleven o'clock, everyone in Smithfield Quarter has heard about the new colored deputies, a few young men barely past their twenty-first birthday, but most in their thirties or forties, drawn by McCully's appeal at Jessie's service or the promise of a new day when the weight of the court and the law will work in their favor. Instead of sixteen local colored deputies, now there are thirty-five. There are no other topics of conversation over midday dinners.

In freedom, most agree, every step forward has always been accompanied by a step back. Notwithstanding the memory of Jessie, a tentative confidence settles over the colored men in the courthouse.

Recruitment to the cause is on the upswing. New men join and stay in town even as they send their families back home. The carpetbaggers and politicians have long since run out of guns of any kind to issue, and they encourage the Colfax late-joiners to bring whatever weapons they can get their hands on. They are careful with their patrol assignments, mixing the more experienced in with men newly recruited, the unarmed in with those who have carried weapons for weeks, and young in with old. They are short on rations, still living off yesterday's feast, but they pool what they have. Women and children promise to forage for supplies to bring back to their men.

There is a great swell of movement out of Colfax. A few days before, white and black families crossed paths, the colored flowing in and the white ebbing out. This time the families on the move are only colored, leaving.

Sam sends Polly back to Smithfield Quarter to pack up and get the boys ready for the ride back to The Bottom. He will take them himself, then circle back into Colfax by evening. No matter what his doubts, Sam isn't ready to give up on the siege. If there is another way to break the grip of the white terror-mongers in Colfax and make a colored school possible, he hasn't figured it out in the eight years he has lived in the town.

It doesn't take Polly long to gather their belongings at McCully's brother's house and organize for the family's trip back home. Green and Jackson help load the wagon, and then they pile in, Sam at the reins.

"Mr. Tademy, we ready to go now," says Polly. She gives him a smile of encouragement, and Sam clucks the horse forward into the afternoon glare, his Enfield by his side.

Mr. Tademy, Sam thinks.

Polly calls him Mr. Tademy because she knows how much it means to him. It is possible to draw strength from a name. Like the moment eight years ago when he started again new. There had been the long time of sleepwalking as someone else's property, of hanging back and holding on, being careful to sweep each day's sameness and indignities out to the margins of himself in a single-minded attempt to protect all that was still free and hopeful at the inner core. Compliant on the outside but waiting for his chance on the inside.

If not for the name, he surely would have broken when he was whipped in the field, or when his first woman was sold away from him and their young sons, but he went inward, dreaming of a different kind of life that bore no resemblance to the one he was forced to live then.

By the time Sam reached the age of twenty, he had become certain of several things. He might be a slave, knee-deep in cotton fields and subject to the desires of master and overseer alike, but he could figure things out in his head that others couldn't, and he knew that when he talked, other men in the field or in the quarter listened to what he had to say. He had been absolutely certain that one day he would no longer belong to any other man.

Sam had sharp memories of his father, memories kept safely hidden in his secret place. His father was dark and powerful, with deep, pitted scars on his face and arms. He knew the man as his father only because he told Sam so, not because he lived with Sam and his mother and brother in their little cabin. This man had come to them late one night, wild and desperate, when Sam was still so young his main work was to run water to the cotton field and his brother, Doe, didn't yet have steady chores. The man was a stranger to Sam, but his mother's eyes had grown wide with some emotion Sam had never seen before, a softness and hardness doing battle on her face at the same time.

"Sam," his mother said when the man calling himself his father burst into the cabin and shut the door tightly behind him, large, ragged breaths coming from his mouth as if his chest couldn't hold them. At first Sam thought his mother was talking to him, but her eyes were trained on the stranger. She didn't move. None of them moved.

"How you get here? They know you gone?" she said.

"I don't have no time," the dark man said. "I come about the boys."

"You running?"

"They selling me tomorrow. I'ma take my chance. You and the boys come with me."

His mother grabbed Sam and Doe and pulled them close into her skirt, pinning them flat against her, so hard that Sam felt the shaking all the way through to his bony chest. "You not taking me or my sons nowhere," she said. "We never make it out."

"Those boys always gonna be mine, my blood."

"Nobody say different."

Sam couldn't figure out what was happening in the small cabin, this strange man's entitled attitude toward his mother, and her acceptance of his right to be there.

"Come here, boys," the man whispered.

Sam looked up at his mother in confusion. He didn't want to go to the stranger. What was he supposed to do? The man frightened him.

"You not taking them," she said again, a clampdown in her tone.

The man nodded, just once, full of disappointment but yielding. "Just a few words, and then I got to get gone," he said.

His mother pushed Sam gently toward the stocky, sweating man by the door, and Doe trailed behind. The man stooped down, eye level with Sam, and took him by both shoulders.

"I's your daddy," he said. "Your name Sam, like the name they give me." The man shook with the power of his message. "And I name you Dara," the man said to Sam's little brother.

"They call him Doe now," Sam's mother said.

"Sam and Doe, those both slave names." The man whispered, but his voice boomed inside Sam's head as if he shouted. "Stretch out your hand."

Sam and Doe were slow to respond, looking over to their mother for a signal of how to act. She nodded, and Sam reached his right hand out for the both of them, feeling vaguely unsafe.

"Spread your fingers apart far as they go," the man said, his speech thick, in a timbre unfamiliar to Sam. Sam complied. "It's like your arm the river, and your fingers smaller rivers running to the sea. The big one the river Nile. Bigger than any river you ever see. We come from the part with the little rivers, call the Nile Delta. Alexandria in Egypt, and Egypt in Africa. That where you from. Not this place.

"We got a real name, a family name. My father tell me, and now I tell you. Keep it here." The man tapped at his head with the broad fingers of his right hand.

Sam's senses were swimming. He saw the scars, more frightening up close than they had been from across the room. It was as if the man were trying to eat him up, inhale his very essence, pressing his urgency on him. Sam's skin tingled, but he lost some of his fear. It was as if they were tethered together in the moment, just the two of them, connected for better or worse.

"This all I got to give you," the man said, "and can't nobody take it away." He squeezed Sam's shoulders so tight they began to ache. "We from far away. We wasn't brought to this country as no slave. We come free, of our own will. We come from the Nile Delta, and my daddy pay passage by his sweat-work on a ship supposed to take him to a land of opportunity. He work boats on the dock, loading and unloading. He come over on a ship had twelve thousand tons of lumber on it. It was a trade. He work on the ship for one year with no pay to come here. He thinking he come to a better place, and they make him a slave after he get here. He born free. My daddy tell me, and now I tell you."

Little Sam still held his hand out, fingers splayed, afraid to move. The Nile River? The Nile Delta? Born free?

"Our real name Ta-ta-mee." The man gently pushed Sam out a little farther away from him, studying his face, but still holding him tightly by both shoulders. "Say it."

Sam looked at his mother. She was busy cutting off a portion of their weekly ration of bacon and tying it up in a cloth rag. Sam could tell she was listening to each word, but she kept her back to them, maintaining a distance, refusing to get between the man and his two boys. Sam wasn't going to get any help there. He turned again to the man calling himself his father.

"Ta-ta-mee," Sam whispered.

"Again," the man demanded.

"Ta-ta-mee."

"One more time, like it fit your mouth."

"Ta-ta-mee."

"Don't never let go of it. That your real name," the man said.

"All's you can do now is whisper, but one day you gonna shout it out so everybody hear, and your children gonna shout it so they remember who they is. Again."

"Tatamee," Sam whispered, wondering what would happen if they found his father here in the cabin. Would they beat him, kill him? Would they kill all of them just for listening?

"You a good boy. You got strong, free, fighter's blood in you. Teach that to your brother, and when you make your own sons, teach them to shout out they name like they know who they is." The man let go of Sam and stood erect again. "You still a fine-looking woman," he said to Sam's mother.

"Good luck," she said, her face still arguing with itself, hard and soft. She handed him the food wrapped in her head scarf. "I pray you make it out."

The man accepted the small bundle and stuffed it in the pocket of his ragged, handspun trousers. He peeked warily out the small window. "Don't forget," he said to Sam. "What your real name?"

"Ta-ta-mee," repeated Sam.

"Hold on to it. You a Tatamee."

As quickly as he had burst into Sam's life, the man calling himself Sam's father was out the front door, out into the deepest darkness of the moonless night.

They never knew whether he made it out of Alabama to a free state, or whether he was caught and taken back to his plantation, but Sam always remembered the last words he heard his father speak.

"You a Tatamee."

By nightfall, most of the colored women and children are already back in their homes. When the steamboat from New Orleans docks later that evening, there are no troops on board, nor is there any word from the governor.

Sam meets McCully bringing the ladder into the courthouse for the evening. The older man looks as tired as Sam feels.

"Long day," says Sam. "I send Polly and the boys on home."

"Don't see nothing from up top but families headed out," says McCully. "No whites left close in to Colfax." McCully has found chewing tobacco somewhere and offers a plug to Sam. "Why you won't be no deputy, Sam?"

"No gain being a deputy. No pay, no extra safety, no longtime work. I'm here just the same."

"Could be something to tell your grandchildren one day," says McCully.

"A name on a piece of paper making some of us deputies don't have nothing to do with nothing," says Sam.

"I thought you was so proud of that name, Tademy."

"Only place I need to see 'Tademy' is on a deed for a piece of land, or on a schoolhouse."

"Opening the court made some folks settle down. Most men held, even if families went back."

"Still don't smell right to me," says Sam. "The Federals not coming."

"That's not what the politicians say," says McCully.

"If troops was coming, they'd be here," says Sam. "Levi say they talking about sending someone down to New Orleans to fetch them up here. That's three or four days, going, talking, coming back."

"Unless the Federals already on their way."

"How long since little Noby Smith heard them men in Summerfield Springs?" Sam asks. "Over a week," he answers, without waiting for McCully to do the figuring. "Eight days, and each time we go on patrol, we see more white posses, more men we don't recognize. Sheriff Nash not gonna sit around forever. Citation or no. The notion of troops marching in here the only thing holding him back. May be acting like the courthouse open for business make us feel better, but ain't gonna stop them."

"Federals got to come, Sam," says McCully. There is a stretched-thin shrillness in his tone; he is plainly exhausted by anger and drained by grief. Sam isn't used to a wheedling McCully, neither confident nor boastful. "They got to come."

"If the governor of Louisiana on our side, why it taking this long to get troops here? I keep thinking he don't care if a fight break out in Colfax. What if he want everybody to see how bad it got here between white and colored, between Republican and Democrat? What if he want to stir up the fight, so's to get more votes next election?"

"You talk nonsense, Sam. Not even a politician got a heart that cold. They Republican, and they owe us."

8

nother endless night, another damp gray morning before the overnight fog burns off, another disorienting wake-up, another day of marching and guns instead of plows and crops. At the afternoon coffee break under the Pecan Tree, Israel unwraps the hard biscuit and bit of smoked bacon that are his meal, eager to share with McCully and Sam what he has just learned on his last patrol.

"They all leaving by this evening," Israel tells his friends, his mouth full. He is hungry and tired, but at least his feet have toughened from the constant walking patrols. The blisters that plagued him have dried up, no longer painful to the touch. "One of them already gone, snuck down to Boyce, waiting till dark for the boat. We not supposed to know."

"What you mean, *all?*" McCully's deep voice carries in the open air, and Israel and Sam both put their fingers to their lips. "*All* who?" he asks more quietly.

"Judge Register, the assessor, everybody come up to Colfax to begin with, except for Sheriff Shaw and Levi. They going for help in New Orleans. The colored boatman gonna ferry them out to catch the steamer."

"We here protecting them, and suddenly they all leaving?" McCully's voice rises again. A pinched harshness is etched into his features.

"Guess it turn out harder than they thought," says Israel.

"Time for us to take charge, anyway," announces McCully. "Colfax our town."

Other men milling around don't even pretend to give them privacy, listening in.

"Why the white man can't give us our forty acres and a mule?" McCully complains. "No matter how much they hold us back, we still here, we still strong. We better at the land, we better at breeding, we better at making do and getting by. And now we got guns and done throwed down the mask. No more patting us on the head like a pet dog or kicking us in the ribs like a stray. This our town. If we got to kill for them to understand, that the way it got to be."

"Don't talk foolish. We don't stand a chance without those troops," Sam says. He lowers his voice, tries to return to private conversation. "Levi staying."

"Levi the one man I'd pick out the lot of them," says McCully. "Let the politicians go and do what they do best. Talk. We never was in this together noway, Republicans or no. And somebody got to go see what keep the Federals away."

"It's a bad sign, all of them leaving at the same time," says Sam.

"We in it now, Sam. What else you think we can do?" McCully flashes some of his old bluster. He is a powder keg of a man ready to stand pat to the last, regardless of consequences.

Israel stays out of the conversation.

* * *

When Israel was eleven, one of his jobs on the plantation in Alabama was to deliver water to the sweating, thirsty men and women in the field, ladling out the liquid with a gourd as he passed between the endless rows of growing cotton. Back then all Israel knew was Low Water, the sprawling plantation with hundreds of slaves where he was born. He called all of the women in the quarter Aunt, and slept in the big cabin with other children who didn't have an exact mother or family to whom they belonged. Israel belonged to all of them on Low Water, and he belonged to none of them, just one more strong buck in training on his way to slide smoothly into a lifetime in the fields.

The overseer was particular about Israel going to each of the field hands to bring them water, one after the other, so they didn't break routine. One day in early spring, the overseer rode up on his horse just as Israel's old wooden bucket gave way from the bottom, the water draining in a quick flush.

"Stupid boy," the overseer said.

"I didn't do nothing 'cept use this old rotten bucket, Massa," Israel protested.

Without warning, Israel felt the sharp sting of the lash cutting into the flesh of his right cheek, and like a door slamming, his right eye closed of its own accord. He forced his eye open again, but his vision was clouded. He felt as if he were trying to focus underwater in a vat of milk. Israel put his hand to his face. The hand he pulled back dripped wet with the dark red of running, pulsing blood.

"You sassing me, boy?" Israel dared not look up, but he knew by the nearness of the voice that the overseer had gotten off his horse. "What my name, darky?"

"Mr. Neely, sir." When he talked, Israel could feel the blood trickle into the side of his mouth, and a slight breeze let loose a stinging circle around his cheek, as if someone had cut him with a straight razor.

Israel sensed quick movement, and he crouched, head down, between the facing rows of cotton bushes. The approaching strides of the overseer were so careless that the white man brushed off several emerging cotton buds from the bloom-heavy plants. Several of the tight, hard buds dropped to the ground, wasted, useless to the harvest now, an offense that would have provoked a whipping if committed by a slave. The overseer loomed directly over Israel, so close that even with his bad eye, Israel saw the rough, raised grain of the overseer's heavy boots. Neely kicked Israel in the side, and Israel crumpled, scraping his tender cheek against the caked, lipped-up dirt of the row. The smart thing to do was lie still and wrap his body into a ball to withstand the blows. Even the youngest slave on the plantation knew that, but a red rage washed through Israel. There was the briefest of moments when he might have called his anger to heel, but instead, he gave the beast inside room to blossom and grow stronger. When the familiar flood of red surged in his brain and the acrid tang of metal lodged in his throat, he yielded, released himself to the swelling song, and gave it free rein.

They told him what happened later, those in the field close enough to see. Israel couldn't remember. How he had blocked Neely's foot before he landed the next kick, throwing the overseer off balance, how the two of them had scrambled ineffectively on the ground, a lumbering, surprised white man and an agile eleven-year-old colored boy, how Israel had bounced up like a coiled spring and snatched the whip from where it had fallen on the ground, walking away in the direction of the quarter, the prize of the whip still in his hands. Young Israel had touched the overseer, but at least he hadn't struck him. That was the only thing that saved his life.

Within the hour, they bent Israel over the post in the central yard, and Neely himself delivered twenty lashes to the young boy's back. The lash gave off a distinctive whistle right before slicing into his flesh. Each blow delivered a bright flash of pain, and the oozing cut under his eye in the shape of a question mark throbbed with its own music, making him dizzy, taking him out of his body. Then they untied his hands and took him back to the quarter, where an old woman salved his seeping wounds. Again Israel's mind escaped what his body could not, so he didn't remember much of that part. Afterward, they talked about him and his defiance in the quarter, and the number of blows, and how there were grown men who couldn't take as many lashes as Israel, just a skinny eleven-year-old boy.

Later, Israel became convinced that Neely hadn't wanted to kill him. The overseer had stopped after twenty lashes, not only because Israel had future value as a slave, but because he wanted Israel's punishment to be of a more personally satisfying and longer-lasting nature. From that day forward, he whipped Israel himself whenever he took the notion, or had him whipped at least once a month. Ten lashes even if there had been no offense, and twenty if he could actually attach a shortcoming. To show Israel his place, the overseer of Low Water said.

For a small handful of men, this repeated treatment might have fed obstinate rebelliousness or a determination to run away. In the case of Israel Smith, the constant beatings accomplished exactly what the overseer had intended. They leeched the fight out of him. They caused Israel to defer to white men. They made him always afraid.

At nightfall, Israel is one of six men assigned to the escort party. They manage to get the politicians away to the steamboat without being discovered, and return to the courthouse without incident, but Israel can't shake a deep sense of defeat. Other men speculate on how long it will take troops to arrive, but Israel wants no part of that. He goes to his sleeping corner in the back room of the courthouse and lies down, pulling his blanket over his head.

He thinks about what the men who oppose the new officeholders are capable of. He thinks of the family he wants to protect at any cost. He thinks of Noby, the storehouse of Israel's greatest hopes for the future, at the dangerous age of nine.

One word ricochets in his brain. *Alone.* They are alone, the colored men of Colfax. For sixteen days, they have been encouraged to stand up for themselves, and promised the help of the United States government. Despite the obstacles, despite incontrovertible proof of violence surrounding them, against the better judgment of many of the men huddled in their own private reverie on the dirty courtroom floor, they have believed. In pursuit of the blind hope of opportunity, they have taken a great risk.

And now they find themselves, all of them together, more alone than they have ever been.

9

S am straightens up to stretch, and immediately, the low, stabbing pain at the base of his spine eases. For every shovel of reddish Louisiana dirt he hollows out and heaps atop the mounting barricades, the resentment building in his chest swells tenfold. The goal is to construct and extend a bulwark three hundred yards in length and four feet high on three sides of the courthouse before nightfall, and Levi put him in charge. The work is slow, and the men who have been assigned are overwhelmed.

It is the Saturday before Easter Sunday, and no one has heard from Cap'n Ward, the assessor, or Judge Register in three days. The last Sam saw was their backs as they fled Colfax, bound for New Orleans. Enough time has elapsed to at least send a message on one of the New Orleans packets that come upriver. Nothing. Three weeks, Sam thinks, three weeks since the carpetbaggers and politicians entered town, asking for the help of the people of Colfax. And now they are gone.

Sam goes back to digging, chopping at the stubborn soil with growing disgust. The courthouse they fight to hang on to is more a symbolic shell than an instrument of the new order. No politicians inside, no elected officials, and no town business being carried out. Even Sheriff Shaw spends more and more time away from the building now that the others have left, staying down at Calhoun's Sugarhouse. Most times the men don't know exactly where he is.

A short copper-colored farmer, sweating profusely, breaks the line of men and leans heavily on his shovel, mopping at his forehead with a grimy white handkerchief. He is part of the detail assigned to fill bags with claylike mud from the river and stack them on top of the barricade to add height around the riverbank side of the courthouse. The man stares into space, propped against his shovel. Sam works his own patch of dirt and keeps an eye on him. Finally, the man stuffs his handkerchief back into his trousers pocket. Instead of bending back over his shovel, the man wanders over to the shade of the Pecan Tree and lies down.

Sam drops his own shovel and moves toward the Pecan Tree, first at a walk and then breaking into almost a full run.

"Keep going," Sam shouts. "Get back to your line."

The man adjusts the straw hat on his head and gives Sam a blank return look. He doesn't move. Sam assumes he is sick, from sun or something catching. His eyes are glazed, barely registering.

"What the use?" the coppery man says to Sam. He looks neither defiant nor sick, just defeated.

Sam quickly closes the distance between the two of them and yanks the man upright by his arm.

"We gonna hold them off," says Sam. He shakes the man, harder than he intends, fighting through the limp resistance to make a connection, to break inside of the man's despair. "But only if we ready. It take us all to put up barricades before nightfall." Sam's attempt at encouragement sounds weak, even to his own ears. There have been too many days of endless marching or rid-

118

ing around the confines of the town limits, muscles straining, listening for any noise, head pounding, attempting to reassure others when there is less and less justification for optimism.

The man's watery eyes find Sam's. "They gonna bring in white men from parishes all over the state and pick us off like ticks from a dog," he says.

"We getting these ditches ready for the troops when they come," replies Sam.

The man is clearly unconvinced, but something in Sam's manner cows him enough to make him rise up, slowly, shuffle back to his place in the line of sweating bodies, and pick up his shovel again.

Men, women, and children pass back and forth between Smithfield Quarter and the courthouse with sacks, building materials, food, and provisions. There are hundreds of colored men around the building, from its front double doors and beyond, stretched across to the Pecan Tree. They dig trenches, stack mud-filled bags as breastworks, gravely practice loading and reloading, and drill with rifles, pistols, and shotguns. Drilling is no longer for show.

Sam trudges back to his own place on the line, not quite able to cast off the deep well of resignation in the copper-colored man's eyes. More and more of the men are coming under its spell each day, each hour.

They make good progress on the barricades. Levi returns to the courthouse midafternoon with a wagon full of supplies, including a large stash of miscellaneous metal, some shiny new and some rusted salvage. The military man relieves Sam and resumes his oversight of the preparations, walking the length of the breastworks, ordering the addition of more sacks to build up the height by a foot in one section and extend the length toward the river. In the main, Levi seems satisfied. He has them unload the scrap from the wagon for deposit at selected spots along the earthworks, pulls several men from the line, and sets them to the task of building makeshift cannons from parts scavenged from the countryside and the general store. They take an old steam pipe and cut it into threes, plug one end of each piece, drill vents, and mount the homemade artillery. A brief, heavy rain kicks up at midday and drenches them through, turning dirt to clotted mud. No one stops to seek shelter.

By early evening, the barricades are almost finished, a crude, wavering line about three to four feet high with trenches behind. Sam seeks out McCully, standing outside under the Pecan Tree with Spenser and Israel Smith. There are always at least two men posted on the roof during daylight hours, but now there are four. McCully comes down and checks in every hour or so, instead of keeping the long solo watches he maintained in the beginning.

"Israel seen hundreds of white men at Summerfield Springs," says McCully to Sam, catching him up on the news.

"Levi took a few of us to scout," says Israel, ready to repeat the story he has told over and over for the last half hour. "More white men than you can count. Guns, horses. Even a cannon."

"What you do?" asks Sam.

"We get out of there. Fast," says Israel. "Levi in with Sheriff Shaw now. There more of them than us. White men not from here mixed in. Some men recognize White League from Sicily Island."

"If troops don't come soon, won't make no difference," Sam says in a soft voice.

There is silence among them.

"Tell me about your school," McCully suddenly says to Sam in the cocksure, bold voice he used before his brother was killed. "How that school laid out in your head?"

"What the school got to do with anything?" asks Sam. "White men gathering at Summerfield Springs. May be none of us getting out of here."

"I'm starting to think the colored school what really matter, outta all this," McCully says.

"These is scary times," says Israel. "Sometime I don't know why we here."

"We here for the best reason there is, so our sons don't have to be," McCully says. "You got to get shed of here, Sam. They's big things you meant to do. You got a plan."

"We all got plans, McCully. We all got the same need to get clear of this."

"You wrong. Most of us just squeezing by, trying to keep going, set up enough room for ourselves. You got in mind moving us all to the fore. Tell us about the colored school," McCully demands.

Sam starts to protest, but on the Saturday night before Easter Sunday, what else better is there to talk about than a vision of the future?

"We get one room, maybe two, not too far in the country," Sam begins. "All colored children be welcome. Parents pool whatever we get our hands on, lumber, stove, coal for winter, chairs, tables, paper, pencils. We find us a teacher with book learning for words and figuring, pay what we can. Just 'cause we can't read don't mean our children got to end the same way. We scrape together enough to buy books for the sharing, and we set aside the time for our children to go to that school, even if we the ones got to work night and day in the field our own selves in their place."

"That's right," McCully says. "I want to be the first you ask if anything need building."

"Me too," says Israel. "Count me in."

The weather turns crisp into the night, with a kick to the wind that whistles through the courthouse while the men try to sleep. About an hour before sunrise comes the unmistakable creaking of multiple wagons approaching, and then sounds of people on the front steps. The flicker of a lantern cuts through the darkness on the other side of the small chest-height window near the front door. Sam is midway between sleep and wakefulness, and he tries to block the picture that springs to his mind, the clear vision of a mob of angry white men with drawn guns bursting through the double doors, come to storm the place. Maybe the troops from New Orleans have worked their way upriver to relieve and rescue them. He grabs his Enfield.

The guard posted outside challenges in a deep voice, and in response, there is a higher-pitched answer. The front door groans open slowly, and a strange procession enters, bringing inside the coolness of the night air at their backs. The intruders carry two lanterns, wicks turned down low, whispering orders to one another, keeping their voices quiet in deference to the sleeping men. They are mostly women, some garbed in Sunday best, fresh collar or scarf or ironed apron, as if they've come to church meeting. There are a handful of older boys and girls, maybe twelve to fifteen years old.

Sam relaxes his grip on the rifle as soon as he sees that it is their women from Smithfield Quarter and The Bottom. Women weave through the courthouse rooms, looking for the men who belong to them. One farmer startles when his wife touches his shoulder, and, still groggy, fumes and sputters, angry that she has not only come inside the courthouse but brings their baby with her. Conversations begin to roll through the courthouse, like a series of clattering runaway wagons, and build in volume. Lucy Smith has found Israel already, and four of them, Israel, Lucy, and their sons, form a frozen tableau of anger and supplication. Lucy, David, and Noby have their heads bowed while Israel whispers fiercely and gestures. Polly has come too and crosses the room toward Sam, followed by Green and Jackson.

"Not a word," Polly whispers to Sam, pressing one of her stubby fingers to his lips while her gaze sweeps the room, absorbing the scene, taking it in.

"Papa." Jackson runs to Sam, stopping just short of his father. "We here to be with you, Papa," Jackson says, his breath short and quick, the smooth, defined angles of his dark face eager.

Sam's two sons stand before him, anxious to be men.

"What can you be thinking, woman?" Sam says to Polly.

Polly comes so close Sam smells the stubbornness on her. "We hold Easter Sunday service at sunrise," Polly says. Her tone pre-empts negotiation. Sam knows her well enough to know that she has already made up her mind. She points to other women making similar explanations to their men.

"This a man's job, Polly," Sam says. "You in the way."

Polly's angular face forms a hint of a smile. In this hard and dangerous time, Sam has almost forgotten Polly's smile. It doesn't seem appropriate.

"In your way?" Polly says. "I pick or swing a hoe almost good as you in the field, Sam Tademy. We been side by side for a long time now."

"This different," Sam says. "Hundreds of white men gathering up in Summerfield Springs. People seen it with their own eyes."

"No safer on the farm than here, with things as they is," Polly says.

"Where the other children at?" Sam asks. "L'il Sam, James, Angeline, William?"

"I left the youngest with neighbors. Jackson pestering every day to come back since leaving town early this week. I do believe if I hadn't brung him, he woulda found a way to come to you of his own accord."

"You all belong home."

"Home where you is, Sam. We decide on that long time ago. And those two boys old enough to fight for what's theirs."

"They not yours to decide for," he says.

Sam has never forced a claim of his greater right to Green and Jackson because they are from his blood and not hers, and she has never treated them as anything other than being from her own body.

Polly sways slightly, and on her face is an expression like the first questioning look from a doe after a hunter strikes home. Disbelief and understanding all wrapped up in one moment. But by the time Polly brings her eyes up to meet his, she has already recovered herself. She realizes she isn't mortally wounded and brings herself back into the fight.

"Me and the boys staying till after church service," Polly says with cool crispness.

The pinch to her lips and the determination in her stance remind Sam how much he has come to depend on this woman.

"Polly, you don't understand." Sam lowers his voice. "They might could come down on us anytime."

"I understand fine," says Polly. "You think I don't know what the men in Summerfield Springs capable of? You the best thing ever happen to me, Sam Tademy, but you not the first thing. Least you got guns here."

Polly touches Sam slightly on the arm and presents him with one of her smiles, meant to soften and reassure him, but the warm curl of her lips can't ease the gnawing at either his stomach or his heart. "We come to make Easter Sunday service soon as the sun break, and then we go home directly after. I promise," she says, gathering the boys to her. "It's not like this the first time we got trouble."

"Blood gonna spill, Polly," Sam whispers. "How many times you gonna make me get my family clear?"

"We ain't clear long as you in here, Sam." Polly seems ready for more argument but pulls back. "We got the need to spend this little bit of Easter Sunday with you," she says. "The others thinking the same. We here now, and we gonna hold service outside and hope the sun chase away some of the cold."

Sam nods, resigned. "Sooner we praise Him, sooner we get you away from here," he says.

Sam remembers the first time he ever saw Polly. She was alone, on foot in Alabama, same as him, heading west, with not much more to help her along on a journey than attitude. She carried nothing. Not food, not utensils, no shoes, no extra clothing, and it was clear she was hungry. Her old homespun dress, dark and colorless, shapeless and torn, frayed to shredding at the collar and worn through at the elbows, looked like it was being held together by sheer will and grime. Her hair was matted, a wild snarl around her head. He couldn't tell how old she was, exactly. Sam's stolen glances in her direction sometimes convinced him that she was in the late part of her teens, but when the light changed, he was just as sure she had seen the better half of her twenties. There was no innocence in that face, but yet it wasn't hard.

She traveled in parallel to him for twenty-six hours before they spoke one word. When Sam stopped to eat and feed the boys, she stopped too. Sam had precious little, but he had managed so far to keep them going by trapping small game, a possum or squirrel, and occasionally a wild rabbit, and he was confident he could catch more each day. He found it almost impossible to continue to ignore the woman who shadowed them, who sat and stared hungrily as he made a fire and roasted their supper of squirrel, but anything he gave to her meant less for his children. She didn't ask, and he didn't offer, until the next day when he caught a possum and halted to roast his good fortune. Again, when he stopped, she stopped, off to the other side of the dirt path they both followed.

"Dangerous, a woman traveling alone," Sam commented. "Some men up to no good on the road these days."

"You asking me to join up with you and your boys?" the woman asked.

Sam was surprised, both by her suggestion and by her forwardness. He was uncomfortable trying to sort out the rest of his reactions. She was much younger than he was, and filthy, but even through the grime caked on her face and the shabby, torn clothes, Sam could tell she was pretty, in a girlish way.

"I asked nothing of the kind," Sam said. "Just saying that traveling alone ain't a good idea for a woman. Though it hard to tell you a woman."

Sam regretted the last immediately.

"You think a woman ought to look best she can, a woman on her own?" Polly said.

"It ain't safe. Why not go back where you come from?"

"Never," she hissed. It was as if her features became indistinct for just a moment. "Never," she repeated.

They didn't speak again for a half hour or more. Sam tended to the boys, getting them bedded down in the woods for the night. The evening weather wasn't too cold or damp, and tonight his two blankets would be enough. The two boys slept together under the same blanket.

"What their names?" she asked.

"The oldest Green. The youngest Jackson," Sam said. He assumed she gravitated to him because she considered him safer than some of the others on the road, an older man with two young sons in tow.

"I seen you all struggling, even you, carrying the little one," she said. "You spare some possum tonight, I help carry the load what you got tomorrow. We take turns carrying Jackson if you want. If you catch game, I find herbs, cook it up, make what you got taste better, stretch out longer. You got a pot, but there's more could come out of it than you know how to do."

Sam wondered what else she would be willing to do for protection or even just a meal. "Ain't you worried what kind of man I is?" he said.

She looked directly at him, what seemed to Sam to be through him, into him. Even in the dimness of the moonlight, Sam felt the power of it.

"No," she said. "I see two choices. Travel alone and travel with you. And you got food."

A little reluctantly, Sam gave her some of the roasted possum he had intended to pack up for tomorrow. She crossed quickly, close to the fire, grabbing at the bony remains of the possum splayed and skewered on a stout branch. It had cooled already, and she didn't hesitate before gulping it down greedily, not stopping until there was only bone and head left.

"We walking till I get us clean out the state of Alabama," Sam said, surprised at himself for sharing this information with the gritty woman across from him. "'Till I come someplace to stop and raise my children. My name Sam."

The woman nodded and smiled, a sweet smile that lightened her face. "Mine Polly," she said.

They just fell in together, as simple as that, and Polly walked beside him all the way from Alabama, step for step. As their walking weeks passed, traveling with his children, they began to shape themselves to each other, seemingly without much effort. By the time they had been on the road for over a month, he had told her of his hopes for the future, his dreams for the boys.

One night not long after they crossed into Louisiana, the two of them sat by the fire while Polly cleaned out the pot from the possum stew she had made. The boys had already fallen into an exhausted sleep together under their blanket, Green tucked up behind Jackson with his arms wrapped around his younger brother. Sam had come to look forward to the transition time after night fell and the boys were settled, a quiet time that on good days meant a full stomach, a chance to rest his feet, and one-on-one talk with Polly. To Sam's surprise, he found himself telling her about Green and Jackson's mother, and how she had been sold away from him the year before, when Jackson was barely two. How he had found her gone one evening when he got back from the fields at dusk, with no explanation. The boys had become part of the plantation, mothered by whatever slave woman was assigned. But then came freedom, and Sam found himself with two small boys he didn't quite know what to do with. But they were his blood, and he was prepared to kill for them.

That night, for the first time, Polly shared too, but only her thoughts of a future, not her past. All she wanted from this life, she said, was a good man she could respect and a family of her own no one could take away. Sam remembered how she looked that night, so young and fearless. But she never said anything at all about where she came from or what had happened to her there, even much later, after they had walked through Louisiana for what seemed forever, and Sam had felt the thick, raised scars that charted crisscrossing paths down the center of her back.

When they met in Alabama, there was frost on the ground in the mornings, but now the days were longer, warmer. Soon the full press of summer would be upon them. It was time to begin a new life, settle down and start living, stop the endless walking, but Sam was afraid to upset the balance he and Polly had together. What if she was far enough from the terrors of her past and didn't need him anymore? They never really talked about what would happen when the walking was over.

When they passed through Alexandria, Louisiana, an area populated enough to need physical laborers, Sam was struck by the town's name, as if it were an omen. He left the boys with Polly while he went to the center of town to ask around.

"I hear Mr. Swafford taking on hands," said one grizzled old colored man, "but he north, closer to Colfax, about a day walk."

Sam made up his mind on the way back from town.

"Soon's I find work, I'm stopping for good," he said to Polly when he saw her. "This place good as any."

Polly waited, saying nothing. She had transformed since Sam first saw her on the road in Alabama. Her clothes were still thread-bare, but she took greater care to smooth back her hair with her hands each morning, tying it back with a scrap of faded cloth. The wildness in her face and her eyes was gone. Both his sons had taken to her. Jackson was so young he had accepted her presence in their lives without question, as willing to take her hand as Sam's. Green still had memories of his mother, but Polly didn't push herself on him, and in time he came around too.

"The boys need a mother, and I need a wife," Sam said. "I'm a good man, willing and able to work hard. I believe in the Lord and expect my woman to do the same, and I'm gonna find a way for my boys to go further than me."

She was too young for him, he thought, but she had a power over him that made him dizzy with longing. And although she had come to share her body with him, she refused to tell him anything about her life before, her slave life. What if the leaving of that life was more important to her than the making of a new one, at least the making of one with him? What if, unlike him, she was still running and not willing yet to be on her way toward something else?

"I got a strong back, and these children, and something else almost nobody else got. I got a name old as any you ever heard, go all the way back to Egypt," Sam told her. "And I'm gonna own my own land here one day, and farm."

Sam realized he was selling too hard, but he couldn't stop talking. As soon as there were no more of his words, she would have to give him an answer, this woman who had taken up with him so quickly. Would it be just as easy for her to keep on going without him? Sam wasn't sure he could bear it if she said no. "If you take me on and take the boys on, my name be yours too."

"Why I want to be call Sam?" Polly asked, puzzled.

She was road-weary, ragged, her coarse hair snarled and tied back with the old kerchief, and she was everything Sam wanted. He offered up his most prized possession to her.

"Not Sam. My *family* name," he said. "From Egypt. From the Nile River. From the Nile River Delta."

Polly waited silently for him to make clear what he was trying to say.

"Ta-ta-mee," Sam said with pride, unwrapping his gift for her approval. He was careful with the sound of it, letting it roll from his tongue as his father had long ago. "That the family name of anybody belong with me. Ta-ta-mee."

"Ta-de-my," Polly repeated, smiling her special smile for him, her face a reflection of the wonder he had always found in the magic of that name. "You, me, and the boys, and more children to come," she said. "The past don't matter no more. We gonna start up a future with that name."

They spill out to the courthouse square in the semidarkness, joining those who camp out on the grounds and others from Smithfield Quarter who choose to come. It is Easter Sunday 1873, and regardless of the predawn hour, word spreads and their numbers grow until they are over two hundred strong. Lanterns dot the landscape, orbs of light flickering, casting shadows over the ghostly, empty breastworks and the homemade cannons and the looming courthouse building in the background. The women draw their shawls over their heads for added warmth, protect their hands in the folds of their garments, and bundle up their children; the men pull down on their hats to keep the wind out.

The Easter Sunday ceremony is brief. The crowd is restless, unable to focus on the here and now when every mind wanders to the future. Without discussion, they instinctively allow no time for speeches, political or spiritual. Everyone feels the urgency. The sun rises as they stand together, streaks of red and gold bands across the horizon, and Sam Tademy asks for the joining of hands. Neighbors, friends, family, and strangers all stand with hands clasped and eyes closed.

"Lord, we stand before You, Your faithful flock, and we praise You. Let Your will be done through us, Your humble vessels. Give us strength to face whatever come. Give us strength to accept Your will. Amen."

Two hundred voices ascend in a slow hymn as they sing of feeble lives at an end and entering God's Kingdom. Everyone hangs tight to each note of "Just a Closer Walk with Thee."

* * *

Hoofbeats pound toward the group outside, and the singing trails off mid-hymn.

"They on the move," a lone colored man on horseback shouts, "coming down from Summerfield Springs. Dragging a cannon on wheels. We got maybe one hour. White men already in Smithfield Quarter with guns."

The service breaks apart in a hundred different directions as colored men rush for their weapons and women and children flood back into the courthouse, holding on to one another. Bowls and platters of food brought for an Easter Sunday feast lay out in the backs of wagons and on wooden tables, uneaten. No one moves them.

The horseman is off his mount and inside within seconds, conferring with Levi Allen. The men make no attempt to keep the conversation private. "Two or three white men for each of us, and they packing every kind of weapon," the scout says.

All eyes turn to Levi. The military man keeps his jaw tight. "Give the signal to pull back all patrols and take your positions on the barricades," he says calmly.

"The women and children," Sam points out. "We got to get them out."

Levi doesn't alter by one muscle the combat-ready expression on his face, but his eyes soften. "Already too late for that now," he says.

Figure 8. Photo of Melrose cannon (Northwestern State University of Louisiana, Watson Memorial Library, Cammie G. Henry Research Center: Francis Mignon Collection, bound volume #115)

10

*I*srael takes up his post, one of several dozen men assigned to the east barricade, parallel to the river. He is at the farthermost end away from Red River, with a clear face-on view of Smithfield Quarter in one direction across the wide, dusty no-man's-land, and a side view of the beginnings of Mirabeau Woods.

Levi Allen is their focal point, barking out assignments. So many men behind the barricades, so many at the three improvised cannons, so many along the path leading to the courthouse, so many inside the courthouse protecting the women and children. McCully and Sam draw duty inside. About two hundred colored men station themselves in and behind the crescent-shaped barricades around the three sides of the single-story courthouse building. They are hidden from view by the deep hollow of the trench below, and above by the mud sacks where they rest the muzzles of their weapons. The only unguarded section around the courthouse is on the west side, nearest Red River, the banks of which Levi deems too slippery and steep for a large body of attackers to gain good access.

Israel waits, looking out from the trenched ring around the courthouse. He and another man are responsible for one of the three small pipe cannons, and he makes sure he has the phosphor friction matches to light the wick in his pocket, at the ready. He has seen the cannon the white men have in Summerfield Springs; it is a heavy weapon, forged and professionally constructed, while this one is small and flimsy, cobbled together from spare parts.

He hears the steady advance of the riders, a symphony of hoofbeats and straining hard snorts of the horses, and then the staccato orders of men in charge dispatching and arranging the incoming riders on three sides of the courthouse. One set spreads out along the lip of Mirabeau Woods, another along the break line of the pecan grove to the south, and the last blocking the entry to Smithfield Quarter, creating battle lines in the open field about three quarters of a mile from Colfax. They outnumber the men in the courthouse and are well armed with a much wider range of weapons—six-shooters, shotguns, and Enfields—and stand or sit astride their mounts under the trees. A few tie up their horses to get down to stretch their legs.

It is surprisingly quiet for a while, with only the nervous whinny of horses breaking the stillness, until into the silence comes the squeak and groan of a heavy object on the move. From his vantage point, Israel gets his second glimpse of their cannon, a medium-size howitzer. Originally a deck cannon on a steamboat out of New Orleans, the ugly, dull brass cylinder has since been fitted out with two big-spoked metallic wheels at the rear for ground transport, and the oversize six-sectioned wheels gouge deep ruts in the soft dirt and weeds as it is dragged into position. Two horses pull the heavy gun forward, and five men surround the weapon, tending it as faithfully as a mother tends a child. They situate the howitzer beneath a tree toward the river near Mirabeau Woods.

"Save your bullets," Levi orders. "No firing till it count. We got women and children here. That cannon still out of range, same as the rifles."

His words don't comfort Israel. The deck cannon rests low to the ground, flanked by buckets of metal bolts and trace chains. Two heavily bearded men, one dressed in farmer's overalls and the other in the often-patched gray trousers that mark him as a former Confederate soldier, fiddle with the weapon, swiveling it first one way and then the other, testing. The farmer pushes down on the back of the barrel, changing the potential arc of the thin, stubby snout, positioning it at a 45-degree angle in the precursor of a practice shot. Then, thinking better of it, he tries an even steeper angle that might deliver the ball in a high curve toward the courthouse. The one in the gray rebel pants shakes his head, dissatisfied, and consults with the second man as they speculate on different trajectories that might land the most direct hit.

For over an hour, the two groups stare at each other across the barren fields between the courthouse and the tree groves, while those in charge debate what step to take next.

Who could have foreseen this deathly nothingness, Israel thinks, this jarring waiting that wears at the nerves and turns the stomach sour?

At ten o'clock there is a commotion in the ranks of the white men, and one of the leaders on horseback trots from line to line giving orders. All of the men on horses dismount to form a human wall eight hundred yards away. They count off, and every fifth man holds the horses' reins for the others.

One man from the line of trees rimming Mirabeau Woods breaks rank and fires a shot from his musket, but he is so far out of range that the cartridge skids harmlessly in the dust in no-man's-land. Across from Israel, Spenser McCullen squints into the sight of his Enfield, squatting down deep in the dugout of a bunker, keeping his head below the top of the stack of mud-filled bags five high along the trench's lip. Spenser raises the rifle to chest height, pops up his head, and takes quick aim. With an explosive cloud of gray smoke, he squeezes off an answering blast in the direction of upper Mirabeau Woods, then jams his body back down into the bunker. It too is an ineffectual shot, with no result. The accuracy of the old Enfield is unpredictable at anything over six hundred yards.

"Not yet," yells Levi as Spenser reloads.

Again they wait, but Israel watches helplessly as white men load a cannonball in the cannon and set a flame to the whiskey-soaked cotton wick. When the ball falls short, they adjust the angle and try again, but even then the weapon is too far away for either of the cannonballs to approach the courthouse or reach the outermost barricades. The white men caucus, but it is clear that if they come in closer from their position at the edge of Mirabeau Woods to make the weapon effective, they will be unprotected, without natural cover. From behind the barricades around the courthouse, despite Levi's protests, there are occasional rifle shots from the colored men to remind them of that fact. The battle goes on this way for the better part of an hour, with the advantage to neither side and neither side willing to back down.

11

*I*ncreasingly annoyed with the standoff and the lack of progress, Sheriff Christopher Columbus Nash and several of his men advance into Smithfield Quarter shortly before eleven. The streets are empty, except for a few stray dogs and a couple of advance scouts. Sheriff Nash chooses one of the houses at random, a two-room shanty at the edge of colored town.

"This the sheriff," he calls from outside, authority embedded in the brittle tone of his voice. "Send out your man."

There is whispering inside. Two minutes pass, and then three, and finally, a wiry man in his mid-fifties with a ragged black cap pokes his head outside.

"Go to the courthouse and bring back Levi Allen," demands Sheriff Nash.

The colored man hangs back, but only for a few seconds. He accepts the white truce flag they press into his hands, and he begins a lonely walk across the stretch of dusty ground between Smithfield Quarter and the courthouse.

"Stop shooting," someone calls from the courthouse side. When the colored man gets to the barricades, they let him through the line and lead him to Levi Allen.

"Sheriff Nash say meet him in Smithfield Quarter," the man relays.

Levi picks up his blue greatcoat and slowly drapes it around his shoulders. "You go tell Sheriff Nash we meet him halfway, in open field," he says. "No more than two other men with him, and we do the same. No shooting."

The colored man starts his walk back to Smithfield Quarter with the message, and the courthouse men bring around three horses so their contingent can ride out to confront Sheriff C. C. Nash under their own white flag of truce. The two groups of men meet in the middle, guns trained on them from every direction.

"What do you intend on doing?" asks Nash.

"Nothing more than before," Levi replies. "Standing. And we are going to stand where we are until we get United States troops or some assistance."

"We got warrants," Nash says. "Give up now."

"Your local warrants ain't no good," says Levi.

"You don't have a chance."

"We got women and children in there. Let them go, and then we settle this."

"Stand down and return the courthouse to us white men who know what to do with it," says Sheriff Nash.

"So you pick us off one by one the way you done Jessie McCullen?" Levi asks. "We do better holding out for the Federals. These men armed and ready to fight. Time's passed when a handful of whites frighten a regiment of colored men."

"Look around," says Sheriff Nash. "Our men come from every parish. We won't never stand for Negro rule, but nobody want to hurt women and children. Give up."

"We got the law," says Levi. "We staying. Let women and children pass."

The two men sit erect in the saddle, brittle. Both sides wait for some small sign of compromise, but there is only silence. The horses fidget, swishing their tails to swat at the flies that bite at their flesh, but the men remain still.

"I give you thirty minutes to get your Negro women and children and any Negroes don't want to fight out of town," says Sheriff Nash finally. "As for the rest of the black devils in there who decide to stay, we are going to get 'em."

"I'll be at the front, so I guess I'll see you when you get 'em," Levi says. He turns his black stallion around and digs his heels into the horse's sides, then trots back beyond the barricade just two hundred yards away.

"Women and children out," Levi shouts as he enters the courthouse. "Hurry."

McCully positions himself directly in Levi's path. "Sam Tademy the man to lead 'em out," he says. He pushes Sam forward.

Sam shakes off McCully's arm. "My place here," he protests, "not escorting women."

"You know the swamps, Sam," McCully says. "Take the women and children and get them hid. They be too busy with us for a while to care, but somebody got to get them a good head start away from here."

"I won't leave now," Sam insists. "Somebody else can do it."

Polly comes to stand next to Sam. She hangs on to their two boys, her face a grim reminder of all the families trapped inside the courthouse.

"Our women and children's bodies not all that need protection," McCully says. His face is hard. "We out of time, Sam. Take them out. Don't never let them forget what we done here, why we come, why we stay. If one of us get through, all of us lift our head just a little. Promise me you look after my wife. And promise Amy be one of the first in your colored school."

"Come out with me, then," Sam says.

"You and me, we both race men, but you on a different path, Sam. Pull as many through with you as you able. I belong here. The days of tipping my hat for the white man over." As if to emphasize his point, McCully removes his trademark fedora from his head and gives the battered brown hat to Sam. "That hat done brought me luck when wasn't no luck to be had. You hang on to it now."

There is no more time for arguing. Sam accepts the fedora. "I give it back when I see you again," he says.

"We got to move, Sam," says Polly, insistent. As frightened as she clearly is, she nods toward McCully, a gesture of gratitude and a trace of pride, and he nods back, but then she is all motion, gone. She and Lucy gather up the children whose fathers remain at the courthouse and herd all those who will leave into a cluster by the front door, cutting short their painful goodbyes.

One woman, forty and childless, refuses to vacate with the others. She takes up a shotgun and stands shoulder to shoulder with her husband at the east courthouse window, while all the rest of the escapees quickly load up the wagons and head out directly toward the line of white men to the north end of town.

12

S am drives the lead wagon, keeping a tight hold on the reins. He already has in mind where he will take his band of refugees, but they have to get past the heavily armed men in their path first. He has arranged the wagons so his is the initial test of whether the white men will honor their word and let the women and children pass. He is closely followed by the second wagon, which Polly drives, and the third, driven by Green. Sam cautions quiet to his terrified load of children and holds the white flag of truce high as he approaches within rifle range of the men by Mirabeau Woods. He has his Enfield under the wagon seat, but it will do him no good against this much firepower if any of the men turn rogue.

"Let them pass," one of the men on horseback says, and the men on foot clear enough room for the wagons to thread through. Some relax their weapons, but others keep them trained on the occupants of the wagon as if they are dangerous. Sam keeps the horse to a steady pace but turns around to make sure the men have let Polly and Green through as well.

Once safely beyond the wall of men, Sam runs the horses as hard as he dares on the rough terrain, heavy on the whip. Following in his wake, Green and Polly maneuver the other two wagons to keep up. The cease-fire allowing their exit is brief, and sporadic shooting starts again as soon as the wagons are out of sight of the courthouse clearing, but no one pursues them. The shots seem random and single, but it is impossible to tell which side fires or which side holds the advantage. Worse, the escapees hear the cannon fire, two times, but again there is an almost calm, isolated grimness to the sound, unlike the fever pitch of battle.

The wagons serve their purpose for the first two quick miles, but eventually, the thicket of pine trees becomes too dense and prevents further passage. Sam orders everyone to abandon the wagons. They loose the horses, panting and lathered, and hide the getaway buckboards in a small clearing at the edge of the woods, covered over with branches. They lead the horses forward by the reins, proceeding on foot by way of less traveled paths deeper into the woods and on toward the swamp. Everyone who is able carries something, blankets or foodstuffs, cooking pots or a small child too tired or bewildered to walk.

Within minutes, they are cloistered within a thick web of pine trees so close together they almost touch, trunk to trunk. In one area of the woods they pass through, the intertwined canopy of massive pine branches twenty feet above the ground blocks out the light completely. One of the youngest children begins to bawl. His mother picks him up and he fights her, twisting his body, shouting, "No, no, no." She can't calm him, but they never break stride, and after a while he wears himself out. Trees change from longleaf pine to moss-heavy cypress, and the ground beneath their feet softens. Sam keeps the group moving, faster than any of them think they are able, deeper into the spongy muck of the swamp. The nature of the air changes quickly, clammy and foul-smelling, as if it is a living thing.

Sam finally stops when they come to a small bog. The ground mixture of moss and peat is soggy and slick but mostly stable. There is a small flowing stream, and the water isn't too brackish. Dead vegetation nearby is dry enough to provide fuel for a fire.

"Stay close and watch for snakes," Sam instructs. The bayou is well known for its black moccasins. Sam does his best to disregard the gunfire in the background. "Gather long branches, leafier the better. This may be where we stay the night."

He breaks them into work units, one group erecting a two-sided lean-to shelter to conceal a small campfire and provide some protection from the wind. Polly, Lucy, and several other women prepare the midday meal, remains of the morning's breakfast which they hastily packed when evacuating the courthouse. Their movements are heavy and slow but full of purpose, although not many are hungry, even the children.

From far away, a single rifle shot triggers a brief, feverish volley before settling back down into quiet. Sam has no words of false cheer to give the group he led out of Colfax. Win or lose at the courthouse, the probability of a Negro hunt by renegade white men intensifies by the hour. Ten minutes pass without another shot, maybe more, but then the silence is broken by another short, sporadic round of artillery.

The distant on-again off-again sounds from the courthouse carry all the way to the far end of Boggy Bayou swamp. The tired, frightened group of thirty shiver against one another, mute, the piercing blasts tunneling deep into their souls, a tangible connection to those they left behind. For the moment, the strategy that makes the most sense to Sam is to stand pat in the uninviting but camouflaging swamp, to stay together as comfortably as they can rather than risk more travel. Here, amid the muck, they won't be easy targets for the white men's bloodlust.

By one o'clock, Sam is anxious to explore the woods around them, unable to stand the emptiness of doing nothing. Since he has the only rifle of the camp, he leaves it with Green and sets out to the north without a weapon. Less than two hundred yards away, he comes across another small group hiding in the swamp, two families huddled close together, shivering. They have already spent a night out in the damp, marshy area, with only two blankets among the eight of them.

"We seen it coming," one of the men says after Sam relates the events at the courthouse that morning. "I told the missus we daren't stay home or go to town. Just cut and run, grab up the children, leave the crops and come out here."

Sam eyes the man's double-barrel shotgun. "Our camp due south," he says. "We got food. You welcome to join us. Your gun be useful." With another weapon at camp, and two more men, he will be free to go farther afield in his scouting.

"Got no fondness for this patch of swamp," says the man. "That shooting done scraped our nerves raw." They pack what little they have and follow Sam back to the camp.

Sam turns the newcomers over to Polly to settle in and heads out in the opposite direction. He makes a broader loop, this time with the comforting weight of the Enfield at his side. The terrain changes again about a quarter mile south, at an outer edge of the swamp, more woods than bog, and the ground firms. He comes across a clearing and what looks like a blanket-town settlement of colored families, packed tight.

A man at the edge of the encampment levels his shotgun at Sam.

"Sam Tademy from The Bottom," Sam announces, holding his rifle away from his body. "We come from the courthouse less than two hours ago, set camp north of here."

They surround him, firing questions so fast he can't sort them out. There are maybe fifty or so in this group, outnumbering his own, and as with his, there are more women and children than men. Most of the men's makeshift weapons—a shovel, a scythe, a stout tree limb—are likely to be useless in real battle. The faces staring at him are covered with the grime of the woods and stretched tight with fear. The assemblage looks as though they have been camped out in the woods for some time, blankets or quilts draped over tree branches or rigged-up poles every four to six feet, and well-established cooking fires.

A middle-aged man in overalls separates himself from the rest. He is stooped, with a nervous eye that never stops watering. He holds up his hand for quiet. "They shooting since morning. How you get out?" he asks.

Sam repeats his tale of the morning's events, up to the noontime confrontation between Sheriff Nash and Levi Allen. "Then the white men agree to let women and children out the courthouse," Sam finishes.

"Maybe they got mercy in they hearts," the watery-eyed man says.

Sam shakes his head. He has carried an unformed dread since noon, when they passed the tree line north of town without being fired upon or stopped. "Letting the women and children go ain't no good sign," he says. Words form for the first time in front of this new group. "Why they want women and children out the way?"

"What you saying?" the man asks.

"I don't know," replies Sam. "But can't nobody stop White League if they get the lead."

Another flurry of shooting breaks out from the direction of the courthouse.

"We got use for another man here," the man finally says.

Sam wants to be back in his own camp, closer to Polly and the boys. If it were just his own family, he would choose to stay totally separate, able to hide more easily, but he is responsible for almost forty people now. There is logic in getting as much firepower in one place as possible, but he can't make himself commit to bring his own group back to these desperate, hopeless-looking people.

"We settled," he says. "I got to get back."

It isn't a long walk between the two encampments, and Sam is surprised by how many small campsites of colored refugees he runs across. There are well over a hundred hiding in the swamp, maybe two hundred, singly and in groups. He repeats as much as he knows to each cluster he meets, and although his eyewitness reports are hours old and shed no light on the current situation, each person devours every scrap of what he has to share.

It takes over thirty minutes to get back to where he left his camp. The shooting drones on in the background. In just a couple of hours, it has settled into a repetitive backdrop, disconcerting and inconclusive. At this rate, thinks Sam, it could take days for any resolution. Precious days during which it is possible the Federals might finally appear. He worries that his group hasn't left the men in the courthouse more of the food for a long siege. At least out here in the open, they have a chance to catch or forage to feed themselves.

It is two o'clock when Sam reaches the campsite. Women are tidying up from the meal, men and older children clearing out debris to create a larger living area. Two young boys play a game of marbles away from the bank of the bayou, where the ground is more firm. Already most of the younger children are bored, their ears grown accustomed to the distant gunfire.

Sam sees Polly in the distance with a group of women, close to the communal fire, her shape outlined by her old olive dress, grown too small this last year. Not far away are Green and Jackson, his pride, their arms full of kindling and moss for the flames. Such an overpowering feeling of relief floods through Sam that he has to stop to catch his breath. He starts toward them, gratitude at his good fortune pushing aside a small piece of the horror of the day.

An explosion punctures the air, and everyone stops dead in their tracks. There is no mistaking the finality of the sound of a cannon. This is the scene Sam carries in his mind for the rest of his days, burned into his consciousness in the middle of Boggy Bayou swamp, a frozen moment when the thankfulness of what he has and the comprehension of what is being taken away occupy the same space. Even from as far away as the swamp, the high-pitched, whistlelike noise produces a heaviness, an expectant pause that goes on and on until it turns unbearable. There is a sickening thud of impact, and then a series of smaller explosions, as of things ripping apart. At first there is stunned silence, and then the pop of shots again, not in unison but discordant and random. This pattern repeats two more times: the blast, the sounds of destruction, the impotent single shots in answer, with silences lengthening in between. The silences are the most unnerving of all. Several of the younger children in the camp begin to whimper.

Sam runs toward Polly. She has already gathered up the children, clutching them tightly against her body, one unit. In the past year, Green has grown to be slightly taller than Polly, but somehow she towers over her family, a fierce protector. She stands with her back to a giant cypress near the edge of the bayou, Green on one side, Jackson on the other. Her face, usually a mask of self-control, reflects naked terror. Sam reaches them just as the second wave of sound hits, a worse cacophony than the first, as if heavy chains drag across the length of the earth, crushing and pounding everything in their path. Sam doesn't know what to make of the noises that come from over the hill. Maybe the troops from New Orleans have appeared after all, bringing down the wrath of the government on the men trying to recapture the courthouse. Or maybe the makeshift cannons they hastily crafted held up in the heat of battle to answer the firepower the white men have at their disposal.

"Gather everything," Sam shouts to his group. "We got to move."

13

From his assigned post along the east barricade, Israel is relieved to see Sam Tademy head away from the court-house in the direction of Mirabeau Woods, leading three overloaded wagons of women and children under a white flag, including Lucy and his boys, crossing the open field and passing through a line of armed men. Thankfully, not a single shot, but after the wagons have disappeared under the cover of trees in the woods, periodic gunfire breaks out again.

A group of colored men comes from inside the courthouse, deployed to the roof, McCully among them. Israel isn't like McCully and Spenser, itching to use his gun. Last night McCully talked about his Enfield rifle as if it were a cherished child, calling it nine pounds of respect. This isn't the kind of respect Israel craves. The long hours of senseless, tentative shooting have twisted Israel's nerves. He feels as if he has been in the trench for days, not hours. There is a flurry of activity around the white men's cannon, and then they wheel the weapon somewhere outside of Israel's line of sight. Another hour passes, and then two. As long as the colored Colfax men can keep the cannon out of range, they are in standoff.

Along the narrow depression of the trench, colored men are spread out every few yards, protected behind the stacked barricades so they can stand at full height to put fresh powder and ball in their muzzle loaders. The close, sulfuric smell is oppressive, and the quiet is eerie, a drawn-out pause in the tiresome game they play.

Suddenly, the earth explodes in a deafening roar. Unlike the previous hollow pops of rifle fire, the pregnant, whistling sounds of objects on the fly shake the air. Israel recoils from the noise, wrenching his shoulder against the back side of the trench. The first blast of the cannon catches all of them completely by surprise. The explosion comes from the side, down by the river, not from the front as expected, taking out the men in the north barricade trenches like so many dominoes stacked on end and set in motion to fall, one after the other.

White men fire from the river's embankment, their approach covered by foliage. Israel sees them moving now, four at least, darting behind cypress trees, shooting at the colored men on the ground, stripped of the cover of the barricades. About a dozen colored men lie flat, dead and wounded both, some still moving but unable to get up. Others run in different directions, as if blind.

"Break for the tree line," McCully yells from up on the roof to the stunned men below. "Away from river side. Run." There is a gap, a narrow possible getaway lane between the men waiting at the far end of Mirabeau Woods in the grove and the river where the cannon fire originates.

Men speed off on foot, cutting across the village roads and fields at breakneck speed. In confusion, a few head directly toward the advancing white men.

"To the woods," McCully screams.

Israel stares dully at the carnage across from him in the adjacent barricade, but his trench line is still mostly intact. He doesn't know whether to stay or run.

Two riderless horses appear from the blind lip of the hill separating the river from the courthouse, and then the squat brass cannon they pull comes into view. There is no longer a barricade to stop them from advancing on the river side.

The man next to Israel fires his rifle, but the distance is too great and the shot worthless. From atop the roof, McCully brings his Enfield up to his shoulder and levels it, taking careful aim at the men three hundred yards away trying to set the wick on fire again. McCully is one of the few with any chance of picking off the men loading and firing the cannon. There are six of them. The torch man is about Israel's age, missing most of his top teeth, so he hands over the powder container for someone else to bite open. He talks to the others around him in an urgent, insistent way, giving orders. His slouch hat is pulled low to his head, his long blond-brown hair, stringy and limp, falling below his grizzled chin.

McCully squeezes back on the trigger, taking the full impact of the recoil with his shoulder. The man with no teeth drops the fuse lighter he holds in one hand and jerks his head around to his right, as if looking over his shoulder. But it is a younger man farther back who falls, wounded but not dead. The long-haired man attends him briefly before turning back to the cannon's fuse.

McCully reloads clumsily. Again he squeezes the trigger, quickly, taking less care with his aim, and the shot goes wide. There isn't even a ripple in the ranks around the cannon, other than two men bearing away the writhing body of the young man. There is another moment of suspension before the second deafening explosion, and then the impact of metal at the edge of the courthouse. The barrel of the cannon has been stuffed with chains, nails, and metal bolts, objects meant to spread wide the destruction, to increase the chances of maiming and killing. A terrible vibration hovers over the barricades, and a scorched smell releases into the Easter afternoon air, like human flesh and hair burning. Several men are cut off from their desperate run to the courthouse. The luckiest have not been killed outright, and can drag themselves toward shelter.

McCully shoots and reloads, again and again, as quickly as he can, getting off a few shots toward the river, his cartridge pouch low. He can only slow the white men, not keep them away, and the mounted horsemen in the pecan grove are now on the move, bringing their horses to a trot and coming in closer from the east.

The white men target McCully. For every shot he manages to squeeze off now, two or three come directly at him, and with each firing, they drag the cannon farther forward up the low, sloping bank of the river. The east barricade still holds, but Israel knows he has to abandon it, like everyone else. The running has a focus now. There are two major streams of retreating men. One set sprints in a panicked, ragged line toward Mirabeau Woods, and the other runs to the courthouse.

Smoke from the cannon hangs heavy in the air. Men shout to one another, hooves thunder, and the smell of gunpowder is so strong it brings tears to Israel's eyes. He has yet to fire his rifle. Out of the noise and smoke, he hears his name.

"Israel. Fire the cannon," McCully shouts. "Towards the river side. Light the fuse."

Israel runs back to the trench. The man he shared the trench with has already fled, and Israel is alone in the dugout with the homemade pipe cannon. He points the mouth of the pipe toward the men advancing river side and, on the second friction match, manages to get the cord alight, waiting for what seems an eternity for the slithering flame to sputter slowly down toward the powder. The smoke is so heavy he can barely see more than a few feet in front of his face, but he is sure the weapon is pointed in the right direction, toward the river. He girds himself for the upcoming blast, when gunpowder will propel the deadly ball toward the attackers. Instead, the cannon shakes apart in a harsh rattle of sticky, spreading black powder. He stares at the defective cannon and then pops his head up cautiously. He is enveloped in the invasive blackness of gunpowder residue. He stumbles as he climbs out of the trench into the open field. Colored men surround him, shouting and running in every direction. His vision blurs, and when he puts his hand to his eyes, he discovers blood trickling down one side of his face. His leg throbs. He is hit.

There is chaos on the battlefield. Dozens of colored men fall in the next few minutes, not only those from the north barricade but men pouring out of all the trenches and running toward the woods. Men behind the embankments scatter in all directions, giving up their position, running blindly for any shelter they can. A mounted horseman chases one of the running men, cutting him off before he reaches the woods and shooting him at close range. A clutch of white men cheer, waving their hats and celebrating their surprise attack, and the south barricade collapses after the next blast from the white men's cannon. Colored men run in all directions, faces frozen in confusion, terror, or astonishment. Exposed wounded litter the flat landscape.

White men on horseback, in small groups and singly, take off after the men running toward Mirabeau Woods, picking off the slowest or the late starters. Some of the fleeing men are lucky, reaching the edge of the tree line and disappearing into the thicket beyond. The white men don't follow them into the woods, as if an invisible line has been defined that they won't cross.

Out of range of long-gun fire, small groups of white men approach the no-man's-land cautiously, starting with the open field farthest away. With a nudge of a boot or the muzzle of a rifle, they turn over bodies to check whether the fallen men are alive or dead. About a hundred yards from Israel, a tall white man with a bayoneted rifle finds a colored man lying on the ground, unable to run but still breathing. The white man finishes him off as methodically as if he is gutting a fish for supper. By the fourth blast of the cannon, dense white smoke clouds Israel's vision as he stumbles and falls, aimless. His leg won't support him. He has no plan.

A cluster of white men slowly advance in his direction, careful to keep out of rifle range of the living. A shot from somewhere kicks up dust between Israel and the advancing men. They pause but come toward Israel again from a different angle. Once more he hears the sharp ping of a warning shot. The men head off after easier pickings, but Israel knows they will be back. He wonders how much time he has left, how long the roof spotters can take aim and keep the attackers at bay.

On the river side, they turn the cannon toward a new target. Israel hears another earsplitting blast, this time toward the courthouse, and the skittering, protective bullets from the rooftop are silenced.

14

*J*t is irrational, and Sam more than anyone else knows it even as he issues the order for the women and children to move to a new location. The cannon blasts are down at the courthouse, not here in Boggy Bayou swamp, but by changing camps, at least they will be doing something. At least they will join their futures, whatever those might be, to the others in the Colfax community. As the grating sounds continue, the group gets to their feet, grabs their few belongings, stomps out the fires, and goes on the move again. Sam doesn't stop to reassure anyone, as he usually would. It is all he can manage to keep himself functioning. The newcomers have packed up once already in the last couple of hours and wordlessly do so again, following Sam's lead.

They march through the woods in a ragged line, men, women, and children carrying blankets, supplies, and cooking pots not yet cool from noon dinner. The squatter swamp city toward which they propel themselves is a community in shock. The colored people in the larger camp sit stupefied around the fire, not speaking, listening to what they believe must be hell come to earth. They make places around the fire for their new campmates.

For an hour, no one moves beyond the perimeter of the camp. They decide against sending scouts, agreeing instead to cluster the women and children in the center of a human circle with the men ringing the outside, holding on tightly to the few weapons they have. For an hour, they wait, muscles tensed and minds numb, nerves stretched to snapping.

From the south, suddenly, a tall, hatless black man crashes through the trees at a run, without caution, wild-eyed, his cotton shirt soaked completely through with sweat, his face contorted with straining effort and exhaustion. Once the man registers that he has stumbled into a large campsite, that he is surrounded by his own kind in the squatter swamp city, he doubles over, hands on his thighs, and takes in frantic gulps of air. Polly brings him a dipper of fresh water, which he guzzles, then asks for more.

Sam recognizes Lawson McCullen. He is a neighbor and McCully's cousin, one of the few colored men who owns his own farm down in The Bottom.

Lawson catches his breath. "They killing every colored man from the courthouse they catch," he says.

A woman in the circle begins to keen, her voice unearthly and unmoored, a vibrating sound that rivals the terror of the cannon fire. As if it is contagious, several more in the camp start to weep and moan.

"We got to keep quiet," Sam cautions, and members of the camp rearrange themselves to try to comfort the more vocal among them. "No government troops?" Sam asks Lawson.

Lawson shakes his head. "Just angry white men," he says. "The cannon turn everything around. After that, anybody could, run. Colored men fall right and left, going toward the courthouse, breaking for the woods. White men circle the courthouse, closing in. I barely make Mirabeau Woods, no stopping, set my eye on the line of trees, keep running. Cannon go off again, earth shaking, more smoke.

"My legs get me to the tree line. Others run too, every which way. Three of us on the barricade take off the same time. Me, Kindred Harvey, Bully Ellis. Kindred, he the fastest, he ahead the whole way. He make the tree line just ahead of me, and the woods swallow him up. I heared him crash through the thicket, breathing hard. I was that close behind, hearing him, but I couldn't see him no more. Just steps from the woods line. Then a bullet come so close, sound like a mosquito. To my left be Bully Ellis."

Lawson locks eyes with Sam. "You know Bully," he says. "Tall farmer down Bayou Darrow?"

Sam nods.

"One minute Bully running, the next he on the ground. Musta took a bullet. On the ground, clutching his side. I only got a few feet more. I keep running. I never seen the white man chasing me, but the horse so close when I cross the tree line, that horse blowing his spit down my neck. Them woods was dark, but I never been so glad to feel pine needles under my feet. Figure we got a chance in the woods.

"One horseback man call out, 'Don't follow. We don't know what they got in there.'"

Lawson stops to compose himself, his big arms trembling. Polly offers him another dipper of water, but he refuses.

"I look back where I just come from. Other colored men breaking through too. No one on horses follow past the trees. I stop and hide behind a tree.

"Bully on the ground still outside the woods. I hear Bully beg, and he lift up his hands to the men on the horses.

"'Don't shoot me again, Mr. Charlie. I bad hurt.' I can't make myself move, watching. I know I got to get going, but can't break free.

"A white man get off his horse. Another hold the reins. He take his rifle by the stock and ram the bayonet into Bully's chest.

The white man don't say nothing, not to Bully, not to the other men. Just get back on his horse like it a day's work."

The group gathered around Lawson listens in silence. None of the mothers move to take their children out of earshot. No one asks questions.

"I start to run again. Don't stop or turn around till I get here," Lawson finishes.

In the background, everyone hears the barrage of cannon fire, one round after another, and those in the camp try their best not to let images form around what those fearful noises signify. Denial is one of the tools that allow many of them to get through that day. Sam can only listen to the terrifying rap and chatter of metal on metal each time they fire the cannon, as if they have set loose the demons of hell to come after the trapped men's souls in the courthouse.

Chapter

15

The open field between Smithfield Quarter and the courthouse is dotted with the lifeless bodies of colored men strewn haphazardly around the grounds, but there are just as many if not more wounded. Relentless rifle fire discourages rescue attempts. Some of the injured attempt to drag themselves to the courthouse as the cannon's blasts fill the air with deadly missiles. Desperate men, not yet quite dead, inch their way to nowhere.

In the short distance between the ruined east barricade and the courthouse, Israel steps over more bodies than he can count. He keeps low to the ground, unable to run, hobbling as he clutches his injured leg. An object passes close to his face—a bullet or pellet, or some of the other miscellaneous flying debris that chokes the sky. He has to hurry before the white men load the deadly cannon again. He can't put his full weight on his leg, and when he trips over another body, he falls in an awkward heap onto the dirt, his weapon lost somewhere in the stampede of bodies trying to escape the cannon. Without the use of his rifle as a cane, Israel can't get himself back up. The hopelessness of his plight begins to sink in.

Still Israel struggles, ineffectively, until he feels a pair of arms in a bear hug around his shoulders, tugging him upward.

"We got to get inside the courthouse," McCully yells into Israel's ear. The noise around them is deafening, coming from every direction.

"Help me to my feet," Israel shouts back, slapping at his leg as if it were a reluctant child that just needs coaxing.

McCully hoists him up, and Israel tests his weight on the un-reliable leg. His trousers are wet with blood.

"Can you walk?" McCully shouts.

"I can make it," Israel says. He begins to limp toward the brick building, but in two steps, his leg buckles and he falls again. "No good," he says.

McCully pulls Israel up once more, this time by his wrists, and drapes Israel's arm around his shoulder.

"Faster if you lean," McCully says. He breaks into a trot, Israel able to do no more than trail his bad leg behind them, using his good leg and foot to help propel them forward. McCully half drags, half pulls Israel, propping him up, and Israel holds on tight with his left arm.

Colored men at each window of the courthouse cover their approach, firing on the white men outside, and they make it inside the building. The double doors barely slam shut before the next cannon blast. In some ways, being inside is worse than being out in the open. The sounds of impact from the explosions reverber-ate within the walls while metal ricochets off tin and brick, end-lessly repeating, as if the world is ending, as if the pounding detonations tunnel in through their eardrums and burrow under their flesh.

Pandemonium reigns within the claustrophobic tightness of the courthouse. Men yell, men stand or sit in a stupor, succumbing to shock. It is a Babel of voices, the volume shrill by necessity to be heard over the conflagration. The men try to reconstruct the events of the last hour from different vantage points. Shouting at the top of their lungs, they debrief one another, disjointed reports of their individual experiences at the east barricade, the southern bunker, the courthouse rooftop. Together, they construct an assessment of their current circumstances. Two hundred colored men of Colfax with forty rifles among them are trapped in the one-story courthouse, surrounded by at least three hundred white men with heavy artillery. None of their official leaders are inside with them. At least twenty colored men lay dead or dying outside in the courthouse square.

Although Israel is in pain, he makes a quick calculation of the scene in the courthouse. Their numbers are split in half, and any man still outside is on his own. Hopefully some can escape by foot to the fields or scatter into the woods. Outside belongs to the white men. Without the check of the barricades, they can set their cannon just out of rifle range anywhere. Instead of cannon balls, they fill the barrel with buckets of metal bolts, nails, and trace chains. Israel listens to the heavy, unpredictable rap and throttle of metallic debris shot from the white men's cannon, ricocheting on the ground and striking the courthouse, an echoing rattle of death. Each time they fire, the chaotic backwash of sound rattles through Israel as if he has been mortally struck.

Once again they are stalemated, the men on the outside and the men on the inside. Over an hour has passed since the first cannon blast, but the white men still aren't close enough to put an end to the siege.

Israel's face is black with the spread of gunpowder caked layer upon layer around his mouth, from biting the paper off rifle cartridges;

his teeth are no longer white, his tongue is no longer pink. He smells nothing but gunpowder, tastes nothing but gunpowder, breathes nothing but gunpowder. The McCullens—McCully, Spenser, and Eli—managed to hang on to their rifles, and they take up positions at the windows, firing periodically to prevent the white men from advancing the cannon or making a run on the courthouse.

Israel sits off to the side in a scavenged chair and makes himself useful, unclogging jammed weapons, reloading for men at the windows. Earlier, he pulled out the metal bolt fragment embedded in his leg, then wrapped his thigh in cloth torn from his shirt. The blood was substantial, but the wound could heal with time, barring infection. Already he is able to hobble around the courthouse.

It is impossible to ignore the bone-hackling racket of the cannon blasts, but in the last hour, Israel has found a way to make his peace with the constant clamor. He once knew a man more afraid of the sound of thunder than of the electric sliver of light that could actually kill him, and Israel had thought the man a fool, and there was a lesson to be learned there. As terrifying as the cannon noises are, the damage from the burning, crashing metal objects can't reach them through the protection of the brick walls. The White League outside can prevent anyone from getting out of the courthouse, but they can't root them out. As long as the colored Colfax men have enough firepower inside, they can continue to keep the men outside at a distance.

Kitty-corner to the east side of the courthouse, two men roll the cannon forward by several feet, trying a different angle. McCully and Spenser both take aim and fire on them repeatedly, until the men pull the cannon back to its previous position. With the same dogged determination he demonstrated on his roof watches, McCully stays by his post at the front window facing east, keeping a close eye out for anyone trying to approach.

Israel Smith limps over to stand beside McCully. "Thanks. For out there," Israel says.

"I wore out my welcome on that roof," McCully says. "I was coming down one way or the other. This way we both get cover."

Israel nods. He shuffles off and comes back dragging his chair. "Sitting's better on the leg," he says.

McCully rests the muzzle of his gun against the sill, alert for outside movement, but he steals a quick look at the wide, bloodied cloth wrapped around Israel's thigh.

"What you think the white men gonna do with us?" Israel asks.

McCully stares out the window toward the tree line. Bullets slap the air, much like the extended skirmish before the first cannon fire of the early afternoon. It is close to three o'clock. McCully doesn't answer.

"Maybe troops show up now," Israel says.

"No troops coming." McCully doesn't take his eyes away from the window.

"They could be on their way," Israel insists.

"They had plenty time to get here." McCully is angry now. "Look around you, Brother Israel. Go one room to the next. You see the men start this fight? Where the politicians? Where the sheriff? Where Levi Allen?"

Sheriff Shaw has made himself scarce in the last week, and no one in the courthouse has seen him at all for the last two days. The last Israel saw of Levi was on the back of his fine horse, riding at full gallop into Mirabeau Woods just after the first cannon blast.

"They bringing help."

"They gone."

"What you think those white men out there going to do with us?" Israel asks again.

"Same they always do. Beat us down. Kill us off one by one," says McCully. "If not today, tomorrow. If not tomorrow, next year. They keep at us. But we still free men till our time on earth done."

"They can't kill us all," says Israel.

"I hope you right, Brother Israel. A death untold is a death forgot," says McCully. "Some got to make it out and bear witness. A truly righteous man can't look at Colfax and call what happen here right."

There is a subtle change in the sounds of battle. Instead of occasional rounds of fire from rifles and shotguns, interspersed with the thumping, crashing sound of the cannon, it is as if all of the white men on the east side are discharging their guns at once. Spenser, Eli, and McCully fire back, shooting as quickly as they can reload, dodging the hail of incoming metal. Smoky-white residue lingering in the air makes it difficult to see.

A white man outside streaks past, a blur. They shoot at him, but he reaches the lowest part of the east overhang of the roof, carrying a small can and bamboo fishing poles bound together, topped with torn-up cotton stuffing from Eli McCullen's saddle blanket, the one he uses for his mule. Why is it here instead of in Eli's storage shed in Smithfield Quarter?

The man throws kerosene on the wooden part of the roof.

"They setting the roof afire," McCully yells. The white man touches the tip of the torch fashioned from Eli's mule blanket to the waiting kerosene, throws the torch farther up on the roof for good measure, and flees down toward Red River, disappearing from view. The shingles covering the eaves ignite.

Israel smells it catch. McCully runs to the side window closest to the flames and twists his big body through, trying to punch off the burning shingles with his hands. A hail of bullets erupts, focused on that single window.

"Keep it going, boys," Israel hears from outside.

"Put the fire out," McCully calls to the others inside. "Don't let it take hold. Shoot back."

Spenser, Eli, and several other colored men discharge rounds to give McCully cover, but the opposing gunfire only intensifies.

"They gonna burn us alive," one of the colored men screams.

McCully peels off his jacket to serve as a strangling rag, then tries again to reach out of the window to the burning eaves. There is an avalanche of gunfire from outside. The fire is no longer explosive, flame to fuel, but it has passed beyond tentative and now blazes greedily, skipping from one spot to another on the roof.

"We done for, 'less we get that fire out," McCully says. He thrusts his upper body out through the window, getting one arm free enough to flap the jacket against the blaze on the roof.

McCully's body twitches with the impact of the first bullet at the shoulder, but still he raises the cloth to take another swing at the flames. He is a tall man, and the reach of his arms is great. He shifts the jacket to his other hand and tries again to stifle the burning material on the roof, but the kerosene has primed the wood, hastening the flames' spread. The next two bullets catch him in the chest and throat. They come from different angles but hit at almost the same instant. The impact opens McCully's body.

"Bring the coon down, boys," someone outside yells.

Spenser McCullen struggles to pull his father back inside the courthouse, and despite his wounded leg, Israel Smith flings himself across the room toward the east courthouse window to help.

16

A slick patch on the floor almost sends Israel Smith slamming into the casement, but he regains his footing, keeps himself from falling. Bits of McCully's wine-dark blood pool on the floorboard planks.

McCully drapes, partway in and partway out the window, arms outstretched along the burning roof, his broad body an easy target drawing heavy gunfire. Israel grabs hold of McCully around the waist and yanks downward, hard. A bullet hurtles past his face and lands somewhere inside the courthouse, but Israel holds on, helping to drag McCully's body through the river of blood on the sill.

Together, Israel and Spenser maneuver McCully away from the window, toward the center of the room, and lay him on his back. Blood spurts pulselike from an opening at the side of the big man's neck, but with progressively diminishing force, creating new plum-colored puddles on the floor. Random bullets smack the side of the building around the window, embedding themselves in the wood and brick, and then the pace of shooting slows.

"Come on now, Papa," Spenser says, shaking the unmoving man lightly. He lifts McCully's head and cradles it in his lap, oblivious to the spreading red drenching his trousers. "Come on."

Several men gather around McCully, but they quickly understand what his son cannot, and they are quiet, creating a circle of stillness in the chaos of the courthouse. Israel stands over the body.

"Spenser, your daddy gone," he says.

"No," says Spenser. He rocks as he kneels, his father's head a heavy weight in his lap.

Israel leaves Spenser hunched over his father's body and limps away from the clutch of men. McCully's Enfield stands propped against the wall, and Israel lifts the weighty rifle in his hands. The long barrel and barrel bands have blackened to an intense, hypnotic deep blue. Some of the other men have chosen to polish the barrels of their Enfields until they gleam, but McCully didn't tamper with the cool certainty of that blue-black.

Men jostle and shove in every room of the courthouse, some arguing, others cursing, a few wordless. No one takes particular notice of Israel. He lifts the blue-barreled weapon, steadies it on the sill of the blood-smudged window, and eases back on the trigger. There is a click, a dull scraping of metal against metal.

The cartridge pouch still hangs from McCully's rope belt, where Spenser slumps, dazed, next to his father on the floor. Israel retrieves the pouch and hangs it from his own belt. There aren't many cartridges left. He returns to the window and loads the Enfield, the taste of gunpowder acrid to his tongue when he bites away the paper wrapping. He slams the cartridge home so violently he jams his thumb, pain radiating all the way up his arm, but this time he yanks hard at the trigger and the gun fires. The recoil is stronger than he expects, the barrel jerking upward for a long moment before thudding back to the sill. The bullet is high and wide. Through the open window, Israel smells kerosene and gun-powder both, strong enough to catch in his throat and force a cough. He stuffs powder, reloads, and fires twice more.

After the effort of those three shots, Israel is spent. Just that quickly, in less than two minutes. He has no desire to shoot the rifle again. All he wants is to be done with this place and to get back to his cabin, and to Lucy and his children.

The smoke from the fire on the roof begins to overrun the inside of the courthouse, and Israel feels the air heat up inside the stuffy rooms. It is as if they are inside a wasp's nest newly smoked and knocked from the eaves, all frantic motion and activity, with-out a leader. Except for the occasional popping of a gun outside, the firing has stopped; Israel knows there has been yet another turning point. The colored men of Colfax have nothing to do other than to vacate the building that will, given enough time, burn over their heads. The white men outside can afford to be patient and wait.

Squatting stock-still over the supine body of McCully, Spenser looks bewildered, oblivious to the bedlam around him. Israel flashes on Noby, on whether his son will also be forced to face a future without his father. He hopes Sam Tademy managed to get the women and children to safety.

"Time to get out of here," Israel says to Spenser, laying a hand on the young man's shoulder.

Spenser doesn't respond, instead pushing with gentle, tenta-tive fingers at the shredded skin of his father's face, as if he can rearrange the crushed bones underneath or coerce his father to pay attention and draw air into his lungs again.

"Rip up your shirt, boy," Israel says.

Spenser stops his mapping on his father's face and stares blankly at Israel.

"For a flag." Israel forces his voice lower, more authoritative. "Rip up your shirt."

Spenser drops his hands to his sides, away from his father, but other than that, he still doesn't move.

Israel stoops to help him to his feet. "Get up, son."

This time Spenser obeys, a limp softness to him. Israel leads him a few steps away from his father's body.

"A flag. We need us a white flag," Israel says. "We got to give up."

Spenser takes off his shirt and hands it to Israel, his movements slow. The material is blotchy with McCully's blood. The front is soaked through, and even the back is speckled with dark red clots. Israel chooses the sleeve most free of McCully's blood and rips it through from the seam. He leaves Spenser and hobbles to the window, waving the cloth back and forth frantically, as if his fervor can ward off danger, change the course of fate. He waves the white flag of truce until the smoke makes it hard to breathe, then he leaves the window to rejoin Spenser.

"The roof gonna give," Israel says. "You and me, we going out together."

Men wave light-colored pocket rags or pieces of clothing from each window. A few wield white pieces of paper they've rippped from the books in the courthouse.

"Don't shoot," an anonymous colored man yells to those outside.

Others take up the refrain, yelling out of the windows, "We give up. We coming out. No weapons."

Spenser seems to come awake all at once, his eyes black and feverish.

"Don't trust them." Spenser pulls at Israel's jacket sleeve. "Stay here. You'll see."

He grabs the ripped shirtsleeve from Israel's hand and rushes toward the front door. Israel follows, elbowing his way through the throng of men pressed near the door, but the passage is tight with the undecided, men afraid to step outside yet unwilling to stay inside the burning building. Israel can't push more than midway through the jostling crowd, falling farther and farther behind Spenser as the young man shoves aside anyone in his way. Spenser elbows one old man at least thirty years his senior, knocking him to the floor. He thrusts open the doors to the courthouse and walks boldly out into the light of the afternoon, holding the limp white sleeve high above his head.

"We surrender," Spenser shouts.

Once Spenser commits, others stream outside behind him, following in the young man's wake, stopping only briefly to fill their lungs with desperate gulps of the clearer, cooler air.

Israel is propelled forward in the pack rushing to get out of the burning building, unable to control his own movements. He is all the way to the front doorway when he hears Spenser speak. There is a hesitation, a pause, not silence but an eerie quiet filled with the rush of footsteps and the panting breath of men in between action. Israel hears a single gunshot, and he is close enough to see Spenser drop. All of the men closest to him stop for just an instant, as if suspended, until the air around them is filled with the sound and smell of bullets. There are dozens of shots, picking the colored men of Colfax off one by one as they stumble through the front doors of the courthouse. Colored men so anxious to exit one minute before now reverse direction, tripping over one another as they try to reenter the burning building. Israel is carried backward in the wave until he finds himself on the floor, knocked on his back in one of the courthouse rooms, like a baby put to crib. He struggles back to his feet and, from the east window, sees colored men run jaggedly across the fields toward the river. Most don't get far before a piece of metal in the back or leg slows them down. Those who are able, continue to run or crawl. Often it takes two or three hits before they fall and stay down.

The rooms in the courthouse warm steadily from the flames. The only choices for the colored men of Colfax are fire, smoke, or lead. Several men dive through the courthouse windows at either side of the building rather than go through the front door and the waiting onslaught of bullets, but they seldom get more than a few feet before being cut down.

Israel can't run for long with his leg wound, and surrender is certain death. He gathers up the three men closest to him.

"I know a place," he whispers. None of the men question him. They just follow.

Israel leads them to the back of the courthouse, to the supply room Lucy cleaned in the early days of the siege. The room is farthest away from where the fire was set, and there isn't as much smoke as in the front of the building. Israel shimmies aside the trunk covering the crawl space entrance and pulls up two loose floorboards with his hands. The other men pry up two more planks so they can lower themselves down into the space, one at a time. Warren Bullitt, a burly man from Aloha whom Israel barely knows, shoves Israel to the side and scrambles into the opening headfirst.

"No need for that," Israel protests, but already more men have materialized as if from nowhere, ready to jockey for one of the coveted spaces. Israel knows he can't control whatever happens. All he can do is make sure he is one of the ones to use his own hiding place. "Set the floorboards back after the last man," he says, and squeezes down headmost into the dark hole, illuminated only dimly by a shaft of light through mismatched sidewall boards.

He crawls through one tangle of dense cobwebs after another, closing his eyes. He can't avoid inhaling the sticky netting full of dead bugs and live spiders, and the webs plug his nostrils and plaster themselves across his damp face. His only consolation is that Warren Bullitt must have gotten worse. The dirt is musty-damp and reeks of mold, but Israel inches forward on all fours until he can go no farther, until he bumps into Warren.

"Dead end," Warren says.

A fifth man wiggles into the hole, and then a sixth, until there is no more room to move, and still a seventh man forces his way in. All of the men in the hole are wringing wet and squeezed up against one another. Israel presses tighter against Warren Bullitt, forced from the other side, and he twists his body to try to create more space. Warren doesn't move an inch, his big frame like a wall of brick.

"Go deeper," Israel says.

"No more room, Brother," says Warren.

Israel starts to cramp from the awkwardness of holding his body at such an unnatural angle. The men above-floor struggle to get the planks back into place over their heads, but there are too many underground.

"On our backs," says Israel. "Hug your chest."

They make a human chain under the floor, side by side, flat on their backs on the damp ground, gaining precious inches by wrapping their arms across their chests as if they are laid out in coffins. Up above, they replace the floorboards, blocking out the light. The men underground stare upward, mummified, unable to distinguish whether the oppressive heat that forces them to shut their eyes to keep out the stinging sweat comes from themselves, their neighbors, or the flames bearing down on them.

A rat comes so close to Israel's face that he can hear the whistle in its breathing, and when he opens his eyes, he sees the red-glared pinpricks of the rodent's flashing eyes. Israel purposefully breathes louder himself, as if to convince the creature that he is bigger and dangerous to tangle with, and for the hundredth time, he wishes himself out of this place, but there is no access to the outside from under the courthouse. There is nothing to do but lie still and wait.

It is likely they will burn to death in this underground grave. The best they can hope for is that the white men, victorious, will put out the fire to save their building before the flames reach the buried men, and they might go undiscovered until after the blood-lust passes. It isn't a great plan, but it is all the seven men have. The pains shooting down Israel's leg have quieted enough to allow him to lie immobile in this mummy box. The fear he has borne all his life has come to carry him home. Instead of panicking, he is calm in the face of death, but Israel wants to live. He wants to see Lucy again. He wants a chance to be a better father to his sons. He wants to rub his cheek scar, the question mark that is his life, but he cannot move. He wonders whether he has chosen the right path in life. Go along to get along.

Has his work with Noby been wrong? He has tried to tame him, to teach the boy to go quiet and look the other way for his own survival. If he could say one thing to Noby now from his underground tomb, it would be "Son, don't never let nobody put their hands on you." It is a tricky balance to be a colored man, keeping both body and spirit alive when the choices you make to preserve the one so often threaten to kill the other.

The seven men lie still, breathing in the close, dank air mixed with smoke and gunpowder and fear-sweat, and wait for a miracle.

Israel doesn't know how long they have been beneath the floorboards, soaked through from both the heat and their own fear, but gunfire becomes sporadic and infrequent. He guesses an hour, but it could easily be much longer or much shorter. Crawling things that Israel can't identify bore into his skin, biting and slithering, stirred up by the heat and smoke.

"Least we not burnt up," whispers Warren Bullitt next to him. The smoke has thinned and the temperature has stopped rising. From under the floorboards, they hear the white men on water brigade call to one another outside, dousing the fire.

"I druther die here than go out to those white men," Warren says.

Israel shushes him and they go back to stillness. The sickening odors of sulfur and burning hair make Israel want to bolt their self-made tomb. He hears the clump and drag of boots over their heads as men walk into the supply room.

"Come up out of there," a white voice says.

None of the colored men move.

The planks creak as the floorboards are pulled up, and a harsh, blinding light streams into the dark hole. To his right, Israel feels Warren quietly scoot farther back into the dark, dank crawl hole. Israel tries not to focus on the fact that Warren has hoarded a few inches of extra space all along. He concentrates on his own body. His muscles are beyond his command, his arms stiff across his chest as if frozen in place. He left the gun above in the courthouse, but he couldn't have used it if it had been in his hand, loaded and ready. They are packed in like summer pickles in a brine jar, and only after the white man yanks out the first one of them nearest the loose floorboard can they even manage to roll a few inches to the right or left.

One by one, sore and dehydrated, the men under the floorboards inch to the opening and emerge to the small audience of white men, unfolding their aching limbs as they try to restore feeling to their bodies. Israel is the last to come out, dragging his game leg behind him, careful not to glance backward into the hole to see if Warren intends to follow.

"There's another," a white man says.

"Drag him out."

"I'm not going in after him," the first man says.

"Fire down under, then," says the other.

The colored men from the hiding hole stand, silent prisoners, and watch as the white man fires two pistol shots into the dark space. They hear Warren scream.

"Leave him in there," the man giving orders says. "Take the others outside with the rest."

The white men herd Israel and the five other men out of the courthouse. It takes several minutes for Israel's eyes to adjust to the glare of the sun. The smells of smoke and charred flesh hang in the air, reminding Israel of hog-slaughtering season. It is all he can do not to stumble and give these men an excuse to shoot. His leg throbs with each step, but he doesn't dare speak or call attention to himself. The grounds around the courthouse are awash in bodies. There are colored men in unnatural poses as far as the eye can see, shot in flight and left exactly as they fell. Israel turns his head away quickly, only to find more of the same in the opposite direction. There are at least one hundred lifeless bodies of the colored men of Colfax, their blood still seeping into the soil around the courthouse.

One of the white men, baby-faced with bad skin, little more than a boy, really, younger than Spenser, smashes the butt of his pistol between Israel's shoulder blades. "Move along, coon," he says. "We got something even better planned for you."

It is a slow march through the ruined town of Colfax, full of detours, and the string of prisoners grows. They add four more colored survivors from just outside the courthouse, wounded but able-bodied enough to walk. Two additional men are discovered hiding in a corncrib in the white section of town, and they are pulled out, bound at the ankles so they can't run, and thrown to the back of the elongating human queue. Most of the fight is leeched from the men gathered in this way, and the rope used to bind them is almost a formality. Their weapons have been confiscated, their friends and neighbors are dead, the fate of their families is in question.

Once stragglers from the vicinity of the courthouse grow scarce, the group pushes on toward Smithfield Quarter. The roads are deserted of colored men, and it isn't until the third house that the captors find anyone home. October White, a man who works at the livery and repeatedly refused to join the cause, lives there with his wife and six children. Israel waits in the middle of the dusty street with the other prisoners, bound together by rope and defeat.

The man who struck Israel with the butt of his pistol is named Jim. "Everybody out," he shouts into the house.

The family exits in a cluster, fearful but obedient, October first, in his patched trousers and with his straw work hat askew. Behind him comes his wife, a pale-faced woman cradling one baby in her arm and carrying another, slightly older, on her hip. Clutching at her long skirt are a boy and a girl, with an older girl who leads her sister by the hand immediately behind.

"We didn't do nothing," October protests. "I never mix in with the courthouse men."

The men bind October and put him with the other prisoners as his wife stands cowed and their children cling to her. October catches her eye and faintly shakes his head, but she knows better than to interfere.

"I didn't do nothing," October says again, but they ignore him and yank the string of prisoners forward.

Israel trudges with the others, his mind a jumble of escape plans, fatigue, and the throbbing pain that branches out from his ankle to his thigh. Their captors are farmers, as young as sixteen and as old as seventy-two, men of the soil, but only a few own the land they work. Israel tries to hear their conversation, tries to extract some shred of hope for the strung-together colored men of Colfax. The round-up squads don't appear to have official leaders, only individuals taking charge.

"I don't belong with them," October White says again. Baby-face Jim smashes him in the face with his pistol, hits him until October falls, blood oozing from his nose.

Narcisse Fredieu steps forward. "That's enough," he says.

"Why you here if you so soft?" Jim asks. "They try to kill us and got designs on our women. I say we string 'em up now."

"Round 'em up is the job," Narcisse says. "Sheriff Nash decides what to do."

Jim turns from Narcisse, addressing himself to the colored

prisoners instead. "No more talking," he shouts before walking away. The colored men closest to October hoist the beaten man up from the ground and prop him between them to get him standing.

The designated collection point is Calhoun's Sugarhouse. By the time Israel's group reaches the property and is thrown in with other prisoners, they number almost forty. They are herded outside to wait for night to fall, tied together by hands and feet with ropes. Israel is bound to Eli McCullen on one side and Clay Murphy on the other, and they stand in a tight clump as white men mill about.

Three white men come from the sugarhouse and jerry-rig a six-foot wooden plank, placing it lengthwise across the windowsill in front of where the colored men stand. One end of the plank is inside the building and the other outside, suspended four feet above the ground under an old oak tree.

"Ready," one of the men calls.

About thirty white men empty out into the sugarhouse yard, jostling one another near the end of the board, as if angling for front-row seats. Baby-face Jim produces a thick length of rope, one end coiled and knotted into a noose, and throws the other end over a low hanging branch, leaving the loop to dangle free above the plank's end.

"You-all boys pay close attention," Jim says to the prisoners.

Israel turns his mind inward to calm himself and prays for deliverance. There are too many colored men to hang them all from one rope. This is symbolic. This is sport.

Two white men continue to fiddle with the plank, positioning the end of the wide board more directly under the tree branch. Scuffling noises come from inside the sugarhouse as someone is forcibly hoisted onto the flat piece of wood. It has to be an important prisoner. Israel wonders if they captured Levi Allen, if their commander will be first to take the board walk.

A white man emerges on the plank with his hands tied behind his back, blinking into the direct light of the setting sun. It is Sheriff Shaw, his clothes so filthy he looks as though he has rolled in mud, his already ruddy face red and constricted. Someone behind forces his head down so he can duck under the upper sill, and the sheriff crouches to fit himself through the window opening. He walks one small step and stands upright on the plank into the rapidly falling dusk. He pauses, disbelieving, until a man behind nudges him at the small of his back with the barrel of his Colt pistol. Prodded, Shaw takes another tentative step forward onto the plank.

Israel has not seen Shaw since Saturday—he'd assumed their sheriff had slipped to safety like the others—but it appears Nash's men captured him before he could get away. Here is their sheriff, a white man, as much a prisoner as the colored men tethered together outside. If the captors will do this to a white man, what is in store for them?

Again Sheriff Shaw is pushed from behind, and he takes two more small steps forward, the unsupported plank sagging under his weight. Inside, a burly white man holds down the anchoring portion of the flat timber, waiting for the rope to be looped around Sheriff Shaw's neck and the signal to let loose the board and release Sheriff Shaw to a tightened noose and a broken neck.

"Don't do this," Sheriff Shaw pleads. He turns to one man in particular. "Bob. Bob Whittington. You know you can't let them do this to me."

The man behind pushes the sheriff farther toward the end of the plank. A horseman fits the collar of the noose around Sheriff Shaw's neck.

"I'm white," Sheriff Shaw says to Bob Whittington.

"You betrayed your race," Bob spits back at the sheriff.

"Bob, wait," Sheriff Shaw says. "You have to step in."

Abruptly, Sheriff Shaw reaches forward and flashes an intricate hand gesture to Bob Whittington. For a long moment, the two men just look at each other, staring each other down. The board stays steady under Sheriff Shaw's feet.

Finally, Bob Whittington speaks. "This man's a Freemason," he says. "Let him go."

Reluctantly, Sheriff Nash nods, and they set Sheriff Shaw free.

Israel and the others outside the sugarhouse watch silently as Sheriff Shaw has his hands untied. Narcisse Fredieu loosens the noose from around his neck and helps him down from the plank. Israel has heard of the Freemasons, a white man's secret society pledged to help one another out under duress, but he can't believe the power that allows the sheriff to go free now. Such is the brotherhood of white men, he thinks.

"Move out," Bob Whittington says to Sheriff Shaw. He is angry, a warning in his tone that suggests he is capable of changing his mind at any minute.

Sheriff Shaw gives a nervous backward glance in the direction of the terrified, filthy, injured, hungry, thirsty group of colored prisoners standing outside Calhoun's Sugarhouse, men who risked everything so he could hold office for three weeks, but he doesn't allow his gaze to connect with any of theirs before taking off from the sugarhouse toward the woods, first in a fast walk, then at a run. Israel watches the sheriff's retreating form, but his mind has already skipped ahead to figure out who will be next.

The white men in the sugarhouse are restless, as if they don't know quite what to do with themselves now that Sheriff Shaw is out of reach. They break into smaller groups, disgusted by his release. Jugs of hard liquor are plentiful, and the white men share them freely, each man taking a long swig before passing the container to the next, their voices coarsening and growing louder. Before long, they eye the prisoners.

"Let's do one of them," someone says.

"Enough," says Sheriff Nash. "We cleared the courthouse. We done enough for one day."

"What's the harm?" says Baby-face Jim, joining his voice to the men from Sicily Island. "We all know they got to pay."

"This is my town, and I decide in the morning," Sheriff Nash says. "They're mine."

Israel's leg throbs with pain, but it seems of little consequence now.

17

They huddle in small groups, dew-dampened quilts suspended overhead in the makeshift tent town along the banks of Boggy Bayou swamp, lost in individual grief. Waves of eyewitness reports pour in about the death or maiming of friend or acquaintance, family or neighbor. The swamp dwellers are spent, as if they have been swept overboard into a violent sea at the height of a storm and washed up at last onto shore, without further reserve.

By late afternoon, eerie quiet cuts the swamp like a chill wind. All the dwellers can do is wait, helpless. The barrage of cannon fire from the direction of Colfax ends, fades to frenzied gunfire, and finally becomes silent sounds of rebellion's end. Fresh accounts of carnage reach those safely outside center city. New stories are added, told and retold as the camp's numbers swell with courthouse escapees and fleeing townspeople.

Each colored straggler, either led or stumbling onto the encampment grounds, adds a different shading to the tapestry of unfolding tragedy, and testifies how the devastation has reached out to touch them. The swamp dwellers, starved for the smallest crumb of new information, refuse to allow any eyewitness rest until he recites a complete list of who he knows for certain has been saved, who he knows to be dead. By the time the sun is on the wane, all of those shivering in the swamp have offered up prayers too numerous to count, some for the souls of their lost men, others with desperate hope for their men's escape.

Almost all of the McCullen men have been sighted, their lifeless bodies identified beyond doubt, felled within the courthouse walls or outside in the no-man's-land that is now a mass graveyard. There are several accounts from different sources of McCully's end, the details similar enough to convince Sam of the story's truth. McCully died trying to put out the fire on the roof, and his son Spenser was the first casualty when men attempting to escape the burning building tried to surrender. With each new version of the same events, Sam almost feels the sting of the bullets and the scorch of the flames. If not for McCully's insistence that Sam take away the women and children, it would have been him. Maybe it should have been him.

Accounts of Israel Smith's whereabouts trickle in, but unlike the reports on McCully, these aren't clear on whether Israel is dead or alive. One eyewitness reports seeing Israel take a bullet in the leg outside the courthouse in the first cannon blast.

"We don't know nothing for sure till we sees it with our own eyes," Polly says to Lucy. All afternoon Polly stays close to Lucy and her two oldest sons, David and Noby. Together the two women busy themselves with food preparation and general cleanup, sending their sons off on small chores to gather kindling or bury refuse, but never outside of their line of sight.

Late afternoon, a young man in his twenties limps into camp and recounts seeing Israel alive inside the courthouse, one of several pulling McCully's body in from a window. The young man was also trapped in the courthouse but jumped out of a side window as the building burned. Despite the waiting cannon, rifles, fire, and smoke, he ran toward the woods, not daring to stop even after he was struck four times by bullets in his thighs and back. He is one of the lucky ones, surviving his flight attempt.

"If this man make it out the building after the fire, why not Israel?" asks Polly. "We got to keep hope," she tells Lucy.

"I pray on it," Lucy says, gathering her boys closer to her on either side, her stomach a conspicuous jutting that will soon enough be her ninth child.

In due course, as the sun grows colder and the news more disheartening, the two women abandon their tasks and sit together by one of the campfires, waiting. Polly gives up her shawl and drapes it around Lucy's shoulders, and Green takes the blanket he and Jackson share and gives it to David and Noby.

Within the hour comes another report that Israel was sighted again, alive, part of a group of captured colored prisoners marched to Calhoun's Sugarhouse by a large covey of white men.

Sam can't make himself sit still. Of all the gruesome accounts he has heard through the day, Israel's saga upsets him most. His mind refuses to release the image of his friend and neighbor repeatedly one half-step away from death. He drinks in every detail of Israel's ordeal, every nuance, a thin tonic to keep him hopeful as he prays for Israel from his privileged post in the swamp. When Sam looks into Noby's face, he sees Israel instead, and it torments him to think of this young boy without a father, the pregnant wife without a husband, Israel's small-woods church in The Bottom without its pastor.

Hiding safely in the woods during and after so many have died leaves Sam no peace. He revels in the fact that he is still alive, so steeped in his relief that it feeds his guilt. He begins to shape the notion of going to look for Israel. His link to Israel feels unfinished, as if there is some action he must personally take.

Near dusk, Levi Allen appears in the swamp camp with a bedraggled collection of eleven armed colored men, some badly wounded. He describes what he has seen from his staked-out position at an entrance into Mirabeau Woods. For over two hours, in the role of gatekeeper and sentry, Levi made sure no white men pursued any colored man managing to cross over into the wooded area. "Giving ours a fighting chance to make it out," Levi tells Sam. "Come a point wasn't nobody else to save but us."

Levi stays just long enough for darkness to fall, and leaves the most injured men at the campsite. Sam leads the military man south to point him toward Boyce, where he can follow the bayou, cross the river, sneak aboard a boat after dark, and slip out of the parish.

"I'm going back into Colfax to find Israel," Sam shares with Levi when they come to the last cross point in the woods.

"White man's blood still running too hot," says Levi. "You likely get caught yourself. What good that do anybody?"

"What if he alive?"

"What if he is?" replies Levi. "Nobody getting them out the hands of the mob tonight. We got to live to fight another day."

Sam gives Levi final directions. "Good luck," he says.

The two men make their farewells, Levi on his black stallion headed south, Sam on foot headed back to Boggy Bayou. He comes across two more courthouse escapees and takes them to the camp as he listens to their testimony.

At Boggy Bayou, Sam checks the perimeters for hostile intruders, watches the women comfort the wounded, and listens again to variations of the same grisly stories of carnage until he thinks he can't stand one more minute of raw human suffering, of unrelieved despair.

"We going hunting," he announces to Green and Jackson, and his sons jump up from their place beside Polly around the fire to join him.

Noby Smith sits off on a log by himself, separate from everyone. He looks small and hunched, lost.

"You too, son," Sam calls to Noby, and the boy looks up, gratitude flooding his face. He runs to catch up to the Tademys,
already on the move.

They rarely speak in the woods, and then only small talk having to do with the mechanics of hunting. The boys are like duck-
lings, with Green in the lead. Jackson falls in behind Green, and
Noby, younger still, attaches himself to Jackson. By the time they
return to camp with two large possums, there are multiple fires lit,
and several communal cooking pots presided over by Polly, Lucy,
and the other women. Sam sets Green to the task of skinning the
possums, and again he makes his rounds. The possum meat is split
among kettles, flavored with roots and wild greens gathered earlier. The women throw themselves into the chore of feeding their
families, an escape into the obligations of everyday chores. They
are all hungry, despite the circumstances, and share the food as far
as it will go, not sure how long they'll have to stay in this place.

"I'm going to Colfax to look around," Sam announces when he
finishes the greasy stew Polly has dished up for him.

Anger pinches at Polly's face, but it is the fear in Jackson's
eyes, so naked as to be contagious, that causes Sam to waver.

"Please, Sam," Polly begs. "What good it gonna do? Stay here
with us."

"Might be somebody need help," Sam says.

"Things settle down some by tomorrow," Polly bargains. "Go
in the daylight. Too many white men liquored up tonight."

"May be too late tomorrow," Sam insists.

"I'm not sorry you here with us 'stead of down there. Politicals
pulled a mean trick, but now we got to deal with the way things is."

Sam studies his wife. Still young, though not so fresh as when
he met her on the road in Alabama, determined and too assertive,
a handful for any man.

"May be we ought to think about moving on from Colfax," Polly says.

"We put ourself in this town eight years," Sam says. He thinks of Levi riding off on his stallion, leaving behind the debacle of the courthouse, the dozens whose blood soaks the ground, their families stranded and adrift, the politicians who will settle in some other place and start again. "Things against us no matter where we is. This my town, and no place else gonna be different till we make it different. A colored man do the best with what he get. Make stepping stones out of stumbling blocks. We make our stand in Colfax."

"In the morning then, not tonight," she pleads. "Think of the boys."

"There ain't no choice," Sam says.

"A man always got choice," Polly says. "Choose us."

"I got to go," Sam says.

Elder B. LaFleur

PASTOR of the FIRST CHURCH of GOD in CHRIST
EUNICE, LOUISIANA 70535
Builder and Pastor of ANTIOCH
Founder of C. H. MASON MEMORIAL SCHOOL
243 Nora Street   Pineville, Louisiana 71360

Gospel Crusade

October 1981

In Colfax, Louisiana, the capitol of Grant parish, there is a sign on the side of the road saying, "The City of the Famous Riot". This was a riot between the blacks and whites in the year 1873. It was ten years after slavery. According to the report, the fast progress of the blacks seemed to be the cause of the riot.

It was reported to me by Deacon James Tademy that nine miles from Colfax Sam Tademy and his brother were released from slavery. Sam inherited the name Tademy from Africa and he held to it. Sam worked hard and purchased land at twenty-five cents an acre. He donated land to build the church and school in his community. He hoped to train his race to live independently wherever they went.

Sam Tademy had little or no formal training, but his philosophy was to "make stepping stones out of stumbling blocks without prejudice". The elementary school emerged into a high school in Colfax.

There were other families that thought progressively in that era such as the Smith family. One of the daughters of that family, Mother S. L. Dorsey, founded this church (Antioch Church of God in Christ) under a little oak tree near Pineville. I was there when the first two souls were saved. I became the third pastor there.

I passed through Colfax in 1935 and stopped overnight with Elder Thomas, a baptist preacher. He told me about the riot. He had residence there at the time. He said God spoke to him and said to go out and catch a horse and he would not be hurt that day. I saw in that that God was making peace.

I consider all that happened to the blacks was showing that God wanted them to fulfill the scripture and stretch forth their hands to God (Ps. 68:31).

I visited a famous pentecostal revival in Colfax being conducted by Elder C. Grimes and Missionary Beatrice Farmearl and Missionary Mary Green. It inspired me to write this circular.

Join in prayer at 4:00 a.m. for problems and advance this world to Christ.

B. Lafleur
The Aged

Figure 9. 1981 letter referring to Sam Tademy

189

18

ost of the white men leave Calhoun's Sugarhouse around suppertime. Those departing on foot and on horseback are the most moderate of the white men, no longer excited by the chase, visibly tired and ready to call an end to the courthouse confrontation, but there are several small, keyed-up groups still energized by the day's events, stoked by liquor. Of the men who pulled Israel and the others out from under the boards of the courthouse, the stout man called Narcisse leaves, and Baby-face Jim stays.

Only a dozen or so of the original captors remain by eight o'clock, the hardest core, swapping stories and reliving high points of the day.

"Cannon keep slipping back down the bank, wasn't sure we could drag it up, but once we got to their blind side, it was like swatting flies in summer."

A white man laughs. "How dumb a coon got to be to hide in a burning building?"

Suddenly, Jim points to Israel. "That one of the coons there played he was dead."

Baby-face Jim tilts the jug and drinks, fixing his stare on Israel. Israel keeps his eyes to the side, prays the man is too drunk to get up.

The conversation sweeps on, past Israel and past the white man-boy. "Today was easy. Just take a little fire to smoke 'em out."

They light the lamps, and a couple of men pull out cards for a game of seven-up. Others, including Sheriff Nash, smoke or spit tobacco, and they all keep drinking. They tap a keg of something, Israel isn't sure what, but the more they drink, the louder they get, working themselves up.

Luke Hadnot shows up at Calhoun's Sugarhouse a little after eight, with three other men from Montgomery at his side. He exchanges pleasantries with a few of the men and then walks over to the line of prisoners.

"You know who I am?" he asks October White, the colored man closest to him.

"No, sir," October says, head down and thin shoulders trembling. His face is already a puffy, battered mess from the beating earlier.

"My name is Luke Hadnot. You seen the white man they took off in a stretcher today outside the courthouse? He was my brother, Smokin' Jimmy Hadnot. You killed him."

October shakes his head violently. "No, sir. I don't shoot nobody. I wasn't never at the courthouse, 'cept with a truce flag to deliver a message for your sheriff. I come right back to Smithfield Quarter, and all day I never leave my house again, not till they come and bring me here."

Luke hits October in the stomach, a sudden, thudding blow that knocks the thin man to the ground. Luke kicks at the felled man until Sheriff Nash pulls him off.

"I remember this man," says the sheriff. "He wasn't one of them."

"That's for my brother," says Luke, and gives October a final kick. He turns to Nash. "Now you sheriff again, what we gonna do with these black devils?"

"We're all sorry about Smokin' Jimmy, but we wait till morning, and then I decide."

"Go on home, Sheriff Nash," says Luke. "You done a good day's work, and now you deserve a good night's sleep. I take charge of the prisoners."

"I don't want no more blood tonight."

"You got my word, Sheriff."

"No funny business till I come back in the morning, Luke."

"I just bunk here tonight, see to it nobody run," Luke says.

"All right, then," says Sheriff Nash. "I leave 'em here with you."

Luke Hadnot and the white men still sober enough force-march the four dozen colored prisoners away from the sugarhouse. They herd them toward the riverbank, not that far from the center of Colfax and the Pecan Tree.

Israel recognizes where they are. Just yesterday the colored men of Colfax gathered here, but tonight the Pecan Tree belongs to the white men.

"We gonna put this old tree to good use tonight," one of the men says.

"I got a better idea first," Luke Hadnot says.

Israel catches the scent of alcohol mixed with Hadnot's sweat. What time is it? Time keeps coming into his head. As early as nine? Late as midnight?

"Pull them out, two by two."

They take the two colored men closest to the end, loosen the bindings from their feet, and pull them away from the others.

"Take their shirts off and put 'em back to back," Luke says. The men who untie the rope, curious, do as he asks, positioning the first pair of colored men so their shoulder blades touch. It is two brothers from The Bottom, Henry and Meredity Elzy. Henry is out of Israel's view, looking out toward the river, but Meredity faces in toward the gathering of men, and to Luke Hadnot.

"You coons kill my brother today," Luke says, his words slurred. "What you think we gonna do about that?"

"No, sir, Mr. Hadnot, sir," Meredity says. "I seen it. We come out the courthouse with a white flag. Your brother got caught cross-ways from the side by a bullet, back from where the shooting was."

Luke Hadnot's face changes expression, his eyes an intense blue that visibly deepens, even in the dim light. "You saying we shot him ourselves in the back?"

Big drops of sweat form on Meredity's forehead. "I just telling what I seen, Mr. Hadnot. We come out the courthouse with our hands up, waving white, and your brother come rushing toward us with a rifle in his hands, and next I see, he grab at his side, toward his back, and fall down to the ground. The bullets what was flying hadn't never stopped from your side."

Luke Hadnot raises his pistol and shoots Meredity in the temple at close range. Meredity crumples to the ground, heavy, like a full sack of rice. Henry turns just long enough to see his brother dead, then takes off in an absurd dogtrot, a short mincing gait toward the river, tripping with each step on the snarl of rope that binds his ankles together. Before Henry has taken five paces, Luke calmly shoots him in the back.

"They made me use two bullets," Luke says petulantly.

Israel is almost exactly in the middle of the long line of roped-together colored men of Colfax. He sees Luke Hadnot load and reload several times, perfecting the game he has invented to kill two men with a single bullet. There is no escape possible, even if the men could devise a scheme to work together. There are fewer white men than colored, but the colored are shackled, and all of the white men have guns. Two by two they are untied and positioned back-to-back while Luke waits for the preparations to finish. Once center stage is his again, Luke practices trick shots, shooting from under his arm, but his balance is shaky and he settles into calling his target beforehand to keep himself amused.

"Head," he calls. But instead of hitting a man's head, Luke Hadnot's bullet hits him in the chest, sometimes the leg. Luke tries again.

"Wasted another bullet," he mumbles, and swears. Luke is mean-drunk, as are most of the white men by now. If a colored man still stands, they prop him upright again, and Luke has another go. The dead pile up, and two white men are assigned to take them down to the riverbank by their hands and feet and throw them into the water.

When it is Israel's turn, hands yank him up by one arm, along with Eli McCullen. They are the next pair hustled to the killing spot. A sudden sharp, rancid odor catches Israel unawares. One of them has fouled himself.

Eli faces Luke Hadnot, and through blurry eyes, Israel takes one last view out over Red River. He and Eli are of similar height. Luke's followers have declared it too much effort to strip the shirts from the colored men before Luke takes aim, but even through his jacket, Israel feels Eli trembling where their shoulders touch.

"Chest," Luke Hadnot calls out.

Israel shuts his eyes. He hears the tinny pop from the pistol, feels Eli convulse, and there is a stinging in Israel's back as Eli falls to the ground. The force of Eli's fall takes Israel down, and he feels the deadweight of the man's body on top of his. There is blood, wet and warm, inching at a snail's pace along his bare hands and face. He isn't sure if it is his or Eli's, but Israel's mouth fills with the warm taste of blood and threatens to choke him, keeping him from drawing air.

"Those two fell just right." Luke's voice. Israel wonders what he is still doing alive to hear it. "Get the next ones."

Israel tries not to cough away the blood blocking his windpipe. If they think he is dead, he has a chance. He has played possum all his life, and now he needs to do it once again for a chance to escape death.

They cart the pair of them toward the riverbank and dump them in a growing heap short of the water's edge, too weary now to carry the bodies all the way down. Israel manages to stay quiet, and the dead man draped across his back shields him from view, but breathing is impossible. He lies facedown with his nose buried in the Louisiana soil, trying to time his frantic gasps to coincide with the noise of the shots from Luke Hadnot's gun. That works for three more rounds of fire. A man cries out when hit and moans in pain until the second shot quiets him.

Israel can't shut out the sounds, but he knows he must fight to keep hold of consciousness.

"I wasn't at that courthouse, Mr. Hadnot," a man begs. Israel recognizes October White's voice.

"Stand him up," Luke Hadnot orders.

October must have dropped to his knees, but Israel hears the gurgle in October's throat and the snap of the rope as one of the white men yanks him back upright.

"I got six children. I work for Mr. Calhoun every day for ten years, even before the war. Ask him. This a mistake."

Israel hears the pop of the gun, the drop of the bodies, the sounds of the next pair of men being prepared.

"Sound just like popcorn in a skillet," one of the drunken men says.

The shooting seems to go on forever. The white men come periodically to the part of the river where Israel lies, and each time he manages to stay quiet. Israel figures they must be down to the last handful of men still alive. He hears footsteps close by and concentrates on keeping himself still, but a thick pocket of phlegm catches in his throat and he gasps several times, drawing fresh nonliquid air into his lungs.

"This one's alive," someone says.

19

*H*e is discovered.

Israel lifts his head to get some relief from the collecting blood. There is no need to strangle when the bullet is so close to coming. He offers up a final prayer. He has done what he can to live, but his time has run out. At least he won't have to listen to any more colored men dying.

The man rolls Eli off Israel with his dusty boot. In his last moment, Israel looks the white man square in the face, watches him draw back the firing pin of a small pistol.

"You know better than to look at a white man, boy," the man says. He aims at Israel's face and, with a hand unsteadied by drink, he pulls the trigger.

Israel feels his right eye implode, and his vision becomes nothing more than the concept of red. He rolls over in pain.

He hears another popping sound and feels a piercing pain in the small of his back. A strange lack of sensation descends on him gradually, like dusk, the passing of day into night. His body is weightless, prepared to drift to the realm of death, but once again his mind stays present. He hears the movement of the men around him, the involuntary sobs and mutterings of the colored men waiting for their fate, the horses whinnying nervously off the banks toward the tree line, the uncapping of the flasks and bottles that the white men pass among themselves, the cocking of a gun. He hears these things, clear and distinct.

He still isn't dead.

Israel enters some other place. They leave him alone again. Without the dead man's weight on top of him, and now that the angle of his head tilts to the side instead of facedown, with concentration, he can take shallow breaths without choking.

"This ain't fun no more, Luke." It is the voice of one of the white men who has done most of the heavy lifting, clearly impatient with the role he has been assigned in clearing away another set of bodies. "Let's stretch hemp with the rest. Plenty of rope."

"Only got three horses," says Luke, his voice slurry. He sounds peevish, as if he hasn't finished his own game and they are making him move on to another before he is ready.

"That's how many left."

Now Israel wills himself into unconsciousness, but his mind won't shut off. His senses are sharpened by the constant pain, not dulled. He hears the white men collect the horses from where they graze by the trees. He hears them gather up lengths of discarded rope lying on the ground, left over from the men held captive but now dead. He hears the scraping of ropes thrown over tree branches. He hears moans from the three colored men as they realize what is in store.

"Take down their pants."

There is more movement now, as all the white men become active. The last three colored men put up a struggle, trying to run, but they are held back. Israel hears the hacking of knife into flesh as the white men cut off the colored men's privates. The moans turn to screams in the uncaring night. Israel feels little of his own body, except the warmish blood in his throat, but it is as if he is one of the three, feeling the drunken stabs at the most tender of flesh with a dirty knife last used for skinning possum. The white men come alive for the ceremony of the rope, an ancient rite etched deep in their communal southern blood.

Israel hears it all, the gashing knife, the bleeding men heaved on horseback, the rope's taut friction over branches, the sudden shooing of horses, the self-congratulatory camaraderie of white men. After the initial burst of excitement and adrenaline, after the three colored men sway suspended in the darkness with their necks broken and faces swelling, Israel hears the eventual damping down of the mood of the white men, a stupored, languid drowsiness of too much liquor and maybe, finally, ample blood.

20

S am leaves his Enfield with Green in the swamp, carrying an old pistol borrowed from a wounded man who staggered into their encampment at dusk. Sam tucks the gun into his trousers' waist.

The woods are alive with movement, men, women, and children traveling singly and in groups, some heavily armed but most not, primarily colored but occasionally white, all antsy, a recipe for collision. The walk from Boggy Bayou swamp toward Calhoun's Sugarhouse is made longer by the need for caution. Sam passes camps of colored people and slips around several of them unnoticed. He declares himself loudly at the more heavily guarded camps, making himself visible to avoid an accidental shooting. The color of his skin automatically identifies him as a man of no threat to the makeshift colored settlements, but each minute he is pressed into conversation is a minute stolen from reaching town.

He comes within sight of the sugarhouse at last, moving slowly and quietly from tree to tree to cover his approach. This is no longer the woods and swamp, the colored havens on this night of horrors. The sugarhouse smells of conquered territory, with Sam the trespasser. There is only one dim lamp lit in the window, and the doors are open wide, swinging back and forth in lazy motion by small gusts of night wind. There is a quiet to the place, and no movement inside. Around the outer edges of the building, a hand-ful of white men in stupefied sleep slump wherever they have fallen. There seem to be neither guards nor prisoners. The prison-ers must have been moved, but where?

Sam veers wide and follows the river toward the courthouse. It has been hours since he heard shots, and he hopes everyone is bed-ded down for the night. As he delivers himself directly into the lion's den, he prepares himself to take off in a run if he comes across white men. Every noise nips at his jagged nerves.

It is well past midnight. The sky is too clouded over for stars, and the moon is only a sliver veiled in mist. The shadowy natural light barely reflects on the water of Red River, and Sam can make out only the few feet directly ahead. He progresses cautiously, focusing on familiar landmarks, and dodges through Mirabeau Woods. Using the white man's trick, he cuts over to the river to approach the courthouse from its blind side. If there are still white men posted, Sam is prepared to retreat back to the swamp, retrac-ing his steps, or maybe to Smithfield Quarter. His plan is uncertain beyond that.

The familiar shape of the upper branches of the Pecan Tree come into view, silent and majestic in the quarter-light of the moon. It is disconcertingly quiet, and Sam is pulled toward the familiar comfort and spread of the old tree.

The closer he gets, the more his skin prickles under his jacket, but still he creeps on. After every step, he pauses, sniffing the air like a hunting dog, alert to sounds and movement, focusing on the distance. A deepening dread intensifies with each passing second.

The air smells scorched, a sickening blend of burnt flesh and discharged gunpowder, singed hair and smoldering wood. He steps forward again, tentatively, his mind slow to catch up to the evidence of his senses, and he stumbles. He looks down, forced to register what he should have seen all along. There is a colored man at his feet, faceup, dead. Another dead man lies sprawled not a yard away. Unmoving forms cover the ground, like logs carelessly left after felling and splitting a tree.

There are dozens of bodies, faces frozen in finality, some with mouths open and eyes shut, some the reverse. The bodies are already stiffened into their awkward poses. Unlike the white men outside Calhoun's Sugarhouse, drunk on alcohol and sleeping off the day's terrors, these men won't wake in the morning. Sam rushes from one to another. Cold, cold, cold. He draws his hand back and tucks it protectively within his jacket. He doesn't want to touch anyone. These are men he knows, men he recognizes, men he stood with shoulder-to-shoulder in the courthouse. Can it be just this morning they took breath, worried about their families, celebrated Easter Sunday, stood firm on principle? Meredity Elzy, Shuck White, Eli McCullen: men sighted along with Israel in the string of prisoners bound for Calhoun's Sugarhouse. Their wives and children are in the swamp, waiting for them to come home.

Sam fights the rising revulsion and lifts his eyes heavenward for an answer. Hanging from the lower branches of the town's Pecan Tree, three limp forms are outlined by the moon, as if their heads are lowered in prayer. Grisly southern trophies. Three puffy, inert bodies swing from different branches, their pants pulled down around their ankles, clotted blood at the groin. Sam forces himself closer, circling the stout tree trunk, identifying each one before he eases them down, one by one. The bodies are deadweight, bloated and swollen, and he handles them as gently as he can, laying them down on the ground at the base of the tree. Their limbs are too stiff to arrange, but he pulls their trousers up to their waists, covers them up. Clay Murphy, Nick Cotton, Lank Pitman. It will fall to him to give an accounting to the families.

Sam listens for noises, any sign that the men who did this are still around. When all he hears is the croaking of frogs by the river, he begins his gruesome work.

He passes among the men on the ground like a shadowy ghoul, turns their faces upward if necessary, enough for a positive identification. For the most part, they are sprawled out and left where they dropped, but there are others stacked on top of one another in some crazy attempt at efficiency. Sam throws up twice as he sorts through the carnage, careful to wipe himself clean with a rag from his jacket pocket so as not to profane the dead. He fights his need to flee, staying to finish his morbid inventory, the dead men's grimaced faces etched in his brain.

He moves from body to body, steeling himself in between each one, pausing to listen for the white men's return. His muscles are taut, prepared to run, but he holds steady, continuing the accounting. He has almost come to the last when he hears a liquid, choking gurgle at his feet. It flashes through his mind that the white men have discovered him. Without looking back, he sprints with all his strength toward the river. Before he reaches the bank, his brain catches up to his reflexes.

The gurgling sound came from one of the bodies. Someone within that mass of death is still alive. Sam is slow to reverse course, needing time to shift his focus from escape to rescue, but he forces himself forward, stumbling in his rush back toward the Pecan Tree. He stoops over the body for a closer look.

It is Israel Smith, and he is alive.

Sam doesn't know how to get Israel from the Pecan Tree all the way back to the swamp. The man is barely conscious, and it isn't clear how close to death he is.

"It's Sam. Sam Tademy," Sam whispers into Israel's ear.

"Sam?" Israel fights to make himself understood. "They cut them before hanging," he says. He sounds like he is drowning, his voice, thick and raspy, surfacing from under bubbles of blood in his throat, strangling on words.

Sam turns away and tries to sort out the magnitude of Israel's wounds in the dim half-light. Israel's right pants leg is stiff with dried blood, but the most severe of the wounds is around his face. A bullet piece has caught him at the throat, and he gasps for breath every few minutes, a terrifying sound. Sam wonders how he possibly managed to stay quiet for so long. Israel's right eye is gone. Nothing remains but a huge swelling of flesh around a socket where the eyeball used to be.

"I think they dead," Israel says, his wheezing words loud and flat in the still air. "The moaning been stopped."

Sam wants Israel to stop talking. For each gurgling sound that comes from his mouth, Sam is beginning to match it with a swelling fear of his own. Soon he will lose the ability to keep himself moving.

"Lucy, my boys?" Israel stumbles over the words, but Sam understands.

"Lucy and your children fine, hid in Boggy Bayou with the others. But you gotta stay quiet now, Israel. They might come back." Sam doesn't know which way to look. There is horror everywhere, no way to escape it. "We got to get outa here."

Sam stares at the blood on Israel's pants, speculating. Did they cut him too, and shoot him instead of hanging? Is he still a man, or did they take his manhood along with his eye? Sam wills himself to stoop down and put Israel's arm around his neck to get him standing, reluctant to be this close, to touch him, as if it is worse to be alive and gelded than dead, as if Sam might catch what the rigid corpses from the tree have. He is shamed by his squeamishness, his selfishness, and sloughs it off. It is up to him to get Israel away and back to his family. If Israel can't walk, Sam will carry him away from this field of death on his back.

"We gotta chance Smithfield Quarter," says Sam.

"Too many white men," Israel says. "They make camp."

"I scout it out, then come back for you."

"Don't leave me here." Israel is insistent, clutching at the cloth of Sam's jacket. The puffy brown flesh around his one remaining eye sags.

The Hanging Tree looms overhead, the dead men's bodies on the ground grown cold and still. Once Sam leaves this place, he isn't sure he will have the courage to return, for Israel or anyone else. The unstoppable stink of death will be worse with the coming of the light.

"Mirabeau Woods, then. McCully got kin there."

"McCully gone," Israel says. "Spenser gone, trying to surrender. They set fire to the courthouse."

Sam doesn't let on how much he already knows. For now it is enough he and Israel place as much distance between themselves and the Pecan Tree as possible. Levi was right. First priority for the survivors is to live to fight another day.

Once they enter the lip of the woods, Sam stops to draw in a cautious breath. They have a long way to go, but at least they are no longer out in the open field, and now there is a cover of trees and bush to shield them. Every fifty feet or so, Israel spits out blood, leaning against Sam when his body shakes with uncontrollable muscle spasms, but they make their way forward, one step after another. Israel Smith provides Sam with more help than he expected on their journey away from the Pecan Tree and toward Mirabeau Woods. They sit down to rest only once, and Sam braces Israel's back against the broad trunk of a sycamore tree.

"Best go," Israel says after a few minutes. "Else I'm done for."

They walk for over two hours through the dark woods, Israel leaning on Sam and dragging one leg, Sam taking on most of his weight. By the time they reach Jessie McCullen's cabin in the woods, step after halting step, Israel no longer talks, concentrating on the bare mechanics of movement. Sam raps hard on the front door of the cabin, waking Jessie McCullen's widow. She answers the door cautiously and takes in Israel's condition in a glance. In the moonlight, Sam thinks he sees a bald instant of either disgust or defeat register on her face, but just as quickly, whatever it was is gone, and she briskly helps Sam get Israel inside.

Without question, the widow takes charge of her patient, improvising a convalescent area in the corner of her front room, cleaning his wounds, making him as comfortable as possible. Israel falls into a deep sleep immediately, and Sam leaves him in her hands, stopping just long enough to accept a cold biscuit and several deep drinks of water from the well. It will be a long walk back to Boggy Bayou. He needs to report what he has witnessed and get early word to as many of the waiting families as possible. Before he can sleep, he will retrieve Israel's family from the swamp and bring them back to the broken man in Mirabeau Woods.

Alone in the sobering darkness on the journey back to Boggy Bayou swamp, Sam wearily retraces his steps. By sunup, there are others on the roads and in the countryside, and the mood has changed from the long night before. A heavy fatigue has settled over Colfax, like a summer morning's thick mist over Red River. Close to town, Sam meets two colored men carrying a dead body between them on a large piece of burlap.

"First light, we went into Colfax. They letting the families claim their men," they tell him.

As repulsed as he is by the idea, Sam decides to detour through the center of Colfax. He considers it his responsibility to report back as much detail as possible to those in his care. He approaches the area around the Pecan Tree, afraid to see the carnage, but already the scene looks different in the light of day.

There are still many of the splayed bodies he walked among last night, but now mounted white men patrol the grounds of the courthouse, watching neutrally, almost indulgently, as colored men and women collect the dead and the lucky few who appeared dead but were only wounded. Relatives and friends jerry-rig litters to cart bodies away for burial, or to tend to survivors' injuries and patch them up.

Sam overhears two of the mounted men remark loudly about the shame of the Colfax Riot, how the colored men who took over the courthouse were radicals and got what they deserved. Sam can't linger any longer. He heads north out of town toward the swamp, tentacles of resentment squeezing in on him, hard.

He reenters their camp in Boggy Bayou swamp on foot, exhausted and full of his loathsome news. Polly and Lucy are still up with a few of the others, haven't slept at all by the looks of it, passing the time in a grim circle around the dregs of the fire. Polly is the first to see Sam and runs to him, almost knocks him over, sobbing so hard she can't collect herself to speak. He holds her close, but she doesn't stop trembling, only able to touch him repeatedly in reassurance that he has come back. Groups of others emerge, swarm to him, including Lucy, flanked by David and Noby. Lucy catches his eye and approaches slowly and calmly, waiting at a respectful distance.

"I found Israel," Sam says to Lucy. "He's hurt bad, but alive, in Mirabeau Woods, being tended by Widow McCullen."

"Praise be," says Lucy. And then again, "Praise be."

Polly disentangles herself from Sam and embraces Lucy, gently this time. The two women sway wordlessly, arms wrapped around each other, until Lucy recovers enough to ask, "Can you take us to him?"

"Of course," says Sam. "I take you directly, but I got a few things to do first."

"Only first is get food and drink into you," says Polly. Already she is up and doing, disappears for only a minute and produces a dipper of fresh water as if from thin air. "And rest for a bit. Look like last night don't include sleep."

"Bless you, Sam Tademy," Lucy says. She takes Sam's hands in her own, squeezes tight. "Me and the boys be ready whenever you is." Lucy straightens up, gathers her sons. "I fix him up some breakfast, Polly." She takes her boys back to the fire to give Polly time with Sam.

"Rest now," says Polly to Sam. She sits on a fallen trunk in the swamp, pats a place beside her for Sam.

As tired as he is, Sam can't bear the thought of sitting. "No time for rest, woman. Too much got to get done."

Polly nods, stands up, and positions herself by his side. "I'm here, whatever you need," she says. "Sam, what you see out there?"

"They already back in charge, calling what happen yesterday a riot," Sam says. "Colfax Riot, my foot. Words matter in how people see, how they gonna remember. Easter Sunday 1873 be the Colfax Massacre, not the Colfax Riot, and the only shame be we didn't get the parish power to the hands of the Republicans."

"Sam, Colfax no place for us no more. Reconstruction nothing but a promise and a test, and now come the sour end."

"White League and their kind always be wherever we is. It up to us, Polly, up to us to stay put and rise again." Sam looks around him at the defeat of their sorry squatters' camp in the swamp, the leaden movements by everyone around him. "McCully and the rest can't be for nothing. We got to make stepping stones out of stumbling blocks."

Polly, unblinking, nods. "Where you go, I go, Sam," she says. "Where you stay, I stay."

Sam is already thinking ahead to the future. This morning he must inform the families of the dead, deliver Lucy to Mirabeau Woods to reunite with Israel, help friends and neighbors retrieve and bury their relations, all before he returns to The Bottom for good. But first, before anything else, Sam Tademy will have his sons shout out their name, Tademy, right here in the godforsaken swamp, for everyone to hear.

They daren't forget.

Figure 10. Gathering the dead and wounded, Harper's Weekly, *May 10, 1873*

Second Lieutenant Geo. D. Wallace,
    Act'g Ass't Adj't-Gen'l, Dist. of Upper Red River, Shreveport, La.:

SIR: I have the honor to submit herewith the list of persons killed and wounded in the parish of Grant, Louisiana, and comprising a few names of those killed in this vicinity, in the contiguous parish of Rapides. These names comprise those furnished in my report in February last; the same were also furnished to Maj. G. A. Forsyth, A. D. C. to the Lieutenant-General, commanding Division of the Missouri. It was impossible to procure the names at an earlier date, as I was compelled to rely on persons over whom I had no control, and was obliged to wait their pleasure and convenience. I am unable to procure data from the upper portion of the parish, as those persons on whom I could rely for such information are afraid to trust to the perils of travel in the "piny woods."

No.	Name.	Date.	Place.	Remarks.
1	Jessie McKenzie....colored.	Apr. —, 1873	2¼ miles from Colfax, La.	Just before riot.
2	More Reed			
3	William Williams........do...	Apr. 13, 1873	Colfax, La........	Colfax riot.
4	H. M. Elzy................do...	....do	....do	Do.
5	Meredith Elsy...........do...	....do	....do	Do.
6	Frank Jones.............do...	....do	....do	Do.
7	Jack Nely...............do...	....do	....do	Do.
8	John Carter.............do...	....do	....do	Do.
9	Mack Brown..............do...	....do	....do	Do.
10	Shuck White.............do...	....do	....do	Do.
11	Barney Brandon..........do...	....do	....do	Do.
12	Kit Smith...............do...	....do	....do	Do.
13	Alex. Tilman............do...	....do	....do	Do.
14	Lauk Pitman.............do...	....do	....do	Do.
15	Kendray Nelson..........do...	....do	....do	Do.
16	Guymo Nelson............do...	....do	....do	Do.
17	Sam Samuel..............do...	....do	....do	Do.
18	Bully Ellis.............do...	....do	....do	Do.
19	Clay Murphy.............do...	....do	....do	Do.
20	Tody Hunter.............do...	....do	....do	Do.
21	Adam Kimball............do...	....do	....do	Do.
22	Philip Harrison.........do...	....do	....do	Do.
23	Alex. Randolph..........do...	....do	....do	Do.
24	Warren Bullit...........do...	....do	....do	Do.
25	October White...........do...	....do	....do	Do.
26	Dun Wilkins.............do...	....do	....do	Do.
27	Jim Bazzo...............do...	....do	....do	Do.
28	Elias Johnson...........do...	....do	....do	Do.

No.	Name.	Date.	Place.	Remarks.
29	Ashel White ....do...	Apr. 13, 1873	Colfax, La	Colfax riot.
30	Eli Jones...............do...	....do	....do	Do.
31	Tom Forster.............do...	....do	....do	Do.
32	Murphy Forster..........do...	....do	....do	Do.
33	Isaac McCullough........do...	....do	....do	Do.
34	Eli McCullough..........do...	....do	....do	Do.
35	Spencer McCullough......do...	....do	....do	Do.
36	Washington Madison......do...	....do	....do	Do.
37	John Hall...............do...	....do	....do	Do.
38	Charles Embry...........do...	....do	....do	Do.

It will be seen that *at least* one hundred and five (105) colored and three (3) whites were killed in the Colfax riot, or in connection therewith, in April, 1873, and about forty-five (45) wounded. This does not include those said to have been thrown into the river.

Respectfully submitted.

ED. L. GODFREY,
First Lieutenant Seventh Cavalry, Commanding Post.

Figure 11. List of killed and wounded, 44th Congress Congressional Record, including Isaac McCullough [sic], Spencer McCullough [sic], and Eli McCullough, all dead (Northwestern State University of Louisiana, Watson Memorial Library, Cammie G. Henry Research Center)

Figure 12. New-York Times, Daily Picayune, *and* New Orleans Republican *1873 headlines*

Part Two

After

Polly

1936

They carry off a handful of the white men what led the shooting on the Colfax courthouse. Took Mr. Hadnot and the old sheriff and some others all the way to New Orleans, but nothing much come of it. The courts down there had colored testify alongside white, telling what they know about that Easter Sunday 1873. Israel Smith get called down and he tole what happen to him since he seen so much, from inside the courthouse and down by the river both. No matter his body broke, half blind and only able to hobble along with a cane, he force hisself to bear witness so his voice be heard and it go to the record. But the more time pass and nothing happen to the white men they charge, Israel end up even more broke in spirit than body.

We heared from Israel each witness sweared on a Bible and tell they story. The stories contrary to one another, keeping with whether told by colored or white, where they was when the shooting start and such, but no matter which way you come at it, couldn't get around the one hundred fifty colored men under the ground, dead and gone. For a little while, we think maybe somebody be brought to justice for all that killing. Them trials and retrials limp on for years, go to the highest court in the nation, the Supreme Court. We get news each time the court say let this one or that one walk away free, till wasn't no one left to put the blame on. Shooting colored didn't have no price, worse than before, 'cause this time, the gov'ment outside Louisiana say it all right. We all knowed Reconstruction was over then, fast in Colfax after that Easter Sunday, and slower but just as sure everyplace else in the South after a while. The White League start calling theyself Ku Kluxers and ride the land without no threat of a lifted hand against them, more bold than ever. Sheriff Nash and Hadnot come back to town heroes, and the whites was mostly happy now they back in charge without needing to worry about the gov'ment looking over they shoulder.

We colored was too busy burying our dead and propping up our living to pay too much never mind. Life keep on, one day to the next. Everybody, but the men 'specially, we got to pull back and walk soft, avoiding relations with white when we was able, and doing the meek down-eye when we wasn't. Don't give them no chance to say we insolent and come down hard again. Didn't nobody talk loud about 1873 in Colfax 'cept the whites crowing about the end of Negro rule. How I sees it, more like we had a slippery hold on the promise of Negro rule, not the rule itself. Anybody what poke they head up too far after that get a visit from the Ku Kluxers, to remind us all what happen if we try to better ourself too much.

Us colored was raw and tender after the massacre, even with each other, and we was scared about the future. Sam Tademy gather his family close and we burrow into The Bottom like we was whistle pigs gone to ground. Anything we was able to do on our own without outside help, we done. We growed our own food and ginned our cotton and Sam rigged up his own gristmill. He build a windmill for us for power. We already had our own well. 'Course that only go so far. They's crops to sell and odd cash jobs to save enough to buy the land Sam so hell-bent on seeing the Tademy name on. Impossible not to rub elbows with white sometime, but we try hard to do much as we can on our own.

Sam Tademy a determined man. He don't say nothing out loud, but I knowed how much he hurt when Israel Smith pass less than three years after the massacre. Some say was as much Israel's spirit as his body what give out, that he just let go. It take a lot to kill a man. A bullet do its dirty damage, but a man learn to live with wounds to the body, learn to live with the loss of a eye, a game leg, pain. Take more time and effort to kill his spirit. A man find it hard to go forward when hope die. Some courthouse men look like the whites what come back after the War Between the States. Shot up, ragged, hurt inside in a place nobody know. You gets what I'm talking? Like they lose they fix on how to live in this world and give in.

Whilst we women watch, some of our colored men disappear. No, you still seed them with the eye, working the field, praying in church, fishing on the bayou, swinging a child, sleeping next to us on the cabin bed, but some other part of them gone for good. The massacre gnaw at who they want to be.

After McCully killed at the courthouse and then his wife die of the fever not one year later, Sam and me bring his daughter, Amy, down to The Bottom to live under our roof, to finish up her raising. But when Israel die, Sam really fix his gaze on the boy children. He sniff after Israel's sons almost much as our own, trying to help them be a credit to they race, get them full of reading and writing to go alongside farming to earn they living. Noby Smith sit around our supper table much as his own sometime. Sam work like three men, but after Israel pass, his talk always come back to building a colored school. He like a dog with a bone about that school. In those days, easy to get beat or kilt over a idea like that, but that don't stop Sam Tademy. He a man always keep his eye fixed on the possible. He never say nothing when they call him a race man, but I know inside he proud as he can be. He call the way he think a duty to his race.

Wasn't none of us sure how the children gonna go into they adult-hood after what they seen in 1873. They was still taking shape, and truth tell, us older folks was busy our own selves struggling with how we *was gonna do in the new way of living. Fear is a cruel master, but hope die a hard death. Don't think we just lay down. Six year after the massacre, two hundred colored men from these parts go to the polls and vote. My Sam march shoulder to shoulder with the others through the crowd of white to shore up the Republicans. Israel Smith already buried by then, but I like to think he'd a gone with them too. Didn't make no difference in the end. By then Republican politicians was on the downslide. Couldn't nothing blow enough life into the party in the South, too many scared. We don't keep back easy, but 1879 the last time any of our men was allowed to set foot in the polls. Sam always say us colored get the vote back someday, that his sons gonna get the chance to vote like he done, but that was fifty year ago and I ain't seen it yet. We running outa time for that. Maybe his grandsons get the opening. Maybe his great-grandsons.*

Most people accept the hand they dealed, dig deep in theyself and carry on, and that's what we done. One thing always sure. Life go on with you or without you, no matter how much you seen. Was a master just as evil as the devil back in Alabama put a heavy choke chain 'round his dog's neck and used to jerk on it hard night or day for no particular reason. Just to watch the poor beast suffer, I think. Meanness. That old dog got to the point he just lay down whenever that man around, like all the fight left him, head hung down and shaking. One day they find his master with his throat tore out and the dog gone. Wait long enough and you reap what you sow. That hold for men. That hold for towns. That hold for a whole country, I suspect.

The same affection Sam and Israel grow when Reconstruction in its last days carry over between the next crop of Tademys and Smiths. 'Course I seed Green and Jackson every day, cook they meals and wash they clothes till they old enough to move out our house and under they own roof and start they own families. Those two brothers never growed out they closeness to each other. I seed young Noby regular too, a tight friend to the Tademy boys. Seed how they all growed up to be fine, God-fearing young men, but wasn't nothing much more for them in Colfax than we had. Colored didn't have too much room to press forward. Was a comfort, though, to see how them three boys lean on one another and come at life the stronger for it.

I think Noby Smith look to Green and Jackson so because of trouble in his own growing-up house. They was poison between Noby and his brother David, carry forward past they youth when they shoulda knowed better and put that bad feeling behind them. Someone on the outside looking in never know the full story, but I think they was rivals for they daddy's attention, and Noby come out the clear favorite. Even after Israel gone, they still can't let the bad blood go. Israel never saw beyond David's pale eyes and fair skin he know didn't come from him. I say you love family no matter where they come from. It ain't right to speak against the dead, but I got to fault Israel Smith for letting that brother-hate breed, or at least for not trying to set them straight before it was too late. Wasn't nothing but his own grievance shining back at him through his sons. But that the way it be, one generation to the next. Like a spinning wheel, go 'round and 'round repeating the same old things.

Figure 13. Colfax courthouse marker, still outside rebuilt courthouse (Northwestern State University of Louisiana, Watson Memorial Library, Cammie G. Henry Research Center)

Chapter

21

1 8 8 2

Sweat inches down the pecan-colored farmer's face, starting at the top of his scalp, under his hat, and makes its way like a troop of stubborn soldiers in a forced march. Rivulets break rank at the stubble of his chin, collecting at the jawline before dropping to the ground or pooling at the collar, fanning out to become dark, salt-ringed stains left behind on the cottonade material of his coarse shirt. Noby Smith is accustomed to the punishment meted out during August Louisiana days in the open field, days that deliver too much sun, never enough shade, and so much water hanging in the air, it may as well be raining. He hasn't broken pace for over two hours; he's adept at tilting his head back or to the side to keep the stinging perspiration from his eyes. Before prodding the mule forward once more across the unyielding soil, he takes off his sopping shirt and ties it around his waist, more a nervous gesture than a sensible one. The leather straps chafe against his bare skin and leave a raised red swipe across his upper body as friction, skin, and perspiration conspire. The metal blade of the plow jerks and successfully pierces the dense crusted ground, but clayish dirt and rocks the size of cantaloupes fight Noby at each furrow.

Two years of drought followed by another year of flood have turned the areas surrounding Colfax an ugly, drab brown, as if temperate sun and moderate rainfall refuse to honor such a place. Three years in a row, cursed, when everyone struggles. Noby picked this long-neglected, miserable patch to work today, as if doing penance under the crush of the midday sun. He is almost far enough away to be out of earshot of the cabin, but close enough for someone to come quickly to fetch him when the time is at hand.

Earlier this morning, anxious, he hovered too close to the small shack he shares with his wife, trying to occupy himself in planting four new rows of sugar peas in the side vegetable garden. After the first few screams, he hitched up the mule and moved farther afield to escape the terrifying sounds, off to the desolate plot he's trying to cultivate now. This scrap of land is little more than hard-packed soil peppered through with rocks, and it lays fallow for a reason, unlikely to ever yield a decent crop. Nonetheless, Noby turns the resistant soil, clearing weeds but not seeding. He can't force himself to budge from his vantage point, this tactical position, mindlessly committing himself to a parallel task as grueling as the one his wife faces inside the darkness of the cabin, but he's unwilling to endure close up the abandon of her pain screams. Emma is tough and stoic. He has never heard her surrender to suffering as she does now, has been doing for hours. His mother gave birth to nine children, four of them younger than Noby, and he can't remember this much upheaval associated with the process. Childbirth is new to his Emma, and he can only hope that his mother's midwifing skills will guide the familiar Emma back to him, that his wife will return to him calm and healthy, she and the new baby.

Sometime soon, within the tight confines of their cabin, Emma will bring new life to this world, a life that promises not only an extension of himself but also of his own father. The birth of his baby turns Noby's thoughts to Israel Smith, and as usual, a flood of images from those last three years of his father's life overshadow the man Noby knew as a boy. He pictures his father sitting up in bed, mute, in the darkened front room of their sharecropper's cabin, or on his better days, in the rocking chair on the front porch, with a grimy black patch covering his right eye. Sometimes Israel refused to wear the patch, his right eye gummed almost shut and terrifying in its hollowness. On those occasions when he walked, Israel leaned heavily on the twisted oak branch he carried at his side. He was able to be on his feet at most only a few hours each day.

For those last three years, Noby's mother, Lucy, took on primary responsibility for Israel, tending him as if he were her tenth child, vulnerable and dependent, cooking down food until it was soft enough for him to eat, changing him, helping him with the chamber pot, taking in washing and fancy ironing by the piece when she could get the work. She didn't complain, she just moved into the breadwinning role.

"Nine mouths to feed day coming in and day going out," she would say. "These children's bellies still get empty no matter what happen in the past."

Noby and David assumed as much of the farmwork and, later, the fieldwork as their size and age allowed. Their father resided in the house with them, all of them, wife and children, but mostly he was not really there. When Noby returned to the cabin in the evening, he undertook his other responsibility, reading to his father, either by the light from the fireplace or occasionally by the light of a precious bit of oil. Noby was clever at scrounging, bringing back scraps of paper with writing on them—old receipts, discarded newspapers, a page from a catalog, a borrowed schoolbook from a neighbor willing to share the prized volume for a few hours. It was only when Noby read aloud that Israel seemed calm and not quite so distant, his mind willing to take a stake in the current world, as if he had stumbled onto a pathway back to the flow of life.

Once, and it had happened only once, not long after everyone wandered off to bed and Noby prepared to do the same, dead on his feet after a long day, Israel called him closer, his leathery hand shaking. The front room was deep in the shadow of evening, with only the light from the moon entering through the single front window and a faint glow from the last embers in the fireplace.

"That day was rigged," Israel said to Noby. His father's voice, barely louder than a whisper, carried a chronic coarseness, but now he dropped the volume even further. "I was wrong, son. Don't never let them put their hands on you."

Noby waited for something more, but his father closed his remaining eye and turned away.

Few of the surviving colored Colfax courthouse men want to share their stories, and the ones who do are immediately shushed by those more cautious. There is a child within earshot, or too much work to do, or a careful life to live. The fear is palpable that somehow the words might carry to the whites, remind them how dangerous these men once were. But it isn't necessary to relive the events, to name the names. Nine years later, retribution still looms large. In the colored community, any public references to April 13, 1873, however veiled, quickly turn dead and silent on the tongue.

Noby's father lived long enough, if you could call it living, to see the end of Reconstruction in Grant Parish, the definitive clanging shut like a heavy iron door, locking out the dreams of the colored courthouse men. Reconstruction passed from potential to unyielding history, a reminiscence, and life in Louisiana returned to its former rigid exclusions. Once open rebellion ended and order was restored, the community slowly shook off the horror. Schools reopened, only for whites, state and parish taxes were collected again, and the police jury, virtually powerless since the fighting, began to exert its authority to undertake the building of a new courthouse to replace the one destroyed during the Easter Sunday battle. By then Israel Smith no longer followed with any interest the goings-on of Colfax, Louisiana, no longer actively participated in the obstinate determination of other families piecing their futures back together in The Bottom.

Noby remembers those days in early spring before Easter and the terror of hiding in the woods, the smallest of details distinct and unshakable, but the whole scorched through in places by the bruising light of time's passage. The intensity of those weeks in 1873 is especially potent in Noby's dreams, enough to bring him fully awake in the middle of the night two or three times a week, unwilling to lie back down for fear of the revisiting. They never leave him completely, the memories. He has trained himself to do without too much sleep.

Today he starts his own legacy. Hansom if it is a boy, and Lenora if a girl. Hansom or Lenora Smith. He badly wants a boy. For six years after his father died, Noby burned with the need to name his first son after Israel. In a moment of brotherly confidence, in an effort to bridge the wide gulf between them, he told David his plan at their father's funeral, sharing with his older brother his desire to honor Israel's memory. David listened, sympathetic, looked him in the face with those cool gray eyes and nodded in support, but when David's own son was born three years ago, his brother named him Israel, as if he had never heard Noby's intent. Now Noby will be forced to settle for a different name.

Hansom is certainly an honorable choice, if it can't be Israel. Hansom Brisco not only saved Noby's life when he was a baby, he is one of the most successful colored men around Colfax, and a worthy namesake. Hansom Brisco owns more land in The Bottom than Sam and Green Tademy combined, an admirable feat.

Another strangled scream from the direction of the house finds its way to Noby, even this far removed in the field. Noby pulls his straw hat down farther, over his ears. He lowers his head, clucks for the mule, and slowly guides the plow forward. There is nothing to do but wait.

* * *

"You got a boy," his mother tells him when she comes for him in the field. Lucy Smith's hair is totally white, sweated through, and plastered close to her head. Her loose housedress has a noticeable dark bloodstain at the hem. When she sees Noby staring at the spot and the alarm on his face, she laughs. "Your son doing fine," she says. "Took his time coming, but now he's here, he not timid."

"Emma, how be Emma?" Noby asks, as his worry shifts to his new wife. Emma is eighteen, same as Noby, a big-boned woman with a burnt-custard tinge to her skin, sturdy but gawky, as if her body is slightly more than she can manage. The real drama of her face is the striking slope of her narrow-slitted, almond-shaped eyes. Her father, China Man Thornton, is the only Chinese man Noby has ever seen, although he disappeared from town shortly after the massacre. When the time came, Noby nervously asked Emma's mother for her daughter's hand in marriage. Her mother said yes, and Emma left them in the front room to dash out to the side yard. With a single-handed twirl, she wrung the neck of a chicken to fry up for their celebration supper. The deal was set.

"She strong, that girl, made for babies, that a fact, but what she need now is rest. Don't worry, I be looking after your wife till her mother come to spell me. Got to get back to my own after that."

By the time Emma's mother, Louisa, arrives two days later, the household is humming with female energy, but little of the bustle is directed toward Noby and his needs. All the commotion mystifies him. There was always a new baby in the house when he was young, spitting up and crying, sleeping and voiding, gurgling and cooing, creating a ruckus, but he is amazed at how much time and attention has to be directed toward this one tiny creature, his son. The baby boy has a thick head of curly black hair and a powerful set of lungs that he uses often, day and night, but to Noby he seems more fragile than he remembers any of his brothers or sisters being at that age. Emma tells him that is only because he just now pays attention.

* * *

Hansom Brisco rides out to the farm a week after the baby comes. Although well into middle age, Hansom is still a powerful-looking man, walnut brown and brawny, with rippling, muscular arms that give confidence he can either guide a plow or deliver a calf.

Noby greets his old friend at the front door with a slap on the back. "You got to be Big Hansom now," Noby says, grinning. "How we tell you and L'il Hansom apart otherwise?"

Hansom looks pleased. "Let me get a look at my godson, see if he look any better than his daddy at that age," he says.

Emma rocks the baby in the front room. She smiles broadly at Hansom and holds up his namesake bundle for him to see.

"You do me honor," Hansom says. "Fine-looking boy. Healthy. Got Emma's eyes too. Thank goodness he take after the mama, not the daddy."

"Difference is, this boy gonna always have enough to eat," says Noby.

Hansom stays as long as etiquette demands, chats with Emma, inquires after her health, holds the baby boy for a few minutes before giving him back to his mother. "Next time I bring the missus and stay longer," he says to Emma. He catches Noby's eye. "Walk me out?" Hansom asks.

Noby clasps the older man around the shoulder and walks beside him to the mare grazing in the front yard.

"David come to me last week asking terms on a piece of my land. Say the two of you considering going in together."

Noby tries not to look surprised. "Me and my brother always talking land. Nothing more important for a colored man than land."

"My hand is out when you ready to get started. Especially now. You know that," Hansom says. "Since the day you wrap your fist around my finger, you been like the son I never had."

"What you done for me and my family already beyond paying back," Noby says. "Emma and me working hard to square the money part of those debts first before adding on."

* * *

After the birth, Emma has a little trouble getting around, nothing serious but enough to keep her closer to home than she would like, and almost three weeks pass before Noby, Emma, and the baby escape the farm for their first real family outing. Jackson Tademy has finally set the wedding day to marry Amy McCullen, and Noby will stand up for his good friend as witness. The ceremony is just immediate family and the closest of friends. Between getting in the crop and the new baby in the house, Noby hasn't seen Jackson in two weeks. Emma bundles the baby, and they make the short wagon ride to Sam Tademy's farm in The Bottom, arriving early, before the minister. It is the first time many of the guests, mostly Tademys, have seen L'il Hansom, and the women ooh and aah over both Emma and the baby.

The heat beats down on the tin roof, turns the farmhouse into a furnace. Within minutes, Emma and L'il Hansom are swept up in preparations inside the house, and Noby drifts outside, where he finds Jackson alone on the back porch.

"Nervous?" Noby asks.

Jackson is slight of stature but athletic, his forehead high, a slight downward hook to the nose, full lips, kinky hair kept close-cropped to his head. The Indian-brown undertone to his skin has turned a bronzy-red from the sun, and he looks especially handsome today. Like his brother Green, Jackson has a distinctive appearance, not just in physical features but in a shared sense of certainty and calm. Except for Green's two-inch advantage in height, they look almost like twins. In fact, they favor each other more as they get older, although they are three years apart. The sharp, chiseled features of Jackson's face are composed, his pants pressed to shininess, and a crisp white handkerchief peeking from his jacket pocket defies the sticky humidity.

Jackson shakes his head. "Not nervous a bit. Just want to get it done."

"What took so long?" Noby teases. "You already old. Twenty

too long to be waiting for the good life. I got me a wife and a baby boy both, and you still in your father's house sharing a single man's bed with your brothers. Amy been on your mind for years."

Noby married when he was seventeen, satisfied Emma was the helpmate he wanted for the rest of his days.

"That's all right," Jackson replies. "Some folks get married just so's they don't have to walk so far on Saturday night."

It is a rare joke from his serious friend, and Noby is pleased that Jackson is in such a good mood. "Amy right under your nose, in the same house, always was too handy for you. Make it easy to put off the wedding day."

"A man got to plan, make hisself ready for the future," says Jackson. "Too many of Amy's menfolk snatched away from her already—father, brother, uncles. My job here on out be providing and protecting, make her life with me built on rock."

"You and Amy a natural pair. Where you gonna live?"

"We stay here at Papa's, on the sleeping porch, until I rent my own farm. A few years more, I be ready to buy my hundred acres."

"Hansom Brisco willing to give me a loan against a plot of his land on Bayou Darrow," Noby says. He debates with himself about how much to admit his misgivings, but he has known Jackson for a long time. "Said David come to him asking after it, but me and Emma already in cash debt to him for getting us through the drought. Can't see going deeper in that hole yet."

"Soon as a man able, he need to get his own land," Jackson says. "Green already working his own place, and he and Papa still talking on starting up the colored school."

"What you think I should do, Jackson? Take on more debt or wait?"

"Ask Green. Or my papa. They the ones know best about land."

"I asked you," says Noby. If there is a fault to Jackson Tademy, it is in refusing to step out of the shadow of his father and brother, underplaying his own value.

"Well, seem to me the real question don't have so much to do with the borrowing. Hansom willing to carry you. Seem like you got your back up more about going in with David."

Noby acknowledges the truth in it. The Tademy brothers are close in ways that Noby feels he will never manage with David.

"How about you? Would you go in with Green on a piece of land?" Noby asks.

"Green don't need me, but I trust him bottom to top. We could work anything out if it come down to it. Papa and Green got the big ideas, bigger than mine. I just want to own a farm, do for my own family."

Noby remembers the day of innocence so many years ago when he and his father left David behind at home to walk to the Colfax courthouse together, just the two of them, and how Noby unlocked the courthouse doors to let the waiting men in. He tries to shake off the image of Israel in his sickbed in the dark front room of their cabin a few weeks later. "You and Green always together, shoulder to shoulder, like brothers supposed to be. I'm not sure David and me got it in us to do that."

"The two of you always been oil and water, but at the end of the day, you family, and family does for family."

The wedding is a small affair, held in the front room of Sam Tademy's four-room cabin in The Bottom. There are twenty guests squeezed into the cramped, sweltering space. Each has some sort of fan, paper or cardboard, decorated or plain, formal or impromptu, some the size of an open hand and inconspicuous, others bigger than a man's head. There isn't even a slight breeze passing through the house, the air so clammy and still that the simple act of inhalation feels like drawing down a lungful of heated water.

The minister is a big man, with jiggling rolls of fat at the jowls and around his midsection, and swollen hands the size of small hams. He fidgets more than any of the guests in the front room, wheezing and sweating profusely. He refuses to take off his dark jacket, as some of the other men have done in the overwhelming heat, sacrificing some small measure of relief and comfort in favor of honoring his official position, signifying the formality of the occasion. During the ceremony over which he presides, he juggles his small black Bible, his white handkerchief, and his stiff cardboard fan, passing them from hand to hand as he uses each in turn.

All the guests suffer through the ceremony, praying not only for a happy life for Jackson and Amy but for the minister to hurry and get to the *I dos* so they can find a less oppressive spot to stand or at least get to a drink to cool them down. Amy makes a radiant young bride, the excitement of the ceremony and adoration of her new husband evident in her broad face. She wears a simple brown cotton dress, neither too tight nor too loose, and has pinned a long, trailing piece of white gauze in her hair that falls along either side of her plump cheeks, follows the shape of her shoulders, and ends down below her waist. Green Tademy serves as best man, and his wife stands up for Amy.

Afterward, Noby and Green Tademy witness the proceedings and sign the papers for the minister to record at the courthouse. The guests linger, though not for too long. There is food, simple yet plentiful, enough to last for several days, but there are chores at home to tend, and the blistering day has taken its toll. After conveying good wishes to the bride and groom, and congratulating the parents, most of the attendees drift away, walking or riding back to their own daily obligations, their own farms, leaving Jackson Tademy and Amy McCullen admitted into the inner sanctum of the married world.

Noby is pleased his friend has found his way there at last.

Figure 14. Jackson Tademy   *Figure 15. Amy McCullen Tademy*

22

1 8 8 6

*I*n the winter of 1886, on the Saturday night after Thanksgiving, Jackson and Amy startle awake. A shrill cow horn blows in front of their cabin. It is close to eleven, and the blast screeches again through the quiet of nighttime. Jackson gets up to look out the front window, protected only by the warmth from his thick union suit, but he knows who it is. Sure enough, Green stands outside, waiting in the front yard.

Jackson's initial groggy irritation evaporates. His older brother's enthusiasm always infects him. Jackson Tademy has grown into manhood the way a child grows into hand-me-down clothes, at first straining to fill out the cloth, but by and by outstripping the limitations of the garment. His growth spurts were late, and when they came, each gave him hope that he had the potential to catch up to the height, if not the stature, of his older brother. He never has. Green holds the edge.

"Come out. We going hunting," Green calls. Both Green and Jackson's smooth skin is the same reddish-brown shade, their cheekbones as high and sharp as if chiseled by a sculptor's knife, wide foreheads that make them appear engrossed in deep, meaningful thought. The particular arrangement of their features conveys an almost regal persona, but Green has an extra sparkle to his eyes that Jackson does not, reflects an amused contemplation of life's absurdities and a warning of impending, good-hearted mischief in the planning.

Green's bloodhound, Jack, sits obediently at his feet, a short, heavy cord of twisted hemp looped around his neck.

"You lost your mind, making a racket, coming this late?" Jackson asks. By then he stands at the front door, and Amy, in her long nightgown, is out of bed too, peeking out from behind his shoulder into the darkness outside. "Decent people already asleep."

"Then let's not be decent," Green says. "Right, Noby?"

Noby Smith steps forward a half-step into the small circle of lamplight and mumbles something incoherent, trailing off. Obviously, he too was asleep before Green's hunting decision.

"No need being in the woods with a gun this time of night," says Jackson.

"How long you gonna act like a woman around a gun, Little Brother? Amy can spare you for a few hours. Right, Amy? 'Specially if there's possum for tomorrow's dinner in the bargain, yes?"

"We still got chicken left over," Jackson objects.

"Then we go for the sport and sell the pelts," says Green. "Better I ask Amy or you, Little Brother?"

Amy speaks up: "There's no gain stepping between brothers." She is extraordinarily fond of Green and always allows herself to be charmed by his sassy talk. "Jackson his own man. He make up his own mind how to spend his time, long as he sitting next to me in church tomorrow morning."

"We not leaving without you, Little Brother. We got a head start on the season. It's possum-hunting time."

"Come on, Jackson," pleads Noby. "Sooner we get out there, sooner I get back to my warm bed."

"Guess I got no choice," says Jackson.

"Bring another lamp and a gunnysack, Little Brother," Green says. "And a couple sweet potatoes."

"Dig 'em up your own self while I put something on," says Jackson. "Second row in the garden."

Jackson dresses for the cold night ahead, grumbling and complaining to Amy as he pulls on his boots, but they both know he looks forward to being with Green and Noby. Regrets won't come until after the rising sun brings light to the obligations of morning.

Green decides to head north. If it were daytime, they would climb trees they know have rotted cavities in the trunks where possums hide to sleep, sometimes fifteen or more feet off the ground. On a lucky day, they might find a possum in a hollow stump almost at ground level, no climbing required. Night hunting is different. Jack is crucial, an impressive possum-hunting dog, steady and reliable, sniffing and scouting until he catches the scent. He doesn't get overly excited, either in the tracking or in the treeing. The hound stalks his quarry until the panicky possum scrambles up the nearest tree to escape, and then Jack positions himself at the base of the trunk, trapping his prey in the branches, barking until the hunters catch up.

Jackson, Green, and Noby walk an even tempo for about an hour, giving the dog his head and following his lead, until they are three or four miles from home. Jackson senses a long night ahead. He is familiar enough with his older brother's moods to sense Green won't be satisfied with one or even two possums. The three friends have hunted together for years, both in daylight and in the darkness of night, and know both the terrain and one another intimately.

"You see now why I call my dog Jack," says Green.

"Why's that?" asks Noby.

"Only one thing on his mind at a time," says Green. "When Jack thinks possum, long as we follow, he lead us to possum. Now, if he was back home, he'd be thinking on the she-dog next door, and if a possum come up and spit in his eye, he wouldn't pay it no mind." Green claps Jackson on the back, rubs his head with his knuckles, grins. "Concentration, one thing at a time, smart and dependable, just like Jackson here."

It is almost as if they are carefree boys, without responsibilities or regrets, not men of twenty-seven and twenty-four. Green got the height while Jackson got the speed. Green is bold and Jackson single-minded. Green developed flair and Jackson doggedness. An instinctive ability to conceptualize the big picture comes as naturally to Green as breathing, while Jackson's gift is his attention to detail. Green is charming and Jackson logical. Green makes things happen, can bend people to his way of seeing even if they are at first baffled by the novelty of his proposed ideas. Green is responsible, as is Jackson, but effortlessly and charismatically, without ever having to resort to heavy-handedness or preachiness.

Jack takes off after something deeper in the woods, and they lose sight of him, but they aren't worried. Jack will let them know where he is when the time comes. Before long, they hear his trademark yapping.

"He got one," Noby yells, and the three of them push through the trees toward the sound, careful not to spill kerosene from the lamps. Jack howls steadily, snout pointed upward at the base of a small sweet-gum tree dwarfed by the pines and oaks on either side. Green lifts the lamp to throw light onto the limbs, and they see the two glistening red pinpoints of the animal's eyes directed at them from a lower branch. The twist of the possum's long ratlike tail arches backward over its own rear end, like a sideways horseshoe.

"It's a clean shot," says Green. "Use my gun and take him, Jackson."

"No," says Jackson.

"You can get him between the eyes."

"The tree's small enough to jiggle him down," says Jackson. He begins to push and pull at the base of the sweet gum, shaking the upper branches. Green shrugs, resigned, puts down his gun, and joins him. Soon all three of them are at the trunk, while the dog circles, yipping all the while. After ten minutes of jerking the tree, the possum loses its hold and comes skittering to the ground.

The possum curls into itself and doesn't move. It is a fleshy, full-grown animal, almost two feet long before adding in the solid whip of tail, and it looks as if it knocked itself out in the fall. Its eyes are closed, and there is no evidence of breathing or motion. Jack snarls and barks but keeps his distance. The possum appears dead, but they have all been fooled too many times to trust their eyes.

"Bring the sack," calls Jackson.

He advances toward the possum with caution, prepared to jump back if the animal is alive. Green and Noby spread the lip of the gunnysack wide, and Jackson grabs the heavy creature by its long tail and lets it dangle. The possum hangs free, without fight, and in one swinging motion, Jackson drops it into the gunnysack. They tie the rope tight around the top to seal it in.

"Our first one," says Green, stretching his arms in front and back to get the blood circulating. "Woulda been easier to shoot it out the tree. For all that shaking you made us do, you get to carry the sack," he says to Jackson.

Green calls Jack to his side with one low whistle, gives him a pat on the head, and sends him off on a new hunt. Again Jack puts snout to ground and sniffs, widening his circle farther and farther out until he has left the men behind. "Next possum be even bigger," says Green.

"This the last one," Jackson says as they keep in the direction of Jack's trail. "Can't be staying out here all night."

"We done it before," says Noby. "'Course, that was before I had a wife and three children at home."

Jack hits the second trail almost right away, no more than fifteen minutes from the first. Once more they hear his baying as he chases his quarry, then the change in his bark when he has it cornered up a tree.

Green, Jackson, and Noby aren't far behind. This time the possum stares down from an old oak, far enough up the tree to make the idea of shaking it out impossible. Jack keeps up a series of throaty howls.

"This one gotta be shot down," says Green. "Who it gonna be, me or you, Noby?"

"Your gun," says Noby.

"Watch how it's done, gentlemens," Green says. Noby and Jackson hold the lamps up to give him as much visibility as possible. Green takes his time, steadying the .22-caliber rifle, aiming and adjusting in tiny increments. The blast when he pulls back on the trigger is deafening to Jackson. He hates guns.

The possum falls from the tree, crashing through the lowest branches of the oak as it picks up speed, bouncing off the trunk. When the heavy body hits the ground, it lands on one side. The bullet has taken part of the head and cheek, exposing the animal's grayish-pink tongue and several dirty, sharp yellow teeth covered with bits of debris and blood. There is no question this possum is dead.

"This spot good as any for the fire," says Green.

Green pulls his knife and skins the second possum, while Jackson and Noby gather up kindling and wood. In no time they have two fires going, one large and blazing, for warmth, and the other lower and slower, for roasting. Green carefully unties the top of the gunnysack and throws the bloody pelt inside, quickly tying it shut again. No use taking a chance with the captured possum. Tomorrow he will turn the pelt inside out, pull it over a long tapered board, and let it dry on the stretcher in the smokehouse. He finds a long, forked branch and skewers the gutted possum, taking the first turn holding it over the slow fire.

When the fire dies down enough, they bury the sweet potatoes deep in the hot ashes to cook, and settle in to wait. The three men sit between their two fires, sprawled on the hard ground.

"Spell me," calls Green, and Noby rouses himself. Green passes the chore of holding the possum above the flame to Noby, brings out his corncob pipe and tobacco pouch, leans his back against a log, and relaxes. They wait in quiet for the possum to cook through and the potatoes to go soft in their skins. Jack lies at Green's feet.

"What you got to say now about how late it be?" asks Green.

Jackson and Noby both laugh. "Nothing beats a warm fire and a rumbling belly about to be filled," says Jackson.

"Nothing better than a night hunt," Green says. "We been doing this together a long time."

"Thirteen years," says Jackson.

"Since we was boys," replies Noby. "Your papa first took us out together."

A sudden silence, heavy and dark, presses down on the group in the woods, as if an uninvited guest has appeared from nowhere and joined them around the fire.

"Nothing like that night," Green finally says. He gets up to throw another log on the fire, poking at it far longer than necessary. The mood has turned sour. Green sits down again. "Shoulda brought the women," he says lightly. "They'd tend the possums while we set Jack loose for another one."

"We got enough," says Jackson. The tranquillity of being in the woods on a clear, untroubled night with his friend and brother is fading away, and he suddenly pictures Amy and the children asleep in the cabin. He wants to go back to them. "We still got the possum in the sack to deal with."

"Tomorrow's soon enough for the flat part of a shovel to its head," says Green.

"Least we won't be picking out lead from the meat of that one," says Jackson.

"We need one more," says Green. "Then we each got one pelt."

"Time to start back. You and Noby take the pelts," says Jackson. "Church come early."

Jackson thinks Green will protest, but his brother begins to break down their little camp, kicking dirt to smother the flames, gathering the lamps and gunnysacks. They walk south, in the direction of home, each lost to his own thoughts. They make good time, already back in The Bottom when Noby calls out "Whoa" and stops dead in his tracks. In the middle of the path, directly in front of them, a skunk stands motionless, tail up, waiting. The wide stripe down its back is unmistakable, a white so bright it seems to glimmer in the moonlight.

The three men freeze.

"You carrying the gun, Jackson," says Green. "Shoot him before he let go the spray."

Jack has gotten ahead, and when he circles back and catches sight of the skunk, he bristles and starts yipping.

"Quit it, Jack," Green says softly. Although the dog doesn't advance, he continues to growl. The skunk just watches them, tail lifted, part of a motionless tableau. It is a standoff.

"Shoot, Jackson," Green scolds. He is angry now. "You the one in range."

Jackson doesn't move, and Green inches toward him slowly. Jack won't back off, and now he barks wildly, makes an abortive lunge at the skunk from the side.

Green grabs for the rifle, snatching it by the barrel out of Jackson's leaden hands. The skunk chooses that moment to release a noxious stream of spray, and Jackson feels a sharp stinging in his eyes and recoils against the sharp, piercing smell. Green fumbles with the grip of the gun and drops the rifle, stock side down. Jackson's eyes burn and begin to water, and he thinks of the disgusting odor and how much Amy will complain about having to get the smell from his clothes. The gun goes off close to his ear, and suddenly, Green is on the ground at his feet.

Jackson drops to his knees. The stench is overpowering, settling over them like smoke, and Jack starts to whimper. Jackson
and Noby roll Green over on his back carefully, but they can't find
a wound. He is unconscious, bleeding from his ear and nose.

"Maybe he hit his head on a rock," says Noby.

"We got to get him to help," says Jackson.

Jackson scoops Green into his arms while Noby retrieves the
rifle. Jackson starts a fast walk, his brother heavy in his arms. He
begins to trot, faster, and then he is running. He hears Noby and the
hound behind him but doesn't turn to see where they are. He runs
in the direction of his father's cabin, closer than Green's house, until
he thinks his knees will collapse, the weight of his brother's body
increasing with each stride. Jackson falls back into a trot.

"Let me carry him the rest of the way," Noby calls from behind.

Jackson hears Noby, is aware of everything. The choking odor
of the skunk spray, the brightness of the constellations in the clear
night sky, the distance he judges to be about half a mile between
his father's farmhouse and where they are, the abandoned possum
in the gunnysack, maybe dead and maybe alive in its sealed prison
back at the camp, the increasing heaviness of his brother and how
stiff he feels in his arms. His practical mind fights with his need to
hold on. He cannot force himself to allow Noby to carry Green.
He can't. It is only a matter of yards to his papa's house. Everything will be fine.

They holler as they approach Sam's farmhouse, calling for
everyone to wake up. It is at least three in the morning, but by the
time Jackson carries Green up the steps and into the front room of
his father's house, Sam Tademy is out of bed and mobilized. Jackson lays Green flat on his back on the sofa, on bedclothes still
warm from his youngest brother, who was sleeping there just a few
minutes before. The front room reeks with the scent of skunk and
the fear they bring inside with them.

"Accident" is all Jackson can say to his father, apologetic.

Sam rushes to his oldest son, laid out on the sofa. Green's face is grayish, devoid of animation, his head rigid and at a peculiar angle to the rest of his body. Dried blood dots his nose, ears, and cheeks. Polly runs into the front room in her nightgown and bare feet, stops short of the sofa. She takes one look.

"Lord, my boy is dead," she moans.

Sam looks from Green's inert body on the sofa to where Jackson is hunched in fatigue, splattered with blood, drenched in the sweat of failure. Sam takes Green's hand, already stiffening and cool to the touch, in one of his own. There is a private moment between father and son before Sam looks to Jackson again in disbelief, stares at him with eyes so dark there seems to be no reflection. Then he turns back and closes Green's eyelids with his free hand.

"I couldn't save him, Papa," Jackson whispers.

Sam never looks up, never diverts his gaze away from his dead son's face. Even so, Jackson feels the chill wind of accusation.

The day after, Jackson sleeps late. Amy comes to him twice, shakes him by the shoulder.

"Your father be expecting you," she says. "Breakfast waiting on the table."

Reluctantly, Jackson forces himself out of bed and reaches for yesterday's clothes on the bedroom hook. All save his jacket are gone. He remembers then that they were splattered with his brother's blood. Amy must have taken them to wash. His other cotton shirt is laid out on her side of the bed, starched and ironed, along with an old pair of patched dark trousers. His jacket is still wet in spots where she scrubbed at the blood. Amy must not have gone back to bed at all after he came home with the news.

They eat in silence, Amy serving. Even the children, young as they are, seem to know that this morning won't tolerate any challenges. Nathan-Green and Andrew don't say a word, and Jackson finds himself lost in his own thoughts, dreading the trip, loath to see his father again. As if the longer he sits at the table, the more unlikely it is his brother is really gone. As if by walking to Sam Tademy's farmhouse, he condemns Green to death all over again.

Jackson rises from the table and puts on his hat.

"Wasn't your fault," Amy says to him as he leaves. "Your papa gotta be hurting too."

Despite the cold, Sam Tademy is on the front porch when Jackson arrives, a horse blanket wrapped around his shoulders.

"Rigging around the waterwheel shaft on the gristmill need mending," Sam says to Jackson before his foot even touches the bottom porch step.

Sam has worked tirelessly for years to carve out a section of The Bottom as a community of Tademys, determined to uncouple his future from the town of Colfax wherever he can. They always have two or three communal projects in the works—irrigating the fields, fashioning a makeshift mill, shoring up the barn, expanding the church, digging a well, rigging up a gin for removing the seeds from the cotton fiber they harvest, building a windmill.

"I'll get on it, Papa," says Jackson.

Polly Tademy comes out to the front porch, drawn by the voices. Her face is full of grief, and her eyes are red and drooped. Jackson is tentative, not certain what to do, but Polly walks down the steps and draws him to her, wraps her arms tightly around him, and doesn't release him.

"Our Green is gone," she says into Jackson's ear. "Back with his Maker."

Jackson is taller than Polly now, but he is taken back to a time when she made him feel small and safe.

"A sad morning, Jackson," she says. She releases him and looks deep into his face. "Amy feed you?"

"Yes, ma'am." The mere thought of going back into his father's house after last night is unbearable. "Green still inside?" he asks cautiously.

"His wife come already and carry him away in the wagon," says Polly. "Mary take the body to their farm. Service be Sunday." She walks back up the steps and stops to tighten the horse blanket around Sam's shoulders, a protective gesture. He doesn't respond. "I'ma bring out some coffee. The two of you needs to talk."

Jackson remains standing at the base of the steps. "Papa, when we was hunting last night—"

"Time running out for me and the school, Jackson," Sam interrupts. "You know how much your brother committed to starting up a colored school."

"That your dream, Papa. Yours and Green's," Jackson says softly.

"We not talking Green now. We talking about you. Why a man so fond of books not ready to take up his duty? Tademy men does three things. We farm, we preach, and we teach. Nothing help the colored man so much as education."

Jackson has heard this all his life, and he believes in the liberating power of education as much as his father and Green. A world of the mind opened up for him as soon as he learned to read, and he can hardly imagine his life without the comfort of words on paper. But no matter, day-to-day reality is an endless landscape of unfurrowed rows to plow, crops to harvest, fences to mend, animals to tend. Yet his father asks a good question. There is a gnawing of something unknown in Jackson, maybe unknowable, that he can't articulate. The absence of some undefined, missing thing in his life hurts him almost as a physical pain. Maybe his calling is as an educator, the direction his father is pushing him so very soon after Green is gone. Jackson knows at a fundamental level that he wants to do more, be more than a farmer. He has a deep respect for men who bring bounty from the earth, and he works harder at farming than anyone he knows, but even when he punishes his body in service to the soil, he feels there is something different, more satisfying, he could do given the chance.

What Jackson loves passionately, besides Amy and the children, is not music, not politics, not farming, but the clean precision of numbers, of groupings. Plowing tires his body, but figuring how a field should be planted, subdividing sections and forecasting the potential yield, calculating probabilities and comparing combinations, those are the things that unshackle his mind and give him joy. He spends hours designing layouts in his head while he labors behind the broad haunches of a mule.

"I want my own land, Papa," Jackson says. "I'm working every hour of the day and most of the night to save enough to buy my first piece."

"Amy a strong girl. She make up the slack, take in washing, tend a bigger garden so you can sell off the crop."

"No woman of mine serve white or work the field," Jackson snaps. "Ever."

He regrets his tone as soon as the words are out. He turns his back to his father and collects himself, then faces him again. "Amy's only job is to take care of me and take care of the children."

"You got high-flying notions, son. Polly wouldn't never stand for that. That woman at my side come flood or famine. You can't shake off your responsibilities. God, family, community. We in service to all three."

"My God help me be responsible to my family," Jackson says, defensive. Jackson won't allow his wife to drain herself as he has seen Polly drained. He believes it is as much a man's duty to shield his wife as to provide food for the household.

Sam doesn't budge. Jackson recognizes the look his father puts on when he lays down the law and expects to be obeyed.

"Colfax need a colored school," Sam says, standing to signal the conversation is drawing to a close. "Not many able to send their children off to Montgomery. We done it for you, scraped so's you get yours, and now Green gone, you the one most able to make a way for others. Those that can, do. Time to step up, son."

Green is less than one day cold, and their father wants to push all responsibility on Jackson. He can't refute his father's logic. He is obligated to family, and community, and has been given more than most. Still, he feels he is being pressed into something when all he wants is to take care of his own. He isn't willing. He isn't ready.

Green Tademy, the chosen son, is dead. Green leaves behind three children and a pregnant wife, and a cleft in Jackson's heart so hollow that he doesn't know how he can possibly fill it.

For twenty-four years, Jackson has defined himself by the yardstick of his family, confident and secure of his place deep in the shade of his father's shadow, grounded in his role as Green's younger, quieter brother. Even after he's married, rented his own farm, and had two children of his own, people in The Bottom see him this way too.

The turnout is large for Green Tademy's funeral, and members of the colored community come to The Bottom from as far away as Pineville to pay their respects. They feel robbed, family and non-family alike. Green represented the best of them—young, God-fearing, intelligent, hardworking, well spoken, respected, sociable.

Jackson stands with the rest of the family at the grave site, shoulder to shoulder with his father, next in line in the broken-legacy chain, in between Sam and his younger siblings, and waits for the pine box to be lowered into the yawning, freshly dug hole. He can't bear to look his father in the eye, as if Sam knows that Jackson's refusal to fire a gun at a startled skunk led to this.

Of all of them, Sam Tademy seems most composed. He has slowed in the last five years as he inches toward sixty-six, more calculation in his step, his hair now totally white under his brown fedora with the heron feather, the hat McCully gave him in the courthouse years before. Others cry, but Sam is a block of stone, and when mourners approach him in commiseration, he extends his swollen, arthritic fingers in a gesture of handshake, but he lets the condolences fall around him without taking comfort. The only weakness he allows himself is his tilt toward Polly, who stands by his side.

At the grave site, Jackson feels like an imposter. If one of the Tademy boys had to be taken early, removed from the world, it should have by all rights been him. He is a poor substitute for Green Tademy.

Days and then weeks pass, and one morning in mid-December, Amy shakes off the gloom and throws herself into celebrating Christmas. She cooks for three solid days leading up to the holiday, claiming a side of pork from Jackson's smokehouse. She picks winter squash and beans, pulls out preserves and fruits canned during the summer, and uses precious sugar from the general store to bake cakes and pies the boys love. She hums to herself as she works, church hymns, and they hold back from talking about Green. Jackson works longer hours than ever, but even he begins to feel a taste of the excitement, despite himself. A bit of the caution and tiptoeing in the cabin dissipates. The boys respond to the change in mood immediately and, with so much sugar coursing through their systems, are constantly underfoot.

After supper on the Saturday evening before Christmas, Jackson decides not to go back out to plow and to enjoy the evening with his family. He settles in his favorite chair by the fireplace and savors the rare idleness. His sons play on the floor at his feet as Amy washes supper dishes in the back of the house. Not used to sitting still, Jackson dozes.

"Nathan-Green!" Amy's scolding voice cuts into his sleep, and he opens his eyes. Amy stands in the hall with her hands on her hips and a dishcloth draped over her shoulder, speaking to their oldest son. "Come away from there right now," she says. "You know not to touch Papa's book."

"That's all right," Jackson says to Amy. "Bring it here, Nathan-Green."

The little boy looks back and forth between his mother and father and gingerly picks up the slim volume, as if there is a trick involved.

"Rough handling of a book won't never be tolerated in this house, L'il Man," Jackson says. "But if your mama or me in the room, and you treat a book with respect, I let you sit beside me and listen to me read. You understand?"

Nathan-Green nods and comes and sits stiffly next to his father.

"Get your brother, and the two of you shout out for me."

This is more familiar territory for Nathan-Green. He jumps up, pulls Andrew to his feet, cups his hands around his mouth, and yells, "My name is Nathan-Green Tademy." He looks to his father for approval. He helps his little brother put his chubby hands on either side of his mouth and prompts him until the two-year-old says, "My name Andew Tadmy."

"That's very fine," says Jackson. "Now the two of you come sit, and we gonna read."

Jackson stabs with the pitchfork at the hard soil packed down from winter and unearths the coffee can buried in the yard behind the cabin. He removes the notes inside and counts. Two hundred and seventy-three dollars. He smooths the money, folds the stack of bills, and pushes them deep into his pantaloon pocket, leaving the coins in the can. He reburies the canister, brushing over the dirt and covering it with debris as if no one has been there. The mule is cooperative when he unhitches it from the plow, and Jackson sets out for Widow Cruikshank's place.

Three workers till in her field. He goes around back and taps on the screened door of the main house, hat in hand, and Widow Cruikshank herself answers.

"Jackson Tademy," she says, as if he comes calling at her property every day. "How's the family?"

Widow Cruikshank is the same age as his father, white hair carelessly pulled back in a bun, the roly-poly outlines of her body barely contained by the patterned shirtwaist dress and white apron over the top. A small girl, her youngest granddaughter, peers out from the folds of her skirt, staring at Jackson with fascination. Widow Cruikshank is long used to living without a husband, surrounded as she is by sons, daughters, in-laws, and their children, who have never moved beyond the boundaries of this farm.

"Fine, ma'am," Jackson says. "Amy sent this mayhaw pie for you. When Nathan-Green seen me carry it out the house, he put up a fuss until she promise to make him another. L'il Man love his sweets."

Widow Cruikshank sets the pie on the table and comes back to the doorway. "Thank Amy for us." She waits, but Jackson doesn't speak. "And your father?"

"Stubborn as ever," he wants to say, but says instead, "He put up a new roof on the church last week."

"And the school?" she asks.

"Hasn't got to the colored school yet." Jackson knows Widow Cruikshank is sympathetic to the idea of educating colored children, but still, it is a mistake to volunteer too much information.

"I know it was a great blow to him when Green passed. That takes the wind out, a child going before the parent. You tell him for me to keep his faith about the school." Again she waits for Jackson to initiate the reason for his visit. "What can I do for you today?" she finally says.

"I come to talk land," Jackson blurts out. "The piece along Walden Bayou. Assuming you still ready to sell."

"It is for sale," she says. "Sitting idle for three years, since the '83 hailstorm. I'd let it go for five hundred dollars. Let's go on the back porch and see what you got."

"Not five hundred dollars," says Jackson.

"There's a hundred acres, a clean bayou full of fish, good planting land for a man willing to work. A good place to raise a family."

"Yes, ma'am, but it flood every year or two, regular. Got to figure on losing some crops, moving the family in and out whenever the water come."

"We all got to live with that," Widow Cruikshank says. "You wouldn't be here at all if you couldn't. Land goes for eight to ten dollars an acre. I'm offering it to you for five because of your family."

"I got two hundred now," Jackson says. He doesn't reach into his pants to pull the folding money out, but the weight and bulk reassure him. "The rest I work off over time."

"That sit fine with me. You not afraid of honest labor. There's even some things around here needs doing, odd jobs. And Amy can wash and cook."

Jackson smooths himself out before opening his mouth. "Yes, ma'am, any work here *I* can do, just let me know, I be here. I'm looking to move my family soon, so I can still plant for the season."

"If you come up with three hundred by the end of the year, I'll take the note at eight percent, another hundred payable the end of '87, and a final payment of a hundred the end of '88."

Jackson makes calculations in his head. He has to buy seed, keep his family and his animals going, risk a bad crop year, maybe two, borrow equipment from his father. He is already plowing his field close to home by the moonlight and entangled in countless Tademy projects. Where will the hours come from? Widow Cruikshank is no nonsense when it comes to her land and her finances, but Jackson knows he is getting as good a deal as he is likely to get. And she is willing to loan him the money over time and give him work around her place.

"Yes, ma'am. Three hundred by the end of the year. How soon I can move?"

"Soon's I draw the papers," she says. "And thanks for the pie. You be sure to give my regards to Amy, you hear?"

23

1 8 9 1

O n a hot, bright Sunday in June 1891, Jackson Tademy finishes his early-morning chores around the farm and joins his family for a breakfast of biscuits, ham, and eggs. Amy gathers the boys, and they set out for the short walk to Mount Pilgrim Rest Baptist Church, just past the last bridge straddling Walden Bayou. Jackson's youngest brother is pastor and Jackson serves as deacon, teaching Bible lessons in the small clapboard building erected by Sam Tademy. It seems everyone is out and about in The Bottom at nine o'clock in the morning, young and old, most on their way to one church or another, or coming back from the bayou with a bamboo pole and a bucket of fresh-caught fish. Others settle on their front porches in advance of the worst of the heat, keeping their hands useful, shelling peas for dinner and swatting flies.

There is a sameness to the weeks and months in The Bottom for most all of the families living there, varied only by change in season and change in crop. For Jackson Tademy, the midweek's backbreak is punctuated by Saturdays spent laboring on his father's farm, and Sunday church service that stretches from early morning into early afternoon.

Soon it will be time to make the trip into Colfax to pay property taxes at the courthouse before they go past due. Each of the past five years, as land registered under his name has increased, Jackson has retrieved an ever larger fistful of coins from the tin can buried in the back under the crepe myrtle tree to satisfy the assessor. In town, he counts out the coins and drops them into the white man's waiting hand, lingering at the side counter for the precious receipt that proves the land belongs to him and no one else for yet another year. On his 142 acres, he oversees two mules, two colts, two yoke oxen, twenty-seven cattle, assorted chickens and pigs, and not only one but two wagons for transport and hauling.

Week in and week out, month after month, Jackson toils in his growing expanse of cotton and cornfields, harvests the grove of pecan trees growing wild on his property, cultivates his vegetable gardens, attempts to keep pace with the ongoing upkeep of the farmhouse by reinforcing a leaking roof, shoring up the sagging porch, or stabilizing the hardpan foundation threatening to sink one corner of the modest four-room cabin he has erected on the southernmost triangle of his land. Without complaint, he contributes his dollars, ingenuity, and sweat in service to the omnipresent parade of communal Tademy projects.

Jackson tends his stock and takes on as many odd jobs for cash, barter, or goodwill as he can squeeze into the day. He often works so long and late that he leaves Amy at the kitchen stove in her nightdress in the morning, and by the time he drags his tired body through the front door at night, she has already changed back into the nightdress for bed. But he is a young man, strong and determined, and no one's life is easy in The Bottom. He has fathered three healthy children, all boys, and planted a fourth due before the end of the year, just beginning to show in the thickening of Amy's waist and the by-now recognizable change in her walk.

Jackson and Amy never miss a Sunday in the small white one-room building at the edge of a clearing in the center of The Bottom. The building smells of dampness, whether summer or winter, equally capable of holding on to the heat and humidity on the hot days or a moist chill on the cold ones, but none among them can imagine spending their Sunday anywhere other than inside the cramped room. All the Tademys worship there, each of Sam Tademy's children and their families. The communal center provides religious, spiritual, creative, and social interaction.

The church is one large unpartitioned space with several rows of long benches and a pine table and single chair for the pastor's corner. Sam insisted the two small windows under the eaves be located high above eye level, so the church is often dim even when the sun is at its brightest outside, both because of the positioning of the building east to west and because the only other opening that admits light is the single door, if open. Jackson would have preferred more windows, both larger so more sunshine could find its way into the room and lower so those inside could look out onto the flat landscape of the Louisiana bottomlands, but Sam was adamant that no such thing take place. "We do God's work inside and out," said Sam, "but while we in the Lord's house, no reason to let the mind stray and be tempted to forget why we come here."

Jackson worries they are late and quickens his step, not wanting to deal with the silent scowl his father reserves each week for whoever is the last of the Tademy brothers to arrive. Jackson carries their youngest boy in his arms so Amy won't have to. She says she feels fine, that it is too early in the pregnancy to make a fuss, and what does he think she does when he isn't there during the other days of the week? But it makes Jackson feel good to lead his family to the church on Sunday, the five of them a unit, healthy and full of vitality, for the entire world to see. Sam Tademy is always first to the church on Sunday mornings, greeting each arriving member as if he is the pastor of Mount Pilgrim Rest, not his son James, welcoming and shaking hands before they pass through the door to go inside.

Jackson rounds the corner of the church, but instead of Sam at the front door, three of his brothers wait outside in the heat, scanning the landscape.

"Papa not here yet," James says. Worry lines the smooth features of the preacher's face. "We send Billy off to fetch him."

No sooner has he finished speaking than they hear the commotion of a wagon, with Billy at the reins and Sam and Polly sitting behind. Sam usually takes pride in walking the ten minutes to the church from his farmhouse, regardless of weather. The wagon rolls to a stop at the front door, and Jackson and James take care in helping Sam down. Sam winces but doesn't complain when touched. His bronzy-brown skin seems grayish and drained of color, and he sweats profusely even though the day hasn't yet heated to its full potential. When Jackson takes hold of Sam's arm, he notices pinhead-sized red spots under the skin on the backs of his father's callused hands, and a small bruise the size of a copper penny at his wrist, just below the sleeve of his jacket. Lately, it seems any contact at all leaves Sam damaged and discolored.

"Church won't wait," Sam says, blinking, his eyes watery and irritated by the sun's glare. This last bout of flu and fever, or whatever it is, has lingered more than a month, and they all worry, but no one can convince Sam to stay in bed.

The brothers help Sam inside the church. They move the lone straight-backed chair, usually reserved for the preacher, alongside the first narrow bench and sit him at the end of the front pew, closest to the pulpit-table. Jackson sits on the bench next to Polly. The church can accommodate forty men, women, and children, if they squeeze in close on the five long pine benches. A flat table covered with a length of cotton material angles the wall farthest from the front door, serving as preaching space and pulpit.

There is Sunday school for the children first, and then they all move into the singing, preaching, and praying. Reverend James delivers a sermon on the wages of sin, coming in at just under an hour, cut short out of deference to Sam's stamina. Shortly after noon, they bow their heads for a final prayer and prepare to return home for dinner. Jackson tries to help Sam outside to the wagon, but his father waves him off.

"Come 'round the house next week before Saturday," Sam says to Jackson. "The gristmill broke again."

"I'll come by today," says Jackson. He thinks of the backlog of chores around his own farm and when he can possibly get to them.

"I'm a little peaked today," Sam says. "Next week good enough."

Jackson is relieved. He still has to lip up the soil in the cotton in the north field, reshoe one of the horses, and mend the fence where it is down in two places, chores that will take the better part of the afternoon and much of the evening.

His relief is short-lived.

"You and me got serious talking to do," Sam says.

Late that afternoon, after the long church services all over The Bottom are finished, Jackson struggles with the plow in the near field while Amy fixes supper. A clattering buckboard wagon approaches the farm in a cloud of dust. It is his friend Noby, wife and five children in tow. Jackson has barely seen Noby, except in passing, for almost two months. Jackson makes a quick calculation. Tomorrow he must clean up the spent cornstalks at Widow Cruikshank's, and unless he finishes plowing the north field before then, he will fall more hopelessly behind. The moon is due to be full tonight, so he decides to take the mule out later in the evening and plow. Jackson untethers himself from his ox and guides the beast back toward the house.

"It's been too long," Jackson says in greeting, clapping Noby on the back.

Between planting, harvesting, hustling work for cash, laboring at the church, and family obligations, Jackson hardly has time to miss Noby Smith, but miss him he does. He and Amy are never at a want for company in The Bottom, surrounded as they are with so many members of his family. Since Noby threw his lot in with his brother David and moved east to Bayou Darrow to jointly farm forty acres, Jackson and Noby have drifted apart unwillingly, two men with good intentions staggering under the weight of making a respectable life, even though they live less than two miles from each other. They attend different churches now, concentrating on their own families and their own business. A conspicuous absence remains, like a missing tooth, an untold joke, or an unshared story, a withered connection.

Noby, rail-thin as he has been since boyhood, grins. "The ride between my place and yours must be shorter in my direction," he says, "since I'm the one broke down to make the trip."

The four older Smith children, nine to two years old, scramble from the wagon, jostling one another, already trying to figure out what there is to do that might prove interesting during the visit. They linger by the side of the wagon, trained to wait for their elders to release them to go off on their own. Emma is the last to climb down, a baby in one arm and a pecan pie in the other.

"She's precious," says Amy, staring for too long a time at Noby and Emma's youngest baby girl.

Amy's wistful glances aren't lost on Jackson. His wife wants their upcoming child to be a girl, since there are so many males in the family.

Amy pulls back the thin gray baby blanket for a better look at little Lenora. "Put on good growth since last we seen her," she says approvingly. "Keep the buttermilk color too."

Emma transfers the loosely bundled girl to Amy, who scrunches her face into a series of poses, almost touching her nose to Lenora's and then lifting away to get the baby to react. "Got your mama's eyes, yes, you do," Amy croons. Little Lenora responds, waving her arms as if she is trying to take flight, sharing quick flashes of a toothless grin.

"Our boys down to the bayou," Amy says to Emma, still able to lose herself in the uniqueness of baby smell and motion, even after three of her own. Amy stares into the dramatic upward tilt of Lenora's narrow brown eyes.

"You hear Mrs. Tademy," Emma says to her brood. "Shoo. Go on down to the bayou with the others while we here, and don't be tearing up nothing."

"I stay with you, Mama," Gertrude says, pressing into Emma's long skirt. The little girl isn't yet three, bold and clearly competing for attention. "You and Lenora."

Amy laughs. "She talking early."

"Early and often," says Emma, shaking her head. "Gertrude got the stubborn thread."

"Just like my Andrew," Amy says. "Got his mind made up about everything and aim to move it in that direction."

"Go on, so adults can visit," says Emma, addressing herself to the small girl, untangling Gertrude from where she clings to her mother's skirt. "Take her hand, L'il Hansom."

L'il Hansom claims his younger sister's small fist, and the three children skip along the worn path, eight-year-old Hansom in the lead. Gertrude gives darting glances back toward the adults to display her displeasure at being banished, and the middle Smith boy follows half a step behind. The children wait until they are almost out of sight before they break into a run, disappearing into the thatch of trees.

"You staying for supper?" Amy asks Noby and Emma.

"We brought too many mouths to feed for that," says Emma.

"Easy to wring another chicken's neck and add more gravy to the pot," says Amy. "'Course you'll stay."

"'Course you'll stay," repeats Jackson. "We got too much to catch up on for a short visit."

Emma looks to Noby, and he nods. "Well, let me help, then," says Emma. "Give me a apron."

Noby and Jackson leave the women and take a walk to the mule shed to smoke. Noby brings out his brown tobacco pouch, the soft, worn material thin from use. He shakes out a thimbleful of coarse tobacco and stuffs the bowl of his corncob pipe.

"Hear there was a meeting last Wednesday night," says Jackson. "I couldn't break away."

In the four square miles of The Bottom, it is possible during the busiest times of the year for faraway neighbors to go without catching sight of one another for days or weeks or sometimes months at a stretch. Nonetheless, detailed goings-on within each family unit, whether of critical consequence like birth, death, or illness, or the not so essential, such as the misdeeds of a wayward child or philandering husband, or successes or failures in dealing with the white man, are preserved and passed along from one household to the next, reported and repeated, absorbed and commented upon as the glue and currency of the community. Out of sight does not equate to out of mind, but firsthand improves the flavor of gossip.

"Come join the brotherhood we putting together," Noby says. "We doing like the whites. Like colored men in New Orleans and other places. There's strength in colored men with character banded together."

"You like a brother already," Jackson says. "If I come to you in need, you surely give, same as the other way around. I got church, I take care of my family. That's enough."

"Still the same old Jackson, keeping to yourself," says Noby. "I know what your father would say if he was here." Noby arranges his face into a serious, intense expression, imitating Sam Tademy. "'A man refusing to step up to his community responsibilities ain't no man at all,'" he says, deepening his voice. He returns to his normal tone. "How your papa getting on?"

"Saw him this morning. From bad to worse," says Jackson. "Don't got good color, bruise too easy, slow getting around. Flu won't go away, but sick or no, he still determined everything happen his way, how he want."

"I got to get over to see Sam Tademy," says Noby. "You lucky to still have him."

"Come back to Mount Pilgrim Rest, you see him every week," says Jackson. "He there each Sunday with the rest of us."

"Emma and me getting used to the little church on Bayou Darrow. Fine enough, but ain't the same as Mount Pilgrim Rest."

"And how Miss Lucy?" asks Jackson.

"Mama's good. Don't seem to age." Noby puffs on his pipe, relaxed. "Remember when we pick up and go, anytime? Spend the whole day hunting? Get harder with six to look after."

"How you and David working out?" asks Jackson.

"Only time gonna sort that out. So far, so good, but he already pushing Hansom Brisco to sell us more land, dragging me in because I'm the one got a little cash."

"Family," said Jackson, in a "what can you do?" tone.

"Family works in the Tademys' favor," says Noby. "Each a you got property."

Jackson's first purchase had been the most momentous, the watershed acquisition that had sealed a mutually satisfying and ongoing land-for-money-and-labor relationship with Widow Cruikshank. No sooner did Jackson pay off one deed in full than he would jump back into the jaws of debt for the opportunity to purchase another small parcel of adjoining land. Sometimes he bought to increase his own holdings, and sometimes to get his brothers set up on their own plots.

"My father skin us alive if we don't do for each other," Jackson says.

"Sam Tademy like a father to me since mine pass," says Noby. "Since before."

"He always glad to see you," says Jackson.

Noby smokes, and Jackson pulls out a nub of pine and a pocketknife and begins to whittle, unable to keep his hands unoccupied. The silence wraps itself around them. Nearby, the voices of the children drift, laughing and playing.

"Don't feel right without Green around to wake us up in the middle of the night to go hunting," Noby says.

Jackson is saved from the need to reply by the sharp clink of the plantation bell at the house. He rigged the bell so Amy can call him in for dinner or supper from one of the far fields, or if there is an emergency. Noby and Jackson don't move to go back to the house right away.

Five boys and two girls come running from the direction of the far field, where a cow just calved, beyond the bayou. L'il Hansom Smith is the oldest, and the biggest in terms of height, but Andrew Tademy runs ahead of the others, outstripping both of the older boys, including his brother Nathan-Green and, of course, all of the smaller children who straggle behind, trying to catch up. Gertrude Smith is the youngest in the pack, since Lenora isn't included. She runs as fast as her chubby little legs will carry her, trying to hold her own, but she falls twice and can't keep up. She doesn't cry, just picks herself up and flings herself in the direction of the house, at the tail end.

Jackson and Noby watch with amusement as the children snake their way to the cabin.

"'Be fruitful, and multiply.' Genesis chapter 1, verse 22. As usual, I got to lead the way," brags Noby, drawing on his pipe, letting the smoke play at his lips and settle deep in his lungs.

"I didn't know we was in a race," says Jackson.

"Who we leave behind what count," says Noby. "That the race that matter. And don't think I gonna let the Freemason idea alone just 'cause you don't understand how important it is yet."

* * *

It turns out to be a fine supper. Amy and Emma have laid out a Sunday spread of fried chicken, rice and gravy, butter beans, and pecan pie, the portions stretched to accommodate both families. Jackson and Amy and Noby and Emma sit at the main table, catching up with community happenings and gossip, enjoying one another's company, while the clump of seven children, L'il Hansom Smith, Nathan-Green Tademy, Oncy Smith, Andrew Tademy, Roger Tademy, Jane Smith, and Gertrude Smith, sit at a makeshift table off to the side in the corner, arranging themselves by age and sex. They are expected to be seen and not heard, and for most of the meal, they manage to keep themselves quiet and beyond the attention of the adults. Only Lenora Smith is exempt from the strict segregation of children from adults, placed in a basket at her mother's side, too young to feed herself and too small to be set adrift in the sea of children.

The conversation meanders, relaxed and unhurried, until, in a temporary lull at the big table, when mouths are full, everyone falls silent at once.

"What's wrong with your sister's eyes, scrunched up like that?" Nathan-Green asks L'il Hansom. His timing is unfortunate. The eight-year-old's voice, though soft, slices through the small room, carrying beyond the intent and anticipated audience. Unfortunately, they all hear, and an awkwardness descends on the room.

"Nathan-Green," scolds Amy. "Come over here right now and apologize to Mr. and Mrs. Smith. A proper little man don't talk about other people."

Nathan-Green pads over to the big table. "I'm sorry," he says. He hangs his head, appropriately chastened and contrite, although he doesn't understand what he did wrong or why he has been singled out, other than having attracted the attention of adults, always a tricky business.

"You excused. Go back to your seat," says Amy.

Nathan-Green rejoins the other children, ashamed by having been called out. He is silent for the rest of the time the Smiths spend at Jackson and Amy's farmhouse, not joining in the children's conversation, throwing an occasional glance in Lenora's direction and the mystery of her slanted eyes, his curiosity aroused, not diminished.

When supper is over, Noby retires to the front porch with Jackson, and Emma helps Amy clean up in the kitchen. Noby and Emma stay so long that most of the smaller children fall asleep curled on the floor in the front room. By seven, when they are ready to leave—a remarkably late end for a farmer's visit—they have to carry sleepy children out in shifts to the waiting wagon.

The adults say their goodbyes, Jackson walks the Smith family out, and they all promise not to let so much time pass before the next visit. Noby, Emma, and their children ride off in the direction of Bayou Darrow. Jackson doesn't wait for them to disappear down the path before turning toward the mule shed. There is still a little daylight he can use for plowing.

Jackson carves out time to go to his father's farmhouse on Tuesday, and together they tackle the gristmill. It is a hot day, humidity clinging to them like hungry ticks, and Sam has his shirtsleeves rolled above his elbows. Jackson counts three large bruises, purple, spread like spilled ink across his father's forearms. The bruises are new, not yet faded like the others. His father doesn't look well, his movements slow and crablike. He tires between every two or three steps and needs to regroup.

"Sit down, Papa," Jackson says. "I do the patch-up myself."

Surprisingly, Sam doesn't argue, his breathing shallow. He sits heavily on a bale of hay pushed against the side wall of the barn.

"Children around here need school," says Sam when his breathing steadies, as if he is continuing on with a conversation, not initiating a new one. "We start small and build from there."

"Take more than yearning to start a school," replies Jackson. "Take a plan. Money to draw and pay a real teacher, some school-books, paper and pencils and chalk and supplies, a steady building to find and keep up. And then how many from Colfax gonna spare their children from the field for months or even days out the year? We start up, all talk, but don't mean what we put in motion got the chance to last."

"Why you fight this so?" Sam asks. "Stop fighting, and we make this school happen. You too young to understand what last and what can't. Green understood."

"I is twenty-nine years old," Jackson says. "Got three children of my own to look out for." The old argument takes on a new edge. "I is not Green. I is Jackson Tademy standing here in front of you."

Sam doesn't respond right away, sizing up his son as if he has stumbled across a foreign, unfamiliar creature. A flinty silence grows between them.

"You think I don't know the difference between my sons?" Sam says at last.

"You blame me for Green," Jackson replies.

Something ugly between them unfolds. Again Sam breaks the silence first. "Son, I only wants you to live up to your potential."

Sam looks old. Old and tired. Have the swollen bags under his eyes always been so heavy, the thickening around his jawline so pronounced? If Jackson met his father on the road for the first time, at this moment, he would see him as nothing more than a worn-down old man of indeterminate age, short and slight of build, for whom you tip your hat out of respect to a long life lived. It is as if Sam's shield of infallibility has evaporated, exposing this ordinary, frail-looking man.

"You want me to live up to Green's potential," says Jackson quietly.

"The Lord give you a gift, and you responsible to use it."

"What gift is that?" Jackson asks, knowing the answer but

delaying to allow himself to cool down. His father will say the same thing everyone says, using the "gift" as a club. That Jackson is smart and steady, as if those traits obligate him to everyone else's cause, indebt him to carry his father's dreams as his own.

"Once you set your mind, tighten down on a notion, you don't let go. Green, God rest his soul, had the gift of dream, to catch a glimpse how the small could be big, and people believed and followed. But you the one know how to plot a course through the impossible. You the stronger one. You a man won't stop until you arrive at the purpose. I knowed that since you was a boy."

Jackson stands mute, blinking back his confusion. He searches his father's face for mockery or, barring that, for a negating comment laced with paternal disappointment. He finds nothing but an old man serving up an observation.

"Time to give you what someone give me at a turning point, so you don't forget how you tied to everybody else," says Sam. "My funeral hat be yours when I'm gone. May be some day it be a voting hat again."

"Yes, Papa." Jackson shows the proper deference, but he takes no pleasure in the idea of owning an ancient hat that has seen better days. He gives the stone wheel a small kick. "I need to come back later in the week to finish patching the mill. Just leave it till I come back."

Sam nods. "Too many give too much already for you to let the gift lie fallow, son," he says.

On Thursday, Jackson is on his own farm putting in posts for a garden fence when his youngest brother gallops onto his land in a panic to tell him that their father has collapsed at the gristmill. Jackson drops everything and takes off at a run. Not ten minutes elapse before he bursts into the yard surrounding his father's farmhouse, winded, races up the steps of the porch and on into the back room of the house, but he can tell immediately by the look on Polly's face that he is too late. Three of his brothers are already there, standing around Sam's motionless body laid out on the narrow double bed he shared for twenty-six years with Polly.

With two fingers, Polly leans over and lightly flicks Sam's eyelids shut. She takes her time, smooths back his hair, runs her thumb down the hollow of his cheek, stares at the grizzled old face as if memorizing every detail. She stands this way for a long time, and no one feels the right to intrude. Finally, she collects herself and looks up to see Jackson.

"The man just too stubborn to wait," Polly says.

Jackson isn't sure if she refers to Sam waiting for him to fix the gristmill or waiting for the few minutes it took him to get to the farm.

"I told him I fix the mill this week," Jackson says.

"I know you did, baby," Polly says.

Jackson wishes she would wrap her arms around him now, make even the worst thing tolerable the way she always has, but she doesn't move away from the body, and Jackson finds he cannot initiate the contact. The day is hot and humid, but Polly begins to tremble as if it is the cold of winter.

"We been getting signs for a while now that his time was coming soon. Wasn't nothing you done or didn't do. Mr. Tademy squeeze everything he could from this life. Wasn't no shame in any parts of it," she says.

"What can I do now, Mama?" Jackson asks.

"Fetch me my shawl, Jackson," she says. "Seem the cold just snuck up in here of a sudden."

Jackson is glad to have some action to take, some excuse to get closer to both his father's body and Polly. He brings the ragged shawl back and places it around Polly's shoulders. She won't leave the body, but he guides her to a chair and she sits.

"You does me a service to go fetch Miz Amy and carry her back to me," says Polly. "I needs a little woman comfort, but I be myself again soon's I catch my breath."

* * *

They schedule Sam Tademy for burial on the following Sunday. Before the service, Jackson rides out to his father's farm to fetch Polly in the wagon. She keeps him waiting in the front room, and he hears her rummaging in the back of the house. When she comes out in her black funeral dress, she carries Sam's brown fedora. It looks even more shabby up close than Jackson remembers. The blue-gray heron feather in the brim is stiff and brittle with age and leans tiredly in toward the hat's dome.

"Sam tell me he want to pass this on to you," Polly says, "the same as McCully pass it to him. Sam always say this hat he wear on the outside remind him what he carry on the inside, but it the Tademy name what make him strong." She fingers the splotchy nap of the fedora. "This hat belong to men could stand up to anything life throw at them. It's fitting to go to you now."

Polly has to stand on tiptoe to remove Jackson's cap. She replaces it with the brown fedora and steps back to take measure of her son. The hat is too big, and it has a slightly gamy smell of sweat, but immediately, Jackson finds a certain comfort in wearing it.

"Now we ready to go," Polly says.

She leads the way out to the wagon and helps herself up onto the buckboard without waiting for Jackson.

Jackson barely absorbs the events of the funeral. People force him to relive his father's final moments in the telling of how he died, even though he wasn't there. Amy never leaves Jackson's side, squeezing his hand at the exact moment he begins to think he can't bear any more. He stands as straight as he can as the new elder of the Tademy clan in his funeral hat, symbolic in his place, this time without his father. It seems the entire town has turned out. Sam has attended almost every funeral in The Bottom, and now that the tables have turned, they flood out to honor him. Jackson sees neighbors he hasn't seen in months, sometimes years. The press of so many well-wishers reduces the impact any one of them can make, and it is all Jackson can do to woodenly acknowledge the condolences and move on to the next. Midway through, he registers his friend Noby standing at the outskirts of the crowd with David, both of their faces contorted and swollen with anger, arguing. Noby shakes David's hand from his shoulder in a brusque gesture before leaving his brother to come forward and join the long line of supportive friends and neighbors.

Jackson sleepwalks, dutifully, during the funeral day but wakes, suddenly alert, later that night. He thinks he hears a cow horn blow, but the sensation evaporates, swallowed up by the stillness of the night. The last remnants of a dream float away, but he is unable to reconstruct it. The moon is full, at its zenith, and the room almost glows with the warm light. Jackson sits up, puts two layers of clothes on over his union suit, pulls on his boots.

"Where you going?" asks Amy. Her sleepy voice at his back is soft, like the calming temperature of bathwater heated on the stove, but Jackson hears the worry.

"Go back to sleep," Jackson says. "There's plowing got to be done."

"You ain't never gonna be Green, and you ain't never gonna be your father," says Amy. "That's all right. You meant to be Jackson."

She doesn't try to stop him from going out of the house, and he walks into the darkness, thankful to be enveloped in the great expanse of the impersonal night. He hitches the small mule, uncharacteristically docile, as if it senses his need; it doesn't fight him, allowing the leather and bit to slip over the slope of its nose and into its mouth.

Jackson plows close to the house, keeping himself steady, turning over row after row, creating deep furrows in the earth.

Green and his father are no longer there, either to lead him or for him to defy. Jackson has spent his life leaning, trying to provide a counterweight to the enormous pull of both Green and Sam. As long as he could respond to either of them, could push back, his life was understandable. Like walking on a stormy day, leaning forward into the wind just to walk upright. What happens when the wind stops? Without them, Jackson isn't sure how he fits into this world. Can he strap on the harness of someone else's hopes?

Jackson pulls back on the leather strap, stops the mule, and listens. Night sounds, nature's sounds. Hooting from the trees, skittering in the underbrush, splashing from the direction of the bayou, hoarse breathing from the mule. Jackson sweats, drenched under the layers of his clothes, and it feels good.

His father talked for years about a commissary for The Bottom, a local store for basic items so the Tademys and their colored neighbors wouldn't have to travel all the way into Colfax. A modest general store on Jackson's property could also serve double duty as a first schoolhouse until they could manage to build a dedicated place for the children. He could begin a colored school, the same way Sam brought the church and gristmill to The Bottom. Jackson could teach, as could others.

They are untrained, but an imperfect beginning is better than a perfect plan that never materializes. No one of them in The Bottom can afford to devote full-time at the start, but with enough hands and enough hearts, it could work.

Jackson gives a soft *git* to the mule, urging her forward again. In the reflective glow of moonlight, he sees the blade of the plow pierce the resistant soil, feels the tug in his shoulders at the kickback of overturned rocks. Jackson keeps at the plowing for an hour more, then two. His mind quiets, and his body numbs to the consistent strain, settling into a repetitive routine. Finally, he believes sleep possible. He releases the tired mule from the harness, puts her up in the shed for the second time that day, and walks back toward his farmhouse.

24

1 8 9 6

Noby Smith purposely comes early, is the first to arrive
on Jackson Tademy's property far in advance of the
meeting. Noby loves the sharp but musty smells of
Jackson's commissary-smokehouse-school, the contrasting and
startling odors of disparate purposes. Mingling scents of rawhide
and tanning solutions compete with the strong perfumes of
tobacco, salves, curing hams, and hard candies. A hint of chalk
dust always seems to linger in the air. Four benches are crammed
in toward the back of the commissary for children engaged in
learning words and numbers during the weekday, and one evening
a month, the benches bear the weight of men during the secret
ceremonies of Colfax's colored Freemasons.

"Emma send me over special. She be glad to get her hands on
the cottonade," says Noby to Jackson.

"The bolt finally come in," says Jackson. "Tell me how much
you want and I cut it for you."

"Four yards plenty enough. Sorry can't be more."

"Don't worry. Amy got her eye on using some for new curtains, and I be able to sell the rest to somebody else sooner or later." Jackson measures out the cloth, snips the end to get it started, and tears the fabric in a straight line. "This the last thing before I clear out your way and close up the store," he says. "Leave you to your lodge brothers."

"Still don't know why you can't join us, Jackson. There's a place for you with the Freemasons. Always has been." Noby can't understand it. Jackson hung back for years, but as soon as he buried his father five years ago, he seemed to come out beyond his own family and embrace the community, though he stops short of joining the colored Freemasons.

"Nothing wrong with the Masons. Just not my nature to throw in with another group. You free to use the commissary when you need, long as it don't interfere with store business or the school. My days is pretty full already. Right now I'm going around to Widow Cruikshank's, see what she got for us. She holding on to a handful of books and some old supplies and odds and ends they done with at the white school, getting ready to throw out. May be better than what we using now."

"I'd offer company, but David's horse come up lame, and I promised to fetch him for the meeting tonight," Noby says. "I got to get home directly and come back."

"Just as well. Better I go to Widow Cruikshank's alone. She know me. Too many of us standing in her yard, she may up and change her mind about giving anything away." Jackson folds the cottonade up for Noby into a neat square and begins to tidy the counter. "So, how you and David doing?"

"Been better," Noby says. "The drought last year almost wipe us out, put us way back, and Big Hansom can't wait much more for some kind of settlement."

"This a hard time for sure, for most everybody in The Bottom. David in just last week for a new saddle, but not too many spending."

"Well," Noby says, at a loss to come up with anything else, "hope Widow Cruikshank come through for the school."

"Just pull the door tight when your meeting done tonight," says Jackson.

After the Freemason meeting, Noby Smith and his brother David leave the colored get-together of men in the commissary and ride home in the same wagon. The trip in was a disappointment. David talked nonstop about his plans for expanding the farm and the best places to find a new work pony, as if he knew a pausing breath would open the door for the discussion Noby really wanted. Each time Noby tried to bring the conversation around to their debt and their precarious position, David changed the subject. During the long meeting, Noby could barely focus on the rituals as their predicament relentlessly sifted through his mind.

He decides to start slow. "We making progress at tonight's meeting," Noby begins. "Eight solid, God-fearing, proper men committed so far."

David agrees. "Our own lodge of Masons." The night is still sticky and warm, but the slight wind created by the wagon's bumpy movement provides a small bit of relief. "May be Jackson Tademy let us use his commissary for the meeting, but it a slap in our face he don't join," says David. "Not like we ask just anybody, only God-fearing family men, leaders in the community. We do like the whites, help each other. May be Jackson think he too good, making money off his neighbors. Wasn't so long ago we help him put up that store. That the least he owe us, holding our meetings there."

"He don't owe us nothing of the kind for a few hours' work," snaps Noby. Already his brother has him riled, before he has even initiated the main topic. Noby settles himself down. "Jackson Tademy the one take the risk running the store, bring in stock don't know when it gonna sell, and he got a right to earn a little something off it. Make everybody's life in The Bottom easier, not having to run off to Colfax so regular. If Jackson don't want to join up with the colored Free-masons, he decide that for himself. He be my friend regardless. And I see you happy to send your children to colored school there."

"Still," says David, "we the leadership. He got a responsibility."

Noby doesn't respond, slows the horse's pace slightly. He doesn't want to get back to the farm prematurely, before he has a chance to confront his brother.

"We got to talk about the land, David. How we pay Hansom Brisco back? Almost three hundred acres' worth of debt now."

"Wasn't me sign no note," says David.

"You and me in this together. We brothers." The horse steadily clip-clops toward home, a familiar route, but Noby keeps his eyes on the road ahead, unwilling to turn and look in David's face. "Hansom need us to repay the loan, at least part. We got to sell off some land if we can. At least half to save the farms."

"You sell whatever you want of your part, Brother," says David. "My part don't got no debt on it."

"That only on paper," says Noby. "We both responsible for the debt, equal."

"Not how I see it," says David.

Noby finally pulls up the reins, stops the wagon, and stares his brother full in the face. David's cool gray eyes reflect no emotion. "You willing to cheat your own brother? You ready to sit by and watch me sell off the old homestead where our father put his sweat, so's you can keep all the other acres in your name?"

"Seem to me the choice of the homestead was made by *your* father a long time ago." The way David lays emphasis on whose father they're talking about is contemptuous. "*Your* father pick you over me every time, every year of your life, always climbing his way over me to get to you. I learn early to take care of myself, and you best learn the same. Israel Smith ain't here to protect you now."

"Why we talking this way? What Papa got to do with it? He was your father too."

David fixes Noby in a steely stare, and the coolness of his eyes become a smoldering pool. "The problem you in is on you to put right, you and Hansom Brisco. I consider my part of the land free and clear."

"My family is on our land. Our mother. Is it really in you to see your mother put out her home?"

"Lucy Smith got a place in my house. I move her myself, your land to mine. She belong in a strong man's house can take care of her."

David's pale, taunting face looms large, and an old, familiar red begins to crowd out everything else for Noby. All of the boyhood scrapes and taunts and fights with David have built to this. If Noby had realized the depth of his brother's contempt, the lingering ulceration of his resentment, he never would have extended himself so fast or thrown in his lot with David.

Noby turns toward his brother and tackles him, hitting him squarely in the chest. They both fall from the wagon seat and find each other again on the dirt road. David is bigger and, although taken by surprise, quickly comes to himself and begins to fight back as they roll on the ground in the darkness. They exchange punches, both leaning hard in to each other, and David lands a blow to Noby's belly, knocking the wind out. David scrambles back onto the wagon seat and takes up the reins, giving the startled horse an expert flick to get him moving. Before Noby can regroup, the wagon gathers speed on the path, and Noby finds himself alone on the dirt road.

He forces himself to calm down and think. Everything he has worked for is in jeopardy, and in the eyes of the law, his brother is not responsible. What David said is true. On paper, all of the debts belong to Noby, are owed by him alone. Without David's cooperation, he will lose his land, his home, and his livelihood.

He gets up, dusts himself off, wipes the worst of the grime from his face, and begins the walk home.

Figure 16. Noby Smith

25

1 9 0 7

Jackson's first response to the smoky scent is drowsy curiosity, a teasing intrusion into his hazy world of sleep. He drifts in a pleasant dream of summer barbecues, and the scorched scent of roasting meat triggers visions of dripping juices from a spit and soft sweet potatoes pushed deep beneath the hot ashes. Inexplicably, he thinks of his father, sixteen years dead, but muffled voices push away the thoughts as his senses sharpen and he realizes the embedded threat of the distinctive smell. He is wide awake in an instant, and his first lucid sensation is relief. There is no crackle of fire or heat to indicate the flames are close. His concern races to Amy, but she is there, right beside him in the bed, snoring softly. She is a heavy sleeper. Her days start even earlier than his, before the break of daylight, and she is usually fast asleep by nine or so in the evening. Jackson pushes at her, insistently shaking her by the shoulder until she stirs, her eyes still heavy.

"Something wrong," he says. "See to Mary. Keep her still."

Their youngest sleeps in the room with them, a baby girl not yet two, and once Jackson is satisfied Amy is alert, he jumps from bed to check on their other children. He calculates the time as somewhere around midnight. Only a couple of hours have passed since he came in from plowing by the light of the full moon, but something is changed. Jackson passes through the empty front room quickly, past the library wall, his row of books stiff and intact on the shelf. He sniffs the air as he moves, trying to pinpoint the precise location of the smoke. It comes from outdoors, not in, becoming stronger every minute, and he hurries to the back room where his three sons sleep. They are men, really, the youngest sixteen and the oldest, Nathan-Green, twenty-four. Jackson shakes them one by one, puts his hand to their mouths to keep them quiet as they come awake. Each stares at him with initial confusion, reacting first to the acrid smoke growing unmistakably stronger, as well as Jackson's gestures of warning, but they take their lead from him and stay put. His sons recognize the layered dangers of the situation. There are white men involved.

Jackson leaves them and treads carefully to the front window to peek outside, gauging his distance from the voices. The white men's figures are outlined clearly in the brightness of the full moon and the added flickering of light coming from the flames racing up the walls of the smokehouse at the back side of his commissary. Jackson hides himself in the darkness of the cabin's interior shadows. Outside are four white farmers from the hill country, dressed in creased and filthy cotton shirts, grimy pants the earthen color of the land they work, and dusty, brownish leather boots. Jackson assumes there are only four men, because of the four horses, but it is never safe to make assumptions. All have dismounted, not more than twenty feet from the house.

Two men stand idle in the front yard, holding the animals, lean work horses still carrying the sweat of the ride, and another two are directly in front of his store, throwing more kerosene on the sputtering flames. The fire blossoms in a blaze of reddish orange.

"Jackson Tademy," a voice calls from the darkness outside. "Come out. You wanna save your store."

For one irrational moment, Jackson is tempted to marshal his sons behind him and storm the men outside, to attack them in a frenzy of righteous indignation. For the briefest instant, it doesn't matter that they have guns and kerosene, or that they can string him up from a branch of the nearest tree as the night's amusement with impunity, or that the issue will never be taken to a court of law. These men—any white man, for that matter—can intrude in his world at any time and burn down what has taken him a lifetime to accumulate.

Between the moon and the gathering flames, Jackson registers details of all four of the invaders, down to the three-day stubble on the chin of the man closest to the house. He is a hill-country Hadnot, the only one Jackson immediately recognizes, but one of the others seems familiar too. The blaze gains strength as it feeds on the new dose of kerosene, creeping farther up the side of the commissary's oak walls.

By now everyone in the household is up and alert, gathered in the front room in their nightclothes, eyes leveled on him. Amy holds the baby tight to her bosom, and the three boys stand at her side, surrounding her within a tight circle of their bodies, whether protecting her or drawing comfort from her isn't clear.

"Jackson Tademy." A different voice, slightly higher-pitched than the first. Jackson understands the dangerous excitement in the tone. "Think you so high and mighty? Come out and show us. Some folks got more than they supposed to. Some coloreds so uppity they need bringing down a peg."

Jackson is caught between the taunts of the men outside and the stares of his family, especially his sons, looking to him. The only one of his children not a witness to this humiliation is Andrew, moved out already and living on his own farm with his new wife. Jackson has spent over sixteen years of backbreaking work and risk-taking to get where he is now, following the template set by his father, preaching the dignity of self-sufficiency and self-pride, building his place as a leader in the community. His livelihood is tied up in the supplies in the commissary, paid for out of his pocket but not yet sold, from harnesses to tobacco, not to mention the winter's pork in the smokehouse. The smell of an entire year's meat roasting and crackling in the fire is strong, much more than a waste, a travesty. To rush outside and save his store is a long shot at best, and to do so to save his pride is foolish, playing in to what those men want. How many times has he preached to his sons to curb their temper, their impulsiveness, to weigh the consequences of rash action?

"Jackson Tademy." Jackson at last places the voice. Jebediah Buckner, a hard-drinking man who lives on the other side of Bayou Darrow, a poor farmer with eight or ten children on a plot barely producing enough to subsist. "What's the point of a coon school, anyhow? No need trying to teach a mule arithmetic."

Jackson should have known immediately that this visit to his farm is about the school. Establishing the colored school took more years and an indirect path Jackson never could have anticipated, delayed season after season by a host of obstacles. After his father died, Jackson put it in his mind to build a colored school in The Bottom, but bad crop years, flood, no money for supplies, and terror of the night riders caused endless delays in getting established. Colored families even thinking of sending their children to a school that didn't yet exist were subject to random threats, and the safety of the children themselves was in question. The night riders reveled in their power. In March, over in Boyce, they ran off the teacher brought in from New Orleans, giving him one day to clear out of the parish for good, and in April they slit the throat of a Frenchman in Aloha for living openly with a colored woman and raising their children in his house. Only after Jackson's best recruitment efforts did five brave students enroll in the colored school, held during the day between nine and one, three days a week for five months of the year at the Mount Pilgrim Rest Baptist Church in The Bottom. Jackson taught the classes himself, basic lessons in reading, penmanship, and arithmetic, using the few books he managed to collect in his personal library, writing out the lessons on the scratched blackboard and stretching the few precious pieces of chalk until they were merely crumbling nubs in his hand.

Jackson feels the burn of his sons' eyes at his back. They are taking their cues from him, and his stomach churns with a deadly mix of adrenaline and humiliation. He keeps himself still and watches the flames reach higher, sees them break through the roof of the commissary, watches as the walls collapse underneath in a burst of sputtering heat. He reminds himself he has too much to live for, too much yet to do to give his life over to the white men outside. If they come for the house, he will have to go out to them, but so far they keep their focus on the commissary.

By the firelight, Jackson sees now that the men have dragged some of the supplies in the store out to the side yard before they set the first match. They begin to load odds and ends into their saddlebags to take home. When it is clear the store is beyond saving, Jebediah Buckner stares into the darkened house one last time. Jackson doesn't move back from the window but keeps as still as he can. The white men mount their nervous horses, touchy so close to the blaze, and ride away from the house on Walden Bayou. On the ground, they leave behind only several badly cracked jars of damaged preserves and a singed half-bolt of material.

The family stays inside for ten minutes more, waiting, careful not to make noise.

"Never fight," Jackson finally says to his sons, as if the store still smoldering is no more than an object lesson staged for their benefit. "Only a fool don't have sense enough to stay away from a fight can't be won." He pulls on his boots and heads outside. "Come on. We got a fair amount of cleanup to do before the daylight," Jackson says.

26

1 9 0 7

J ackson Tademy and his four sons work side by side for an hour to smother the last of the flames with a large piece of discarded burlap, a damped-down old quilt from the house, and the reddish farm dirt they shovel directly onto the worst of the blaze. They weave in and out like ghosts in the moonlight, in cautious silence around the footprint of what used to be their commissary. Thin wisps of smoke spiral upward from the blackened skeleton of the store, and the air is swollen with the stink of cooked meat, burnt leather, and lingering kerosene. With the exception of a couple of cast-iron pots, little from what they kept in the front of the store is salvageable; although the roof has collapsed, the fire has skipped over a few items toward the back.

Jackson tries to shake the disquieting feeling that he has been here before, standing in the wake of destruction, toothless in the face of untouchable enemies, surrounded by his sons. He knows he has not, but the phantom memory stays with him and goads him nonetheless. He pauses, leans on his shovel.

"Shout out your names," he demands, the necessity of the request overriding everything else. Jackson hasn't asked his sons to do this in years, but with the strangling smoke filling his lungs and stinging his eyes, suddenly, nothing is more important.

"Shout out your names," he insists, ferocious.

They only look at him, his sons, as if they have confronted an angry bear in the woods and are in those first few critical seconds of developing a strategy for survival.

Nathan-Green is the first to respond, cupping his soot-coated hands around his mouth. "My name is Nathan-Green Tademy." It comes out a deafening whisper, the silence of the night and the backdrop of hissing, burning wood amplifying the words.

"Louder," commands Jackson.

"My name is Nathan-Green Tademy." This time his son's words carry and become large living things, an echoing roar that surprises all of them.

"Every one of you," demands Jackson, and in turn, each of his sons shouts his name.

Jackson still isn't satisfied. They have been working through the night, and they are physically and emotionally spent. The flames are mostly out, and the gray dawn provides enough light to see.

"We wasn't brought here as no slave, in the beginning," Jackson says. "We come here from Africa, from Alexandria in Egypt, from the Nile Delta. We come on a boat, free men, working our trade in the sunshine.

"Squat down closer." His sons gather around him, and with the tip of his abandoned shovel, in the charred mess at their feet, he draws a triangle with a thin, wiggling stem that trails downward. "This here the Nile Delta," he says, and points to the triangle. "And this the Nile River." He points to the stem. "Breaks apart into all these streams in the delta and run out to sea."

Jackson looks from face to face, each a distorting mirror of different parts of himself. He sees in those wary young faces that they are a little afraid of him in his current frame of mind, that their growing understanding of their precarious position as colored men in 1907 Louisiana burrows in a deep, corrosive path toward their core. They want to believe their father is strong. They need to believe themselves safe, even though that assurance is impossible.

"We lost the name for a while after coming here, but my father, Sam Tademy, give us our name back after the war. Same name we had when we was in Egypt. May be one man got the power to burn down a store, take our property, but can't nobody take away the Tademy name. Tademys was born to be men took serious. Don't forget. Don't never forget. Don't never let your sons forget when the time come."

Jackson is so weary he can barely straighten up. "Go on back inside and catch a couple hours' sleep," he says to his sons. "We got a full day ahead."

Noby Smith shows up just past dawn to find Jackson alone outside by the store site, separating debris into retrieval piles.

"What happened?" Noby asks Jackson, assessing the blackened ruins. "I smell smoke a mile away."

"Jebediah Buckner and some others," Jackson says. He doesn't volunteer anything else, doesn't think to ask why Noby has come.

Wordlessly, Noby takes off his jacket and joins Jackson in the rubble. The two men walk around the destruction, poking into the carcass of the building with long oak poles, turning over layers of charred wood, exposing hot pockets where flames still smolder, pulling what they can from the wreckage. Toward the back, facedown and buried beneath a singed horse blanket and a thick coating of ash, they find a slate blackboard. Jackson turns it over. The smooth, hard panel still has a part of the children's last copy-out lesson written in smudgy chalk.

Jackson lets it fall back into the ashes. "Gone," he says quietly.

"We build the commissary once, we build again," says Noby.

"They just come to burn it down again," says Jackson. He hasn't slept at all since first awakening to the smell of smoke last night, and his mind is slowed by the finality of what lies before him.

"Least nobody get hurt. Could be worse," Noby says. "We can fix all those things they put their hands to."

"You wasn't here," says Jackson. "My family the ones living through them men on our land like they own it, trapped inside the house in the middle of the night, watching and waiting on whatever Buckner and the others take it in their heads to do. As long as they know we keeping a colored school, they coming back."

"The school what they come for?" asks Noby.

"That, and they don't like to see a colored man with nothing. Not like the school a success. Only six students, and even they can't come regular."

"Those six teach six more," says Noby. "Almost sound like you ready to give up."

Jackson continues to poke around in the ruins with his pole, hits something hard, finds two more glass put-up jars with a congealed, bubbling mess inside, too hot to handle, cooked in the flames. "I got to think about my own. There's no more money to spare to buy goods to start up the store again, our winter meat is gone, and one charred slate board not enough to keep a colored school going. Better to teach one by one, without catching the white man's eye."

"The slate board coming out whole be a sign," says Noby. "If not you, who else in this town able to keep up a colored school?"

"Not no sign," says Jackson. He has streaks of black soot crisscrossing his pants legs up to thigh level, and his hair is almost white from settling ash. "A sign be more students full-time, not snatched back into the field come harvest or sickness at home. A sign be books don't have pages torn out and water stains so bad a student can't read all the words. A sign be read-ing books that got words with more than three or four letters and real thinking in them."

"Every dream got to have a start place," says Noby.

"Well, I'm not in the dream business. Not no more. Not if a dream mean my sons got to see me brought low by any riffraff want to cross my path."

"Not brought low," says Noby. "Since when you don't listen to your own sermons? Turn the other cheek, say the Bible."

"The school gonna stay closed."

"Your school mean everything to colored in Colfax, Jackson. It go way beyond the six students. Just to know we got a place and a right where our children go further than we able to take them."

"You know much as me, Noby. All your children get education at home at the hand of their father."

"But that's not true of most. The colored school matters."

"The school gonna stay closed," Jackson repeats.

"One man can't rightly ask another to take on risk, for hisself and his family, but this community in bad need of a school. I'm not sure why I was put here on this earth, 'cept to cheat death and bring forth children, but you put here for the colored school. I'm sure of that," says Noby.

"We try again when the time right," says Jackson. "Mine the family in harm's way, not nobody else."

"Not true," says Noby. "The school be community business. We all got a stake. Neighbors come tomorrow if you ask, help you rebuild."

"Still too raw," says Jackson. "And I won't hear no more on this particular subject. Could as easy be my house, not just my commissary." Jackson changes the subject. "What you doing here so early, anyway?" he asks. "Word don't travel that fast."

"Don't matter no more now," says Noby.

"What?"

"I was coming to see if you was in a position to buy half the part of the farm I got left." Noby looks around at the smoldering heaps, the piles of salvage at their feet. "I see the answer to that one for myself."

"You already sold most all away already 'cept the piece you living on. What you and David going to do?"

"I got to pay Hansom Brisco back on the loan right away, or he in trouble with his own land. I can't leave him hanging after all he done for me and mine. David don't care about none of that, long as he got his piece free and clear. My part of the farm gone, just like your commissary gone. That's the naked truth."

"We in the same fix, then," says Jackson. "Set down a peg or two from where we thought we was headed." Noby's misery somehow made his own seem smaller. "What you do without the farm?"

"I'm going 'round to the icehouse, see if there's paying work for me there, then find a farm to rent."

"They won't let colored deliver ice," says Jackson.

"Not deliver. That's Roy Hadnot's job. I'm not foolish enough to tangle up with that. But Hadnot almost always sloppy drunk now, shortchanging customers, scaring the children on the route, letting the ice melt out from under him while he sneak off to the bottle. Mr. Fletcher got to be looking for someone to count on to actually do the before and after work. Chopping ice from the river, packing the sawdust, loading, cleanup. No reason can't be me. I done plenty odd jobs in off-season for Mr. Fletcher before, he know me. We get along fine. Long as I'm not in front."

"Emma know?"

"No need to tell her till I got something to say," says Noby.

"Good luck. Sorry about the farm. Wish I could help more. Time to get the boys up, anyway. At least come on in to breakfast and eat with us. Amy fix plenty."

"Can't," says Noby. "We both got our hands full, and I still got to go see Mr. Fletcher."

* * *

Jackson shakes off as much of the soot from his clothes as he can before going into the house. He draws water from the well to wash away the worst of the char and smoke, but the sobering reality of the long night still clings to him. His children, little Mary and the boys, sit waiting for him, and Amy dishes up a bowl of thick porridge for him as soon as he crosses the threshold.

He resists the temptation to linger as he passes by the shelf he has built in the far corner of the front room, resists the urge to run his hands over the neat row of fragile, musty books housed there. His family waits for him, and he must not disappoint. He owns six books, upright side by side on the shelf, two very slim volumes and four thick, braced on one end by the wall, and on the other by a smooth river rock, and each is precious to him. His favorite is the oldest, a worn undersize book, so small it almost fits his hand, with black tape at the spine and the edges of the green cover so worn the cardboard shows through. *Sheldon's Primer*, it reads on the front, with a picture of a white girl sitting on a pillow holding a doll. Inside are the letters of the alphabet and reading lessons, the same lessons he uses still to teach the children in his school, the book from which he learned when he and Noby were small boys, and from which he gave his own children their first reading lessons. Jackson glances at the other titles in his library, each special. In front of him is *McGuffey's New Fifth Eclectic Reader*, with its rough cover and uneven texture of the title's raised lettering. There is a curl to the crimped, rounded border, and a reddish coloring to the outer edging of the bound pages within. Jackson yearns to lift the largest book from the shelf by its tattered cardboard spine and hold it. The glue is crumbling, visibly separating away from the original tightness of the pages. He wants to feel the weight and heft, the mere holding like a blessing.

Instead, he joins his family at the table and sits down to eat. They all concentrate overmuch on the food in front of them, avoiding one another's eyes. For most of the meal, they don't talk at all. No one dares to be the first to bring up what pulses among them like a tender tooth, best left alone.

"I'm thinking on taking the wagon over to Widow Cruikshank's this morning," Jackson tells Amy.

"She got more work?" Amy asks. "I thought you finished mending the fences for her last week."

"No work today. But she do have a encyclopedia she selling." Jackson pushes away the rest of his porridge. He isn't very hungry. "A big set, nineteen books, only missing a few parts, got descriptions on most every subject inside. Two dollars and a couple weeks moon work plowing her north field, they be ours."

"So you keeping the school open?" asks Amy.

Jackson feels all of them around the table waiting on his answer. "I'ma shut the colored school down," he says.

"All our savings tied up in that store, and the heat haven't even died down off the burnt-up roof out there," says Amy. "If you shutting the school, why you buying something we can do without and don't have no money for?"

Jackson bangs his open hand on the wood table, making a noise so sudden and sharp it startles everyone, including himself. "Opportunity come when it come, not always when things is easy," he says. "Them books is for the library. Just because the school shut don't mean everything got to stop."

"We don't got two extra dollars," Amy persists.

Jackson pauses. "I'm a rich man," he finally says. "Money only matter what it buy or who it feed."

"Pride don't fill a empty belly," Amy says.

"A full belly don't make a man," replies Jackson.

"Jackson Tademy, you gonna do what you gonna do," Amy says. "A man always seem to find a way to get what he already decided he want. If you so set on those books, I know the widow give me some washing or ironing. You getting too old for moonlight work. We in need of money, but you already loaded up beyond what you able to handle."

"I told you, no woman of mine gonna work in the field or clean up behind white, no matter what, and that be the final word," says Jackson. "My wife's only job be looking after me and the children."

He jams his hat down low on his head and storms out of the house, barely glancing at the smoldering remains of his commissary, on his way to Widow Cruikshank's farm.

Chapter

27

1 9 1 1

One steamy summer afternoon, three months to the day after her marriage to Nathan-Green Tademy, Lenora Smith Tademy finds herself alone in the front room of Jackson Tademy's farmhouse. She cannot believe the luxury of having the only two-story house in The Bottom all to herself. She has become comfortable in her new daily routine and what is expected of her. Her time of violent sickness in the morning has passed, and although the baby growing in her belly sometimes drains her of energy, for the most part, she feels strong. At Amy's insistence, they have their own room, Lenora and Nathan-Green, separate from the others, a situation so unexpectedly freeing that Lenora sometimes finds herself giddy with the selfishness of it. She and Amy have come up with a scheme to divide the household chores, or, more precisely, Amy decided, since she prefers the cooking and outdoor work to scrubbing and washing, which Lenora doesn't mind at all. This particular morning Amy has taken her little girl fishing down at the bayou, and Nathan-Green is out with Jackson for the day to work the far field.

Lenora finishes scrubbing the kitchen floor, airs out the empty back bedroom just as Amy instructed before she left, and carries her soapy water bucket into the front room. She uses the back of her callused hand to unstick the sopping wisps from her damp face and away from her eyes. She is self-conscious about her eyes and wishes there were some way to hide them. The offense isn't in the color, a warm brown like most everyone else's, but in the steep tilt and narrow almond shape, and in the heavy upper lids that almost hood the smallness of the opening below. They are her mother's eyes revisited, a cause of torment when she was growing up. Lenora is sorely aware of the double takes and stares whenever she meets someone new, as they try to figure her out, to determine her lineage.

The day is blistering. At least it isn't wash day or, worse, ironing day, the two chores where there is no escape from the fierceness of the sun and high humidity. But it is July, Louisiana-summer hot, and the sweat that runs in rivulets from her armpits to her waist and beyond makes the damp material cling to her body and stick in crevices that force her to be on constant lookout to make sure no one can see her. Lenora hates Louisiana summers, hates that every breath drawn feels as if you're inhaling liquid flames through your nose, hates that the heat sucks the life out of you and makes the simplest task a superhuman effort. Lenora isn't the type to complain about the weather. She doesn't do well with conversation at all, doesn't like the way talk either deadens a subject or spins ideas off in unexpected directions, demanding something she doesn't want to give. The possibility of other people focusing in her direction, expectations rising, judgments ready to be made, is enough to keep her as far away as possible from those she doesn't know.

Since she moved in, she has explored all of the areas contained within the walls of this house on Walden Bayou. She is perpetually in motion, doing whatever needs doing, never still from first light to eyes shut, washing, cooking, scrubbing, sewing, tending, mending, ironing, mulching, weeding, picking, canning, milking, feeding, making herself available to Nathan-Green and the needs of the household. But Lenora likes the tranquil corner of the front room with the bookshelves best, almost as comforting as church. She carefully dusts the neat rows of Jackson Tademy's books, lingers as she runs her hands across the spines of the set of encyclopedias. Papa Jackson feels about each one of his books the way most in The Bottom feel about the sanctity of the Bible.

"Jackson say what's in those books set our minds free," says Amy.

Her mother-in-law stands in the doorway, watching her carefully, bamboo fishing pole in one hand and a bucket of dead fish to be gutted and fried up in the other. Amy came in so quietly, and Lenora was so engrossed, that she missed the warning sounds of her mother-in-law's approach.

"Mrs. Tademy," says Lenora, unsure whether she is in trouble for dawdling.

"You live here now, child," Amy says, "married to my son. His bride be my daughter, so again, you call me Mama Amy. Two Mrs. Tademys in this house just cause confusion."

Lenora nods. It takes some getting used to, the transition from thinking of her mother-in-law as first Mrs. Tademy, and then Miss Amy, and now Mama Amy. Sometimes Lenora still can't believe she is married. The transition from one family unit to another only a few months prior hasn't been as traumatic as she feared, not yet anyway, aided no doubt by the fact that she knows Jackson Tademy's household almost as well as her own. Because the two families are so close, Smiths and Tademys, because her father, Noby, and her new father-in-law, Jackson, are lifelong friends, more like brothers than neighbors, Lenora feels as though she has grown up with the Jackson Tademy farmhouse as her second home. The Tademy children are as much an assumption in her life as her position embedded within the middle of the pack of her twelve brothers and sisters, from L'il Hansom to Martha Geneva, twenty-five years apart.

"You aching to read one of those books?" Amy asks. She comes closer to Lenora.

"No, ma'am," says Lenora quickly.

"It's all right if you are," says Amy.

Lenora shakes her head violently.

"I knows how you feel. Jackson think more of those books than he do some people," says Amy. "Sometimes I'm tempted to hold them myself, just to see if I can figure out what kind of magic they got, see if it rub off. If I didn't know better, I'd think Jackson put more store in his private books, his *library*, than anything else." She pronounces *library* carefully, an exotic word become familiar.

Lenora nods.

"Why don't we say from here on, when we split what need doing around here, you the one carry book duty," Amy says. "All that being careful and reaching hurt my back. You got more patience for the work than me."

Lenora has seen Amy embroider tiny stitches on a pillowcase, interweaving the different-colored threads in an intricate pattern, or crochet complicated doilies for the sofa to protect the furniture from head oil. Almost every day, Amy sits motionless at the bayou for hours, waiting for the fish to bite. If there is one thing she doesn't lack, it is patience.

"Yes, Mama Amy," Lenora says. "That be fine."

Amy pulls out her scaling knife and takes the fish bucket to the front porch. "Come help, Lenora," she says. "I got a full day in the kitchen today. We got a important guest coming."

Lenora follows and waits. Amy motions her to sit and pushes the bucket toward Lenora with her foot. She passes her the knife. "Must be you curious who coming to pay us a call," says Amy.

Lenora nods, takes a medium-size catfish from the bucket, and makes the first long cut.

"My son don't marry no chatterbox," says Amy, "so I go ahead and tell you. Jackson's mama gonna come live with us. She been like a mama to me too, took me in when my real mama die. Jackson and me brought up in the same house, in Sam and Polly Tademy house down on Bayou Darrow. You know that, I expect? Sam die when you such a baby, you too little to remember him, but Polly Tademy familiar."

Lenora nods.

"Well, Polly getting on in years, and now we got the chance to pay back some of what she done for us, we bringing her here to live. Since Jackson add on the second story, and all the boys but Nathan-Green move out, we got more than enough space. That room at the back just right for her."

Lenora likes Polly Tademy, an old woman who speaks her mind. She concentrates on the task in front of her, and before long, all the morning's fish are scaled and gutted.

"Mama Amy?"

"Yes?"

"Papa Jackson ever gonna open the colored school again?"

Amy sighs and leans back in her chair. "If I got anything at all to do with it, the answer be yes. But truth told, only so much a wife able to carry out with a Tademy man."

Lenora married late. Nathan-Green was twenty-eight, and Lenora twenty-one, and compared to the others in their families and in the community, both were leave-behinds in the quest to start their own lives with spouses and children. Lenora Smith and Nathan-Green Tademy each thought of the other as the best they could do. They came together more as a result of proximity and the closeness of the two families than any overwhelming pull toward each other, although they were connected by certain similarities of personality—a reflexive willingness to accept rather than grab or shape whatever life extended to them. Left behind, and with the slightly sour taint of being left over after a lifetime of growing up together, Nathan-Green finally began to court Lenora, taking his time in the easygoing pursuit. Although he showed no signs of interest in any other girl, or of faithlessness, it took Lenora's panicked announcement that she was expecting his child to bring him—to his credit, not unwillingly—to the marriage table. They called in a preacher and wed within the week, in the front room of Noby Smith's house, Lenora wearing her Sunday dress. She gathered her scanty belongings, including an extra housedress, a nightgown, a set of undergarments, one for summer and one for winter, her Sunday hat and pair of white gloves, a hairbrush given her by her mother, Emma, on her wedding day, a laying hen donated by Noby to her new farm home, and she moved with her new husband into Jackson Tademy's house. One day she was nothing more than a middle child, distinguishable only as the daughter of the iceman, a visible and coveted occupation, and the very next day she claimed her position as a married woman.

Much had been made of her sister Gertrude's marriage at sixteen to Nathan-Green's brother Andrew six years prior, by everyone's judgment a golden couple full of plans and ambition, a match that held promise for not only the families involved but the community as well. Lenora faded into the background, found it impossible to be visible alongside Gertrude, rigid and exacting in her view of so many things, and vigilant about defining and keeping everyone in the appropriate place. Lenora's older sister demanded attention and, as a result, more often than not received her due. It hadn't been easy growing up in the Smith household in Gertrude's shadow. Lenora and Nathan-Green had that in common too, an inability to command center stage, growing up in houses where one sibling so clearly outshone all of the others. Lenora was comfortable behind the scenes, never resentful of Gertrude's domination.

Nathan-Green and Lenora get on well enough. Nathan-Green

never mentions her long stretches of silence, or the fact that she so seldom exchanges words with him beyond the basics necessary for everyday living together. She is sure he actually prefers the scarcity of communication and their fixed roles, and a stoic, silent wife who never complains.

Although Nathan-Green signaled his participation in the community by the taking of a wife, he is not particularly proficient in the active upkeep of a marriage, not in the way of her parents, Noby and Emma, or Jackson and Amy, whom Lenora admires for their true fondness for each other, still evident after all these years. Nathan-Green isn't mean to Lenora, doesn't beat or berate her as she knows some husbands in The Bottom do their wives. He seems mostly indifferent. She is an assumption in his life, a fulfillment of expectation, the signpost of a milestone encountered and mastered, an examination passed. Lenora performs her wifely duties, and when Nathan-Green ventures out beyond the boundaries of the farm, for a friendly game of dominoes or to a church social, he leaves her home. Her silence makes her complicit, as if she accepts the wisdom and justice of being ignored, and in truth, although she is lonely, her expectations are low in terms of her own happiness. Lenora understands all of this, even so early in their marriage, the same way she knows it will be her children and not her husband who will eventually shape her days and define her domain. The first one stirring now in her belly was quick to catch, and she assumes there will be many more.

There is a part of her that longs for what Jackson and Amy have together. But Lenora is no Amy. She can't speak up in Amy's sweet way, she doesn't inspire the protective qualities to blossom in her husband the way that Amy does, without artifice or guile; and Nathan-Green, with his dreamy demeanor and tendency to accept whatever is dished up, much like Lenora, is very far removed from having the determination, ambition, or cleverness of his father.

Lenora observes Jackson and Amy at every opportunity, committing their little personal rituals to memory, replaying them in her mind while she darns Nathan-Green's socks or beats together the cornmeal and cow's milk for corn bread. At the end of each day, when the sun finally drops and darkness starts to fall, Amy sits on the porch swatting at flies, waiting with what seems to be infinite patience, supper prepared and ready to warm again on the back of the stove. When Jackson returns to the farmhouse, leading the mule or the ox, there is a private moment that passes between the settled married couple, a reassuring quickening and glance as each drinks in the existence of the other. They don't touch or speak, and before Jackson passes the porch on his way to the shed, Amy pushes up from her rocking chair to go inside and dish up his supper.

Already Lenora's father-in-law talks about setting Nathan-Green up on a plot of land, a piece of the south field for him to build on and cultivate as his own, as he did with Andrew shortly after he married. Most brides live for the day they can have their own place, when they no longer have to suffer the cramped quarters and constrictive rules implicit in living under a mother-in-law's roof. But not Lenora. She wishes she could go on living with Jackson and Amy forever.

28

1915

The wakening morning sheds the gray of night, and a crimson lick of sun fires the sky and pushes the temperature to over 80 degrees, a mere hint of what the rest of the day will bring. Horse hooves echo in the silence, a steady clip-clopping breaking the sluggish stillness of morning. Three white children, somewhere between the ages of six and nine, two boys and a girl, burst through the front screen door of a recently whitewashed house not far from the center of Colfax, running pell-mell toward the buckboard wagon outfitted in back like a house on wheels, pulled by a dapple-gray mare.

"Here come the iceman! The iceman here." The children run around the wagon like puppies, all eagerness and little control.

Noby is in a foul mood, a mood he can't show his customers or the children of his customers. He makes his movements deliberate and small, both to conserve his strength in the face of the inevitable heat buildup, as well as to keep himself in check. He has been up transferring the heavy blocks of ice from the icehouse since four-thirty this morning, stewing all the while as he planned a strategy for the confrontation with his brother later in the day. Every time he thinks of David, he tastes red at the back of his throat.

It is helpful to see the children almost dance around his wagon, unable to contain their excitement. For this delivery, at least, he can relax a bit. It is the stops when no one is around and he must go into a white person's house alone to deliver the ice that make him uneasy. It occurs only infrequently, but anything can happen, any accusation made, and it will be his word against a white's. He knows his customers, has serviced most of them for over four years, and they are used to him, but there is always the possibility they will say they left the quarter for the ice on top of the icebox when they didn't, or that he never made the delivery at all, or worse. Noby sets the wagon's wheel brake, throws the iron weight from under the raised seat to the road, and climbs down. He ties the reins to the weight to keep the mare from wandering off and fixes the feedbag over her snout.

He preferred the old arrangement with Fletcher, when Noby only made deliveries and Fletcher himself collected the money, but the inefficiency of recircling the route an extra time bothered both of them, a colossal waste of hours when they both know Noby is capable of delivering and trustworthy in collecting.

As if the day isn't already like the inside of a boiler, Noby wears a long leather apron that goes from his neck to his boots, and a leather pad over one of his shoulders to bear the heft and chill of the ice block. Noby climbs on the back of the wagon and takes the long, shiny ice pick from his apron. He hacks at the block of ice, chipping away until he has the perfect size to fit through the door of the icebox. Except for the butcher shop and the apothecary, Noby doesn't rely on the diamond-shaped cardboard ICE cards left out in the windows of each home, specifying how much ice to leave, twenty-five, fifty, or a hundred pounds.

Experienced, he knows the exact block size to cut for each of his customers. He pulls out his tongs, snapping each side securely onto the sides of the ice, and hoists the heavy block to his shoulder.

Noby balances his load and kicks a few shards of ice with the toe of his boot to the end of the wagon for the waiting children. They stay out of his way until after he jumps down from the back of the wagon. Noby doesn't have to say anything. It is understood that as soon as he is in the house, the children can rush to the back of the wagon and pick out the biggest pieces of shaved ice to suck on.

Noby enters through the back, nearest the kitchen and the icebox. The icebox is dingy white and stands up on legs high enough from the floor for the water pan to slide underneath.

The delivery doesn't take long, but by the time he comes back outside, the three children have moved to the front steps, ice pieces in hand and cooling the insides of their cheeks. They watch Noby with large eyes, content. He puts the tongs back in their holder, takes the feedbag off the horse, pulls the iron weight back in the wagon, and climbs up. A sharp snap of the reins and a few clicking sounds get the old horse moving, jerking the wagon forward, on their way to the next delivery.

Before turning the bend, Noby glances back one last time. The oldest boy is already busy, shoveling the steaming pile of road apples left behind by the mare and storing them to dry, to be used later to spread in the garden for fertilizer.

It has taken years of proving himself, and harassment from others around Colfax who wanted work as steady as ice delivery, but Noby is the one who landed the job. He has a regular route, and Jim Fletcher pays cash money each and every month for a job normally given to a white man. The work requires a strong back and a pleasant disposition, but Noby also has to project that he won't tolerate disrespect, not from the children who follow him around all morning hoping to steal shavings to pop into their mouths, or older men who would steal a cube of the precious ice if they could get away with it. The constant damp and cold, even on the hottest days of summer, first in the icehouse and then sliding the blocks onto the wagon for the deliveries, have stiffened up Noby's hands, turning them a strange mottled color somewhere between the caramel brown of his face and a bleached-out color closer to that of the sodden sawdust in which he packs the ice. It is worth the discoloration, and the circulation-deprived pins and needles he often feels in his arms, and the muscle strains of his lower back. He is fortunate to have the job, and he knows it.

Fletcher tried him out as a delivery man in an emergency, years ago, when the regular man didn't shown up, a victim of the bottle the night before. Before that Noby worked in the icehouse, chipping and sawing, hauling and storing, stacking and packing, always stunningly numb and cold while everyone else roasted outside. In the beginning, Fletcher made his own rounds once a month to collect the money from the people on the route, complaining when a customer couldn't pay out for an entire month of deliveries. Even when Noby had nothing to do with reconciliation of accounts, he kept his own books, although he didn't know to call it that. Once he finished reading the weekly *Colfax Chronicle*, he jotted his records in the margins, maneuvering the close-scrawled figures around the newsprint by date, name, and amount of ice delivered. He subscribed to the newspaper for one dollar a year, a weakness and indulgence made easier by the ongoing demand for the ice work, especially when he became the permanent delivery man. There are sixteen ongoing, good-paying customers, most clustered in Colfax— the apothecary, several commissaries, and a butcher shop—but he delivers as well to private residences as far away as Selma. Most individual families do without ice, cannot afford twenty-five cents for a delivery, but there are a few well off enough to have iceboxes. If they empty the big pan underneath to catch the dripping water twice a day, a single clump of ice, a hundred pounds or so, can last for at least half a week, sometimes all week long.

Once Fletcher made him the permanent iceman, Noby devised his own scheme for covering the rounds. He starts early in the morning, before the sun can dwindle his merchandise, comes all the way back to the icehouse several times during the day, unlike the previous delivery man, who allowed much of Fletcher's profits to melt away out of the wagon. Noby divides his delivery territory into grids and takes out only as much ice on any single trip as will keep under the blanket in the beating sun.

Noby goes out on his ice rounds every Monday, Wednesday, Friday, and Saturday. Not only does his constant exposure covering the length and breadth of Colfax increase his reputation for dependability, it gives him first access to other odd jobs that come up around the parish and even beyond. Above all, the iceman job is respectable, and he does better than many of his friends and neighbors, but that can't compensate for the inescapable fact that he no longer owns a single piece of property.

By early afternoon the last of Noby's ice is gone, the wagon filled with the soggy sawdust that is all that remains at the end of his delivery cycle. Noby swings wide to make his way back home; most of his customers live far from The Bottom.

"Just one more stop before resting, girl," he says to the mare.

Noby finds it helps to talk to his horse, his daily companion; to work out his moods with the faithful beast. The little mare is tired, and so is he. He points her toward The Bottom, for David's farm. Her ears prick back and she picks up her pace, knowing they head in the direction of home.

He pulls up to an expanse of land along Bayou Darrow, planted out in corn and cotton, not an extravagant homestead but certainly a respectable one. Noby goes straight for the house, a small four-room cabin with a sleeping porch attached to the back and a raised porch at the front. David's wife is on the front porch, sitting in a rocker, shelling peas in a bucket on her aproned lap.

"Hello, Miz Susanna," Noby says to his brother's wife. He

doesn't get down from the wagon and tries to keep his voice casual. "Mighty hot today."

She looks flustered for a moment but quickly regains her composure. "Noby," she says. "It's been such a long time." She smiles a small smile, but it is clearly strained, encased in embarrassment.

They are stiff and reserved with each other, neither wanting to say too much, but the next move is his. He is the one who is forcing this.

"Yes," says Noby. It isn't her fault, and she doesn't deserve the brusqueness, but he can barely tolerate standing on David's land. Looking his brother's wife in the face reminds him of David's deceit. Her only crime is to have married David, but still.

"Mama Lucy inside, but she sleeping."

"How she be? She didn't come out to church last week."

"Don't worry, she just under the weather," says Susanna. "Eighty-five, and except for a touch of catarrh, she stronger than you or me. Cough be gone in a day or two, and she be up and around and in the front pew again Sunday coming."

"David here?" Noby asks.

"In the pecan grove," she says, a little too fast, obviously relieved that he will leave her alone and go to his brother.

Noby touches his hat. "I'll find him," he says.

He knows the layout of the parcel, has studied it on the surveyor's map in the courthouse and walked the length and breadth when he knew David wasn't there. Almost three hundred acres, land that should have been his. Land purchased only because of Noby's crushing debt, not David's, debt that still holds him in its grip.

Just beyond a clearing east of the farmhouse, David and his four boys harvest pecans, shaking the trees until the nuts fall and then collecting them from the ground. David looks older but retains the slim, fit build he has had since he was a child. The chronic paleness of his skin has turned slightly muddy in the sun. David isn't afraid to work, Noby will give him that, but the sight of him sweating on his own land, able to bear the fruits of his labor, is almost more than Noby can stand. Noby is tempted to turn around and ride home. What good can this do?

David looks up, holds a hand up to protect his light gray eyes from the glare of the sun, coolly registers Noby on the ice wagon. He doesn't wave or smile, just drops his corner of the burlap sheet, motions to one of his sons to take his place, and walks over to where Noby waits.

"Noby," David says, tight-lipped. He is still a handsome man, even with his strange eyes. He is in his early fifties, two years older than Noby, and his face is unwrinkled, though he spends so much time in the sun.

"I come to see about you helping pay down the debt," says Noby.

"It's not my debt, Brother," David says.

"We was both on the land, not just me."

"That's not what the courthouse say," says David.

Now Noby rents back the small plot where he lives, not big enough to farm, barely adequate to reside. He was forced to raise his children on diminishing land, foreclosed a piece at a time, paying back what debts he could, since he held the paper and the obligation. David walked away, leaving Noby to succumb to the creditors alone. Noby and Emma still have four children at home, three girls and a boy, the youngest only eight.

"This the last time I ask. You doing good now. Do right by me," says Noby.

"This a old argument, and I got work," says David.

David stands for a moment, staring at Noby, his face unyielding, and finally turns to walk toward his sons and his pecan harvest.

"You dead to me," Noby calls out to his brother's back.

Figure 17. Noby Smith

29

1 9 1 8

Noby positions his wagon at the back of the long waiting line for loading at the quarry. He has already spent the better part of the early afternoon shoveling the first load of gravel into the wagon bed, delivering it out near The Bottom, and getting back to the quarry for another load. After this run, he can call it quits for the day. The pains between his shoulder blades and shooting down his legs are forceful reminders of the fact Noby isn't so young anymore, but he is dependable, and white men still come to him when they want a job done right. Today is good work. He has already finished his ice deliveries, and the extra dollar will come in handy.

Up ahead, four wagons wait to dump and weigh, three driven by white men he has seen around town or at the quarry before. The fourth wagon is driven by Jupiter Hall, a colored man from The Bottom. Noby and Jupiter have worked side by side for years, on one project or another, for farmers who can afford to hire out help.

"Slow today," the farmer in the wagon directly in front of Noby says, making conversation to pass the time. Wash Honeycutt has a small place south of Colfax, and Noby helped him once in the difficult birth of a calf.

Noby smiles and tips his hat. "Yes, sir, Mr. Honeycutt."

"Who you hauling for this time?"

"Mr. Swafford," Noby answers.

Noby starts to cramp, and he decides to walk a little to stretch out his muscles. The line won't move forward until the men ahead finish their shoveling. The circulation comes back into his legs, and he stands by the side of the wagon, eating the last of the dinner Emma packed for him when he left the house that morning. The cold biscuit and ham take away his hunger but do nothing to help him endure the merciless heat.

The long line of wagons inches forward for the better part of two hours. While he waits his turn in the full force of the sun, Noby maps out the rest of the day in his head, his wide-brimmed straw hat pulled low over his forehead. Once he shovels the gravel into his wagon, it will take maybe thirty minutes to get back to Swafford's, and then he can head home to Emma with the dollar in his pocket. She will have chicory coffee for him, and he will sit down for a leisurely read of yesterday's newspaper. A day well worth the sore muscles.

Up ahead, Wash Honeycutt throws the last bits of gravel into the bed of his wagon and pulls off the wagon brake. Noby is next.

"All yours," Honeycutt says to Noby, snapping the reins. The horse strains under the heavy load, and for a moment Honeycutt can't get him moving. Noby grabs hold of the horse's harness, leading him while Honeycutt prods again with the reins. The heavy wagon lurches forward just as another wagon arrives at the quarry. The white man at the reins doesn't stop at the end of the line but drives his wagon directly to the front, closest to the pile of gravel, Noby's spot.

"Move aside, coon," he says.

Noby recognizes the man as one of the many Hadnots around the area. Noby always has trouble keeping himself in check around a Hadnot.

"Excuse me, sir, I am next," says Noby. He steadies his voice to strike the balance of claiming his rights without provoking a white man.

Wash Honeycutt, not yet clear of the quarry, pulls his horse to a stop, still partially blocking the way. Now there are three wagons in the logjam, and none has clear access. "No call to cut line, Simon. We all waited our turn," says Honeycutt to Hadnot.

It is a generous gesture, and Noby senses the mood of the waiting men on his side, colored and white. There is a workman's code that lies beneath their dealings with one another at the gravel pit.

"No son of Canaan going before me," says Simon Hadnot. He flicks the tip of his whip across his horse's back and maneuvers his wagon around Honeycutt's.

Wash Honeycutt remains where he is, outmatched, his heavy wagon at an awkward angle. He doesn't drive away, but he doesn't challenge Simon Hadnot again either.

"Yield," says Hadnot to Noby.

The familiar red begins to take form in Noby's mind, radiating out until his skin tingles with the rage. He climbs back up on the seat of his wagon and takes the reins in his hands.

"No, sir," says Noby. "I been waiting 'most two hours. My turn next."

"You back-talking me?" Simon Hadnot is honestly surprised. "Best get out my way, boy, 'less you don't mind leaving this life early."

There are about a dozen white men at the gravel pit, loading, unloading, and loitering. Hadnot turns to them, plays to a larger stage. "This boy going against a white man. What this parish coming to? Who's with me?"

The response is mixed. Some are ready for a confrontation under the hot sun, but others just want to load their gravel and be done with it. Noby no longer tries to calibrate the tempo of the crowd. The red has already staked its claim, taken hold of him. His mind, body, and senses pulse to their own beat.

"Move aside, boy. Don't make me get down," says Hadnot.

"I will not," says Noby. The muscles in his face are so taut he can hardly move his jaw to speak, his body coiled in intense concentration. He sees the insult of Simon Hadnot's slouch hat, the entitled, sun-chapped face, the big rabbitlike teeth. Everything else recedes, noise and onlookers and quarry.

Hadnot jumps down in one agile, fluid motion, seeming to cover the short distance between the two wagons in less than a blink. He yanks Noby by the arm of his shirt, jerking him from his perch on the wagon seat, and Noby finds himself looking up at Hadnot from the ground. He isn't quite quick enough to roll away as Hadnot brings his boot to Noby's ribs.

"Enough," cries Wash Honeycutt, but Hadnot kicks again.

The sharp edge of the pain sharpens Noby's senses, the power of red coursing through his brain and body, focusing him on the easy target that is Simon Hadnot. He springs up from the ground, sore ribs forgotten, and flies at Hadnot, tackling him around the middle, bringing him down onto the sharp stones and dirt of the quarry. He briefly registers the astonishment on Hadnot's face and, with all his might, slams his fist into the center of the remnants of Hadnot's smug smirk. Noby hears the crunch of bone, the surprisingly soft give of facial structure, and he draws his fist back and punches Simon Hadnot again, harder, not sure if the vivid scarlet swimming in front of his eyes is the man's blood or a reflected manifestation of his rage. Noby's hand stings, gashed raw by something sharp. The stinging brings Noby back to himself, enables him to see the scene as others will. Simon Hadnot, a white man of Colfax, lies on the ground writhing, moaning, his face a bloodied mass, teeth broken and spilled on the ground like discarded wood chips, and a colored man delivered the blows. A hand at Noby's back jerks him up by the neck of his shirt and away from Hadnot on the ground.

A circle of white men surrounds Noby. Even those who were indifferent or sympathetic toward him when Hadnot began his bullying are outraged now. Beyond the close-in circle of hostile white faces, Noby sees Jupiter Hall, the only other colored man at the quarry, still at the reins of his wagon, his dark face a mask of passivity. Noby reads more from Jupiter's demeanor than in the anger of the men closer by. Jupiter's situation is precarious. He can't call attention to himself by leaving, and he can't rush to Noby's defense or the same fate will fall to both of them. All Jupiter can do is wait and see what happens, where the white men will take the situation next. All Jupiter, one of his colored Mason brothers sworn by the secret ceremonies of fraternity to come to Noby's defense, can do is wait and see if he can pick up the pieces, if there are any pieces to pick up.

The circle of white men tightens, not a single friendly face among them, and with a quick seizing of his stomach, Noby realizes he is done for. They will never allow this affront to the race, a white man down on the ground at the hand of a colored, no matter what the provocation. The fight seeps from Noby then, not only because he is outnumbered or because the flood of red rage fueling him has dissipated, leaving a bad taste of inevitability in his mouth, but because he carries forward the cautionary weight of over a hundred years of conditioning deep in the marrow of his bones. Like Jupiter, he waits, and the wait is short.

Simon Hadnot stumbles up from the filth of the gravel pit and breaks through the knot of white men. The lower part of his face is smeared with blood, some congealed already, and some sprouting fresh rivulets over his chin and down the front of his shirt.

"Now it's your turn, boy," Hadnot says, his eyes wild with fury.

The snaking menace in the white man's voice sends shivers through Noby, and he tenses his body for the blows. Softly, he recites the Twenty-third Psalm.

Hadnot pummels Noby, bare knuckles to his face, his stomach, fists to his kidneys. When Noby falls, Hadnot kicks at him, and Noby instinctively curls himself in a ball until he is hoisted upright and straightened out by other men so Hadnot can come at him again. Strangely, there isn't much yelling or noise of any kind, not by the crowd of men or from the surroundings, only the dull thuds of landed punches, as if the birds and insects have stopped what they were doing until the beating is finished.

Noby loses touch with the present and stops cataloging his injuries. His broken nose and cracked ribs are the least of the pain. He just hangs on. *Yea, though I walk through the valley of the shadow of death, I will fear no evil . . . thy rod and thy staff they comfort me.* He loses track of who hits him, his eyes swollen so shut he can barely see. Noby thinks suddenly of his father, of Israel Smith, how he hobbled around the cabin on his one good leg in his last years, broken in body and spirit, and he realizes what a luxury that was, to still be alive under any circumstances. He will not be so lucky. Already he feels his life force leaking away.

"If he not dead yet, I'ma finish him," Noby hears Simon Hadnot say. "He's mine. I got to wash this blood off. Watch him till I get back."

The successive waves of new pain stop, and the tight squeeze of sweating bodies pressing in on him thins. There are no blows or kicks or jabs to his body for another minute, and then another, and Noby almost slips into unconsciousness from the unexpected dearth of bright explosions to his face, his groin, his back.

"Might's well stay down." Wash Honeycutt leans close to Noby's ear, his voice a whispering buzz. "Hadnot hurting too, gone to patch himself up before he come back to see if you really dead. Why you gotta hit him?"

Noby drifts, his mind not quite able to put everything together. He is still alive, but when they come back, they will finish him for sure. If he doesn't get out beyond the reach of Hadnot now, he is as good as dead. Noby tries to pull himself up but can't balance himself sitting, let alone standing. He grabs the hand of the man leaning over him and gives him the sign, pushes the blood out of his throat so he can say the password.

Wash Honeycutt stares at Noby, first in surprise and wonder, then in anger and confusion. Noby has given the Masonic distress signal to a white man, as if they are brothers. The white men have their lodge of brotherhood but don't acknowledge the right of colored to conduct the same practices, even in secret. A brother is bound to help a brother, but not across race lines.

Noby makes one last desperate gamble. "Jupiter," he says. He points weakly in the direction of Jupiter Hall, still in the quarry with his horse and wagon. "He a colored brother."

Honeycutt struggles with conflicting emotions. "Simon Hadnot a hothead fool," he says finally. He rises and walks to Jupiter's wagon. Noby can't hear the conversation, but Wash Honeycutt and Jupiter Hall lean in close, conferring, before Honeycutt walks off in the opposite direction.

Jupiter pulls his rig near Noby, looks around warily. Everyone is in the quarry shed, including Honeycutt. "Can you get in back, Brother?" he asks.

When he moves, Noby is so nauseated and dizzy he can hardly stand, but he manages to stumble to his feet. "I need help," he says.

Jupiter gets down and drags, pulls, and pushes Noby into the bed of the wagon, laying him flat on the planks, throwing a filthy horse blanket over him. "Hold the sides," Jupiter says.

Jupiter scrambles to recover the reins and gives the horse a guarded *gee* to get him going. Caution for the battered man's condition comes second to the need for a rushed retreat. Once they are about two hundred yards away from the gravel pit, Jupiter picks up the pace, brings the horse to first a full trot and then a gallop, and heads for The Bottom.

Noby aches, the pain coming in waves so intense at times that all he can do is close his eyes and pray as he grips the crossbars of the wagon to prevent himself from crashing into the sides. The bumps and pitch of the wagon toss him about, reopening wounds and inflicting new ones, made worse by rolling on the sharp edges of loose gravel that bore into his exposed skin. The next hour is critical. It is too risky to take Noby to his own house, the first place the white men will look. Instead, Jupiter makes a beeline for Jackson Tademy's farm. It is only a matter of time before the search begins and The Bottom is crawling with white men set on retribution.

Noby can't prevent the avalanche of random thoughts and memories that come to him unbidden, feeding the crushing fear of his impending death at the hands of a white mob. Noby hears his father's voice deep inside his head, giving conflicting commands: *A man control himself; then he don't have nothing to pay for later*, but also *Don't never let them put their hands on you*.

Noby doesn't want to die. His mother, Lucy, says he knows how to cheat death, but this time he doesn't have the physical strength to escape. One eye is swollen totally shut, and he can barely see from the other. Mercifully, the wagon stops at last. Noby hears voices, then feels familiar hands on him, pulling him upright out of the muck of gravel and blood that has become his refuge. There are four who help him climb from the wagon bed, buttressing him upright between them so they can walk and drag him to shelter. It takes his daughter Lenora, Amy Tademy, Polly Tademy, and Jupiter to get him into the mule shed, propped up against a bale of hay. The house, any house, is too dangerous, and this is only the first stop of many if he is to survive the long night.

"White men come soon," says Jupiter. "This wagon got to get hid."

"I take the wagon to the woods," Amy says. "Jupiter, you take the horse and go tell Emma we got Noby here, safe. She got to stay put."

"What Noby do?" asks Polly.

"Hit a white man at the gravel pit," says Jupiter. He throws a saddle on Jackson's mare and cinches it tight. "Hit him twice."

Amy shudders. "They see you help him away?"

"Only one, I think," says Jupiter. "Wash Honeycutt turn his back so's I could collect Noby out of there, but I don't know how long he'll hold. A white Mason doing a good deed for a colored Mason. Darnedest thing I ever seen."

"Well," says Polly, but she leaves the thought unfinished, unwilling to pass judgment too early. "We don't got much time. Hide yourself tonight after you leave Emma's."

Amy, Polly, and Jupiter leave the shed together, Jupiter leading the saddled horse. Lenora stays behind. She strokes Noby's hand, crying softly, the expert fingers of her other hand seeking out the most brutalized places on his body that need patching first. Noby winces, the pain springing back to life under her probing fingers, but at the same time he feels safe in the hands of his daughter and of friends.

Noby hears the urgent ringing of the old plantation bell on the porch and the clipping of hooves away from the shed as Jupiter rides off. Before long, Polly returns with two buckets of water, one for cleaning his wounds and one with a dipper for drinking. She rips up a bedsheet for bandages.

"Make him ready to travel," Polly says to Lenora. "Amy's hiding the wagon. When Jackson come, he figure out where we take your papa next."

They talk as if Noby isn't there, but his mind is starting to clear. He can't escape a second time from the white men at the quarry. To have any chance, he has to leave the parish.

"Get me to Sidney," Noby says.

Both his sons work at nearby train stations. Nineteen-year-old

Sidney Smith works in Alexandria, almost thirty miles away, and twenty-one-year-old Aston works closer to home at Boyce. It is one of the best possible jobs for a colored man just starting out, cleaning the toilets and assisting the red-capped porters who have seniority.

"Sidney get you away, Papa," Lenora says, excited. "He know a lot of people at the train."

Noby holds to this fragile thread of hope. If they get him to Alexandria, he can hide on the train and escape not only the parish but maybe the state of Louisiana.

Lenora's face goes stiff, and she puts her finger to her lips, warning him to quiet. She throws the nearest horse blanket over Noby, hiding him, the second time that day that he is buried within the scratchy, stinking folds of horse sweat and straw, like a shroud. Lenora tiptoes to the doorway of the shed.

"Papa Jackson, it's you," she whispers. Her voice is so full of relief that Noby can't help but feel a little heartened too, as if his boyhood friend has the power to make the last hour disappear, to somehow wake him from this nightmare.

Lenora lets Jackson and Nathan-Green into the shed, and when she uncovers Noby, tugging at the blanket as if performing a magic trick, the open air feels intoxicatingly fresh.

"What happened?" Jackson asks.

"He got in a fight with white men," Polly says.

"Then you got to run," Jackson says to Noby. He is all business.

"Alexandria," Noby says. "Sidney get me out."

"How long you here?" asks Jackson.

"Less than a hour."

"How bad?"

"I hit a Hadnot. They gonna come," says Noby.

"No, how bad a beating?"

"I can't walk far, but I'm breathing," says Noby. "Keep passing out."

"Still," says Jackson, considering, "you never make it all the way to Alexandria without somebody seeing. Boyce half the distance, mostly woods. We get you on the train there and send you to Sidney in Alexandria." Jackson picks up the reins and bit to hitch up the mule to his wagon. "Sooner you gone from Colfax and The Bottom, the better." He rattles off a list of things to do, mumbling to himself. "We got to get word to Sidney, let Emma know."

"Jupiter brung Papa," says Lenora. "He off to tell Mama now."

"Where's Amy?" asks Jackson.

"Hiding Jupiter's wagon down the bayou. May be they know Jupiter at the gravel pit too," Polly says.

The water in the first bucket is already bloody, but Lenora manages to clean out most of the cuts and stop the worst of Noby's bleeding. She wraps strips of the sheet around the deepest wounds, careful not to tie them too tightly. Amy comes back, assesses the scene at a glance, and takes over from Lenora.

"Aston got a train pass for Boyce," Lenora says. "Somebody got to go tell Aston at the sawmill to prepare Sidney. They won't think nothing of me. I'll go."

Noby considers this girl, his daughter, almost thirty but so shy since childhood that she barely speaks except to him and Emma, and even then spares her words, as if to say too much is to risk something precious. Lenora isn't frail, but she is fragile, and she is offering to do something beyond her own imagining.

"They know you the daughter. I'll go," says Nathan-Green. No one would have expected Nathan-Green to volunteer. "My wife don't belong in the middle of this, not with white men on the prowl." It is out of his character to play an active part where there is both danger and choice involved. "Where the mare?"

"Jupiter took her."

"Hansom Brisco lend you a horse, just get to his farm," Noby says.

Nathan-Green takes off running, moving fast on foot between the rows of corn and then disappearing into the dense piney woods.

"We stay here at the house, in case anybody come looking," says Polly. She pulls Lenora to her, steadies her. "If they show up here, they find a old helpless woman, don't know nothing. I got a few tricks left, come to that."

Jackson pulls the wagon close to the shed, and he and Lenora help Noby to his feet. They put him faceup against the planks in the back and cover him with hay, rigging up a hollow area around his face so he can breathe. The sun is lower in the sky, but the air still throbs with Louisiana's wet summer heat, and Noby throws off sweat, feverish.

"We got about a hour and a half," says Jackson. "You can make it?"

Noby grits his teeth, tries to block out the ripples of pain and the stale smell of moldy hay forcing his throat to constrict. "Just get me on the train," he says.

Jackson gathers up a last handful of straw to sprinkle lightly over Noby's face, hide him completely from view. "Sorry, old friend. This ain't right," he says. "You more a part of this town than anybody."

"Wait," says Noby. "Wait."

Jackson stops and leans closer, the last of the hay stalks limp in his hand.

"The school," Noby says. "The time come for the colored school."

"We got to make haste," says Jackson. "They be on your trail any minute."

"What about the school?" Noby persists. "Jackson, please. Make our passing through this life be about something. Our grandchildren worth they own school. Promise."

"First things first," says Jackson. "I got to cover you now, Noby. Get you away."

"I can't come back," says Noby. "Tell Emma I'll send word."

Jackson nods, his face unyielding, and places a thin layer of hay on top of Noby's face. It feels to Noby as if Jackson is burying him alive, consigning him to a world without light or family or anything he has ever known.

30

1918

E mma, is Noby here?" Sheriff Clinton asks.

    The sheriff's tone is neither harsh nor dismissive. He asks the question as if he already knows the answer, as if they each have a part to play and he is bored already with his assignment. Like everything else that has thrown itself at her in the last hour, his demeanor is a surprise. Emma expected worse, has anticipated the ransacking of her house and the calling out of herself and the children for the entertainment of the white men. She manages to keep herself calm only because of the children. They take their cues from her.

    The morning on Bayou Darrow started like any other, full of chores to perform, children to take care of, animals to water and feed, meals to be cooked, floors to scrub. Wednesday is bake day, and Emma was up before dawn, trying to get a jump on the heat. She has her apron on still, streaked with flour and small, curling bits of dried-out dough. The smells of yeast and freshly baked loaves linger in the air, smells she usually loves, but they no longer appeal. The cow refused milking this morning, a bad omen she should have recognized, but she packed up a dinner pail for Noby and watched him ride out in the wagon bound for first the icehouse and then the gravel pit on a paying job for Mr. Swafford. The day ran smoothly, flowing as she flowed, in harmony with her rhythm.

And then Jupiter, as lathered as the horse he rode in on, galloped onto the farm to deliver his breathless synopsis of Noby's predicament. It took only a moment for Emma to comprehend that her world was irretrievably wrong side out, that her husband might still lose his life if they didn't figure a way to smuggle him out of the parish. And now she stands facing the sheriff of Colfax, not sure what to say.

The sheriff is a big man, a man with a webbed network of broken capillaries along his ruddy cheeks and a nose that spreads across his face like melting ice cream. Emma knows him by sight. Everyone knows who the sheriff is, but she hasn't dealt with him this close before. She is afraid of this white man standing with impunity in her doorway, with the power to do anything that crosses his mind. Behind the sheriff is another white man who gapes at her openly, as if she is a treed possum. He shifts from one foot to the other, the skin of his face bruised a mottled purple, with a freshly split lip, shockingly crimson and poorly tended. Unlike the sheriff, the man makes no pretense of cordiality, too angry and agitated to extend the least courtesy to the family of the colored man who dared strike him. Simon Hadnot is the most dangerous kind of white man there is, looking for any outlet. Farther out in the yard are six more mounted men, waiting with an assortment of shotguns and pistols, a hastily formed posse.

The sun is still strong, even this late in the afternoon, enough to throw a glare. Emma forces herself not to look in the direction where Jupiter rode off thirty minutes before. She summons an expression of slow-witted ignorance. Her daughter Martha

Geneva twines herself in the long folds of Emma's skirt, sucking at her thumb and slowly rubbing her nose with her index finger, peeking out while staying as far from the white man as she can, but unwilling to leave her mother's side.

Married thirty-seven years, and the day Emma has dreaded since the wedding day is at hand. Noby is a good man, a good husband, but he has to fight hard to keep his temper from flaring if he feels disrespected. Pride and stubbornness are a deadly combination. Noby forces himself to smile as needed in order to get by, insincerely, the same as everyone else, but he has a brittle inner core, a rigid boundary of "no trespass." Noby cannot tolerate being pushed around, and Emma has always prayed he would never forget himself in his dealings with whites, the one thing she feared most.

"No, Sheriff Clinton," says Emma, "he ain't here. I ain't seen Noby since he left this morning. You can look if you want."

Sheriff Clinton and Simon Hadnot enter the cabin. At one time, fifteen people lived under this roof, from babies in cloth diapers to aged grandparents, but it never seemed as crowded as at this very minute. These two white men fill the space in a way that they as a family never did. Emma positions herself in a corner and throws her arm around Martha Geneva's trembling shoulder, pulling her daughter as deep into her skirts as she can.

Simon Hadnot upends the rocking chair in the front room. The spindly chair totters absurdly for an instant, as if it has gotten a second wind, but then it crashes to the floor and stays put.

"Simon," Sheriff Clinton says, "go wait with the others outside. I'll handle this by myself just fine." He sounds weary but patient, as if scolding a disobedient puppy who doesn't know any better than to chew up the master's boots.

"This time the coon ain't gonna get away," declares Simon Hadnot.

"We know what happened at the quarry," says Sheriff Clinton. "Go outside and let me do my job."

Simon Hadnot throws a warning look in Emma's direction, and the terror of that glance makes her go weak inside. Martha Geneva, who has been quiet up until that point, begins to cry. Not a full-throated wail but quiet sobs she tries, unsuccessfully, to choke back. She trembles against Emma, clutching hard through the skirt and holding her mother's legs in a vise, pinching with her little fingers until she breaks the skin. Emma wraps her apron around Martha Geneva's shoulders. It is all she can do.

Simon Hadnot reluctantly walks outside. Sheriff Clinton moves through the rooms of the house in a leisurely way, giving each a cursory inspection. Emma follows on his heels at a distance, not close enough for him to claim she is interfering with his search but not so far away as to lose the thread of what he is checking. She doesn't know what to expect. When he comes to the children's bedroom, Willie Robert sits on the cot, perfectly still. Her son stares at the sheriff with large, liquid eyes, and the sheriff nods as if acknowledging an unpleasant but necessary task. The civility of the small gesture throws Emma into confusion.

The sheriff moves on and enters the bedroom Noby and Emma share. He stoops to lift a corner of the beige chenille bedspread. Emma has sewn the spread generously, large enough to fall to the floorboards on both sides. The sheriff barely bends over far enough to take a reasonable look under the bed. He doesn't upend the thin mattress, or examine under the overturned washtub on the sleeping porch, or so much as glance at several places large enough to hide a clever or desperate man, almost as if he doesn't care whether he finds Noby or not. And yet he doesn't leave. Sheriff Clinton stands, leans against the wall toward the rear of the cabin, pinches three fingersful of tobacco from the pouch he keeps in the pocket of his jacket, and fills his cheek.

It dawns on Emma that the sheriff is stalling. She isn't sure if he thinks Noby might come riding home into their waiting arms for an easy capture, or if it is possible that he delays to convince those on the outside that he has performed a more thorough search. She prays to keep herself steady, prays for every extra minute that passes, time that might make the difference between Noby getting away and the men outside catching up to him.

After about ten minutes, Sheriff Clinton strolls to the front room. "Noby made a big mistake," he says to Emma. "A shame. He's a good man."

Sheriff Clinton rejoins the posse outside, and they ride away. Where, Emma doesn't know. Willie Robert comes into the front room, waiting for a sign, an explanation of what just happened and what comes next. Emma rights the rocking chair and sits down hard. She reaches for Martha Geneva and Willie Robert, gathers them beside her in the chair, and holds tight, letting the back-and-forth motion calm them all.

Emma knows that almost every colored person in The Bottom will help get her husband away if they can, but there is nothing more she can do directly. She holds on to her children and prays. The sheriff's behavior seemed almost sympathetic, even though he heads the posse intent on hunting Noby down.

It is a puzzlement.

Figure 18. Willie Robert and Martha Geneva Smith, Ellen and Elmira Tademy

Figure 19. Emma Smith

31

1 9 1 8

T he trip to Boyce underneath the load of stinking straw in the bowels of the roasting wagon is unbearable, but at least it is uneventful. Jackson and Amy keep off the main roads, cutting through isolated wooded areas where the wagon wheels dig grooves in the mud. The detours make the likelihood of running into a posse more remote, but the ride takes longer and the terrain is more bumpy. It seems to Noby as if days and not hours have passed between this jolting ride to the train station and the incident at the gravel pit. No matter what position he tries to assume, his ribs ache and his wounds throb in protest, draining what strength he has. The grasping ache behind his eyes makes it impossible to think clearly, and the overpowering stench from the bales of straw makes it increasingly difficult to keep from either gagging or sneezing. Slowly, gradually, he begins to focus on the new parameters of his universe, recognizing with numbing certainty that the only two paths open to him now are death or exile.

He is in despair at the possibility of fleeing the only home he has ever known, leaving behind the Louisiana land his father so bitterly fought for, abandoning his wife, Emma, and his mother, Lucy, still scratching out a widow's living in The Bottom. This dawning acceptance is far worse than all of his physical wounds. Noby is fifty-four years old, strong enough to competently perform in a sought-after young man's job, a young white man's job, delivering ice to the people of Colfax. He was tested early and established himself as a valued member in his colored community, a deacon in his church, trusted enough by the whites of Colfax to be in demand for steady cash work. He has brought thirteen children into the world and lived to see most of them already settled, married, with children of their own, and held on to a wife he is able to lie down alongside each night and look to each morning without regret. It isn't fair, and he waits for the old familiar red to rise, but it is a puny thing now, dimmed, no longer carrying its previous power to cloud his mind and provoke him to strike out. The finality of his predicament dilutes the destructive force he has wrestled with and tried to control all his life. It leaves in its wake a man frightened of losing everything.

The wagon stops, and Noby hears the indistinct buzz of distant voices and the mechanical sounds of the apparatus of a train yard. Steam hissing, metal striking metal, lonesome voices calling out departures to places far away. He is familiar with all of it, so proud that two of his sons found positions at train stations that he once bought a ticket and rode in the colored car from Boyce to Alexandria and back again, just to be a part of the glory of their employment.

There is a bounce to the wagon when Jackson and Amy climb down from the bench seat, and Noby hears Jackson's retreating footsteps as he walks into the train station. He assumes Jackson will survey the scene, look for members of a posse, assess the risk, and refine their plan. Waiting, Noby nods off more than once, each time waking to panic. He isn't sure how long Jackson has been gone, only that the precision of time no longer works properly for him. Everything seems to float, and there are no new clues or comforting sounds he can identify to anchor his mind. Noby wonders if Amy is still beside the wagon or if she has gone away as well, leaving him alone. His cocoon under the hay drives him toward some form of madness, an unmooring. Just when he thinks he would undergo anything else rather than stay buried and ignorant of what is happening for one minute longer, he hears footsteps and another wagon rolling toward theirs, coming closer and stopping nearby. The familiar weight of Jackson and Amy on the front bench once more comforts him with the sense of someone in control of his destiny. Their wagon begins to move, slowly, away from the noises of the train station, the grinding sounds dimming with the steady clopping of the horse's hooves and the clatter of another vehicle following.

The wagon stops again. Several pairs of hands unbury Noby from his tomb of hay, moving aside the larger bales, carefully digging him out. They pull him upright, but his body is slow to obey. The stiffness and unresponsiveness of his trunk and limbs insulate him, yet as soon as he is touched, all of the pains he has come to expect in the last few hours are set loose.

"Papa, we got a way to get you out." It is Aston, his son. Noby would weep with gratitude if he weren't so fatigued. "We work it out. Sidney, L'il Hansom, and me. It's the best way."

Noby looks to Jackson and Amy. The drawn-tight muscles at Jackson's jawline betray his rage, and Amy's studied composure cannot mask the pitying sadness reflected back at Noby through her eyes. Whatever this plan is won't be easy. Noby has trouble following a straight line of thought. His sons worked what out? Sidney is east in Alexandria, Louisiana, and L'il Hansom now lives to the northwest, in Oklahoma.

"We got to put you in a coffin," Aston says. "If they check colored cars, you too beat up to miss. Even if we pull your hat down low over your face. This way you go in the boxcar. Nobody check that but us, loading and unloading."

"How he can breathe?" asks Amy. "He burn up in there."

Aston points to the crude pine coffin in the other wagon. "We doctor the box," he answers. "A Mason work the funeral detail and give this one airholes, pack it down with ice and sawdust. Least going out at night be cooler, and we put the coffin in the refrigeration car. We pack up drinking water for you in there too." Aston either has the optimism of youth or is trying to put the best face on a bad situation. "The train already in the station and leave for Alexandria in one hour. We gonna load you up and get you in the boxcar now, before more of a crowd come. Sidney know to get you on the switch train to Oklahoma, and by the time you get there, L'il Hansom be ready to pick you up when you get to the last stop."

Noby doesn't allow himself to dwell on the thought of the long, sweltering ride encased in a tight coffin from Boyce to Alexandria. It makes the short trip to the train station underneath the hay seem easy by comparison. A boxcar in the Louisiana summer is bound to be upward of 100 degrees, more if the refrigeration unit fails, as they so often do. There is the added danger of the transfer, changing trains, one boxcar to another on a different track, being maneuvered around the Alexandria station, maybe as the corpse he is pretending to be. Another ride crammed in close quarters from Alexandria to Oklahoma could finish him off, if the beating by a gang of white men, smothering by hay, and stewing by coffin haven't already done the job, but Noby has to admit that the plan does have a small chance of working.

Noby chuckles.

They stare at him, his friends and family, uncomprehending, and he finds that funny too. He begins to laugh, taking in deep breaths of air. He is caught short by a sharp bruising pain around his midsection, and he forces himself quiet. Instead he just smiles, a silly grin he knows to be inappropriate.

He must be getting better, he tells himself, either that or he has taken a turn for the worse and delirium has taken root. Images of Israel, his father, crowd Noby's mind, the broken man with the cane hobbling around the cabin where he grew up, afraid to go outside. Although his father faced the mercilessness of a white mob and escaped with his body, they robbed him of his spirit, and he lived out his days as an old man, afraid and subdued. Noby witnessed the decline up close, and he refuses to repeat the pattern. He refuses to be defeated in the same way. To keep the fear at bay, to keep himself intact, he chooses to recast the situation, to see it in a different light. There is a certain absurdity, a certain humor, in his plight, however macabre. His mother has always told him he has cheated death from the time he was a baby, and he will do it again. He is sure of it.

Figure 20. L'il Hansom Smith

Figure 21. Aston Smith

Figure 22. Sidney Smith

32

1919

The wintry end of 1918 and the first few months of 1919 prove colder and more punishing than usual for central Louisiana. Small lakes freeze, and crops lay dazed in the field. Slender icicles weep from rooftops in The Bottom, and the trees stand stark and brooding. Jackson Tademy's fifteenth grandchild is born during the worst of that winter, at the beginning of 1919, but even the joyous sharing of another family addition cannot lay to rest Jackson's aching hunger to sit on the front porch in quiet celebration with his old friend Noby Smith, the boy's other grandfather, now so far away. If Noby were still in Colfax, thinks Jackson, he would be harvesting ice for summer selling, sawing out and storing the precious cold pieces in the icehouse, layering the blocks with coarse sawdust from the sawmill to prevent them from melting.

Last year, when the loss was fresher, Jackson thought about Noby every day, but now his mind turns to his friend only when he stumbles on a trigger, an association, a reminder, like a bruise that seems free of pain unless you push too hard on it. Jackson carries on conversations with his friend in his head as if he still resides a short walk away instead of in exile. But life takes on a different tempo without their easy patter, possible only with someone who has shared every stage of your life as you've lived it, someone who can understand more than you put into words, without explanation or apology. At least Noby has sent word back to them that he is safe in Oklahoma, that even the worst of his physical injuries is beginning to heal.

Noby's wife, Emma, has joined him there, at least temporarily, and she will see after him, but trouble brews closer to home. Lucy Smith, almost ninety, has somehow come to blame her son David for Noby's abrupt departure and is refusing to stay under his roof. She has asked Noby to send Emma back to The Bottom. It is a mess.

The year moves forward, winter finally giving up its grip, and at the beginning of April, the sun breaks free from the shrouding dark clouds, and the air warms by almost thirty degrees, a heady relief. But by the second week of April, rain has begun anew, and for two straight weeks, it pours every day. The river steadily rises, higher and higher, monitored almost hourly by those in The Bottom. Everyone knows the evacuation will come early this year. The warm spell is sure to melt the ice upstream at a rate too fast for the banks to handle, and the fierceness of the downpours clinches the inevitability of flood.

At first Jackson calculates they have a day or two more before high water engulfs The Bottom. He and Nathan-Green work as a team, without friction, preparing for the flight to safer ground. The rain is steady but light, with only gentle winds, and father and son work in harmony to erect a raised wooden platform behind the farmhouse, high enough off the ground where many of their leave-behind possessions will be out of harm's way from the seeking waters when they come, but not so high as to be unstable.

They have become used to falling asleep to the monotonous,

hypnotic pinging of rain on their corrugated tin roof, but in the night, the world outside turns wrathful, as if the devil himself flings hailstones the size of watermelons at the Tademy household. It is a frightening sound that terrifies the children and opens at least half a dozen additional roof leaks that will require patching later, as soon as they return from high country. The nonstop downpour throughout the long night accelerates the evacuation timetable.

The women—his wife, Amy, their daughter Mary, his mother, Polly, and daughter-in-law Lenora—divide the last of what they need to take with them to the tent city in the hills. They carry a sack of cornmeal, foodstuffs from the rebuilt commissary, clothes and blankets, bed dressings, a couple of pots and pans, matches, three of Jackson's books wrapped in oilcloth that he refuses to leave behind. Since daybreak, the women have been separating everything into piles, so much to carry with them, so much to leave behind that will hopefully escape the destruction of the rising floodwaters, so much to send ahead when it comes their turn to use the neighbor's boat later in the morning. Lenora packs as quickly as she can, her hands adept at tying up the carrying parcels, but there are constant interruptions. All five of Nathan-Green and Lenora's children are underfoot, excited in the way children work themselves up to be when adults in their midst are anxious, all but the youngest, a baby boy who sleeps the deep sleep of a three-month-old, though he is sure to wake up soon demanding to be fed. He is a small, willful baby with a bullet-shaped head and Indian-brown skin, like his father. They named him Nathan-Green Jr. but call him Ted, to avoid confusion with the duplicate name.

The wind howls in the background, making a terrifying racket. Inside, Amy and Lenora struggle with the old front-room sofa, their best piece of furniture, lifting it off the floor, flipping it upside down, and lowering it, legs up, on top of the elevated wood surface of the dining table, hopefully high enough. Outside, Jackson and

Nathan-Green secure the last of their leave-behind belongings. Whereas yesterday the rain fell constantly, gentle and measured, today the wind whips the rain around in ferocious sheets, and walls of stinging wetness slap into their bodies as if they are on the receiving end of a fighter's punch.

Year after year, they go through the same exercise, but the fastening of the oilcloth in the face of this morning's screaming gale is trickier than usual. As they stretch the tarp over the top, an end gets away, flicks out of reach, sudden as a cracking whip.

"Tie down your end," Jackson yells into the storm. "If Andrew here, it be done already. Stick to it. For once."

Jackson regrets his words as soon as he says them. Since Noby left The Bottom, Jackson seems to find himself much closer to anger all of the time, especially with Nathan-Green. He looks to his oldest son, the one who should be clearing the path for the others. On the day Nathan-Green arrived in this world, mewling and kicking, Jackson conferred upon his son the honor of Green's name to give him strength. But Nathan-Green Tademy seems not up to the challenge. He is who he is. Jackson tries to adapt to that truth, although he finds it difficult to make peace with the disappointment.

Nathan-Green's only reaction to his father's criticism is an obstinate clamping down on his teeth and a press-together of his lips, but he doesn't utter a word in his own defense. He keeps his head down and tries again to secure his end of the rope. His passivity frustrates Jackson even more.

The time has come when Jackson feels he must orchestrate the passing of his life's work, as his father did with him. All of his children except Mary are fully grown. Andrew is the most capable, serious, stable, driven, but his oldest, his stunted son, has never managed to grow into his potential. Nathan-Green is thirty-six, and he, Lenora, and all of their children still live in Jackson's home.

How can sons be so different? Of course, Jackson knows the answer, and he even sympathizes. Wasn't he once in the same situation, buried deep in the shadow of a brother upon whom all hopes were pinned, all expectations channeled, all opportunities first allocated and passed along to him, like a hand-me-down jacket, only when they no longer fit? Wasn't Green the heir apparent, and didn't Jackson take stock and come into his own when circumstances demanded?

It is against the Lord's plan not to love your own children equally, but Nathan-Green and Andrew have so little in common that it is difficult to believe they were raised in the same house, that both come from Jackson's seed. Andrew, so ambitious and responsible, so able to see possibility in the smallest opportunity. Able to lead others in moving forward not only his family but the Negro race as well. And then there is Nathan-Green, so absent, not in body but in spirit, willing to drift along whichever way the current pushes, as if his eyes are sewn shut and his arms bound, as if he has no say. Barely able to do for his family, unwilling to provide his wife, Lenora, with as little as a visiting dress so she isn't ashamed to leave the house.

Nathan-Green pulls the last piece of rope taut and ties it off with a double knot. Finally, the two men manage to cover the platform, encircle it with more rope, weigh down the pile with rocks heavy enough to keep the edges from working loose, and anchor the tarp as tightly as they can.

"Let's get down from here," Jackson says. "Not much time left. Pull the wagon 'round."

They climb from the platform, water running off the brims of their hats in streams and penetrating the slickers they wear over their coats. When they reach the ground, the two men split off in different directions, Nathan-Green running toward the barn and Jackson making his way toward the house.

Jackson stumbles through the door, bringing the bitterness of the storm in with him before he pulls the door shut against a blast of biting, cold air and heavy rain. He is drenched through, dripping muddy puddles on the floorboards, his hands chapped and raw from the ropes.

"We going *now*," Jackson shouts over the high pitch of the squall. "Over land."

"What about the boat?" asks Amy.

"Can't wait no more," Jackson says. "Get the children and animals together. Nathan-Green bringing the wagons out front. Anything not ready stay behind. River too swole to chance any more time here."

Once the Red River releases its overflow, the floodwaters will spill the banks and rush over the low ground. The potential speed of the capricious waters holds everyone in The Bottom in its sway, preparing for the worst. Men, women, and children, young and old, black and white, must make their way to higher ground, salvaging whatever they need for the siege, limited by what they can carry or load in the boats, driving their animals hard to set up tent cities in the hills until the water recedes. Sometimes they must stay away for a month or more.

Jackson checks the shelf that holds his books, his library. He takes one last look. "You pack the others?" he asks his daughter-in-law.

Lenora already has the children at the front door, ready to thrust herself into the drenching storm and load the last of the goods into the wagon. She stops to nod at Jackson. She cares for his books as carefully as she cares for his son. Jackson trusts her completely to protect what is his.

"Then let's get gone," he says.

The Tademys jostle over soggy ground in the heavy wagons, driving the horses harder than Jackson feels comfortable, but they have run out of time. Twice the wagons stick in the soupy mud, so clogged with the claylike sludge that they are forced to clean and dig out the spokes before they can continue on toward the hills.

Jackson drives the horses hard, cracking the whip over their ears. Normally, he treats his animals, whether mules, horses, goats, oxen, or dogs, with almost courtly respect, expecting them to work as hard as he does but giving them their due.

"You and the beast in a partnership," Jackson often says. "Both parties got responsibilities."

Once past the lowest of the bottomland, Jackson lets up slightly, and he and Nathan-Green both get out and walk at the head of the small caravan to lighten the load, leading the exhausted animals forward at a slower pace. There is an ominous rumble of water in the distance from the direction of their farm.

They ride and walk south and east for two hours. The rain doesn't let up, but the terrain changes, from the endlessly flat bottomland to mounds of rolling hills covered with pine trees. Looming ahead of the caravan, the crown of one of the most pronounced hills looks as if a field of giant Easter lilies have sprouted there, white-topped forms spiking up from the ground. They are close to the tent city.

They ride into the midst of the makeshift community, quickly find a small vacant area in the colored section, and settle, deciding to leave most of the supplies in the wagon until morning. It is too wet and miserable to unload. Even in disaster, white and black keep separate, huddling into their private enclaves, as if loosening the established boundaries can plunge them into uncharted territory as treacherous as the floodwaters that drive them to the high ground. Jackson and Nathan-Green spread a thin tarp on top of the muddy ground. Water seeps from below, and rain assaults them from above, already compromising the largest piece of oilcloth they save for a tent. Jackson tries to build a fire, but the wind and rain make it impossible to keep lit.

The children huddle together in a row, exhausted, wide-eyed, and shivering, looking to their mother for assurances they will be warm and safe again soon. Emma, Ellen, L'il Jackson, Archie. Ted, in Lenora's arms, seems to be the only one among them able to sleep peacefully, his small world simple, defined by the thickness of his blanket, his access to body heat, and the easy availability of his mother's breast.

"I'm cold, Mama," says Ellen to Lenora. The children are wearing all of their clothes, layer on layer, and there is nothing to be done, no dry garments to change them into.

As much as Jackson misses Noby, he acknowledges that Lenora must have it worse. She comes from a family of thirteen children, yet she is almost like an orphan, her birth family flicked away from her like the water a wet dog shakes from its fur. First her father, then her mother and siblings. Earlier in the year, when Noby Smith sent for her, Emma left Louisiana for Ardmore, Oklahoma, taking the two youngest, Willie Robert and Martha Geneva. It isn't clear if any or all of them will ever come back to The Bottom.

Lenora's brothers Aston and Sidney drifted away from The Bottom shortly after, not forced into exile, as Noby had been, but by their own choice, as if the community had a catching disease against which they were determined to protect themselves. After getting Noby away by train, Aston and Sidney left for good, taking up permanent residence in Alexandria and Boyce. They have put The Bottom and Grant Parish behind them without looking back. Even their visits are scarce, as if they can't bear to step foot where their father was nearly left for dead. Lenora has lost the comfort of her father close, and her children have lost their grandfather before getting the chance to know him. At least he lives.

A couple of years ago, before Noby's exile, it snowed, an oddity in Louisiana, and Jackson recalls how the Tademys and the Smiths gathered at his farmhouse. Amy, Polly, and Lenora made buckets of ice cream, packing the scarce snow and coarse salt in a metal container, using the butter churn as an ice-cream maker, cranking until the handle resisted, transforming everyday cow's milk into a wintertime treat. The children begged for more, as everyone would expect, but so too did Jackson and Noby, two older men on the front porch enjoying themselves as if their childhood had been handed back to them. No one could get enough of the frozen concoction, and the women made batch after batch for as long as the snow held out.

Ted wakes and starts to cry. They are almost on top of one another under the oilcloth, without space, no place to go.

"Why that boy crying all the time?" snaps Nathan-Green. "Can't you keep him quiet?" he says to Lenora, who tries to shush the baby, but Ted won't be pacified, his milk cry strong and unrelenting.

"Babies cry," says Jackson crossly. "Let him be."

Nathan-Green turns his back to the others, lies on his side, and settles in to sleep.

Under the oilcloth, on the soggy ground, barely escaped from the barrage of rain, Jackson acknowledges the wealth shivering beneath the tent's leaky canopy. Three generations. Jackson Tademy, Nathan-Green Tademy, and Ted Tademy. The past, the present, and the future. They fit together, if uneasily, all the fierce protectiveness of family, if not necessarily the acceptance.

Jackson has been negligent, waiting too long for life to unfold in the exact way he has envisioned it. Twelve years have passed since his first commissary burned to the ground, taking his father's legacy of the colored school with it. He and Noby have grandchildren who will grow up without the benefit of formal education, and he can no longer hang back in the blind hope that his firstborn will step up to the task. There is another generation hard on the heels of Nathan-Green's, and others in The Bottom and Colfax need what Jackson knows is in his grasp to provide. If Andrew is the son who slips into the role of successor instead of Nathan-Green, so be it. Community is as important as family.

Jackson forms the words he could not force himself to utter on the night of Noby's departure from Colfax. Out loud, Jackson says to his grandson, now sleeping, "I promise."

Though his voice is soft and the storm rages outside, they all hear him, stare at him, not understanding. He leaves them to wonder without clarification. The man to whom he would like to explain is gone, and the baby boy who needs to understand is too young. Jackson is firm in his resolve and absolutely clear about what he must do.

They return home three weeks later, the rain a memory and the sun at their backs. Water stands in puddles along the saturated ground, but the mud has become firmer with each passing day. At the height of the deluge, the churning water sprayed halfway up the walls of the cabin, leaving rust-colored residue stubbornly clinging like vines crisscrossing the wooden surfaces. They shovel and scrape, sweep out the thick layers of left-behind mud, cart out the big furniture for the sun to dry, open the windows to air out the house, and scrub down the floors and walls to avoid further mildew. They retrieve their belongings from where they battened them down on the makeshift scaffolding behind the house. Soggy fabric, damp for weeks under the tarp, has produced a foul-smelling mess. Everything will have to be washed and properly dried, but there is little long-term damage. The foundation of the house held, elevated on cinder blocks, and the floodwaters didn't warp the porch too badly. They find nothing major missing, and, except for a smashed piece of Amy's crockery, a favorite, their damaged belongings won't be so difficult to replace. They lost a few chickens, but all in all, this flood isn't as bad as many they have lived through in the past.

The Tademys carry on the best they can, as they do every year, picking up the pieces and going forward. Sometimes, concedes Jackson, that is all that can be done.

Figure 23. Tademy Road sign, Colfax, Louisiana

Chapter

33

1925

It is just too hot to stay inside his farmhouse, Jackson thinks, upstairs or downstairs. Even the collar of his newly ironed shirt has given up its starched stiffness, and he is drenched. At least today is Saturday, a day away from the schoolhouse. Saturday and his sixty-third birthday, a double indulgence. Amy and the women have been busy in the kitchen since last night, barely pausing to rest, putting pots to boil, baking three-layer cakes, frying up not only minnows from the bayou but chickens and fritters as if it is Sunday. Soon every one of his children and their families will descend on his farm for his celebration birthday supper.

Aided by his cane, Jackson goes out to the back porch, hoping for a breeze.

Andrew's wife, Gertrude, a substantial woman with her head done up in a scarflike turban, dominates the back stoop. Gertrude stands, imposing, overseeing the cranking of ice cream by several of his grandchildren. Polly, too old to stand on her swollen feet for long, sits alongside, queenlike in her rocking chair, shucking a small mountain of corn ears, pulling off the husks and silk of each before moving on to the next.

"How you feeling this morning, Mama?" Jackson asks.

"Shoo," Polly says. "You mens need to get out the way, let us do our work."

Jackson is at a loss. His birthday, and he finds himself an interloper in his own house. He joins Andrew and Nathan-Green on the front porch, but he is restless.

"Let's us go into town, see the high school," Jackson says to his sons. "By the time we get back, may be they be ready to treat a man like it his special day. We even take the wagon."

Ted, his six-year-old grandson, peers at him from the front stoop, eyes wide with desire. Jackson goes to the library shelf in his front room and comes back outside with an ancient-looking slender blue book with a tattered cover. He tucks it into his jacket pocket.

"Follow me, L'il Man," Jackson says. "You going with us."

Nathan-Green rehitches the horse, and they take Andrew's wagon. Jackson situates himself on the back buckboard, and Ted wiggles in to sit close beside him. Jackson sits up straight and plants the length of his black leather shoes on the wooden face board to brace himself. Ted straightens his back and holds his legs out, suspended in air, although his bare feet won't reach far enough to touch the wooden cross-plank. Jackson loosens his collar. Ted wears a coarse white cotton shirt sewn by his mother, loose at the front, but he fusses with the material around his neck, repeats Jackson's gesture, as if he too has a collar to loosen. The four of them set off down the narrow piney woods road, past the half-dead oak tree split by lightning, and on along Bayou Darrow leading to Colfax.

"Comfortable, L'il Man?" Jackson asks.

"Yes, GrandJack," Ted answers.

Jackson takes the frayed reader out of his jacket pocket and passes it to Ted. "Read out page thirty-seven to me. Careful, that book be older than you."

Ted handles the book gingerly, knows not to open it too wide and risk any pages falling out.

Dan has a cod-fish in a pan.
The pan is a tin pan.
This is a big cod-fish.
Dan has a mop in his hand.
Dan will mop the wet step.
The mop Dan has, is a rag mop.

He closes the book and looks to his grandfather for approval.

"You coming along fine," says Jackson.

"GrandJack, when does I get to go off to high school?" asks Ted.

"When *do* I go off to high school," Jackson corrects.

"When *do* I go off to high school?" Ted parrots.

Jackson laughs. "Not at six," he says, but when he sees the stricken anguish on Ted's face, he adopts a less dismissive tone. "You got brothers and sisters ahead of you, and you not old enough yet. You learn everything you can in my elementary school in The Bottom, and wait your turn for Andrew's high school in town. Only so many be boarding in Colfax at a time. But you keep racing that mind like you do, and I teach you extra myself out of my personal library until it time for you to go. You already better at reading than most. Tademys is special, you know."

"We come from Egypt," Ted offers.

"Tademys got a long line of history to live up to," Jackson says. "We come from Egypt, in Africa." They ride in silence for the better part of an hour, until the woods thin and they see the first signs of town.

They keep to the wide dusty main thoroughfare, bisected

by the railroad tracks, toward Smithfield Quarter on the other side.

"Take the route past the courthouse," Jackson says.

"We don't have no call to go into white folks' part of town," says Nathan-Green.

"The boy need to see it," says Jackson. "Colfax our town too. Do like I say."

Reluctantly, Nathan-Green turns the horse toward a side road and keeps her at a steady pace. They pass the old Pecan Tree, a landmark with its spreading canopy of branches, and Jackson has Nathan-Green pull up well short of the courthouse square. Three white men sit in straight-back chairs in front of the courthouse building in the shade of the overhang, barely moving, except to fan the flies that linger too long or wander too close to their faces. A day this hot doesn't lend itself to much more than swapping stories and chewing tobacco. The white men keep their eyes on the wagon, watch the three men and the young boy to see what they will do. Across the street from the courthouse is the newspaper office, but it looks deserted.

"Your relations fight to hold on to their rights on this very spot," Jackson says to Ted. "Some make it out, some don't. They was brave men."

Ted stares at his grandfather, questioning, but that is all Jackson is willing to burden the boy with today.

"We best get gone," Jackson says to Nathan-Green, and his son giddy-ups the horse. But when they pass closer to the courthouse, one of the men in front calls out to them.

"Whoa," he says. "What bizness you boys got here?"

It is Andrew who speaks up. "No bizness," he says. "Just on our way to the other side."

"Ain't you that teacher fella, over to the colored school?" the man asks.

"Yes, sir," says Andrew. "We going there now."

"Well, stay over where you belong," the man says. He leans back, tips his chair until the top frame rests against the courthouse wall, and puts his hat over his face.

Again Nathan-Green urges the horse forward, and they head for Smithfield Quarter.

"Young man, never fight," Jackson says to Ted. "When you see you getting hot, count down from ten to one inside your head. Only a fool don't have sense enough to walk away."

Once they cross the railroad tracks, the land slopes downward, more prone to flood. Four houses from the end, just past the first row of rough-hewn cabins, is a whitewashed building, smaller than the surrounding houses, but brighter and more pristine. It has been freshly scrubbed down with a fresh coat of limewater that makes it appear to almost shine in the sunlight. Off toward the back is a small vegetable garden, poled off and flagged with crop markers. Each time Jackson sees the colored high school, he gets the same familiar quickening in his chest. The Grant Parish Training School, dedicated to no other purpose but to teach children, a giant stride from one corner of his commissary of so long ago or the small elementary school he runs in The Bottom.

Out front, in the full force of the sun, a colored man in a wide-brimmed straw hat ax-splits logs into potbellied-stove-size pieces to add to the neat row of stacked pinewood piled along one side underneath an overhang. He is shirtless under his overalls.

"Brother Boyd," Jackson calls out in greeting.

The man stops working and tips his hat. "Jackson, Professor, Nathan-Green," Nep Boyd replies. "And who this little one be?"

"Nathan-Green's boy," says Jackson. "Nathan-Green Tademy, Jr., but we call him Ted."

"Today my day to see after the school," Nep explains. "We don't see you much this spring, Jackson. Used to be every week."

"I be staying closer to home these days," Jackson says. "Colfax a little far now. Since Andrew move into town, he take over. My boys carry on the school just fine."

"Well, good whenever we sees you," says Nep Boyd. "The Tademy name hold up special to mean colored education in Colfax. Don't think we all not thankful for it."

Jackson nods. "Come on, L'il Man," he says to Ted. "See where you coming one day."

Inside, the one large room is divided by a partition that goes three quarters of the way to the ceiling. A row of hooks lines the walls, and an iron potbellied stove and a large rectangular table fill the communal space. Two large blackboards and a series of mismatched long wooden benches dominate each of the sections. In a careful hand, MR. TADEMY has been written in chalk in large block letters at the top of one of the slate blackboards, and PROFESSOR TADEMY on the other.

Jackson walks from one space to the other, marveling.

"We just raise up the wall inside, Papa," boasts Andrew. "Makes it easier to separate the grades. This old stove not quite up to the task of heating the whole building, but we do better one day."

Jackson picks up a small pot in the corner, half full of brownish water, and holds the pot out accusingly to Andrew.

"A new roof leak, but nothing a pot underneath can't handle," his son says. "Just haven't had time to patch it yet."

"Better to treat the disease than the complaint," says Jackson. He throws the water out into the front yard. "These children learning more here from you than just their letters."

"Yes, Papa. We get to it."

"Sooner better than later," says Jackson. "If I'da knowed, I'da brought my hammer and some wood. We all busy, but at least half-dozen men I can think of come help you if you ask. Nep Boyd be on it this afternoon."

"Yes, Papa."

"And how you coming along, Nathan-Green?" Jackson asks.

"I teach the youngest ones," Nathan-Green says. "We got thirty students, come from far away as Pineville."

"One son principal and the other teacher," says Jackson. He takes one last look around the small space. "Now I'm ready to get back to The Bottom and celebrate my birthday."

Figure 24. Colfax colored school, Willie Dee Billes, front row, seventh from left

*Figure 25. Andrew "Professor"
Tademy*

*Figure 26. Nathan-Green Tademy,
Sr., and four of his eight children:
clockwise, Jackson, Archie, Odessa,
and Ted Tademy, hand on hip*

34

1 9 3 3

"Stop sniffing 'round that Billes gal," Aunt Gertrude says. She speaks proper, in the way both she and Uncle Andrew affect, worrying over every slow word, drawing out each syllable, as if their lips are trained show horses, prancing. "What she possibly want with the likes of you?"

For three months, since Ted came to live in Colfax with his aunt and uncle, Gertrude Smith Tademy has ridden him hard. He endures the constant carping so he can stay in school. True, life is better than when he first arrived from The Bottom. In the beginning, he had to endure the brief humiliation of being put into seventh grade with younger students, even though he was fourteen, but that didn't last beyond the first school day. Just last month, and for the second time, his uncle Andrew advanced him another grade, to ninth, not because Ted is the principal's nephew but because he so clearly outstrips the other students. The lessons in the higher grade are more interesting, challenging, particularly mathematics. The teacher quickly discovered that Ted could hold long columns of figures in his head and produce a sum without writing anything down. She sometimes makes him perform this stunt, problem after problem, but the truth is, he doesn't mind. He has acquired enough of a school reputation that the sandy-haired girl he fancies talks to him in a friendly way now. Sometimes she even lets him carry her dinner pail on the walk home, and although he knows he isn't the only boy afforded the privilege, it is progress.

Ted tries to keep out of his aunt Gertrude's way, makes himself scarce when she is close at hand, but she is around most of the time. Gertrude spends weekdays at the schoolhouse, teaching classes and helping with the administrative workload, leaving two hours early to cook supper for the family. At night she rules the roost at home, parceling out criticism, disappointment, and chores. Ted endures all of her fault-finding, her picking at him no matter what he does, but she has escalated her advice-giving since discovering he is sweet on Willie Dee Billes.

"You got to keep your mind on your lessons and off that fickle Billes girl or you won't end up no better than your father," she finishes. Aunt Gertrude inflates, full of the import of what she has to say. As Ted watches, she seems to become bigger, the way birds puff themselves up on cold mornings.

Ted doesn't know where to begin. In only one sentence, Aunt Gertrude has managed to insult his father, himself, and the girl who, without trying, has wrenched control of his heart.

Andrew Tademy has blossomed as principal of Grant Parish Training School for Colored, expanding the elementary school Jackson Tademy started, while his older brother, Nathan-Green, barely scrapes by. Nathan-Green sometimes teaches the lower grades and sometimes farms in The Bottom. Andrew, stoked by his own inner fire and pushed by Gertrude, owns a house in Colfax and the land beneath it, while Nathan-Green lives on a piece of land given him by their father to work. An indifferent farmer, Ted's father is capable enough, but without any deep passion. What he does best is create more children.

His mother, Lenora, soft of voice, is as different from her sister Gertrude as Nathan-Green is from Andrew, two physically unalike sisters married to two temperamentally unalike brothers. Gertrude continually remarks, reproachfully, on Lenora's quiet demeanor and lack of ambition for her husband. Two Tademy brothers and two Smith sisters married, so dissimilar that had they not been surrounded by a town preoccupied with family lines and assumed connections, they would have done no more than tip their hats to each other if they met in the street.

"What's wrong with Willie Dee Billes?" Ted finally asks. He feels a vague unease that he hasn't rushed to his father's defense first. But he doesn't know how to respond to everything at once, and the web of relationships between his parents and their siblings is a larger, more long-standing, and more complicated quagmire that he isn't eager to slog through.

"Just another high-yellow gal with her nose in the air. Stay away, you hear? That girl never give you the time of day anyhow."

Gertrude has generated a list of people her family can associate with, and under what circumstances, and a far longer list of those they are warned to keep away from for one reason or another.

"She's my friend," says Ted.

"Not so long as you living under my roof, she isn't," replies Gertrude.

Gertrude puts her hands on her wide hips, glowering at Ted. This isn't the first time they have come to an impasse. Ted feels a swirl of red begin to bubble deep within himself.

"Then I got to go," he says before the red rage has time to release and carry him off to some unpredictable place. He turns his back to his aunt and quickly snatches up his nearest things, his cotton jacket, his other shirt, and a borrowed textbook. He moves fast before she can regain her wits and come after him with the strap.

Ted trudges toward home with his small bundle of belongings thrown together and tied up in his jacket, all the way from Colfax to The Bottom. With each step of the two-hour walk, he realizes what a mess he has made. Maybe in Colfax he is labeled a country boy and poor relation, but he has waited years for his turn to break free of the constrictive confines of The Bottom, to shed the ill-fitting farmer-in-training persona thrust upon him, to finally venture beyond the limiting drudgery and sameness that nibbles away at his core. And now, because of his temper, he walks back toward that life, no one to blame but himself.

When he comes to the half-dead oak tree split by lightning just beyond the Walden Bayou bridge, Ted turns right instead of left. Rather than go directly home to his father's cabin, he makes his way to GrandJack's two-story house at the edge of the bottomland.

GramAmy sits on the front porch, bowie knife in hand, cleaning the fish she caught that morning in the bayou, and GrandJack stoops over a row of sugar peas in the garden at the side of the house. They are old, his grandparents, both over seventy, but they have a gentle way with each other that gives Ted a feeling of stillness and peace, as if nothing bad can happen when they are around. Each visit starts with a treat from the back burner of GramAmy's stove, maybe tea cakes and a strong cup of chicory coffee, or a long-simmered pork stew and sugar tea. They assign him chores whenever he comes by, water to tote, eggs to collect, vegetables to pick, or the cow to milk, and he is glad to help them out. After, he sits alongside GrandJack and listens to his advice. GrandJack always has advice.

"L'il Man," his grandfather calls to him when he sees Ted tramp up the path toward their farmhouse. Jackson Tademy stops to lean on his pitchfork, his initial pleasure in seeing his grandson suddenly replaced by suspicion. He wears a wide straw hat as protection against the sun, and his fresh blue coveralls have smudges of mud from the garden. GramAmy keeps his grandfather in starched and ironed clothes, whether he goes out to work the field or into town for business. "Why you not in school?"

"The books they got not even good as yours, GrandJack," Ted says. "And I won't stay with Aunt Gertrude no more. She don't think I'm good as them."

"She *doesn't* think, L'il Man." His grandfather always corrects Ted's speech, although Ted doesn't quite understand how Grand-Jack can so consistently find the errors in his grammar but then turn around and make the same mistakes himself when he is doing the talking.

"Aunt Gertrude doesn't think I'm good as them," Ted repeats. "Uncle Andrew on my side, but I can't do nothing right for her. Trying to tell me who I can see and not see, how to act."

"L'il Man, don't be disrespecting your elders to me or nobody else. And you going to stay in school. Too many paid too steep a price for you to turn up your nose at the opportunity."

"School's all right," says Ted. "But I won't stay with Aunt Gertrude."

"Whoa, now. Draw back on the reins, telling me what you will and will not do," Jackson says. The old man sheds his friendly expression. "You not too old to whup."

"Yes, sir," Ted says. He drops his jacket to the ground and takes the pitchfork from his grandfather's hands, tilling the row where Jackson left off. The only sound between them is the strike of metal in dirt and the soft catch of the earth as he turns the soil. After a few minutes, Ted speaks up again. "I was hoping may be somebody know someplace else I could live for the school term."

"Somebody? When you turn into such a brassy little man?"

The older his grandfather gets, and the more infirm he becomes, the looser he gets in bearing and banter with Ted, as if they are almost equals.

"Why you call me L'il Man, GrandJack?"

"That's what you are, that's what you always been. A little man. Go to the Bible. No boys and girls in there. God made us all in His image, men and women, splendid. You not a boy, you a man in training, close to coming to your own. Don't never let another man calling you boy take you down to his level. That his ignorance, and you got to be wary around it, but his blindness don't have nothing to do with who you are."

Ted loves the sound of his grandfather's explanation each time he hears it.

"Your aunt Gertrude got her ways," Jackson says. "If staying with her the only means to keep you in school, that's what you do. And no complaints. Understand?"

"Yes, sir," Ted says, cowed.

"Hitch up the horse. We going into Colfax and straighten this out. No need bothering your mama and papa until we know which way this likely to fall."

Now Ted is cautiously excited. "Yes, GrandJack."

"Pay respects to your grandma first, and let's get gone."

"Yes, GrandJack."

Dear Willie Dee,

Today in geography class, Professor Tademy told us about the world. He showed us a globe, a way to hold everything that is the earth in the roundness of your hands. I never heard of some of the places he talked about. Colfax is not all there is. Neither is Aloha or Alexandria or Montgomery, or even Louisiana.

There are things I think about, especially at night when the quiet gets strong. Solving a hard arithmetic problem. The smell of my GrandJack's library on his farm in The Bottom. The last minutes of a fast basketball game when both sides match up the same. The way you smile and build up to a laugh, like rolling thunder but without the noise.

You remind me of one of the people in a book my GrandJack let me borrow from his library. They don't have the book here at school. Her name was Eliza, and she had long hair too.

I moved out of my Aunt Gertrude's house and live with a nice couple close to school. Nep and Annie Boyd like me in their house. They say I am young, and I do errands and fix things. Her cooking is good, especially the three-layer jelly cake.

I hope you and me can be friends.

Sincerely,

Nathan-Green (you can call me Ted) Tademy, Jr.

It is his sixth draft, and Ted knows if he doesn't give Willie Dee the letter soon, his nerve will pass. His thoughts organize themselves better when he puts them down on paper first.

Ted folds this latest version and writes "Willie Dee Billes" in large script in his neatest penmanship on the outside.

At school the next day, he slips his first of many letters into the storage compartment of Willie Dee's desk and hopes for the best.

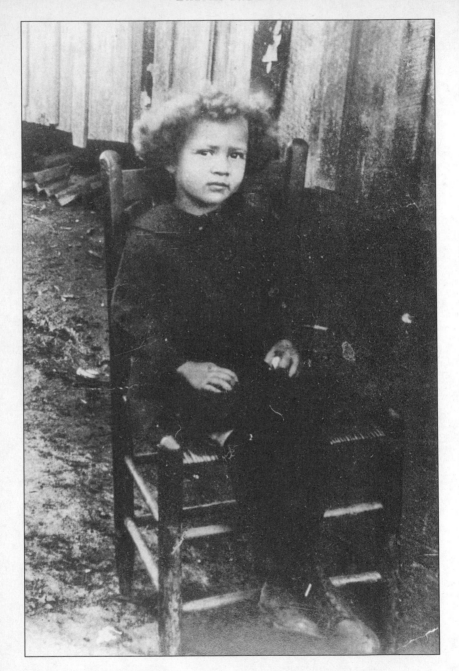

Figure 27. Willie Dee Billes

STATE DEPARTMENT OF EDUCATION

OF LOUISIANA

ELEMENTARY SCHOOL CERTIFICATE

This Certifies that *Willie Dee Billis*

has completed the Elementary course of Study of the Public School System of Louisiana as prescribed by the State Department of Education, and is, therefore, eligible to promotion to the high-school grades of State-approved high schools, and is awarded this certificate as evidence of graduation from the elementary grades of the

Colfax Colored School of

Grant Parish.

Given this *20* day of *April* , 193*4*

NOW White.
President, State Board of Education.

Snable
President, Parish School Board.

L H Harris
State Superintendent of Education.

S. C. Shaw
Parish Superintendent.

A. M. Hopper
State Supervisor of Elementary Schools.

A. J. Tademy
Principal

Oscar Allen
Governor.

Figure 28.
Willie Dee Billes's
elementary school
certificate, 1934

Figure 29. Gertrude Smith
Tademy, Andrew "Professor"
Tademy, and Mary Tademy

35

1935

Early in the spring of 1935, time finally catches Noby Smith, that old dodger of death's heavy hand. On a breezy but bright Easter Sunday, they reserve the first four pews inside the poorly lit preaching room of Mount Pilgrim Rest Baptist Church for the kin of the man in the coffin, brought back across state lines into Louisiana in the rear boxcar of the Texas & Pacific.

The pecan trees haven't quite yet come to bloom, the definitive signal that the last of the sudden morning freezes are behind them, but today's crisp brightness and unfolding warmth are a welcome backdrop to the massive turnout for the funeral. At daybreak, for Easter sunrise service, Ted's father played for a smaller congregation on the church's wobbly black piano, his stubby fingers surprisingly fluid atop the yellowed, cracked keys, and once again he sits at the piano's smooth bench for the afternoon memorial service. His music ushers in the latecomers.

Every available surface inside Mount Pilgrim Rest is crammed with arrangements of spring's early-budding wildflowers. Indian paintbrushes compete with clusters of blue chicory, yellow daisies surround clumps of elegant daylilies at either side of the raised pulpit, and tangles of blue irises in large containers encircle the choir box.

Ted Tademy waits impatiently as more men, women, and children from The Bottom and Colfax, and what looks to be all of the colored Freemasons in Grant Parish, arrive, find seats, and settle in. This gathering is the largest collection of old people in one place at one time he has ever seen, as if every colored person over the age of sixty, regardless of infirmity, has come out to the church. They will follow the body to the colored cemetery in Bagdad for the next part of the service, and after, a smaller group of family and friends will meet at Grandma Emma's house near Walden Bayou.

More than anything, Ted wanted to be sitting next to Grand-Jack to witness the final return of the grandfather he never had a chance to meet, but earlier, when he approached the front of the church, his mother, Lenora, cut her eyes to a pew two rows behind the honor seats held for the family elders. He obeyed, squeezing into a space farther back, between his brothers, but not before he heard Aunt Gertrude whisper to his mother loudly, "Uncle David better not show his face in here. Not here and not at the house, even to see Mama Lucy."

Ted knows the story, as does everyone in The Bottom. How his great-grandmother Lucy refused to stay under one son's roof after the other had to flee. How Emma returned from Oklahoma without Noby to care for his aging mother. How, regardless of David Smith's success, his Freemason brothers no longer welcome him.

The new widow sits in the middle of the first long pew. Emma has pulled her white hair straight back from her high forehead and smoothed it down, but even though thinned by age, stray strands still flaunt their coarse wildness. Profound lines etch deep into the contours of her face. The long black shapeless dress she wears, the staple of every practical country woman, accentuates the undertones of yellow in her skin. Her upsloped, slanted eyes, shaped so like Ted's mother's, are dry.

Because Ted is restless, on the lookout, he may be the first to see the old man enter the back of the church. The man hesitates, but only for a moment. Although the dark three-piece suit he wears is newer than most of those to be found in the congregation, and his shoes are good-quality leather, barely scuffed, in other ways, time has not been kind to the man. His hands tremble, always in slight motion, and his pale gray eyes water without letup. He does not look well. He walks directly to the front of the church, to the first pew, but none there greet him warmly or make any effort to create a place for him. He says a few words to the widow, and Emma murmurs something back. Finally, Polly Tademy raises her hand and beckons, presses closer to Jackson, and makes room for the man on the end. By now all eyes in the church are trained on the front pew. David Smith is Noby's brother, after all. By rights, he should be here.

A narrow shard of sunlight from the window accentuates the deep copper-brown tones of Jackson Tademy's face, which will darken even more as summer catches hold. He carefully dabs at his eyes with a crisply ironed white handkerchief, stiff with starch. He says nothing to David.

At last the service begins. After several piano melodies, a strong voice solo by Aunt Gertrude, and endless remarks by the minister, there are a parade of testimonials for Noby Smith, Colfax's first colored iceman. Like all funerals in The Bottom, this one goes on for a very long time. Old men and old women totter up to the front of the church with slow steps, or lean on the available arm of a church deacon. Lodge brothers pay tribute to Noby's good works and industry, widows recall his kindnesses and sense of community. Still, regardless of how often the words *good* and *proud* and *brave* are repeated, Ted can't grab hold, can't decipher who his other grandfather really was beyond generalities.

Once everyone has had a chance for a say, the minister leads them in a final prayer, and the service concludes. Ted's father plays one last tune on the piano, and the congregation files out, reassembling in the small vestibule of the church and flowing outside into the sudden chill of the afternoon. Attendees express their condolences to the immediate family, visit for a bit, and then some hurry off home to their waiting Easter dinners.

Ted lingers in order to offer his services to the family, but David has already taken Polly's arm to escort her.

Again Polly motions to David, who leans in close, putting his ear almost to her mouth, but Ted is standing close enough to overhear. She whispers, "You paid your respects, but now you not welcome. We gonna carry him home from here."

To David's credit, he doesn't falter or drop her arm, but slowly walks Polly to the waiting buggy outside. She is one hundred and one, and although she insisted on coming to the church and is still able to walk short distances on her own, she won't accompany them to the graveside.

Once outside, Jackson places his old brown fedora on his head. The ancient hat has lost its original shape, caved in beyond repair near the back, where a blue-gray heron feather, hopelessly faded, is secured by a fraying band around the brim. The hat is so threadbare in one patch that Ted can see clear through the material to GrandJack's scalp. The hat gives off a musty smell that follows in GrandJack's wake. Ted's GrandJack is a meticulous man, particular about his person and his clothes, but nonetheless, he wears the badly preserved brown fedora to every funeral he attends.

Jackson leans heavily on Ted. One group spilling out of the church sets off immediately for the cemetery, plodding down the wide dirt road at a slow stride. As the pallbearers load the casket into the waiting wagon, Ted helps GrandJack and GramAmy twist and squeeze into the cramped backseat of the lone automobile, a shiny black 1930 Chevrolet sedan that belongs to Ted's brother-in-law. Emma is adamant in her refusal to ride in the devil machine; she is shepherded instead into a horse-drawn buggy and driven away. Ted walks behind with several others in the wake of dust kicked up by the vehicles. Once they arrive in the section known as Bagdad, everyone leaves the road and walks for the last quarter mile into the cemetery, an uneven patch of overgrown land encircled by a short rotting fence of pine pickets. Homemade grave markers populate the area, some stone, most wood. The pall-bearers carry the casket onto the grounds next to a freshly dug hole, six feet deep and three feet wide, marking Noby Smith's ultimate resting place.

"Noby Smith survived, unlike so many of our other men," the minister says. He looks as if he will say more but instead takes out his handkerchief and wipes at his face. "Finally, he can rest in peace. At long last, Noby Smith has returned home. Amen."

Ted's last sobering image of his other grandfather is a crude wooden box lowered into the ground by four pallbearers, the snatches of legend as cold and flat as the man inside the crate.

About thirty of the mourners return from the cemetery on foot or in a convoy of buggies, buckboard wagons, and horseback to Grandma Emma's farmhouse. Food has been spread out on tables inside, and more dishes arrive with each visitor—a three-layer coconut cake, crawfish casserole, butter beans in rice, still-warm candied yams.

Ted has lived with the specter of Grandma Emma's absent husband for as long as he can remember, although Noby Smith has been decades gone from Louisiana. Over the years, Ted formed pictures of his other grandfather in his mind, speculating on whether Noby could be as smart or wise as GrandJack, whether the tales they told about him were exaggerated or true. Ted always thought he would one day get a chance to meet the misplaced man who continues to hold sway over the lives of the Tademys and Smiths both, as if his other grandfather just wandered down to the commissary for tobacco and would show up again, unannounced, when he tired of the conversation around the cracker barrel. But now Noby Smith is dead, and Ted will never know firsthand whether he favored his predecessor, in facial features or carriage, in speech or temperament. Whenever the flooding red rage descends on him, especially when Ted was younger and his tantrums had more power to sweep him away, his family has shaken their heads with regret. "He got Noby's temper," they say.

Ted has just turned sixteen and is short for his age, although not so short he has to suffer the indignity of a nickname like Half-pint or Peewee. His do-or-die hustle on the court, so unlike his quiet demeanor off, assures his place on the high school basketball team, but he is convinced that another growth spurt, just one or two inches more, would go a long way toward improving his performance both on the squad and with the girls, specifically the sandy-haired Billes girl. Ted is skinny but muscular, unable yet to grow the kind of mustache he knows will confer increased stature. His future hasn't yet shaped up with the substance or speed he longs for, and he is keen to get on with his life in some pursuit that doesn't involve horses or plows or crops or unruly children and a chalkboard.

Every so often he is tempted to just pick up and go away from this town, hop a freight train and ride to wherever the tracks lead. But today held his interest, a mystery. There was something thick and dangerous enveloping the church, hidden just beneath the veneer of polite words, festering underneath the niceties, and he wants to listen to what the adults talk about over dinner.

Another wagon pulls up outside, and Ted offers to carry the flat pan of ollenberry cobbler to the women inside. He maneuvers up the front steps, past the porch where GrandJack and a cluster of old men congregate, and makes his fifth delivery inside the house. Grandma Emma has pulled up a chair and sits by Great-Grandma Lucy's bedside in the front room, stroking her mother-in-law's thin hand. The old woman looks so delicate and shrunken that Ted almost believes he can see through the sagging folds on her thin arms where they lie limp atop the fancy starburst-pattern red quilt. The quilt is brought out only for company. As soon as the guests leave, it will be carefully refolded and stored.

Ted slows his steps as he passes through to the kitchen. His great-grandmother is not only alert but talking to his grand-mother.

"He say he never step foot back in Louisiana, long as he live," Lucy insists. "Say he never come back."

"He dead, Grandma Lucy," Emma explains. "Your son is dead." She waits for the old woman to grasp the meaning of her words before continuing, feeding her one fact at a time. "Died in Oklahoma."

"Dead," Lucy repeats. "So many dead." Her eyes, clouded, are sunk deep in a face ravaged by age.

"Noby say to bury him where he born," says Emma. "He put aside money for the burying here, not in Oklahoma."

"Oklahoma?"

"The body be here. In Bagdad Cemetery."

"God bring my boy home?" Lucy finally asks.

"Your son, my husband. God bring Noby Smith home to us at last."

"Couldn't keep them brothers in the same room," says Lucy. "I lay that at Israel's door. A father 'sposed to love his sons equal."

"That's all behind us now, Mama Lucy."

"Lord, that man preach," Lucy says. "You hear him preach?"

"Yessam, Mama Lucy," Emma says. "You thinking of Noby's father with the preaching."

"Why he don't preach for us now?" Lucy pushes.

"We talking about your son, not your husband. Noby, your son, he dead, Grandma Lucy," Emma says patiently. "We bury him not a hour ago."

"Dead?" Lucy says. "Nothing but dead piled far as the eye can reach. Bones still coming up from the courthouse ground."

"You mixing together your husband and your son, Grandma Lucy. Noby's father got out the courthouse. No need bringing that up. We mourning Noby today."

Emma continues to stroke Lucy's hand until the old woman calms and closes her eyes, but now Emma's face is set tight and fierce. Ted doesn't say anything, just slips past unnoticed as he carries the cobbler to the kitchen.

The back room is a hive of activity. Ted's mother, Lenora, is in the kitchen with the rest of the wives and daughters, wrapping the casseroles and bowls of stew to guard against bugs and to keep pilfering hands from getting at them, covering the biscuits and three-layer cakes with towels to keep them moist. Since the telegram informing them of Noby's death from consumption, and his wish to be buried in Louisiana, Lenora has drawn even deeper into herself. She gives Ted an absent smile when he delivers the cobbler into her hands.

Unwilling to stay tucked up behind the women, Ted drifts back outside to the front porch, where Jackson and the other old men hold court. Ted finds a place on the lowest of the front steps, his chin almost level with GrandJack's feet. Emma's front porch shelters the oldest of the old from around Colfax, most seventy and above. A small parade of women brings out plates of food for their men and then retreats back inside. They split off cleanly, women from men, tending to the needs of guests, visiting among themselves, mourning in their own way.

GrandJack sits erect in a straight-back pine chair, dressed in his Sunday best, his dark jacket smooth, a sharp crease steamed into his pants, a freshly starched and ironed collar, the old, mis-shapen brown fedora pulled down snug on his head. Ted feels as if he is eavesdropping, an invisible youth sitting here among his elders. Even his father and Uncle Andrew, well into their fifties, younger by a generation, seem out of place.

"Buried Easter Sunday, of all days," Jackson says. The older men nod their graying heads in agreement, knowingly, a heavy sadness to the acknowledgment.

"The past don't let go," says a man in the group. He looks to be in his early eighties, but his age is difficult to determine. The features of his cocoa-colored face are thin and sharp, although he has a weak chin and has lost all of his upper teeth. He wears a stiff straw hat, and tight, woolly pillows of white fringe poke out underneath.

"Not supposed to," says Jackson. "If we let the past go, how we know about those hundred colored men march down to Colfax and vote after the Civil War? My father and Noby's father done that."

"I remember," the old man says. "I was one year short of twenty-one, too young. I couldn't vote that first time, but I remember. Wasn't safe." The old man pauses, his rheumy eyes lingering on Jackson's face. "I knowed your daddy. Noby's too. Good men, willing to stand up."

He leans back in his chair, closes his eyes, lost in his own memories. No one else speaks, waiting. "I voted, though," he finally says without opening his eyes. "Twice." He leaves his faraway state behind, is with them again. "We vote Republicans in to Colfax in 1872 and stood down Democrats trying to steal the election in '78. Wasn't no more voting after that."

"I never got the chance to vote," Jackson says. "Not even the one time."

"Colored could vote, GrandJack?" Ted asks.

Nathan-Green shoots him a withering warning glance for

silence in this gathering of elders. "Keep quiet and listen," he says.

"Least L'il Man show interest," snaps Jackson. Ted doesn't remember ever seeing his grandfather this testy. "Your daddy never had curiosity," he says more deliberately, directing his comment to Ted, leaning back in his chair. Jackson shifts his focus once again, looks squarely into Nathan-Green's face. "You never got your sons to shout their name," Jackson says, accusing. "How he going to know who he is? You let tradition die, too lazy to honor the past. Andrew know better."

The two middle-aged brothers, Nathan-Green and Andrew, sit motionless on the front porch, side by side. They are as quiet and unresisting as if they are ten years old, caught dipping their finger into the butter churn. Silently, they endure their father's rage. "Letting go of the past is like letting go of the Lord," Jackson says.

Nathan-Green looks away, says nothing in his own defense.

Much of this is lost on Ted. It has been a long day for everyone, starting before dawn with preparations for both Easter Sunday and the funeral, and then a full day spent at the church and cemetery. There is tension in the air, the mingling of memory and regret loosening tongues and outing thoughts long unsaid, but airing family business in public is unexpected and out of character.

"Was a time colored men vote just like white." Jackson addresses the group at large again, continuing his thread of thought as if the awkward moment didn't happen.

Ted wants to draw attention away from his father, still smarting with the shame of a public reprimand. "Was Grandpa Noby in the riot, GrandJack?"

Jackson Tademy's face pulls back into itself, his lips tight. "Wasn't no riot," he says slowly, his voice a harsh whisper. "Don't never let nobody tell you it was a riot. I was there. Your grandfather Noby was there. Our fathers was both there. It was a massacre."

The word *massacre* still rings in Ted's head as Grandma Emma bursts through the front door of the farmhouse, the wire screen banging behind her.

"Come help me, Ted," she says. "Take the plates out for the hog."

It is a strange request, the women's work she asks him to do, but he has no recourse but to obey. He collects as many of the dirty dishes as he can carry, stacking them one on top of the other, and takes them behind the house to scrape the half-eaten food into the pig's slop bucket.

"No need to stir up that old mess today," Emma hisses to the men on the porch once Ted is gone. "Leave that boy out of it, you hear?"

Figure 30. Lenora Smith Tademy

*Figure 31. 1936
basketball
champions, back:
Irving Hall, Ted
Tademy (center,
holding basket-
ball), Willie
James; front:
Owen Brew, I. V.
Billes*

36

1 9 3 5

Jackson unhitches the mule and walks in from the field toward the house. The day is bracing and chilly, but the wet season hasn't arrived, not yet. A string of crepe myrtle trees marks a path all the way from the house down to the edge of the bayou. It is so late in the season that their gauzy dark pink blooms are almost gone. Amy sits in her usual spot on the front porch of their farmhouse, framed by a cedar tree on one side and their mulberry tree on the other, swatting now and again at the last of the fall flies. Polly rests in the rocker kitty-corner to her daughter-in-law with her eyes closed. Jackson never tires of the familiar scene, of Amy waiting for his return, of his mother still spry enough to get around by herself, although slowly, after a century of living, both waiting for him. Amy embroiders a green-and-red-threaded pattern on the edge of a cotton pillowcase, her nose so close to the wood hoop it looks as if she is trying to smell the material. She hears him approach, lifts her head, and smiles.

"Nathan-Green's boy inside," says Amy. "Into your books again. Walked from Colfax and been here since directly after school."

"What he want?" asks Jackson.

"Won't talk to no one but you," replies Amy. "But I think it about college."

"He going," says Jackson.

"Ted the one to talk to, not me. May be he quiet, but he stubborn just the same."

"He a Tademy all right," adds Polly, drawing herself awake. She has lost the last of her teeth, her lips cave in around her gums, and her eyes are so clouded over she has trouble making out anything beyond shapes, but she is still observant.

"Sound like the two of you got the boy all figured out," says Jackson.

"His way fool some into thinking he just going along easy on the ride of life, but quiet don't mean he don't got appetites," says Polly. "If there something he want, he fix on getting to it no matter what other folks throw in the path. I sees something in that boy."

"Just let me shake off the day's dust," Jackson says, "and then I'll talk to him."

Jackson creaks when he walks now, his bones and joints in combined protest to all he has forced them to endure over the years. When he was younger, he thought he could go on strong forever. If he moves slowly now, deliberately, putting thought into each motion, if he swings his feet out of bed before trying to push himself up in the morning, if he adjusts positions often, though only slightly, whenever he sits for long periods, he can keep his aches and pains at a tolerable level. There is no denying he has gotten old. He and Amy both. Polly, on the other hand, seems to go on forever.

Jackson spends more time now thinking than doing. It used to be that the days were so overfull, he'd hitch up the mule and plow half the night by the light of the moon. Turning the soil and turning his mind at the same time. Amy sometimes scolded when he stayed out too long, but she always fixed him a big breakfast come morning—minnows fresh-caught from the bayou, biscuits and syrup, soft, runny eggs fried in bacon grease, thick, warm milk from the cow, hot chicory coffee. "A skinny man with a big appetite," she'd tease. It pleases her to coddle him, to cook his favorites, to iron his shorts and handkerchiefs, rub his feet, darn his socks, in the same way it has always pleased him to keep her from either the fields or a white woman's kitchen. They came to agreement on this point early on. His wife's only job is the Tademys, himself and the children. They never once violated the bargain, not in fifty-three years.

Getting old means the gradual mutiny of his body, and too much time spent in the mazelike warren of his head, but all in all, Jackson knows he has much to be thankful for. He is at peace with God, never misses a Sunday going to church, owns the land he works, reaches out to help his neighbors whenever he can, and is fortunate enough to pull through life in tandem with a woman who fits him.

For years he has worked tirelessly to breathe life into his father's dream, and now Colfax has its own colored school, run by his son, a school his grandchildren and maybe their grandchildren can attend. Jackson has given each of his five offspring a good start, more than anyone would have thought possible when he was coming up, and given a plot of land to each of his sons to develop for themselves. His children. The mistlike haze of nostalgia thins, and reality intrudes. The specifics of his children don't conform to his tidy accountings of his life's blessings, but each has become a teacher, albeit of differing ability, interest, and application. Though he loves all five of his children, he harbors disappointment and regret too.

Still, a new crop of Tademys is maturing, a new breed, not grounded enough in their understanding of the past or appreciation of the land to suit Jackson, but with an impatience that isn't all bad. There is no clear heir apparent yet, the way Andrew emerged so early as the obvious one to take over Jackson's work, but then Jackson himself was late in his own development. These new ones, the next generation, bear watching and cultivating.

Of all his grandchildren, Ted visits the farm and Jackson's library most often. If Jackson allowed it, his grandson would have three or four books pulled down from their places on the bookshelves at once, spread out at his feet, reading passages from first one and then another, like a hummingbird sampling nectar in a newly blooming field.

"One at a time, L'il Man," Jackson warned for years, until Ted understood the books would be there whenever he was ready. Three shelves full of knowledge, waiting for a beneficiary.

"He waiting on you," says Amy.

Jackson leaves Amy and Polly on the front porch and goes inside to the front room of the farmhouse.

Ted crowds seventeen years old, almost good as grown, and Jackson finds him curled up on the floor, his back to the wall, legs pulled up in an inverted V to provide support for the book, his favorite posture since Jackson taught him to read at age six. Ted once told Jackson that losing himself in the library was as good as playing basketball. Ted approaches each new addition to Jackson's library in the same way, indirectly, patiently, postponing the pleasure, warming to the idea of the book in his head before ever allowing himself to touch it with his hands, sometimes delaying by a matter of weeks the moment when he finally cracks the spine of the book to read the pages inside.

Jackson has accumulated more than fifty books over the years, not always in the best condition and seldom new. In Jackson's view, a used book holds the promise of information in the same way as a new one, at a fraction of the cost. He owns a few volumes of fiction, not his favorite reading, but most of his collection are dense, impressively bound tomes, many purchased as incomplete sets. Three sturdy pine shelves run almost the length of the wall, one above the other in neat rows. They hold encyclopedias, almanacs, teachers' manuals, and several progressive-farmer magazines. He also has a special set-aside place for newspapers, a stack three feet high, curled and badly yellowed at the edges, with articles Jackson has saved for one reason or another. Only he is allowed to touch these, since one of the oldest newspapers almost turned to dust in his hands. Some go back to the last century.

Preoccupied with his reading, Ted doesn't look up when Jackson enters the room. The book in Ted's hands is the *Encyclopaedia Britannica*, one of twenty-four in a set, an impressive purchase missing only five of the original volumes.

"L'il Man, don't never exchange health for wealth," Jackson says as he eases himself into the chair. "Health not for sale. You just turn around and spend up your wealth trying to get it back."

Ted looks up. "Not a good day, GrandJack?"

"Good as I got a right to expect, I guess," says Jackson. "What brings you all the way out here to see us?"

"Just reading and thinking. A couple years, I'll be graduated, GrandJack."

"So what you gonna be? What you gonna do with your life?"

"Something different, GrandJack," says Ted.

"Nothing finer than teaching."

"It's just . . . What I like is to make something where there wasn't anything there before."

"Like farming? Turning a crop? I see a lot of progressive in you. Let me make a progressive farmer out of you."

Ted shakes his head. "More like building a chicken coop or raising a house. Cutting the wood, figuring angles, how many pieces there need to be, how it comes together. Planning the roosting shelf, pitching the roof right so the water runs off but not too fast."

"Plenty of that on a farm," says GrandJack.

"But I don't see farming the rest of my life," says Ted. "Maybe go away somewhere else, find a different kind of work."

"You got to eat, L'il Man. You got to settle down with a good woman and take care of your children. You got to stake your claim. What you thinking about after college? You partial to where you teach?"

"There's no money in teaching, GrandJack."

"The goal isn't money. No education, no progress."

"I'm not sure I want to go to college, GrandJack. All that time in school, and all I do is come back to teach kids here. They just going to be farmers anyhow."

"You say that like it poison the inside of your mouth. Farming not good enough. Teaching not good enough. Tademys known for teaching, for bringing the word to the next generation."

"There's got to be something else besides teaching," Ted says. "Or farming."

Ted sees the disappointment in his grandfather's face and goes quiet. He has admitted to his grandfather, of all people, how much he dreads the rhythm of the lives he sees played out every day in Colfax.

"If I go anywhere, I guess Grambling be the school," Ted says. It is clear he is throwing out a bone, lacking sincerity, in order to avoid the familiar argument, avoid scraping the scab covering an old sore.

"What you learning today in the books, L'il Man?"

"Look GrandJack." Deep wrinkles crease the wide expanse of Ted's forehead, and his eyes flash with the challenge of the young. "They lied."

"We don't allow that kind of talk in this house," Jackson warns.

"Sorry, GrandJack." Ted points to the book he holds and offers up the offending volume. "This can't be right."

Jackson understands immediately. NAZAR–NEGUS. He balances the heavy weight of the open book in his hands.

There are several pages, long passages under the heading of NEGRO in large capital letters. Jackson can no longer read the small print in these books, but he remembers the first time he came across the description years ago. The sketch off to the side of the text is the head of a man, full-face forward, who looks like an exaggerated version of his neighbors, of his friends, of his family, but the lips are too puffy, the hair too coarse, the eyes too round, the skin too shiny-dark.

"It says we smell different than normal, that we're lazy, intellectually inferior, and . . . more."

"Read it out to me, L'il Man," says Jackson.

Ted hesitates, reluctant.

"Reading out loud sometimes bring in the light," Jackson says. "Read out in a strong voice."

Ted reluctantly obeys. "'Negro children were sharp, intelligent and full of vivacity, but on approaching the adult period a gradual change set in. The intellect seemed to become clouded, animation giving place to a sort of lethargy, briskness yielding to indolence.'" Ted doesn't stumble on the words, but he is clearly uncomfortable. "'We must necessarily suppose that the development of the Negro and white proceeds on different lines. While with the latter the volume of the brain grows with the expansion of the brainpan, in the former the growth of the brain is on the contrary arrested by the premature closing of the cranial sutures and lateral pressure of the frontal bone.'"

Ted pauses, embarrassment taking the volume of his voice down to little more than a mumbled whisper. "'Deterioration in mental development is no doubt very largely due to the fact that after puberty sexual matters take the first place in the Negro's life and thoughts.'"

"Go on," says Jackson. "When you read, read loud and clear."

Ted shifts uneasily but continues. "'Though the mental inferiority of the Negro to the white or yellow races is a fact, it has often been exaggerated; the Negro is largely the creature of his environment. It is not fair to judge of his mental capacity by tests taken directly from the environment of the white man, as for instance tests in mental arithmetic; skill in reckoning is necessary to the white race, and it has cultivated this faculty; but it is not necessary to the Negro. The mental constitution of the Negro is very similar to that of a child, normally good-natured and cheerful, but subject to sudden fits of emotion and passion during which he is capable of performing acts of singular atrocity, impressionable, vain, but often exhibiting in the capacity of servant a dog-like fidelity which has stood the supreme test.'"

Ted balks, refusing to recite more. Jackson remembers how he felt when he first read those same passages. It was the matter-of-factness, the irrefutability of the statements, the absolute respectability given to this view of himself and the people he knows, that disturbed him most.

"Better you understand what people take in their heads to teach," says Jackson.

"Is that encyclopedia true?" Ted asks.

"Does it describe people you know? Me, your grandmothers, your father, Uncle Andrew, yourself?"

Ted shakes his head. "I get mad sometimes."

"Any white folks you know ever get mad?"

Ted laughs, a small, nervous chuckle, but it softens the mood. "Yes, sir."

"That encyclopedia over twenty-five years old, got some old-time ideas in it, but wasn't no excuse even then for coming up with that foolishness." Jackson takes the book from Ted, closes it, and replaces it on the shelf. He pulls out another thick volume from the uppermost shelf, its somber green binding embossed with gold lettering, and hands it to Ted. "How about this one?"

Ted handles the hardback carefully, reading from the spine. "*An Era of Progress and Promise.*"

"That's right. Sometimes you got to dip your bucket in more than one well to get it full. This book old as the other, but they come at things a different way. Turn to page five-sixty-three. Read to me from under the title 'Inventors and Inventions.'"

"'A list of three hundred and seventy inventions by Negroes was furnished for the Paris Exposition of 1900. Granville T. Woods of Cincinnati, whom someone called the black Edison, has twenty-two patents listed, in electricity and telegraphy. Elijah McCoy, of Detroit, has twenty-eight inventions relating to lubricating appliances for locomotives. Miss Miriam B. Benjamin, of Massachusetts—'"

"That's enough. Go back and read the rest later. You ever hear of Granville T. Woods before? Or Elijah McCoy? Or Miriam Benjamin?"

"No."

"They sound to you like inferior people whose brain squeezed together the older they got until they ended up stupid?"

Ted laughs again. "No, GrandJack."

"Read under 'Farmers and Farms.'"

"'Forty years after emancipation, about one fourth of the Negro farmers had become landowners.'"

"You know your way around a farm. Anything you ever come across about planting or harvest or livestock so easy to do you can afford to be lazy and still hold on to the land?"

"No, GrandJack."

"Think for yourself, L'il Man. Some people make up reasons we can't be on the same level as them, even drag history into it. So we got to remind ourselves how good we is. That's education. Keep reading, L'il Man, and don't you get bothered because you see somebody's 'fact' on a piece of paper, not if it sounds contrary to your God-given good sense. Those books written by men. More ways to color how a man think and how he choose to explain his 'environment' as there are flavors of honey. Why you think I collect all these books? The purpose of the written word is to help you flesh out those things you know and those you don't. Understand what I'm saying, L'il Man?"

"I think so."

"Good," Jackson says. "Everybody different, that part is true, but not divided out by race. We got some lazy ones, some slow in thinking, some turn their backs on God, some willing to act the fool. So do white. But we got those who make inventions, who come up lightning fast with numbers, like you, plenty working hard and making things better for their families and their community. God the only one with absolute truth. Use the brain He give you to do more than figure out arithmetic problems. Figure out right and wrong."

Ted sits up straighter, folds the book closed, prepares to return it to its place on the shelf.

"We not ready to let that book go yet, L'il Man," says Jackson. "One thing more. In the back, they list Negro colleges. Our race go to one of those and come out trained. A man that want to better himself got to be addle-headed to ignore those pages. And I don't have no addle-headed grandsons."

"I don't want to be a teacher, GrandJack," Ted says.

"When you grown, you choose what you want. We not talking about teaching yet. But you gonna be made ready for the test of life first. Tademys is special. You special. We try hard to collect the many, but I won't lose the one," says Jackson. "We put a lot in you, L'il Man. College one of the prices you gonna pay for it."

Ted breathes hard but holds his tongue.

"You give me your word, that's all it take," says Jackson. "We don't need to talk about it again."

Ted stands, puts the book back into its assigned space on the shelf, turns to face Jackson squarely. They are the same height, grandson and grandfather, both small men by society's conventions, one growing, one shrinking.

"You not up to defying me on this, L'il Man."

The small farmhouse room seems airless and muggy. A fine sheen of perspiration coats Jackson's face, even though the cool of fall is already in the air. He keeps his gaze steady.

Ted blinks first. "Yes, GrandJack," he says. "If you want me to go, I'll go."

"That be settled," Jackson says, satisfied.

37

1 9 3 5

*T*he day after Christmas, Ted rises early. The household in The Bottom is up and about, but subdued, as if yesterday's overeating, visiting, and activity have drained everyone's reserves. Excess still hangs in the air. His mother, her cotton robe pulled tight against the cold, has already milked Bessie out back and stands waiting by the stove for a pan of water to come to boil. His sisters, in a rare show of idleness, sit around the kitchen table in quiet conversation, without so much as a mending cloth in hand. His father pokes distractedly at the glowing embers in the fireplace. His youngest brother snatches up what passes for a homemade football, a mass of tightly wrapped material scraps, and Ted and his other brothers follow him outside, and they throw easy passes to one another despite the puffs of clouded cold they exhale until their mother calls them inside.

After breakfast, Ted announces, "I got to go out for a while."

"You got chores," Lenora says.

"I need to return something to Willie Dee Billes. From school. I do my chores soon's I get back."

"You hear your mother," says Nathan-Green. "You need to stay put."

"A walk do the boy good," says Lenora, coming to Ted's rescue. "Long as you not gone too long." She gives Ted a small, conspiring smile.

Ted walks in the direction of Colfax, flags down the Greyhound bus on Highway 71, and heads north to Aloha.

School is out of session until after the New Year, and Ted's mind is made up. It is time to make a move, something beyond the furtive letters slipped into Willie Dee's waiting hand. The campaign for her heart has been slow, uncertain, and sometimes painful. She is fourteen today, the age of choice, when friendship has the potential of becoming more, but of all the boys who buzz around her, Ted knows he isn't highest on her list. She spends time with him when other, better offers haven't yet come her way. She is nice enough to him, but Ted isn't fun like Willie James, or popular and sociable like Owen Brew. His biggest rival appears to be Robert Hadnot, from one of the colored Hadnot families in The Bottom, a handsome older boy she's been spending too much time with lately. Ted has his playful side, but he can never hope to win her on that score. His strategy so far—keeping up an amiable friendship while waiting for her to come of age—requires updating. Now that she is fourteen, he needs to seize the opportunity to formally court her.

He has five cents saved for the inbound bus trip, an extravagance, although his intention is to walk back and save the return fare. He wants to arrive at the end of the nine-mile journey without carrying the stink of the road with him. Willie Dee's house is two miles or so from the main road, going east; he isn't sure exactly where it is in the woods. He's never been there before.

The bus is on holiday schedule and long in coming, but when

it finally clatters down the highway, Ted flags it down. There are only two others on board, and he takes his seat in the back, nearest the rear exit. When he sees the sign for Aloha, he pulls the cord and the driver lets him out. From there Ted heads north away from the main road, away from Red River. He knows at least that much. He approaches a young white boy, maybe seven or eight, who sits alone outside a dilapidated house in the woods.

"Excuse me, sir," Ted says, taking off his cap. "Where's the Billes house?"

The young boy motions. "Down yonder, can't miss it. Look for the path for their car."

Ted thanks him and moves through the light brush until he comes to a tamped-down trail, wide enough for an automobile, and follows the rutted road for another half mile. He spots the mailbox first, with BILLES printed boldly in white paint on the curved metal, next to a lean-to shed off to the side of the main house. There is a cutting stump with a double-sided ax, and a tall stack of chopped firewood, pine and oak mixed, in between the shed and the house.

Willie Dee's oldest brother, Theo, is outside, tinkering with an old car parked beneath the corrugated tin roof of the shed. Despite the cold, he wears only a thin, grease-stained undershirt.

"Hello," Ted calls. A well-fed yellow dog barks, but without conviction, and comes to Ted, nuzzling his snout under his hand, begging to be stroked. Ted is afraid of dogs and doesn't move.

"Hello, yourself. Come back, Jasper."

"We met in town once before," Ted says. They met when Ted walked Willie Dee to her uncle's house after school. "I'm Ted. Ted Tademy." He makes a move to shake, but Theo raises his hands apologetically, showing the oily grease on his hands and arms.

"Next time," he says.

Ted is relieved. He can't get his palms to stop sweating.

"Ted Tademy." Another of Willie Dee's brothers steps out from the shadows of the shed. Ted knows him from the basketball team.

I. V. Billes is popular, self-assured, outgoing, cordial, everybody's best friend, president of his class, the favorite of all the girls. "What brings you all the way out here?"

"Come to wish your family a happy holiday," Ted says.

"The whole family?" The two brothers exchange a look, a devilish smile hanging between them.

Ted lets the moment ride.

"Have a seat on the porch," Theo says. He leaves the car hood and wipes his hands with an oil-soaked cloth. "Maybe you came to see the whole family, but I suspect you might want that to include my kid sister. I'll go get Willie Dee." Another smirking glance passes between the brothers before he disappears into the house.

Ted talks basketball and cars with I.V. while they wait. It is easy conversation, and interesting. There aren't many who own an automobile in Colfax, and Willie Dee's brother recounts the benefits of a Chevrolet over a Ford.

It isn't long before Willie Dee pushes open the screen door to join them outside on the front porch. Just the sight of her makes Ted's heart do a two-step inside his chest. She has on a blue dress that ties in the back and falls to just below her knees, with a scruffy pair of black house slippers on her feet. There is a very large hole at the waist of the dress, where the seam has given way. Her long hair is partially sectioned off, looped in separate curls, and held by a number of shiny metal clips on one side, falling free on the other. Ted has never seen her look so untended, so ungroomed.

"What you need me out here for?" she calls to her brother through the door, her voice dripping impatience. She freezes when she sees Ted sitting in the rocking chair, staring. She is caught, unsure whether to flee back into the house or to act nonchalant and proceed out onto the porch.

Another amused glance passes between the brothers. "Looks like you have a visitor, my gal." Theo doesn't bother to hide his great satisfaction at orchestrating such embarrassment for his little sister.

Willie Dee turns tail and stumbles back into the house. Ted hears snatches of frantic whispering inside, two distinct voices, one distressed and petulant, one authoritative and calm.

"Tademy."

"Bring your guest inside."

"I didn't invite him."

"Now."

"Not like this."

"No time to change. Just the hair."

Ted and the brothers pretend not to hear. When the silence outside and the whispering inside become too awkward, I.V. speaks up.

"What time you start out this morning?" he asks.

"Just after breakfast," Ted replies.

The conversation lapses again.

"The bus wasn't running a regular schedule," Ted says.

A very long five minutes later, Willie Dee comes back outside. Her thick sandy-colored hair has been combed out quick and loose around her face and down her back, and she has slipped into a pair of Mary Janes. She wears the same dress but holds her hands in front of the torn seam.

Ted stands. "Happy birthday," he says to Willie Dee, as upbeat as he can muster. Everyone stares at him, and he is unsure what to do next.

Willie Dee cuts her eyes at her brothers, her face pinched in a warning of the future injury she plans for them.

"We got the car to work on," I.V. says, chuckling, not intimidated by her in the least, and the two brothers go off to the shed together.

"What are you doing here?" Willie Dee whispers to Ted.

Ted is flustered. Willie Dee is angry, not even attempting a cordial greeting. "It's your birthday," he says simply, as if that explains everything.

"I know what day it is," she says. "That doesn't mean you can just show up here unannounced."

Ted's mind whirs, like the spinning toy his father made for his little brother for Christmas, but he is speechless. To turn around and go home this soon will surely be rude. Not to mention the fact that he hasn't yet established his intent.

Eva Billes's voice comes floating out from the interior of the house. "Willie Dee, bring your company inside for tea cakes."

"My mother says to invite you in," Willie Dee says, making clear by her tone that what she would do, left to her own devices, and what her mother decrees are two very different things.

Ted doesn't relish the upcoming scrutiny, but if he hopes to truly court Willie Dee formally, he has to meet her mother. When Willie Dee reenters the house, Ted follows to the front room where Eva Billes stands, waiting.

She is an imposing figure of a woman, taller than he expected and solidly built, her long dark skirt covered by a white apron. By reputation, she is a formidable force, willing to lend a hand to anyone who needs her help. She is known for her capabilities in fixing things, whether a tattered dress or a marriage that needs shoring up, and it is said that people go to her, black and white both, for a dose of good common sense they can't necessarily find elsewhere. She is ginger-colored, neither convincingly dark-skinned nor light enough to be considered fair, the inky blackness of her coarse hair parted straight down the middle, perfectly, as if she understands the deep importance of measuring out precise and equal portions. Her hair is fashioned in a twist on either side, held back by hairpins, but a few inflexible steel-gray strands go their own way, refusing to be tamed. She smiles at Ted, a welcoming, genuine smile.

"This is Ted Tademy, Mama," says Willie Dee, as if reciting a school lesson.

"How you related to Professor Andrew and Miss Gertrude, Ted?"

"My uncle, ma'am. My father's brother. My father is Nathan-Green. Senior. I'm Nathan Green, Junior. And Miss Gertrude, she's my aunt, my mother's sister. We live in The Bottom." The first test is always to clarify your people.

Eva Billes nods appreciatively. "Colfax owe the Tademys for the school."

"Yes, ma'am."

"Have a seat, Ted," she says. "Make yourself comfortable."

Ted looks around the small front room. There are several choices. In the corner is a pine rocker, and next to that a plaid-patterned armchair with crocheted doilies covering the skinny arms. Along the wall, under the front window, is a yellow-green upholstered couch with two thin cushions. He chooses the couch and sits.

"That's my brother's nightbed," Willie Dee says.

Ted jumps back up.

"Sit," says Eva. "This is daytime." She throws a fierce warning look in Willie Dee's direction. "What bring you out to see us today?" she asks Ted.

This is harder than Ted thought. He should have practiced before he came. "Willie Dee's birthday," he says. It sounds weak, inadequate to his own ears.

"That's right," says Eva. "She just missed being my Christmas baby."

"Yes, ma'am," Ted says.

"I'll leave you young people alone, then," says Eva. She disappears toward the back of the house, and Ted hears the rattle of dishes and the slosh of water from a bucket.

"Why didn't you tell me you were coming?" whispers Willie Dee, annoyed.

Ted's mind races, full, but his tongue idles. What exactly can he say? That he came to start the courting process? That since she doesn't seem glad to see him after he made his way to her house, he doesn't know what to do? That he is bewitched and can't seem to free himself of thoughts of her? That all he needs is a little encouragement on her end to marshal his composure and go about this in a more rational way? That he is a good person with the best of intentions, and she could do no better, even if he doesn't have the outward trappings? Ted shrugs.

Willie Dee pouts a little and ignores Ted as if he isn't in the room, punishing him for surprising her. Ted settles deeper in his seat, his hands on the cap he took off to enter the house. He tries not to be obvious about using the cap to wipe the sweat from his hands.

Willie Dee gives in first, the quiet obviously disturbing her more than it does Ted. "Why did you come if you don't have anything to say?" she asks.

Again Ted shrugs.

"How can you write such beautiful letters and not talk?" she demands.

She called his letters beautiful. "Did you have a nice Christmas?" he asks.

Willie Dee launches into a description of the length of material she got as a present, enough to make a dress and scarf, her impressions of the choir singing at the church service in the evening, the coconut cake her mother baked, the pecans they sugared that were all consumed within thirty minutes of coming out of the oven, until she realizes she is doing all of the talking. She stops.

"How about your Christmas?" she asks Ted.

"It was good."

"Good how?"

"We had a lot to eat," says Ted.

He doesn't know how much more of this he can stand. It isn't as if he doesn't know just how badly he is failing to impress her, but he can't think of a single thing to talk about. He wishes he

Figure 32. Eva Billes

could go somewhere with a piece of paper and pencil and script out what to say. As he turns his cap around and around, he hears her mother clear her throat from the back of the house. Why has he come? If he could turn invisible and disappear, he would gladly do it.

Willie Dee turns her head and pats her foot. Ted spins his cap. After about twenty minutes of silence, Eva Billes comes back into the front room with two tall glasses of sweet tea and a plate of warm tea cakes.

"I say again how much I appreciate what your people done for this town," Eva Billes says to Ted. She welcomes him with her kind expression, into her house, into her confidence. "They sure done wonders with that school."

"Yes, ma'am," Ted says, uneasy. The mother is much nicer to him than the daughter.

"The Tademys is good people, serious people," she goes on. "I'd like to see some of that steadiness rub off on Willie Dee, calm her down a little."

It comes to Ted clearly then. Maybe Willie Dee Billes isn't bowled over by him so far, but he has time on his side, and he is a man on a mission with a clear goal. He hasn't counted on the good fortune revealed today, that her mother could be his greatest ally. For a woman with a fourth-grade education and ambitions for her children, association with the Tademy name and its strong, prestigious links to the beginnings of colored education in Colfax has benefits, and the wishes of the mother count.

How many times has GrandJack told him that persistence is everything? If Ted remains patient, keeps his focus on the long term, and stays in good graces with Eva Billes, Ted is convinced he has a chance with Willie Dee Billes yet.

38

1 9 3 7

Ted is part of the small clutch of teenage listeners huddled around the RCA Victor radio in Nep and Annie Boyd's front room. Outside is heat and humidity and boredom, but inside is the wonder of the music. There isn't another band quite like Duke Ellington's, not singsongy and formulaic like the other popular radio performers, but fresh, infectious, sultry, and earthy. Jungle-style.

Robert Hadnot stands and pulls Willie Dee to her feet, and the two of them Lindy-hop together to "It Don't Mean a Thing (If It Ain't Got That Swing)," quietly, so as not to disturb the others listening. Ted tries not to stare at the obvious enjoyment on Willie Dee's face, the half-smile, the parted lips, the long hair swept back high off her face, wispy tendrils tickling the back of her neck, the slight sheen of sweat on her upper lip, the occasional flashes of abandon as she shakes her hips in time to the music, the brief glimpse of taut calf muscle as she kicks back one leg and then the other. If Willie Dee's mother knew she was dancing in plain sight of this handful of boys and girls, Eva Billes would get the strap first and ask questions later. And Ted himself is complicit. After school, he let them into a house that isn't even his to listen to the radio, unchaperoned, but otherwise he fears losing his tenuous hold on Willie Dee. Ted can't dance, but he will use whatever he can to stay within her orbit. He does have access to a radio.

When the song finishes, Willie Dee collapses not on the sofa, where her best friend, Fern Lee, sits, but on the floor, tomboy-style, pulls her legs under her, and arranges her dress to cover her knees and boots. Robert circles around and sits next to her, laughing. Robert is older than all of them, back from a year at Louisiana Negro Normal and Industrial Institute in Grambling. The age difference notwithstanding, Ted recognizes the hunger in Robert's look, one Ted unsuccessfully tries to mask himself. Infatuation. Robert whispers something in Willie Dee's ear, and she throws her head back, laughing, the gap between her two front teeth exposed. Ted looks away briefly, but he can't stop himself from stealing another glance.

"Different houses taking in some of the band members overnight," says Fern Lee. "Too bad we can't stay up late enough to see one of them."

Willie Dee is keyed up, her face still flushed from dancing. "We should drive past Calhoun's barn tomorrow night," she says. "Nothing this exciting going to happen again in Colfax anytime soon. People coming all the way from Alexandria, Natchitoches, Montgomery, even Shreveport to see Duke Ellington and his band in person, and afterwards they're gonna dance till they drop."

"We can't go," says Ted. Why does he always have to be the serious one? "They catch colored hanging around, they hurt us sure."

" 'Course we won't hang around," says Willie Dee. "If we get a car, we just drive along slow with the windows down on the public road. No telling what we see or hear. Maybe we see the Duke himself."

The next song from the radio is "Mood Indigo." Under normal circumstances, Ted would have shut out the world and flowed into the music, but he needs to pay attention. The direction of the conversation is veering dangerously.

"Betcha Robert could find a way to borrow a car tomorrow night," Willie Dee says. "We could all go then."

"I can drive," says Robert, "but my uncle's using his car tomorrow night."

Willie Dee makes a pouty face. "Sounded like such fun."

"I could get my brother-in-law's car," Ted brags. The moment the words leave his mouth, he regrets them.

"Your mama not going to let you go out with me in a car," says Robert.

"She will too, if Ted comes," says Willie Dee. "The four of us just say we going to a movie in Alexandria. You in or not, Ted?"

Ted is accustomed to Willie Dee using him as a shield. He doesn't particularly like the role, and he especially doesn't like the idea of deceiving Eva Billes. She is his strongest ally, and he risks the depths of her ill will if something goes wrong. On the other hand, if he says yes, he will be with Willie Dee.

"Only if we really go to the movies after," says Ted. A part of him wants to catch a glimpse of Duke Ellington too, or hear a snatch of a tune by the great swing band, live. "Only if you promise we don't get out of the car or dawdle."

Willie Dee claps her hands, like a little girl with a new toy. "It's settled. Tomorrow night we see the Duke," she says.

At five o'clock on Saturday night, Ted drives up to Willie Dee's house in Aloha in his brother-in-law's Chevy. His best shirt is pressed and his shoes are wiped down. Willie Dee's father, T.O., a slight, pale man with straight wispy hair and a small potbelly, sits on the front porch in a rocking chair.

"Evening, Mr. Billes," says Ted.

T.O. nods, goes back to his whittling. "They waiting on you inside," he says.

Eva Billes serves him tea cakes and lemonade while they pass the time in the front room, and she makes small talk. Shortly, they hear footsteps on the porch stairs. Eva is up holding the front screen door open before Robert has a chance to knock.

"Evening, Miss Eva," say Robert Hadnot and Fern Lee, politely, almost in unison. Robert takes off his cap. Eva Billes seems to tower over everyone.

"Come in," says Eva, sweeping them into the room. "Sit. You got time to visit before the evening picture show start." They settle on the couch, and Eva sets the plate of tea cakes on the small coffee table between them. She entrenches herself in a side chair and produces a small ball of grayish-green yarn and two needles and begins to knit.

"How's your father, Robert? Last I hear, he miss a month of Sundays at church. Might have to go over and offer my help, see if he sick, if he need anything."

"He just tired from working double at the mill, Miss Eva. He stay home on Sunday morning, but the rest of us go to church."

Eva purses her lips, unsatisfied. "What you plan for this evening?"

Robert, smooth around parents, answers. "We going to the picture show in Alexandria. Not so many chiggers in the seats as upstairs in the colored section at the Colfax theater."

"We want to start out for Alexandria before it gets too late, Mama," Willie Dee says nervously. "No telling how much traffic is on the road."

"How they persuaded Duke Ellington to come to Colfax, I'll never know, but the whole town lost their minds over his band and their devil's music," Eva says.

"They on tour all the way from New York City, just finish playing in New Orleans," says Robert. "Wish we could see him."

"That's foolishness. And even if they allowed colored, would be a waste of good money put to better use. Just don't take the road near Calhoun's barn," Eva says, "and then you don't have to worry about no traffic."

"Yes, ma'am," says Ted.

"You young folks go on, then, but you be back by ten," says Eva. She rises from her chair, and they all get up. "Come home right after. I know I can count on you to be responsible, Ted."

Eva Billes walks them outside and they pile into the car, the two-door black 1930 Chevy sedan that Ted has borrowed from Walter Jerro, his sister's husband. Willie Dee and Fern Lee squeeze into the back, and Robert takes the passenger seat. Once they hit Highway 71, they head directly for the largest building outside Colfax, a huge storage space built on the old site of Calhoun's Sugarhouse. Streams of vehicles move in the same direction—automobiles, wagons, tractors, trucks—and park by the side of the road or in the open fields. Some people arrive by foot, mostly young, and others by horseback, all white, all ready for a memorable Saturday night.

"Drive slower, Ted," says Willie Dee from the backseat.

All of the windows are down, but there is barely any movement of wind, no relief from the August sun. Although it is almost six o'clock, the sun is still strong enough to beat fiercely down on the car, and the air is gummy with humidity. Already Ted's good shirt is sweated through.

Singles, couples, and small groups wait in a long line for admittance through the front double doors of the warehouse. A stocky white man in overalls, a little older than Robert, collects the money for tickets before allowing anyone past.

"Robert, isn't that your cousin on the door?" asks Fern Lee.

Robert is clearly uncomfortable. "Yeah, that's Lucius Hadnot." He doesn't say anything more, and they let it go. The white Hadnots don't acknowledge the colored Hadnots, even if they descend from the same tree, even if they live in the same town. The practicalities of their lives are separate.

From the car, they hear the vibrations and the melody of music. Ted picks up the smooth, sly arrangement of "Rocking in Rhythm." Several couples waiting outside begin to Lindy-hop, and others share flasks or jars of moonshine.

Willie Dee almost has her nose on the side glass pane of the car. "Circle around and let's pass again," she says.

"We're going to Alexandria," says Ted.

"Nobody's paying attention to us," says Willie Dee. "Just one more time."

Reluctantly, Ted turns the car around and heads back toward Calhoun's barn.

The line outside is shorter already, and this time they don't hear music spilling from the building in the same way. The doors must be closed. Ted slowly drives past, so slowly he has trouble keeping the car in gear. The engine sputters and coughs but doesn't die.

"Look, look," Willie Dee squeals. She clutches the back of the seat and points out the window. They all stare in that direction. Standing, leaning on the side of the barn, is the most elegant colored man they have ever seen, in a white tuxedo with tails and a blinding white shirt. His sleek, straight black hair glistens, is plastered back to the side, away from his face, and a cigarette dangles from his lips. "It's the Duke! He is so handsome."

While Fern Lee and Willie Dee congratulate each other over their good fortune of a Duke sighting, Ted sees Lucius Hadnot focus for the first time on the colored teenagers in the car that doesn't belong.

"Get us out of here, Ted," Robert whispers. "Hurry."

There is a sickening sound of grinding gears, and Lucius Hadnot begins to walk toward the road, toward where they sit unmoving, baking in their metal trap. Ted gives one more yank to the gearbox, and the Chevy spurts forward, once, twice, and then in a relatively smooth glide away from Calhoun's barn.

"We saw Duke Ellington in person!" Willie Dee says. She is radiant in her excitement.

The remainder of the ride to Alexandria is uneventful.

By the time the four of them arrive in Alexandria, pay for tickets, and climb upstairs to the colored section, the movie already flickers on the screen, a silly Marx Brothers film called *A Day at the Races*. They hunch down when they pass the projector to get to their seats, but they still get angry shouts of "Sit down" and "Be quiet" from angry patrons when they block the light and throw their own shadows against the screen. They haven't missed much, and the plot is thin and easy to follow. They are still keyed up from their adventure at Calhoun's barn. After the movie lets out, they don't linger in town but immediately head toward Colfax. The girls in back chatter, and Robert and Ted struggle to make small talk.

"You going to Grambling?" Robert asks.

"Yeah," answers Ted. "Next month."

"How you getting up there?"

"Hop the rails."

"That's what I did too," says Robert.

There is a popping sound from the right front side, and the car shimmies on the road before coming to a shuddering halt.

"It's the tire," Ted says knowingly. "My brother-in-law keeps a spare one in the back, only been patched twice."

Robert and Ted leave the girls in the car and examine the damage as best they can in the dimness. If not for the full moon, the road would be pitch-black. No other cars or wagons pass. Fortunately, the reflected light is enough. Ted produces a kit from the back, including a jack and tire iron. They roll out the patched-up spare and set about jacking the car up, loosening the bolts, and replacing the ruined tire.

They don't talk as they work, performing swiftly as a team. When the new tire is on, Ted is ready to get back in the car and head for home. Inside the car, the girls chat with ease.

"Say," says Robert, "walk over here with me for a minute."

Puzzled, Ted follows him to the side of the road, where they are still in visual range of the car but out of earshot.

"I expect you in for learning more than you think in college," says Robert. "Long as you stay up at Grambling, you be all right."

"I be back holidays," says Ted.

"Well, stay away from Willie Dee when you come back. She don't want you," says Robert.

"How you speak for what she want or don't want?" replies Ted. "I got just as much right as you to see her."

"Not the way you thinking about," says Robert. "Just 'cause your family put on airs in Colfax don't mean she's for the likes of you. Wait until you get to Grambling. The Tademy name don't mean nothing there."

"Take it back," says Ted.

"Wasn't you what started the colored school here, anyway. You all puffed up to no purpose. I say again, Tademy don't mean nothing."

Something reckless and wild bubbles up in Ted. A red swirl of emotion takes shape in front of his eyes, and there is a buzzing in his head. Sensing the change in Ted's attitude, Robert Hadnot raises the tire iron, clearly determined to use what has become a weapon.

Willie Dee and Fern Lee stand watching by the side of the road, their expressions a curious mix of morbid fascination and anticipation. Ted isn't sure when they abandoned the isolation of the car, how much they have heard.

"Somebody got to take the Tademys down a peg," Robert says.

Ted considers throwing himself at Robert, punching and kicking to land the first blow, consequences be damned, but he backs

Figure 33. Ted Tademy stands behind the hood of Walter Jerro's (brother-in-law) 1930 Chevy; Ellen Tademy Jerro, front

Figure 34. Ted Tademy as a young man

himself away from both the insult and his anger to take a look at the situation with his rational mind. Robert Hadnot is not merely pretty-boy handsome. He is older and bigger, a muscle-bound mill hand with a weapon in his hands. He has a good four inches of height on Ted, and a gritty determination. But Robert is no bully, no thug. The circumstances have gotten out of hand. If GrandJack were here, he would say, "Always two ways to skin the same cat."

"How you think it looks, you with a tire iron and me with nothing? You think that makes you look like a big man in front of the girls?" Ted circles around and positions himself so that he is between Robert and the car. He wants Robert to be able to see Willie Dee. He has to trust she won't egg him on. "Don't make any difference whether they know the Tademy name at Grambling or not," Ted goes on, "long as I know what it means. Don't make sense to get in a fight about it now."

Robert hesitates and finally lowers the tire iron. "Let's get the girls home," he mumbles, and strides off.

Relieved, Ted follows toward the car. Willie Dee stares at him, assesses him. He senses more than sees the change. Willie Dee is looking at him in a new way. He wouldn't go so far as to call her new attitude a reciprocation of his feelings for her, but it is a thawing, a reconsideration. It is admiration. It is respect.

39

1 9 3 7

Pounding storms have swept over The Bottom almost without break for the last two weeks, and the saturated soil of the pasture is slick and marshy, sucking at the leather of Jackson's boots. He moves slowly, a diminutive outline against a dense cluster of pecan trees in the north field, not far from his two-story farmhouse. He has become shorter by at least two inches in the last year alone, his shoulders hunched as if coaxed down by a pulley toward the ground, his walk dependent more and more on the oak-branch cane he carries all of the time. He is an old man, alone, surveying his acres, the prideful expanse of land, buildings, and equipment that has taken years to amass. Jackson leans heavily on his cane, pausing every few steps to catch his breath, but he keeps pushing himself forward nonetheless. A vicious, convulsive cough shakes through him.

His grandson appears at a trot from the house, easily catching up to Jackson by cutting across the wide meadow at a diagonal. "GrandJack, can I help?" he offers.

"Walk beside me, L'il Man," Jackson says. "I got to make the last round."

"We looking for anything special, GrandJack?" Ted says. "Maybe you should go back to bed. I'll see to whatever needs doing out here."

"Not this time, L'il Man," Jackson says. His breath comes in raspy gulps, as if someone is pinching his nostrils shut. He stops to study Ted's face, all seriousness and concern.

Jackson gives in to another coughing attack, a deep, harsh hawking that consumes him and sets his thin chest vibrating. Shaken and a little surprised at the force of the assault, he briefly loses the thread of the conversation and can't find his way back.

"L'il Man, whatever you earn, you save it for a needed time," Jackson finally says.

Ted nods indulgently and comes to Jackson's side, holding his arm at the elbow.

"You wait on up to the house," Jackson says. "I be back directly."

"GramAmy said bring you back."

"I got things to finish. By myself."

Ted hesitates, reluctant to leave his grandfather out in the field, maybe even more reluctant to face Amy without having brought Jackson.

"I say go along, L'il Man." Jackson makes his voice hard, commanding. Ted turns back, and Jackson continues on his slow, hobbling walk. He walks all the way out to the lightning-split oak tree that marks the beginning of his property, across the Walden Bayou bridge until he can see the better part of the north fields, and down past Mount Pilgrim Rest Baptist Church. His muscles throb, the pressure in his chest is almost unbearable, and he shivers, finding it difficult to control the constant fluttered motion of his hands. He doubles back and heads toward the farmhouse.

It is dusk by the time Jackson drags himself up the front porch stairs, where Amy and Ted wait. They rush to him, one on each side, and put Jackson to bed in the back room. The moist heat of a fever pours from him.

Jackson reaches over to Ted and grabs hold of the sleeve of his jacket with trembling fingers. "We got one more piece of business, you and me. Go to the closet upstairs and carry back my brown hat."

A look of alarm makes a quick journey across Ted's face. "Who died, GrandJack?"

"Never you mind, L'il Man. Just don't rough-handle the hat. It's been on this earth far longer than you. Top shelf."

Ted retrieves the hat and brings it downstairs, carefully wrapped up in a length of thin gauze. He carries the whole bundle to Jackson. Amy backs away from the sickbed to give him room.

"Unwrap it," Jackson says to Ted.

Ted lets the cloth fall to the floor and perches the hat on his knees.

"Tell me what you see, L'il Man."

"Your funeral hat, GrandJack."

"What else?"

"An old brown hat with a heron feather stuck in the brim."

"A man I once knew would call that a failure of imagination." Jackson summons up his concentration. "This here hat start out clean and sleek. Just something to keep a man's head covered and warm. Mr. Isaac McCullen, your great-granddaddy, he come by it after the newness already gone, but he freshen it up with this feather. If McCully alive to hear you now, he be upset to hear you call it a heron feather. Maybe to you or me it look like it come from one of the waders floating in the swamp, but he swear it come from the phoenix bird. Some say no such bird, but McCully, he tell the story of a phoenix live in the desert for five hundred years, die in a fire it sets to blaze its own self, so a new phoenix can spring from its ashes."

"You believe that story, GrandJack, about the phoenix?"

Jackson props himself up in bed, leans forward, holds the fedora out just inches from Ted's nose, angles it between himself and his grandson. "I believe this hat just waiting. Mr. McCullen give this hat to my father, and my father give it to me, and once I'm gone, the hat gonna come around to you. Whoever own this hat got a job to do, beyond themselves or even their family. Whoever own this hat got to push forward and reach out for others not as strong, bring them along too."

"Why you giving Mr. McCullen's hat to me?" asks Ted.

"This not a gift, L'il Man. This hat a responsibility. Names of men you never gonna know lay buried in the ground for you. Can't change the past, but don't mean you not in somebody's debt. This hat mean no matter how much time pass, no matter how dark it seem, you not allowed to turn your face to the wall, throw up your hands, forget. You a man now, and it be time to turn your mind to men's things."

"What you asking me to do?" asks Ted.

Jackson leans back on the bed. "Your day coming, and when it does, it be clear to you. A man sometime don't know who he is until somebody expect something from him. We all expecting in abundance. Don't disappoint."

Jackson closes his eyes, and he floats for a time in the sweet relief of letting go. He is tempted to give in now, to gladly follow the force that tugs him elsewhere. He already told Amy last night that he would soon meet his King, that wherever he goes, he will wait for her to join him. He never thought he would have the luxury to walk his land, to measure out the sum of his life and impart without hurry his last words, and now he is calm, at peace.

Amy fusses with the covers in an effort to make Jackson more comfortable, smooths a cool, wet towel across his forehead, bringing him back to the here and now. He hears her pull a chair to the side of the bed, and then she takes his hot hand into the coolness of hers, but he needs to leave all of that behind. Now he needs to consume himself with the selfishness of dying.

Now he is ready.

STATE DEPARTMENT OF EDUCATION

OF LOUISIANA

Class IV-AA

No. 191

FIRST GRADE CERTIFICATE
VALID FOR FIVE YEARS
(NEGRO)

This Certificate is issued to   Nathan Tademy, Jr.

by the State Department of Education of Louisiana, based upon the following requirements:
Approved 2-Year Teacher-Training Course
Graduate   Louisiana Negro Normal, 1939   Total Credit   36 hours

Eligibility: This certificate authorizes the employment of the holder to teach in the elementary grades of any school. It does not authorize any teaching service not expressly authorized on the certificate.

Baton Rouge, La., July 26, 19 39

State Superintendent of Education.

Director of Certification.

500 Sets 7-39 M12,800C96

Figure 35. Nathan-Green "Ted" Tademy's teaching certificate

Figure 36. Ted Tademy, U.S. Navy

Figure 37. Willie Dee Billes Tademy and Ted Tademy

Figure 38. Ted and Willie Dee
Tademy, with daughters Joan
and Theodorsia Tademy

Figure 39. Willie Dee with her children (clockwise) Theodorsia, Joan, Lee, and Lalita

Figure 40. Nathan-Green and Lenora's grown children: Odessa, Ted, Ellen, Willie, Elmira, Archie, and Jackson at family reunion, 1978

Figure 41. Willie Dee and Ted Tademy, 1980

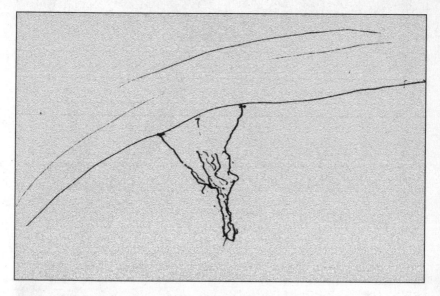

Figure 42. Nile Delta, drawn by James Tademy, age ninety-three, in Pineville, Louisiana, 2003; first drawn for him by his uncle Jackson Tademy

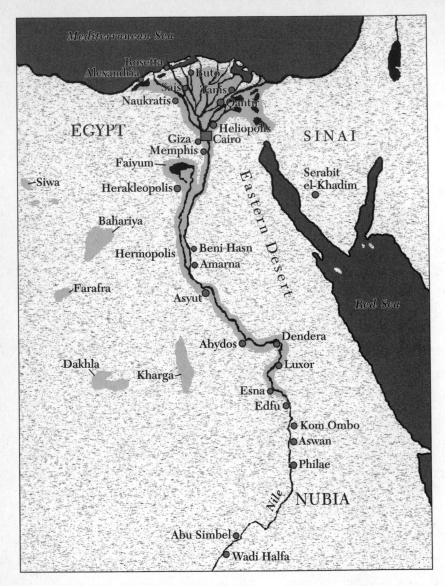

Figure 43. Nile Delta as it existed in the 1800s

Author's
Note

Some family stories are gloriously specific. With great pride, a family member repeats colorful details of an ancestor's life, passed down for one or two or three generations. If a researcher is very lucky, another branch of the family fills in gaps, embellishing and confirming or adding a heretofore unknown nugget. But there is also a different type of family story, lacking shape and enthusiasm, only stingily disclosed, rationed within vague hints or whispers, and only then with great reluctance and obvious discomfort by the teller.

So it was with my attempts to understand my ancestors on my father's side. When I was growing up, and later, as an adult, I became obsessed with tracking down every branch of our family tree, and both types of stories were laid out before me. Certain family episodes were repeated almost verbatim, regardless of which parent or aunt or uncle or distant cousin recited our history. Sam Tademy and his son Jackson always inspired deep reverence and pride, starting with Sam reclaiming the Tademy name after the

Civil War—hanging on to the closest phonetic pronunciation he could get to his original African name—and quickly followed by the father and son starting the first colored schools in Colfax, Louisiana. Whenever Noby Smith was mentioned, first he appeared as a sickly baby who'd been laid out in the back of a buckboard wagon to die but was rescued and nursed back to health by Hansom Brisco and his wife. That story was inevitably followed by the tale of a fully grown Noby, beaten within an inch of his life by a white man at a gravel pit and saved only because his family and Freemason brothers spirited him out of the state to Ardmore, Oklahoma, before a white posse could kill him.

The accounts given of my other great-grandfather were not nearly as satisfying. Ellen Tademy Jerro, my father's sister, still lives in Louisiana, and on my "roots trips," I would stay at her house in Colfax. No matter how many times I asked her about Isaac McCullen, the most conclusive response I could ever elicit was a single statement: "There used to be a lot of McCullens around here, but not anymore."

The census records for Isaac McCullen stopped after 1870 in Colfax, Louisiana. Searching for further clues, I visited the Colfax library, the Colfax newspaper office, and the Colfax courthouse, located at one end of the small, dusty town. Outside the courthouse was, and still is, a prominent marker, a state historical landmark:

On this site occurred the Colfax Riot in which three white men and 150 negroes were slain. This event on April 13, 1873 marked the end of carpetbag misrule in the South.

Taken aback, I began to do parallel research on the Colfax Riot, only to discover that the few easily obtained records were all reported from a very specific point of view—the voice of a southern town thankfully purging itself of dangerous troublemakers. I visited the Colfax cemetery, where there is a massive marble obelisk memorial almost twelve feet high dedicated to the three white men who died on that day:

Erected to the Memory
of the Heroes
Stephen Decatur Parish,
James West Hadnot,
and Sidney Harris
Who Fell in the Colfax Riot
Fighting for White Supremacy,
April 13, 1873

I returned to my aunt's house that evening upset and somewhat testy from my day's research. I asked Aunt Ellen about the Colfax Riot and what she knew about it. Only then did another piece of our family history dribble out. "Our people were there," she volunteered for the first time. "Some got out, and some didn't." To this day I don't know if she knew any more than that, but it was the full extent of what she was willing to share. Those words have haunted me from the first time she uttered them years ago. They haunt me still.

I determined to try to imagine the lives of my ancestors—former slaves and then, at long last, United States of America citizens—within the context of this horrific incident. One prominent historian, Eric Foner, calls that Easter Sunday 1873 "the bloodiest single act of carnage in all of Reconstruction." This novel attempts to overlay the rich anecdotes passed down in my family lore with the times in which they unfolded, a blend of fact and fiction told from the point of view of people whose voices were lost in official records. I want to honor those who were able to reemerge from the "scary times," to push forward with their lives from one generation to the next. From the comfort of my privileged life over 130 years later, I can still barely comprehend what they had to endure, but I acknowledge I am here only because of their stamina and resolve. They gave their all for me, without knowing me, and for that I am eternally grateful.

Acknowledgments

Novels don't come easy, but they can be coaxed into the world with the help of voices that are, thankfully, outside of one's own head.

My agent, Kim Witherspoon of Inkwell Management, and her trusty aide Eleanor Jackson believed in this book at a time when belief was hard to come by, and they helped me shape the final product. Gratitude to my editor for the second time, Jamie Raab, and the rest of the gang at Warner Books.

A very special thanks to Joan Tademy Lothery, my sister, who is always my first reader during the early, tentative, and terrifyingly fragile stages of writing a book. And to all of the other helpful readers along the way, from the first draft to the eighteenth. You know who you are.

I could not have created this work without my aunt Ellen sharing our family stories and her encouragement to document them. Ellen Tademy Jerro just passed in 2006. Neither she nor my father lived to see the publication of this tribute to their family, but they were both proud people who always knew exactly where they came from.

Joel Sipress, professor of history at the University of Wisconsin-Superior, provided invaluable help and insight in researching the Red River region during Reconstruction, beginning with his work *From the Barrel of a Gun: The Politics of Murder in Grant Parish*, and his subsequent generous offer to share his unpublished manuscript, "The Triumph of White Supremacy: The Politics of Race in a New South Community." Mary Linn Wernet, head archivist at Northwestern State University in Natchitoches, Louisiana, helped me get my hands on several of the documents that appear in the book, particularly the list of dead and wounded on that fateful day in 1873.

And thanks to my new(ish) husband, Barry Williams, who gave me his support during both the best and worst of writing days. He made me want to hurry up and finish so I could come out and live life with him.